ANOTHER MAN WILL

Also by Daaimah S. Poole:

Another Man Will

What's His Is Mine

Somebody Else's Man

A Rich Man's Baby

Diamond Playgirls

Ex-Girl to the Next Girl

What's Real

Got A Man

Yo-Yo Love

ANOTHER MAN WILL

DAAIMAH S. POOLE

Kensington Publishing Corp.
http://www.kensingtonbooks.com

DAFINA BOOKS are published by

Kensington Publishing Corp.
119 West 40th Street
New York, NY 10018

All Kensington Titles, Imprints, and Distributed Lines are available at special quantity discounts for bulk purchases for sales promotions, premiums, fund-raising, and educational or institutional use. Special book excerpts or customized printings can also be created to fit specific needs. For details, write or phone the office of the Kensington special sales manager: Kensington Publishing Corp., 119 West 40th Street, New York, NY 10018, attn: Special Sales Department, Phone: 1-800-221-2647.

ISBN-13: 978-0-7582-4623-3
ISBN-10: 0-7582-4623-4

First trade paperback printing: September 2012

10 9 8 7 6 5 4 3 2 1

Printed in the United States of America

Allah, for the gift and making all things possible

Dedicated to my family & friends
Where would I be without you?

CHAPTER 1

Crystal Turner

"Dana, don't forget that I have to take the DNA test tomorrow."

"Right, right, okay. I'm glad you reminded me. I have a meeting, but as soon as I'm done, I'm coming straight to you. Ooooh, I hate Kenneth so much for making you go through this."

"I know, but once he gets the results, I think he will step up and do what he is supposed to do."

"He better, because this doesn't make any sense. My beautiful niece doesn't deserve this, and neither do you. I'll see you tomorrow."

"Okay, see you then," I said. Then I took a few deep breaths and prepared to go back into work. I was on minute eleven of my fifteen-minute break, and I didn't need another write-up. I hurried back inside.

I boarded the elevator and rode back up to my floor, the ACR Cable Vision headquarters. I thought about what my sister Dana had said and had to agree that nobody should have to go to court to prove the paternity of their child. Let me take that back. In some situations paternity tests were very necessary, but not in my case. I knew Kenneth Dontae Haines was the father of my three-month-old daughter, Kori. I was positive because we were in a committed relationship for several years, and during that time I wasn't with anyone else. I asked my younger sister, Dana, to go with me because she was levelheaded, and I want to have support just in case he brought his sometimes bigmouthed butch sister, Syreeta, with him.

Negotiating a maze of cubicles, I made it to my desk with only a minute to spare, just enough time to log back on to my phone. I put my headset back on, and instantly my phone began ringing. The air-conditioning made it very cold in the building, so I put my gray wrap sweater over my skinny frame and began taking calls. "Thank you for calling ACR Cable Vision & Internet. This is Crystal. How may I assist you today?"

"I have this blue screen on my TV," the caller complained. I could tell from his voice that he was old. I didn't know why people always called about the blue screen. They knew what the blue screen meant. It meant that they hadn't paid their cable bill.

"Okay, I'm reviewing your account," I said, as if there was a chance that there was mistake, but I knew better. "Unfortunately, your account is showing that you have a past due balance of one hundred and eighty-nine dollars." I hated giving the old man that bad news.

"What! Is that for one month?" the old man asked me.

"No, sir. Two months."

"Hmm. I gave my grandson the money, and he didn't pay the bill! Now I'm about to miss all my shows. If I mail you a check today, will you turn the cable back on?"

Aw, this was so sad. I hated this part of my job.

"No, sir, full payment is due at this time. However, I can take a check by phone."

He made an irritated sound. "I can't see this goddamn number on the check. Look, never mind. It's a shame how y'all rob the elderly. Can't even watch my television. All I can do now is just sit here and look at a blue screen." He grunted in aggravation. "You goddamn robbers, making people pay to watch TV, anyway."

I heard the man continue to mumble, and then he hung up on me. *Just one of our millions of loyal, happy customers,* I thought as I took the next call. I'd been a customer service representative for five years. The only really good thing that came with the job was the free cable and Internet. As I answered the caller on hold, I waved to my returning coworker, Gloria. She always tried to pop her head over my cubicle and make conversation between calls. But I wasn't interested. I kept it at "Good morning," "Hello," and "See you tomorrow."

I was more of a loner. I barely spoke to my supervisor, Delphine. I kept to myself, and I didn't have a lot of friends. My kids kept me busy enough. I didn't have time for catty, petty, drama-filled women. That was why I didn't deal with any of the women on my job. I'd seen it happen so many times. Two coworkers were besties; then the next thing you knew, they were enemies, telling everybody on the job each other's business. No thanks! The same women that ran to your desk with juicy news about someone would do the same thing to you. I came to work and then went home to my babies—Kori, who was three months old; Nasir, who was five; and Jewel, who was nine.

After work the pending test was still on my mind. I just couldn't wait until all the dumbness was over. I just wanted to be happy. Ever since I was a young kid, all I had ever wanted was to have a family and be happily married like my parents. My mom and dad had been together for thirty-five years. You'd think I'd follow in their footsteps, but it was hard for me to stay with anyone for more than a few years. I had three kids and three different baby fathers. The minute I told someone this, they automatically formed a negative opinion of me. Sometimes it bothered me, but most times it didn't. I hadn't planned for it to turn out like this. I had really believed that I was going to be with each one of my children's fathers forever, but it didn't happen that way. So, I just got up and went to work every single day and provided for my children as best I could.

Jason, who was my oldest daughter, Jewel's, father, and I were together from eighth grade until I was twenty-one. Jason got locked up when I seven months pregnant. When he first went away, I did the jail thing: the visits, sending letters, putting money on his books. But he eventually told me to stop. He said he didn't want to hold me back, and to go and live my life. That was eight years ago. He still had another seven years to go before he got out.

Then there was Maurice, my son, Nasir's, dad. I really cared about Maurice. He was very smart and motivated. I met him in the coffee shop down the street from my job. We were truly opposites. He was working on his third degree, while I had finished only high school. Initially, we were inseparable. He taught me so much about the world, and I really thought we had a chance. I was in love with him, but something about our relationship couldn't work. I think it was because Maurice saw me as his little project, like I was his "ghetto girl," whom he was going to refine. I wouldn't have minded being his project, but he wasn't trying to make me a better person. He was trying to mold me into something that I wasn't. After a while I got tired of him talking down to me. He wasn't physically abusive, but I knew he would never consider me his equal. His treatment of me probably bordered on emotional abuse. He rarely gave me money for Nasir, and he married some older woman, so I just acted like he didn't exist.

And lastly, there was Kenneth, the deadbeat baby daddy of my youngest child, Kori. In my defense, I could honestly say that Kenneth begged and pleaded with me to have his child. I loved my daughter, but I wasn't ready to be a mom again. I was actually on birth control, but obviously, it didn't work. I had planned on aborting her, but Kenneth cried. The man actually shed tears, whole tears. Trying to make me feel guilty, he said, "You had two babies for dudes that didn't love you. I'm the one here with you, loving you and your kids, but you wanna kill my baby?"

So I caved and went through with the pregnancy. And at first it seemed like we were going to make it. Kenneth was great during my entire pregnancy. He went to every doctor's appointment, was in the delivery room, holding my hand, telling me to breathe and to push when I went into labor. Kenneth even cut the umbilical cord and began kissing and snapping pictures of our baby daughter as soon as he saw her. He was a doting father for the entire half hour before his sister, Syreeta, arrived. Once she got there, everything changed. From my hospital bed, I saw her in the corner, whispering to him. I didn't know what they were talking about, but I soon found out.

Syreeta had a major issue with Kori's complexion. She said my baby looked like she was mixed with something, and that she was too light to be Kenneth's child. Now, I would admit, usually when two brown-skinned people had a child, you got a brown baby. However, I was smart enough to know about something called genes. Genes could cause traits and characteristics, like a child's complexion, to skip a generation.

Unfortunately, Kenneth and Syreeta weren't aware of these things, because all of a sudden Kenneth started having doubts. He was asking me questions like "Is Kori mine?" "Did you cheat on me?" "Why is she so light?" I thought it was funny, because when would I have time to cheat on him? I had a full-time job, two kids, and since Kenneth practically lived with me, he got a lot of my time and attention, as well. A part of me understood that in his sister's mind, she was looking out for her little brother, but Kenneth should've stood up like a man and told his sister that Kori was his daughter. He should have, but he didn't.

He asked me to take a DNA test, and I told him to kiss my

ass. I asked him if he could just look at her and see that she was his. She had the same mouth, ears, nose, and had a head full of hair, just like him. But the only thing he could think to say was, "I don't trust a face test." Then he mumbled something about this bull on his job who got burnt that way. His denial of his daughter was unacceptable. He even refused to sign her birth certificate, so I broke up with him. My response to all of that was, "Fuck you." I wasn't about to poke or swab my baby for him or anyone else. If he didn't want to be bothered, then fine. It was his loss, not mine.

I eventually changed my mind and agreed to have her tested, and I suggested that we order an at-home DNA test. We could get the results online or in the mail, but Kenneth wouldn't go for that. He said that his sister had warned him that with an at-home test, I could tamper with the results, and so they wanted an official test done by professionals. So tomorrow was D-day, and I hoped we could finally put all this ghetto mess behind us. He'd have proof that Kori was his child, and his sister could shut the hell up.

CHAPTER 2

Dana Turner

The marketing firm I worked for was having its annual customer appreciation dinner at the Arts at Piazza in downtown Philadelphia. It was a big event where we got to wine and dine with our clients, all on the company's tab. Meeting clients socially was always good. They were relaxed and not in business mode. You could do the right amount of schmoozing without looking like you were kissing up to them.

The night was going extremely well; actually, the night was almost perfect. I was wearing an off-the-shoulder, lilac-colored dress that hung great on my size six curves and accented my cherrywood brown skin. I had on my favorite pair of peep-toe shoes, which made my five-three look like five-eight. My beautiful, big layered silver necklace was making a grand statement and rested right above my cleavage. My long, wavy weave was pulled up into a sloppy, loose bun, which was set off with just the right amount of makeup.

The food was delicious; the cocktails had the perfect blend of sweetness, and only a trace of liquor was detectable. I was in the great company of my coworker Reshma Patel and her fiancé, Zyeed, and my other coworker, Leah Oliver, who had brought her boyfriend, Stephen. The only thing that was off was the empty chair that was next to me. It was reserved for my no-call, no-show date, Todd.

Leah was from rural upstate Pennsylvania. She was bubbly and fun and always made me laugh with her off-color humor. She had a few freckles, rust-colored hair, and brown eyes. Leah and I had interned together, and Reshma had come in a few months afterward. Reshma was a quiet, sweet-hearted first-generation American of Indian descent. We all got along so well, yet we were all so different, but we made the perfect little marketing dream team.

We all worked for Millennium Concepts Agency. We provided marketing and branding services for small and large companies—from the huge billboards you saw on highways to the tiny advertisements above your head on the train.

"So where is that boyfriend of yours, missy?" Leah inquired.

"He should be on his way. I was about to call him and see where he is," I said.

Reshma grabbed my hand and tried to contain her laughter as she pushed her straight black hair in front of her wheat skin to block her smirk. "It's okay, sweetie. You can stop lying. We know you don't really have a date."

I frowned. "Reshma, this is not funny. That's really sad that you would think I would make up having a date. I told you, Todd said he was coming. He'll be here."

Reshma looked at Leah and made a face. They both began to laugh at my expense as their guys stood around, looking bored and making light conversation with one another.

My eyes were focused on the entrance. "I'll be right back. Let me see if he is on his way," I said as I excused myself from the table. I was trying to act nonchalant, but I was so angry at Todd, I could feel my blood pressure rising.

I exited the crowded party, hoping to see Todd parking or

walking toward the restaurant, but no such luck. I didn't see him. So I called his phone and listened to it ring about four times and then heard, "You have reached Todd Montgomery. Unfortunately, I'm not available. . . ." I listened as I looked up and down the street once more, before leaving a message. "Todd, where are you? I hope you are on your way. I'm still at the Arts at Piazza on Fourth Street. Call me and let me know what's going on." I really hoped Todd would make it. He said he would. But he said a lot of things. Todd was not my real boyfriend. We were in a six-month relationship about a year ago; then things got complicated. Our relationship was going so good. I mean, really, really, really well. But then work got in the way.

He said our relationship was taking up too much of his time and that he needed to focus on his architectural career. He said I required so much and he couldn't give me everything I deserved. So we semi broke up but never stopped seeing each other. Our relationship was downgraded to that fuzzy place commonly referred to as "friends with benefits." Which meant that we hooked up occasionally. I kept thinking if I hung in there for a while, he'd realize that we should be back in an official relationship. Plus, I loved a career-driven man, and Todd was definitely that. Believe me, there were far worse things that a guy could be doing besides working nonstop. Especially in this economy, when so many people couldn't find jobs and others were losing their homes. And I knew he didn't have anyone else, unless she lived under his desk at his job. But then it was evenings like this one, when he stood me up, and it didn't seem worth it or fair.

I walked back to the party, and my phone rang. Todd's name appeared on the screen.

"Hey. Are you on your way?" I asked.

"No, not exactly," he said.

"What does 'not exactly' mean?" I already knew what that meant, but still I asked.

"Sorry. I can't make it. Listen, don't be upset with me. I can't leave this office. I have so much work. I really want to be there with you, but my work is my priority."

Instead of giving him the artificial "Okay. I understand"—that was what I usually said—I just gave a defeated, "You never can make it, can you, Todd?"

"Why are you being sarcastic, Dana? What do you want me to do?"

"I don't know. You promised me. I told you about this party how many weeks ago? And you said, 'I promise I'll be there.' "

"Yes, I said I would be there. However, I can't always predict what's going to happen. Things change on a daily basis at this company. . . . Once again, I'm sorry, Dana. I have to go. I didn't eat, and I'm very frustrated. I'll be at the office for a while. Feel free to stop by."

"Okay," I said as I twisted my mouth and tried to control my anger and not let tears escape my eyes. He wasn't able to be with me, but at least I could be with him later. I felt a little better, even though I was at another event alone. I walked to the restroom to make sure my eye makeup hadn't smudged. Leah and Reshma were exiting the ladies' room.

"We were looking for you. Are you okay? So is he coming?" Reshma asked.

"No, he is working."

"Well, one thing is for sure, when you get married, you will be provided for," Leah joked as they walked me into the restroom. I began to fix my clothes and reapply my eyeliner and blush. I tried to remain calm, but I was so upset.

Leah looked at me in the mirror above the sink and said, "Dana, I can't understand why you put yourself through this. You are a beautiful girl. You can find someone else.

"You deserve a real boyfriend." Reshma giggled, breaking the serious tone.

"You guys are full of jokes tonight."

"No, really, you need to be dating, having fun. You need a

guy that doesn't stand you up all the time," said Leah. "You're beautiful, you have a great personality, and you're successful. I'm sure lots of guys would love to date you."

"If it was only that simple," I snapped back at them. "Listen, ladies, there aren't that many black men like Todd."

"And what is that supposed to mean?" Reshma asked.

"It means it is different for us," I replied.

"What do you mean, us?" said Leah.

"Us means black women. We don't have as many options as you guys. There aren't thousands of black architects running around Philadelphia."

"I don't believe that. That's just a myth. It's all the same. There are as many jerks who are white men, Asian, and Indian men as there are those who are black," Leah responded.

"Nope, not the case. There are plenty of white men for you to marry and lots of Indian men for Reshma. I have to work with what I have. Todd is a great catch, and I'm not letting him get away."

"Great catch or not, he doesn't treat you well. Seriously, I don't like seeing my friend upset," Reshma said.

"I have to say one thing. You won't find anyone as long as you won't let go of an old relationship," Leah retorted.

Reshma nodded her head in agreement and said, "Remember that crazy Indian guy I dated before I met Zyeed? After him I didn't think there was any hope that I was going to ever meet anyone—and now I'm getting married in two weeks. As a matter of fact, there will be a lot of single guys at my wedding."

"And I could introduce you to one of Stephen's friends if you like," Leah added.

"I don't want to be hooked up with anyone. I'm happy with what and who I have. And besides, I want a black man."

"You're telling us you'd rather have a so-so good black man over a nice guy of another race?" Reshama asked perplexed.

"Yeah. I mean no. I just want a good man, but I would prefer if he is black. Besides, I have one, and we are not having this discussion anymore."

"If you say so." Leah looked at me like I wasn't making sense. I wasn't . . . but I was. I knew what I wanted.

I left the party and stopped at Todd's favorite restaurant, Laverne's, to pick him up dinner. He always got the classic turkey-spinach burger, sweet potato fries, and a strawberry milk shake. *He's going to be so pleased that I brought him dinner*, I thought.

Todd worked on the twenty-second floor of a tall office building at Twentieth and Market Streets. The building was lively during the day, but at 10:00 p.m. it was eerie and empty. I said hello to the security man, signed myself in, and rode the elevator up to his floor. I walked down the hall and could see Todd steadily working. I tapped on the glass door, and Todd came and opened it. He gave me a quick kiss on the cheek and said I looked beautiful. I was glad that he noticed.

"You said you hadn't eaten, so I stopped and got your favorite."

"Wow, and I'm starving. Thank you, sweetheart." He took the food out of the white paper bag and took big bites out of the sandwich and stuffed the fries in his mouth. As he ate, I admired the blueprints lying out on his desk and the color model on his computer. I was always so amazed at the intricate drawings that eventually became buildings.

"What project is this?"

"The new athletic center for Temple University. The deadline is next Friday, and we are so behind. I'm going to be working nonstop on this. There is so much that has to be done."

"Oh, this is what kept you from being with me tonight," I said as I poked out my lips.

"Yeah, this is it."

"I really wish you could have been with me tonight. I get so tired of going places alone. My friends at work think I'm lying when I say I have a date. They think I'm making you up."

"I don't know why. We've all met before. They know that's not true."

"Yeah, they were just being extra silly tonight, I guess. So, how much longer are you staying here tonight?"

"Actually, I'm trying to get out of here now. I have to be back in here by seven, and what I have left, I can do from home. Do you want to meet me there? I'll be home in, like, half an hour."

"Okay."

At Todd's loft, he continued to work and I didn't distract him. I took off my dress and cute shoes and showered. Once I was out of the shower, I put on one of his T-shirts, and I watched television in his bed, making myself comfortable. Todd was right in the other room, but I wanted him closer. I could smell his scent on his sheets. However, I knew not to bother him or force myself on him while he was in work mode. When he was ready to come to bed, he would join me and I could show him how much I missed him.

Around 2:45 a.m. I got the nudge I was waiting for. I was barely awake when he began lifting my T-shirt over my head. The room was dark. I couldn't see Todd, but I could feel his hands all over my breasts. Once his hands touched me, everything was right in the world. I forgave him for standing me up, making me angry and embarrassing me in front of my friends again. I was so caught up in the moment that nothing else mattered.

"You ready for me, baby?" he murmured in my ear.

"Yes," I responded sleepily as I wrapped my arms around his neck tightly, sliding my body down on him, until he was all the way in. My pulse sped up the moment our bodies connected. My clitoris was pressed hard up against the base of him. I could feel hot sensations coursing through me. I was just enjoying the way he gripped my waistline and controlled my body, moving my hips as fast he needed to.

"Todd!" I moaned as he panted on top of me. Our bodies

were sweaty. The sex was so good, and I was just enjoying it so much that I couldn't help whispering, "Baby, I love you and don't want to be without you anymore." I waited for him to respond and say he loved me, too, and he needed me, as well, but he didn't speak. More strokes brought out more emotions. I couldn't control how I felt or what I was saying. "I love you so much, Todd. I miss you when we're not together. Baby, we really need to figure out what we are going to be."

Todd still remained quiet and placed his finger over my lips and kept pushing his firm body in and out of mine. I didn't like that he was ignoring me. I couldn't let it go any further without him giving me an idea of what we were doing. He had to explain why we just couldn't go back to being a couple.

I pushed him off of me mid-stroke, sat up, folded my arms, and asked, "Todd, when are we going to be together again?"

"Let's not talk about this right now please, baby." He pushed me back down and squirmed back in me and began our beautiful experience again.

I was becoming a little frustrated. I felt like crying, but tears only made Todd upset. So I kept them in check and momentarily forgot all my troubles by focusing on the pleasure on the horizon. Within minutes I exploded. My body shook so hard, I thought I was having a damn seizure. All the shaking I was doing must have excited him, because a few seconds later he collapsed on top of me. We were both satisfied so it was the perfect time to ask him the status of us again.

"Todd, what are we doing?"

"I don't know."

"You do know. What is this? Where are we going?"

"Uh, Dana, can we talk about this later?"

I said okay, but the minute he was in the shower, my brain started spinning again. I began to get angry and I decided I didn't want to spend the night. If he couldn't define us then I didn't want to be bothered with him anymore. I huffed loudly as I threw my dress over my head and slipped on my heels. Todd walked back in the bedroom in his open navy robe, brushing his teeth.

"Where are you going?" he asked with a mouth full of toothpaste.

"Home."

"Why?"

"Because I can't keep getting hurt by you. I asked you a simple question, and you can't answer it."

He stepped back in the bathroom and spat out the toothpaste and said, "That doesn't mean you have to leave."

I didn't hesitate. I finished getting dressed and walked out the door.

"Dana, hold up," Todd called. "Wait. Let me throw on some shorts and walk you to your car."

The cool summer air was refreshing and woke me as I climbed in my white Honda Accord coupe. Todd made it to my car door just as I started the engine. I rolled down the window and waited for him to speak.

"Yes?" I said, staring straight ahead.

"What's wrong with you? Why do you always get like this? I told you I don't want a relationship, not with you or anyone else, right now. You know what we are."

"No, I don't know. That's why I'm leaving."

"Dana, you're being extra . . . Just call me when you get in."

I wasn't thinking about Todd right now; he frustrated the hell out of me. I pulled out of the parking space and dialed Tiffany, my friend since college. We had been roommates at Maryland Eastern Shore. In college we shared books, food, clothes, and gained a lifelong friendship. If her mother sent something for her, it was for us, and vice versa. I missed college, the good old days, when I didn't have a lot of responsibility and every day was a party. Nowadays Tiffany was sometimes up in the middle of the night, doing lessons plans, preparing to deal with the twenty-one kindergarteners in her class, and we would talk. I took a chance and called her.

"What's wrong? Why are you calling this late?"

"Todd is the problem. I'm just leaving his house. He stood me up again, and then I asked him where our relationship was going and he acted like he couldn't speak."

"Dana, he always does this to you. I don't like Todd for you anymore. He had all this time to get himself together and still hasn't. When are you going to realize it is never going to be the same?"

"I know. I was just hoping that maybe one day it would. That's what's kept me around. I hoped that one day he would change. He is everything I want in a man and husband. And I'm not in a rush to leave him, because what else is really out there, anyway?"

"You have a point, I guess. But is a little of something better than nothing?"

"I don't know."

"You should think about it. Good night."

I drove back to my apartment and went inside. Now that I was in my apartment, lying in my cream silky sheets alone I regretted leaving Todd's. I should have just continued my fantasy with Todd until morning. But no, I shouldn't have—because he was not giving me what I wanted. What I wanted was for a man to treat me like royalty. Like the love of his life. Like I'm the only thing that matters. Like how my daddy treated my mom. I wanted a good man who took care of his family, like my father.

My dad, James Turner, worked long hours at the Tastykake factory to provide for my mother, me, and my two sisters. Tastykake was a well known Philadelphia baking company. My dad would bring us home treats all the time, including Butterscotch Krimpets and lemon pies. Every time he got his paycheck, he would take all his girls out. And on our birthdays he would give us a hundred dollars and let us pick out whatever we wanted at Toys R Us. My dad was the closest thing to superman. He could do no wrong, and even now he still treated my mom like a queen and me and my sisters like princesses. I guess they didn't make them like him anymore.

It was morning, and I didn't have time to think about last night with Todd. I had to concentrate on my presentation at work. I was in my office's huge conference room. It had three large windows and a twenty-foot-long, shiny maple boardroom table that could seat ten on each side. I pulled down the projector and made sure everything was set up for my 10:00 a.m. meeting.

Reshma and I had thirty minutes left to prepare for our PowerPoint presentation. We were scrambling to get our notes together for our initial meeting with Cell Now. Cell Now was doing really well in the southwestern part of the country, and the company wanted to expand its services in the region stretching from Philadelphia to Atlanta. We planned to do a viral campaign through social media and have lunchtime contests and giveaways at local colleges. The service was good, but the phones were kind of cheap. Still, they were highly marketable to the eighteen-to-twenty-five demographic.

Our presentation went okay, though I flubbed a few lines of my prepared speech and then the computer kept freezing. I had to present most of the figures from memory, instead of being able to refer to all the attractive graphs and charts I had prepared. Overall, it still went well, I thought, as everyone from Cell Now exited the boardroom. They seemed excited about our ideas. I would know in a few days if they were going to go with our agency or not. I looked down at my cell phone. I had to hurry up and get to Eleventh Street to meet up with my sister Crystal.

"We are ordering food. Do you want Greek today?" Leah asked as she tapped on the door to my office.

"No, sorry. I have to go take care of something with my sister."

"Is everything okay?" Leah asked.

"Yes, everything is fine."

I arrived at the family court building to find it crowded, with long lines in every direction, and they made everyone go through a metal detector. I was truly annoyed by the way the horrible, power-hungry security people kept speaking to me. They were very demanding and questioned me. "Take off your earrings." "Do you have any change in your pocket?" I gave a hefty security guard an evil stare, and he responded by saying, "Miss, I'm just doing my job."

After the invasive security screening was over, I finally was able to go upstairs. I walked into the room and saw Crystal, her baby daddy, Kenneth, and his sister. I gave Kenneth and his sister both a stone-faced glance. I had to make sure they knew that my sister had support.

Kenneth should be executed for having the audacity to deny that he was Kori's biological father. However, Crystal should have known better than to mess with a nothing ass like Kenneth. Crystal was a classic example of a middle child. She wanted to save the world, be nice to all, and help everyone, but honestly she needed to save herself. Every relationship she had ended in disaster. And, of course, it was never her; the men she chose were always the ones to be blamed. But I blamed her for picking such horrible men. She believed everyone had the best intentions for her, and obviously, they didn't. I'd been telling her this her whole life. Sometimes it was hard to believe she was not adopted, because it didn't seem possible that two people who were less than two years apart and had been raised in the same household could turn out so differently.

CHAPTER 3

Yvette Turner-McKnight

Some women hated to walk past groups of men, because no matter what you were wearing, they found a way to objectify you. I wasn't one of those women. I would not say I welcomed it, but I couldn't help the way I was built. Early on, I just embraced it. I had always been tall for my age and built like a little woman, my mother would say. My father would always try to make me wear baggy clothes and didn't like the way boys looked at me, wanted to walk me home, and rang the phone for me. He hated it so much, he tried to keep me under his supervision as much as possible. I was not allowed to spend the night at the house of a friend who had brothers, and I could never get off the porch. All my dad's efforts were in vain, because I was still boy crazy. I moved out and married at eighteen and left my younger sister, Crystal, to deal with my punishment. My dad put a tighter vise grip on her life. She couldn't do anything or go anywhere. That didn't work, either, because she got pregnant early and the dad went to jail. By the time they got to my baby sister, Dana, my dad had refined his approach and molded her into the perfect overachiever.

I walked past a group of men who worked at the same

place I did. They were dressed in dark blue Dickies pants, work boots, and T-shirts and were leaning against the dingy white work truck. They were staring at my short, tight, tan pencil skirt and my navy and white short-sleeved blouse. The most noticeable glance came from Hector. His eyes were roaming up and down my legs, and he didn't look away, which made me feel slightly uncomfortable. I had asked him before not to stare at me like that.

As I made my way past them, one of them called out, "Yo, Miss McKnight. Can you tell Frank we are burning up in these work trucks? They need to be serviced. It's ninety degrees outside. They have to get this AC fixed. I shouldn't be sweating like this when they got all that money."

"Okay, I will. I'll let him know."

"Please, 'cause someone should tell him that air-conditioning is not a luxury. It is a necessity."

"Okay. I'll call him as soon as I go in the building."

"Miss McKnight, I have to give you my time sheet," Hector said.

I didn't bother to turn around. I just kept walking and said, "Make sure you get it to me by the end of today."

I sashayed off of the showroom floor, filled with hanging rugs on display and living room, bedroom, and dining room sets, and headed upstairs to my office. I worked as the front office/human resources manager—and any other title they decided to give me—for Zinoloi Rugs, Carpets, and Exotic Furniture, with seven locations in New Jersey, Delaware, and Pennsylvania. Mr. Zinoloi, the owner, was really nice and gave me a job almost nine years ago, and then he retired and his son, Frank, took over and started cutting corners everywhere he could, like not getting the air-conditioning fixed in the work trucks. I entered my spacious office and dialed him. He never answered, so I left him a message.

"Hey, Frank. Listen, the guys are complaining that they don't have air in the trucks. Please give me a call so I can get approval to have them repaired." Before I could complete my sentence, Hector walked up to me, grabbed my butt, and lightly bit my lip. He was a twenty-four-year-old, sexy-ass Puerto Rican from Kensington—a rough North Philly neighborhood. He had a low, wavy haircut and a trail of colorful bad-boy tattoos going down both of his muscular arms. From afar, someone would mistake Hector for a thug, but he was not one. He was one of the sweetest men I knew. He would be my man if I hadn't married and wasn't now divorced, and if he were a few years older and didn't have a girlfriend and a kid. Because of all our obstacles, he had to be content with just being my YB, or young boy.

"You better be careful and make sure no one followed you up here," I warned.

"They didn't. They made a McDonald's run. So we have, like, ten minutes."

"Uh-huh. Where is the time sheet?"

"Right here," he said as he patted his pocket, where part of a bulge was visible.

"Stop playing."

"I'm not playing. The way your ass was moving in that skirt . . . it took everything in me not to grab you. How's my lady doing, anyway?" he asked as his hands glided up my skirt massaging my ass.

"She's great. She misses you."

"Tell her I was thinking about her this morning in the shower."

"Okay, I'll be sure to let her know."

"When can I see her again?"

I walked from beside him and said, "Hector, I have a lot going on. I don't know. Sometime soon."

"How you going to give her to me, then take it away?"

"I'm not taking her away for good, but she can't right now. Hello. I just went through a divorce, Hector. I'll call you tomorrow. We will get together then. I promise you. Right now I have a lot of work to do."

He gave me a kiss on my cheek and told me he was holding me to my promise. I had a seat at my desk and began to prepare checks to pay a few dozen invoices. My work phone rang and interrupted my work flow. I hoped it was Frank approving those new air conditioners. But it wasn't; it was my best friend Geneva. "Are you going to come to Caribana and party with us Trini style?" Geneva asked with a fake island accent.

"I told you I can't go to Canada. I have so much going on right now."

"Vette, you need this trip. Every year I go, and every year when I come back, you complain that you should have gone. This is going to be the closest we'll ever get to Carnival. You're a newly divorced woman that needs some fun in her life. Plus, we want this to be your divorce party weekend."

"My divorce party weekend," I repeated back to her. "Who came up with that idea?"

"Stacey did. She is getting you a cake with a dead groom to sit on top of it."

"A dead groom. Really? You know what? That actually doesn't sound like a bad idea. Can you put the real dead ex on a cake, too, for me?" I laughed.

"Vette, you are crazy. Come on and go. We're going to have fun. Please come."

"It sounds like fun, but I have a few things called bills standing in the way. This is my rent check."

"What about your check from the house?"

"That check didn't come yet. It will be here any day. I have to call the Realtor."

"Vette, come on. You haven't been anywhere this summer. It will be fun with all three of us. You are going to miss it. Think about it. . . . When will be the next time all of us will be able to get out of town at the same time?"

"I don't know. Probably never."

"You're right—never—so you have to go."

"Let me see what I can do. Maybe I can pay everything when I get back. I'll think about it. Who's driving?"

"Stacey is driving."

"Good. Because you drive too slow. Give me a minute. I'll call you back."

I giggled a little at the thought of a divorce party and the fact that I was thirty-three years old and about to be twice divorced. If you started as early as I did, it was easy. I married my first boyfriend straight out of high school. He was leaving for the army, and I wanted to go with him, so we got married. Six years later I had two children and was divorced. I couldn't blame Doug for anything; it wasn't his fault that it didn't work. I was bored with him and tired of moving all around the world, and I cheated on him. Now, looking back, I should have worked it out. He was a very good man. My first ex-husband now lived in Panama City, Florida. The kids had just got back from spending their summer vacation with him. He was a good guy and father. He sent me money for them and coparented from afar.

I went into my second marriage like I was going to make it work and be a good wife. What a mistake! His ass cheated on me like crazy. My ex-husband Phil was a bus driver for SEPTA, and in case you didn't know, bus drivers had fans and groupies, too. Their fans were the ladies that sat daily in the front of the bus and talk their ear off the entire ride. Well, one young girl took a liking to my husband, and, well, he couldn't resist. She was only nineteen and was so in love, she knocked on my door, claiming she was pregnant by my man. This little girl knew everything about me—where I worked, my schedule, my kids' names, what kind of car I drove—and she said she had been to my house several times. So of course I wanted to leave my husband for cheating on me. But when I confronted him, he assured me it was over.

Most women that got cheated on were somewhere crying and asking why. I did the opposite: he cheated on me, and I said, "Oh, that ain't nothing, boo. I'll cheat on you, too, and I'll do it better." So when the opportunity presented itself for me to get revenge, I did . . . with Hector. Phil knew how to give it but couldn't take it. The minute he learned I had an affair, the world was over. I'd forgotten to turn my ringer off, and Hector had texted me all these messages from YB on my phone. They said that he was falling in love with me and couldn't wait to fuck me again. I came out of the shower, and Phil was in tears. He cried, "How could you? How could you think about being with another man? What? I don't satisfy you?"

I didn't know what to say. I tried to tell him I cheated because he did, but he was furious and was not trying to hear my argument. We had a long discussion that night, and he said he forgave me. I believed him at first, but then he would come in the house, slamming things and picking fights with me. Of course, I always said, "You cheated first!" But all he could say to that was "I'm a man." I guess that meant he got a pass and I didn't. He constantly questioned me about what YB stood for and who YB was, but I told him it didn't matter and we should work on our marriage. I promised him the cheating was a one-time occurrence and not a full-fledged affair. He would have died if he knew it was with someone on the job.

And I think our other issue was jealousy and him wanting to compete with me. He was envious of the relationships I had with my parents and my sisters. He would always tell me I was lucky I had good parents, because his mother and father had neglected him and had let him raise himself. His parents chose drugs over him and I think he almost resented the fact that my parents were there for me. Then there were other signs throughout our entire relationship. For instance, if I said I was thinking about going to the gym, then he suddenly got interested in lifting weights. If I said I was thinking about buying something, he would go buy the bigger, better version. We were having a lot of problems, and we finally went to counseling. I thought it would save us, because for a little while everything got good again, but it didn't last. Then reality set in: Phil would never get over the fact that another man had touched his wife.

So, after all the cheating and counseling, we decided to just get a divorce. We agreed on no high lawyer fees; we did a do-it-yourself divorce. It wasn't like we were rich, and we didn't have a whole bunch of possessions. The only thing we gained in our marriage was our house. Our house was a brick single-family home in Cheltenham. It was on a tree-lined street, with a big front lawn and a double garage. It was a few minutes outside of Philly, but it seemed like it was miles away. Our neighborhood wasn't affected by the recession, and we were fortunate enough to have equity in our house. I wanted to stay in the house, but we both needed the money to move on with our lives. We were going to split the profit and then go our separate ways. My share was twenty-five thousand dollars, and with that money I planned to find a house to rent, pay my daughter Mercedes's, tuition for the year, get a nice used car, fix my credit up, treat me and the kids to a few things, and put the rest up.

In the meantime, while I waited to go to the real estate settlement, I got a temporary small apartment with a month-to-month lease and put most of my big things in storage. All of this divorce stuff was so aggravating. I regretted meeting and marrying my ex Phil. I regretted our big, expensive wedding. Had I known I would be divorced after only three years of marriage, we would have just said "I do" at city hall.

During the drive home I realized Geneva was right; the summer was almost over and I hadn't been anywhere. My rent was due, but I could pay my landlord as soon as I got back with my next check. I needed to go on this trip. I called Phil to find out our exact settlement date. I hated his voice, the way each syllable came out of his mouth.

He didn't say hello or anything. He just answered, "Yeah, we are going to the settlement sometime next week."

"Okay. Well, I wasn't calling only about that. I was making sure you were okay, too."

"I'm fine. Yvette, don't act like you like me or even care about me. When I get the exact date and time, I'll call you," he grumbled, and then the phone went silent. He was a nasty, miserable-ass man. That was exactly why I was happy. I wasn't with him anymore.

I dialed my mom to see if Brandon and Mercedes could stay with her and my father for a few days. My father answered the phone, and I put on my baby voice, which had worked on him since I was three.

"Daddy, where's Mommy?"

"She is in the living room. Why? What do you need?"

"I don't need anything, Daddy. I was just wondering if maybe the kids could come over for a few days."

"Uh, I don't see why not. Sure, no problem. Where are you going?"

"Just getting out of town for a bit. You know, with the divorce and everything, Geneva thought it would be a good idea for us to get away and relax."

"Yeah, that sounds good, and I'll be home this weekend. Your mother won't mind. You can bring the kids. We'll probably get Nasir and Jewel, too."

"Okay, I'll bring them over now, because we are leaving first thing in the morning."

Now that I had a sitter, it was time to leave Frank a message letting him know I wouldn't be in tomorrow, and call Geneva back and let her know I was going.

I was now extra excited and began packing for my trip. I had so many things I needed to do. I had to do something with my hair, get a pedicure, go to the bank, pick a few things up from storage, and drop the kids off. I called down the hall to my son. Brandon was fourteen and was starting high school in a few months. He thought he was grown, but he was still part baby. He came in my room, smelling like an entire basketball team after practice.

"Go pack. You're going to Mom Mom and Pop Pop's for a few days."

"Why?"

"Because I'm going out of town with Ms. Geneva and Stacey for a few days."

"Man, I don't want to go over there. It's boring! Pop Pop's going to be telling all those back-in-the-day stupid stories."

"You don't have a choice. You can't stay here by yourself."

"Can I at least take my Xbox?"

"I don't care. Take your game, but take a shower and get ready."

My daughter, Mercedes, whom we all called Mimi, wouldn't be as hard to break the news to. I could leave her anywhere as long as she had a few books to read, her skates, and a rope. Mercedes came in my room, bouncing and lively. She was very thin and smaller than the other nine-year-olds in her class.

"Mom, where are you going?"

"On a little trip with Miss Geneva."

"Where are we going?"

"To Mom Mom's."

"No, Mom, please. I don't want to go there."

"Too bad. Get ready. I think Jewel will be there, too!"

"She will?" Her attitude changed a little, like maybe she could deal with her grandparents if her cousin was with her.

"And whatever you do this time, do not talk to her about Santa Claus not being real or her dad's college."

"Okay, Mom, but there isn't such a thing as Santa Claus, and her dad is in jail, not college. Why does Aunt Crystal tell her that stuff, and why does she believe it?"

"Because she does, Mercedes. Just go get ready."

I pulled up to my parents' West Oak Lane home. It was a semidetached brick home. The neighborhood had changed a little, but it was still a decent area, where everyone worked, trimmed their hedges, and swept in front of their home. My mom came to the black iron security door. I could tell she was surprised to see us. I was tall caramel brown and shapely like she was, but I didn't inherit her thick brown hair, which she kept flipped up at the ends.

"What are y'all doing here?"

"Daddy didn't tell you? The kids are staying over for a few days."

"Your father doesn't tell me anything. But, of course, they can stay." My mother reached her arms out to Mercedes and Brandon. Mercedes gave her a pathetic hug, and Brandon quickly patted her side.

We walked in the house that I grew up in. Everything was still the same: My parents still had the big black sectional, next to the the wall unit that took up the entire wall, pictures of all our proms, hung on the wall. The pictures reflected a time when we had long ponytails, missing teeth, too many barrettes, and hadn't quite grown into our looks. My dad came out of the basement. He gave me a quick peck on the cheek.

"Daddy, why didn't you tell Mommy we were coming?" I asked.

"Oh, I forgot."

"Brandon, your grandfather was just saying he was going to call you to see when you wanted to finish working on the planes in the garage," my mother said.

Brandon looked over at me like, *Why, mom*? I turned away, laughing to myself.

"Here is some money if they want to order a pizza or something," I told my mom.

"A hundred dollars for pizza?"

"Yeah, Mom, and if they need anything else. Call me if you need me. Love y'all."

"Yeah, bye, Mom," Brandon shouted with an attitude as he lowered his eyes at me from the top of the steps.

Mercedes pouted, her lips poked out and her arms crossed.

"Don't worry about them. They'll be fine," my dad said.

"I'm not worried." I wasn't worried. They could spend a few days with their grandparents while their mother had much-needed fun.

Chapter 4

Crystal

It was a quarter to one, and the line was already wrapped around the corner of the family court building. I wasn't excited about taking a paternity test, but at least my sister would be there with me. The only problem with Dana was she thought she knew everything and she didn't. I never got why she was always in someone else's business and giving out advice. She was not married, either, and didn't even have a steady boyfriend that I knew of, but she was quick to tell someone what they were doing wrong in their life. However, she was the first one to go to college in our family and had a really good job and a nice apartment, but that didn't make her life perfect.

I walked into the dreary beige room filled with rows of empty, blue, hard plastic seats and sat in the back. I wanted to have a full view of the room when Kenneth arrived. I looked out the corner of my eye and saw Kenneth and Syreeta walk in the room. He gave me an evil stare, like I was the enemy. Behind him was his manly looking sister, Syreeta. She was skinny and tall, dressed in sagging blue jeans and an oversize orange polo shirt. Her brown hair was two inches long and slicked back with gel.

Kenneth made me so angry. Here he was, a few feet away from his only child, and he wasn't even acknowledging her. I had to put my head down and try not to let them get to me. But even with my head down, I heard Syreeta say something like "That baby ain't yours. Look at her." Instead of responding to her, I gave Kori her bottle and checked the time on my phone, because I was only minutes away from the truth.

A few moments later I heard the click of high heels approaching. I looked up and saw my sister. I smiled and spoke to Dana very loudly. Kenneth and Syreeta looked up, and I gave them a look like "What now, bitches? I have back up, too." Dana grabbed Kori from me, gave her a kiss, and started playing with her, which garnered more hateful stares from "the uglies."

Finally, this older black man came into the waiting room and called out, "Mr. Haines and Ms. Turner, follow me please." I stood up and grabbed Kori and followed him down the hall. The man took us into a small room and instructed us to have a seat. A woman with a white lab coat came in and began to explain the testing procedure.

"I'm going to insert this in your mouth, and I need you to hold it against the inside of your cheek for me. Okay?"

We both said yes and took turns opening our mouths and being swabbed. Afterwards the lab worker inserted the swabs into vials and then sealed them. She scribbled a few things down the side of each with a black marker and said that she was done and that we would receive our results in two to four weeks. I was surprised it took only ten minutes. I thanked the lady and gathered Kori and my bag and began walking out the door. Kenneth was right in front me. I had so much I needed to say to him. I sped up a little and tapped his shoulder.

He turned around, backed up, and said very rudely, "What's up?"

"So, when you get the results, are you going to come and get your daughter?"

"Yup, but if she ain't mine, then it is a done deal and you better not say anything to me"

"I don't say anything to you now. You are ridiculous; you know this is all stupid and unnecessary."

"No, I don't. That's why we are here."

I didn't know why I was still shocked that Kenneth was acting like an ass. "You are a fucking idiot," was all I could think to say.

"Whatever," he said as he flagged me, pulled up his sagging pants, and then bent the rim of his hat down and said to his sister, who was waiting for him, "Man, let's get out of here."

She rolled her eyes at me one last time, and I just shook my head.

"Kenneth, you got this," she had the nerve to tell him. "I don't know why chicks be trying to blame babies on dudes. You don't have anything to worry about."

I couldn't hold back anymore. Syreeta was always saying whatever the hell she wanted to someone, and no one was supposed to respond.

"Why don't you stay out of this, Syreeta? Kori is his. She is your niece, whether you like it or not."

She walked over to me, pointing her finger in my face, and said, "That's yet to be proven."

"Nothing needs to be proved. I know who I slept with, and so does your brother. You weren't there." I stood toe-to-toe with her and looked her directly in her face, as if to say, "Try me, bitch."

Kenneth grabbed Syreeta, and Dana began pulling on me. Syreeta was still talking trash, but I was happy that I had finally stood up to her.

"Girl, you lucky I don't feel like getting a case, because I would smack the bullshit out of you," Syreeta yelled.

"Syreeta, please! You still a woman, and I will fight you like one. Like I said, you need to mind your business."

"I ain't got to mind shit," she said like she was ready to throw a punch, but Kenneth grabbed her before she did. She kept trying to yank her arm away from him, screaming, "Get off me. I'm cool. I ain't even got time for this dumb bitch. She the one who don't know who her baby father is."

All she was doing was a bunch of hollering, making herself look foolish. People were staring, shaking their heads, and the security guard was on his way over. I thought I had won our match and felt like I had a victory, until she screamed, loud enough for the entire family court building to hear, "Crystal, your ho ass is nothing. You hear me? You have three babies and three baby fathers. Ain't none of them with you, and no one will ever want your ass. Because you're just a whore-ass baby mom. Okay? Just a baby mom. You're not a girlfriend. You're not a wife. You're just a baby mom. Find out who your baby daddy is before you say anything to me. Okay. Let's get out of here before I snap on a bitch," she said and then walked off.

I wanted to give a quick rebuttal, but I couldn't think of anything to say back to Syreeta that would hurt as much as the words she had just hurled at me. I did have three baby fathers, but I wasn't a whore. And I knew for sure she had slept with more men than me, and she was a lesbian, but nothing came out. Her words stung, and she was kind of right. I wasn't a girlfriend or a wife. I was just a baby mom.

On Fridays I usually ordered pizza or made some kind of finger food for the kids. It depended, because my children were picky. On different days they decided what they would eat and wouldn't eat. Sometimes I'd end up making three meals: one for Nasir, one for me, and the other for Jewel. My mom said, "Don't fix a bunch of different dishes. Make them eat what you cook," but I didn't want them to be hungry.

While I prepared the ground beef for our tacos, Nasir played with his toys in the middle of the living room floor and Jewel entertained Kori as she sat in her bouncy seat. Jewel was my little helper, my big girl. She was only nine, but she was always telling me that when she grew up, she wanted to be a teacher and a mommy like me. She had a very nurturing personality and always helped me with her brother and sister.

My house was a three-bedroom house. Initially, I was renting, but then my landlord retired and sold it to me before she moved to Florida. It was a nice home on a quiet block, but by the time Kori got big, I was going to have to move because there wouldn't be enough room.

My living room had a big green love seat and sofa. In the middle was a large rug, which the children played and watched television on.

"Nasir, we are going to clean this living room and then your bedroom tonight. Okay?"

"My room is clean."

"No, *clean* means everything off of the floor and out from under the bed. We are going to clean this entire house."

My house wasn't dirty, but it is hard keeping everything together. But as long as we had a clean kitchen and bathrooms, who cared if there were a few toys on the floor? I didn't. I'd rather spend time with my kids and take them out for a day in the park than make them spend the day cleaning.

"Hey, Mom," I said, picking up the ringing phone after checking the screen.

"What are you doing tonight?"

"Cooking tacos for the kids and trying to clean the house."

"Dana told me about what happened in court. Don't worry about Kenneth or his sister. But I know one thing. He has to help you with that baby or he is going to deal with me.

Anyway, I didn't call to talk to you about that. I just wanted you to know I have Brandon and Mimi over here, so if you want, you can brings yours over, too."

"The kids? Tonight? Mom, that's okay. I already started dinner, and I don't have any plans."

"It's Friday night. You had a long day, and you need a break. Bring them kids over here."

"No, Mom. I'm okay. Maybe next time."

"Next time, I don't know about that. I'm not going to call you every week and beg to watch your children."

"Okay, I'll bring them over after they eat."

I welcomed the break my Mom was about to give me, but I didn't have anywhere to go. Jewel would be happy to spend time with Mercedes, even though you could never tell they were the same age. My niece acted just like her name: spoiled and entitled. Yvette bought her everything; she even got her hair and nails done and my little girl still plays with dolls.

Mercedes was waiting on the steps for us to arrive. She called out to Jewel and ran over to the car as soon as she saw us. Her hair was in long rod curls and she was wearing all pink. Jewel was as excited to see her and jumped out of the car to hug her cousin.

"Mercedes, look at you. You look so pretty," I said as I gave her a sideways hug and grabbed Kori out of her car seat.

"Thank you, Auntie Crystal. Can I hold the baby?"

"Let me get her inside and I'll let you hold her."

I walked in my parents' big home. You could see both the kitchen and the dining room from the front door. It was one big, open space. Every time, I walked through my parents door I felt like time stood still and I was a kid again. My nephew Brandon had already taken over my mother's television with his game. I spoke to him, but he was too busy killing people on his game to respond.

"Look at my baby. She is getting so big." My mom grabbed Kori, who then began to cry.

"She is probably still hungry. That's why she being fussy." I got her bottle out of her bag, warmed it up, and gave it my mother, and she began feeding her.

My mom looked down at Kori as she fed her and shook her head and said, "How can a man not want to be a part of this precious baby's life? Now that you took the test, explain to me what's going to happen next."

"We'll get the results, and everything should be okay after this. It will prove she is his."

"Okay, he better hope so, because he sure has a lot of nerve. I'll tell you, these men today have lost they damn mind. Making babies and then not taking care of them"

"Yeah, well I think he is going to get it together. At least I hope."

I talked to my mom a little more, then went upstairs to put the kids' bag in my and Dana's room. It was the back room. My half was the right side, and her half was the left. We used to jump on the bed and stay up all night in this room, sharing so many secrets, dreams about who we were going to be who we would marry, and where we were going to live. Back then I would never have thought my life would turn out like this.

"Mom, I'm going to get out of here."

She gave me a kiss on my cheek and asked if I had packed enough diapers.

"Yeah, and I already made the formula, so all you have to do is put the bottle in warm water for, like, two minutes and it will be ready."

"I raised three babies. I'll manage."

"I know you will. Thanks for taking them, and I'll be here first thing in the morning," I said as I was leaving and tried to figure out what I was going to with my free time.

Chapter 5

Crystal

I was ready to go pick up my babies. Being home alone and listening to the sound of nothing was boring. It was only nine, but I was ready for bed. The sound of Syreeta saying, "You're just a whore-ass baby mom" was still ringing in my ear. I started thinking of everything I could have said back to her but still couldn't think of anything that would have hurt as bad.

I needed to go somewhere, get out of the house. The only friend I had was a girl name Portia, whom I went to middle school with. We talked here and there. Whenever I ran into her, we would always exchange numbers and she would always say I needed to go out with her. Maybe she was out and I could meet up with her. I called her, and Portia answered with all this noise in the background. I could barely make out what she was saying over all the loud music. I asked her where she was and what she was doing.

"I'm at Rascals. Come down. We're having a fish fry for Jeremiah's football team."

"A fish fry? That sounds so very country."

"It's not country at all. We're raising money for the team's new uniforms, and it is Wagner's unofficial reunion. You should come down, too."

"I probably won't remember anyone from Wagner, girl."

"That's why I have my yearbook. Come on, Crystal! If nothing else, come out and support my son. Get a platter and leave."

"All right. Okay. I'll come down. Let me get dressed."

An hour later I was walking through the door of Rascals. Rascals Lounge was what most people would consider a hole-in-the-wall hood bar. It was crammed with people and had loud music and the aroma of fried fish and fries. A thick girl with a silver ball piercing right over her lip was collecting money. I paid fifteen dollars; she gave me a ticket and pointed in the direction of Portia. As soon as Portia saw me, she rushed over and gave me a hug.

"Who did you come with?" she asked.

"No one."

"Okay. Then come over here with me." She had envelopes filled with tickets and dollars hanging out of them. She was multitasking, talking to me, texting, and greeting other people as they walked by. Over the music she leaned into me and asked me if I wanted a drink.

"No, but thanks. I'm going to get this food and probably leave."

"No, you have to stay out for a minute. I need someone normal near me."

"Why you say that?"

"Girl, everybody here I see from Wagner looks so old and fat. I'm, like, 'I know we didn't go to school together.' Anyway, you look good. You can't tell you had three babies."

"Thanks, but I feel like it."

A skinny older man approached us both and said, "Ladies, I got that MAC lip gloss and some smell goods." He pulled an assortment of lip gloss and an array of perfume out of a yellow plastic bag. I was thinking, *Who would buy lip gloss off a man in a bar?* when Portia pulled out her money and bought a bottle of perfume and some lip gloss. The man thanked her, and right after he left, a girl with a big belly came over. The big-bellied girl had a brown drink in her glass. It didn't look like soda, either.

"I know you not drinking and you pregnant, Rhonda," Portia said.

"Please. All my kids had a sip, and they're all fine. It's okay to drink when you pregnant, just not every day."

"Right. If you say so. Well, thanks for coming out and supporting my son, girl. Make sure you get a platter. Take one home for your husband."

"Yeah, I might as well get him one, too." She paid for her platter, gave Portia a hug, and walked away. As soon as she turned her back, Portia whispered to me that Rhonda's baby was going to come out with twelve toes. We laughed, and then Portia tapped one of the bartenders and told him not to serve Rhonda anymore.

Everyone was approaching Portia like she was the queen of the bar. We talked about our kids and jobs and then she saw someone she knew.

"I haven't seen him in years. Tap that guy for me," she told me.

I tapped him, he turned around, and I said, "She wants you."

He looked over and said, "Portia Stevenson."

"You can tell when you went to school with somebody. They always yelling out your first and last name," said Portia. "What's up, Rell? Where Shareef at?" They leaned into one another and gave each other a quick friendly hug?"

"He doing good. Got a wife and a son."

"For real? When you see him, tell him I said, 'What's up?' "

The man said that he would, then Portia told me she would be right back and the guy turned his attention to me. He asked how I had been.

I didn't know him, so I said faintly, "Fine."

"So now you going to act like you don't know me? I sat behind you in sixth grade, and we had Mr. Hafler, the science teacher that had that real bad dandruff. Tell me you don't remember that."

"Yes, I remember him, but . . ."

"But what? You don't remember *me*? Terell Glover? How can you forget me? We used to go together."

"We did not," I said, laughing.

"We did. You were my girl for, like, a week. You broke my heart, but I got over it."

"I didn't. You are lying."

"No, you was my girl. But, anyway, you're still looking good. Pretty as ever. No more big plaits in your hair, huh?"

I laughed some more, wondering how he remembered the ugly big braid my mom would give us when she didn't have enough time to do our hair. "You have a very good memory."

"What? The Turner girls? How could I forget? Y'all always were sitting on the steps with y'all's pop. He always had that look, like, 'Don't look at my daughters.' Your older sister was real, real pretty. What was her name?"

"I don't know. Now are you going ask me about my sister?" I asked playfully.

"No, hold up. I remember her name. It was Colette."

"No, you're wrong. It's Yvette."

"Okay, so I'm talking to the sister I always wanted, anyway," he said, flirting with me.

And I fell for it, because I started to blush.

"Do you still live around here?" he asked.

"No, I live in West Philly now."

"So what are you doing with yourself?"

"Like work?"

He nodded yes.

"Uh, I work downtown at ACR Cable Vision. I'm a customer service rep. How about you?"

"I just got out of the army. I did two tours in Iraq, one in Afghanistan."

"Wow. How was it?"

"Really hot. Just think of the hottest summer day times ten."

"Whew, that's hot."

"I just got out about a year ago, broke up with my girlfriend, and moved home. I was stationed at Fort Bragg in North Carolina. I was going to stay down there, but I missed being home with my family."

"Really? I think I would love to move outside of Philly, see something different. I've never lived anywhere else."

"Yeah, but it gets lonely. So do you have any kids?"

"Yeah, I have a son and two daughters."

"Wow, three kids. I knew someone would marry you."

I snickered quietly. "Kids, yes, but I'm not married, and me and my children's fathers aren't together."

"Oh, okay. I understand how sometimes relationships just don't work out. I don't have any kids yet, but how old are yours?"

"My youngest just turned three months."

"Three months. So you just had a baby."

"Yup, I did," I said self-consciously. Judging by his facial expressions, I knew what he was probably thinking. *You just had the baby, and you not with the dad already.*

"Well, I'm about to get a drink. You want one?" he asked.

I let him know that I was okay, and he walked to the other side of the bar and told me he would be back. However, I knew he wouldn't be back. Who would be interested in someone with three kids?

Surprisingly, Terell returned with his drink and my platter, which Portia had sent over with him. I ate my food, and for about an hour we reminisced about back in the day, and he insisted on making me remember who he was.

"I bet you remember my cousin. She was two grades ahead of us. Octavia Glover. She used to always fight everyone."

"Oh yeah, now I remember you. You were short."

"Yeah, I grew up. I prayed every night, 'Please let me be

taller than Octavia.' We were her cousins, and she would try to fight us, too."

"What is Octavia doing now?"

"Now she is beating prisoners up. She is a corrections officer now in New York."

"That's good. Well, Rell, I didn't plan on staying this long. I'm going to find Portia and leave. It was nice seeing you again."

"You, too. I can walk you to your car if you like."

"Okay."

Terell Glover escorted me to my car, and then he gave me his number and told me I had to call him to let him know I had got in the house safely. I called him, and we were on the phone for the next two hours. He was funny and interesting, but I was becoming sleepy. I let out an uncontrollable loud yawn.

"Am I that boring?"

"No, I apologize. I'm just so tired. I had a long day."

"I understand. Well, good night, Crystal Turner. I wish I could see you before you go to sleep."

"See me where?" I asked.

"Come see you at your house."

"You just saw me and talked to me two hours straight. You're going to come to my house at four in the morning? It's too late."

"You are right, but it would have been nice," he said in a little boy voice.

"Well, if you really want to see me, I guess that would be okay."

"All right. Text me your address and I'll be on my way."

I texted him the address and began to straighten up my home. I was a little nervous about seeing Rell again, but actually kind of happy to have some male company.

About twenty minutes later, I peeked out the window and saw a black Dodge Charger pull up in front of my house. Rell got out of the car. I opened the door.

"You got here fast," I said as I turned on the television and the fan and he sat on the sofa.

"I didn't want you to fall asleep on me."

"I wouldn't have fallen asleep on you."

"I couldn't tell, the way you was yawning. I didn't want to take any chances." Smiling appreciatively, Rell looked me over. "You still looking pretty, I see."

"Thank you. I couldn't have changed that much. You just saw me."

"You most definitely didn't. So are your kids asleep?" he said, looking around the living room at their pictures.

"No, they're with my parents. I have to pick them up early in the morning."

"Oh, so I don't have to be quiet?" Being silly, he raised his voice.

"No, you don't have to be quiet."

"Well, where your baby's pop at? Y'all really not together?"

"Nope, we not together. What about you? I know you had a girlfriend down in North Carolina."

"I did, but she got rid of my baby and didn't tell me about it."

"So you broke up over that? Why did she get an abortion?"

"I have no idea. I'm not sure she knows why she did it. I think she was just used to being with dudes that didn't care or didn't want any kids. But she should have known better than that. I would never leave my baby, like my dad left me."

"Your dad left you?"

"Yeah, he left my mom while she was pregnant with me. I don't care about him. I never met him. My mom kept it moving and raised me and my brother on her own. So, anyway, after she did that, I couldn't look at her the same. We started having problems, and we just broke up."

"Well, my daughter's father kind of did the opposite. He begged me to have my daughter and then demanded a blood test. I gave him one, just to shut him up."

"Yeah, he sounds like a clown, just like her. After all that, I just left her everything, even my car. I just knew when I got back here, I would start over and rebuild everything. I'm staying with Mom and driving my brother's car for now."

"You left her with everything? Should have at least taken your car."

"I probably should have taken the car. I regret it a little, but it's nothing for me to get everything again. I'll have another car and be on my feet in no time. I do have some money saved up, so don't worry—I'm not a bum."

"I didn't think you were, but what kind of work are you going to do now?"

"I have a few things lined up. My brother is trying to get me in with his job. He works at Seisman Bread Company. I already had one interview. I'm just waiting for them to call me back. It's one of those companies where you have to know someone to get in, but once you in, you can make so much money. My brother's wife went to college, and he makes more than her now. He be killing it with overtime. They got a nice house and three cars."

"Yeah, companies like that are good to work for. My dad just retired from the Tastykake factory. He did make good money." I noticed him look in the direction of the fan. "Are you hot? I can turn the air on."

"No, the fan is fine," he said as he took his shirt off. I was able to get a look at his muscular arms. He had just enough muscles to make my mind wander. As vulnerable as I was feeling, it probably wasn't a good idea to have him in my house, sitting next to me on my sofa. I hadn't had sex in six months. Three months before Kori was born and the past three months, because I was going through all this with Kenneth.

Rell moved close to me, and his hands wandered down to my leg. I didn't have the strength to stop him. His fingers felt good rubbing the outside of my neglected body. Mmm. I could feel my heart rate changing when he started blowing and kissing in my ear. I even shivered a little when he unhooked my bra, unleashing my heavy breasts.

I hadn't even realized that my hands had started traveling down his body. My right hand caressed his pants back and forth as a lump became firm against his jeans.

"Why don't you take it out," he murmured in a seductive tone that I couldn't resist.

I didn't need a lot of encouragement. The next thing I knew, I was unzipping his pants and investigating his package with an eager hand. I gasped. His dick was long. Women loved to say that they wanted something big and to announce what they would do with it when they got it, but most were afraid. Something made me feel bold. I didn't have the excuse of being drunk, so all I could say was that I had been in a sex drought for so long that I needed a man! I wanted to feel good. My entire body was shaking with anticipation.

"Do you have a condom?" I whispered, my words coming out unsteady.

"Yeah. In my wallet." He stood, took a condom out of this wallet, and then rolled it over his oversize length, and still managed to keep his lips on mine, kissing me passionately.

We didn't even make it out of my living room, and I didn't care. He held my waist as he hoisted me right on top of his thick erection. My insides were already juicy when he steered his head toward my delicate insides one inch at a time. I spread my legs open and pulled him in deeper. He slid in a few more inches of his luscious manhood, and my hips started moving in a demanding way that let him know I could handle some more. He wasn't completely in, but that didn't stop him from thrusting forward. His belt made jingling sounds every time his body slapped against mine. I felt like I was going to fall off the sofa.

"You feel like a virgin, baby girl. Damn, this pussy is good!" he shouted as his body rammed deep into mine. He kept his fast pace for another fifteen minutes and his body trembled to an orgasm.

After we finished, I showed him to the bathroom. I was wearing a little smile of satisfaction as I cleaned up our mess, picking up clothes and the condom wrapper. When he came out of the bathroom, he kissed me and picked me up and took me up to my bedroom.

Rell made love to me again—slowly this time. Afterward, I lay in his arms, feeling so peaceful and satisfied. I looked over to my left, at the clock, and realized that it had been hours since I had been reintroduced to Terell Glover. To be honest, I didn't know what to think. I wondered how long this feeling of sexual euphoria would last. I knew I would have to pick up my three-piece soon, and my dream would be over. But at the moment, I was enjoying the warmth and security of his strong arms and didn't want to let go.

CHAPTER 6

Yvette

"What took you so long?" Stacey yelled as I placed my luggage in the trunk of her silver Chevy Malibu. I had two bags filled to capacity with all the shoes, makeup, dresses, and accessory options I might need for the weekend. "All of that for three days? Really, Vette?" Stacey asked.

"Yes, I want to look nice for all three days."

"Always the diva," Geneva chimed in.

"Be quiet. You begged me to come. Now that I'm here, be happy and stop complaining."

"No one is complaining, Your Highness. We bow down to the queen, Yvette." Geneva laughed as she bowed graciously from the front seat.

Geneva was my girl, and Stacey was her friend. We were all friends, but I was way tighter with Geneva. I had known them both since elementary school. We were the pretty girls that everyone wanted to befriend. Geneva married her college sweetheart, Eric, and had two young children and was lucky enough to be a stay-at-home mom. Out of all the couples I knew, I thought her marriage was almost too perfect.

She and Eric still went out on weekly dates and liked each other.

Stacey worked for the state and was married, too, but not happily. She didn't have any children and stayed with her husband because he paid the bills. Stacey was cool; she just was cheap, and not a sensible kind of cheap. She would go across town to save a nickel on dish detergent. I didn't have time for that. I felt like you should live life to have fun and not cut corners.

Now that we were on our way, I was excited and couldn't wait to get to Toronto and enjoy a fun-filled weekend with my friends.

"So, Ms. Trinidad, tell us what we should expect," I said to Geneva.

"Yeah, you got me going and I don't even know what it is like. Are we too old? Are we going to feel out of place?" Stacey asked.

"No, not at all. It is all ages. The entire weekend is going to be one big Caribbean party," Geneva said. "As a matter of fact, we need to start this divorce party, aka single lady weekend." She handed me a big red gift bag from the front seat.

"What's this for?" I began digging in the bag and pulled out a big chocolate-colored dildo, Bath & Body Works lotions and sprays, condoms, and cherry-flavored massage oil.

"That's your single lady gift pack," Geneva explained.

"This is not a single lady pack. This is a freak pack. I will take the Bath & Body Works, but I don't need the dildo. I still have Hector. Thank you very much. I was actually supposed to get with him this weekend."

"Oh, yes, sexy-ass Hector. That's a fine young boy," Stacey added.

"Oh, my God, you sound like an old, desperate cougar and a pervert, Stacey." I burst into laughter just as my phone began ringing, and it was none other than Hector. "Hey, baby," I said, shushing them.

"What's up, Ma? What time am I going to see you?"

"Change of plans. I'm out of town. I will call you when I get back."

"Out of town? When are you coming back?" he asked, disappointed.

"In a few days."

"A few days? I really have to wait to see you? This right here is the shit that I don't like with you, Yvette. You always get me all hyped, then cancel on me."

"Look, I'm not home. Sorry. There is nothing I can do about it. Listen, I'm in the car with my friends. I'll call you later."

"Whatever, man." He could be mad all he wanted to. I didn't care. I could deal with him and everyone when I returned.

"What now, Stacey?" I said.

"Oh, nothing. I just love it. Love them and leave them. Take the dick and run. How many women have men waiting for them as soon as they get a divorce?" Stacey said.

"Be quiet. He's not waiting for me. He still has his girlfriend, and I'm not interested in being with him full-time, anyway. He's a kid, only twenty-four years old."

"I wish I had me a twenty-four-year-old," Stacey replied.

"Girl, me too. Yvette, you got to teach us what to do," Geneva said.

"Okay, turn this car around. I got to get out. You both sound like the oldest thirty-two-year-old grandmoms I've ever met." My phone began ringing again. I looked down, irritated, to see if it was Hector again. I was going to cuss him out.

I didn't bother looking over at Stacey before she said, "See what I mean? He's calling back again. Damn, you have him whipped!"

It was not him. It was my job. "Hey Frank."

"Hey, Yvette I know you are off, but I have a quick question for you. Do you know when Edwin Mitchell is supposed to return off of disability?"

"No, I was waiting from another letter to come in from his doctor."

"Okay, well he called me a few times today, asking did we receive anything. I think he is bullshitting us anyway. He doesn't need four months off for something falling on his toe. Do me a favor, when you return to the office send me all his info, because if he don't get back on the job by next week he is fired."

"All right Frank. I'll take care of it as soon as I get there."

I hung up the call and I did really seem like the popular girl because Frank was calling again, but this time I wasn't going to answer. I wasn't on the clock and nor was I accepting any calls the rest of the weekend. It was time to party.

Stacey pulled into a gas station and made it known that she needed toll and gas money from us. I was going to give her money as soon as we got to an ATM, and I didn't need a reminder, but her petty ass kept hinting around, which aggravated the hell out of me. As soon as we got a few feet away from her car, I began to question Geneva about her friend's ways.

"I don't know why she felt the need to ask us like we were children," I said. "What grown person gets in another grown person's car and does not pay their own way?"

"Shh, be quiet. She might hear us," said Geneva.

"I don't care. I can't take her penny-pinching this weekend. I'm serious."

"Let's just give her money and be done with it," Geneva replied.

We paid for the gas and grabbed gum, Nerds, chips, and a few waters.

"Stacey, we put eighty in the tank. That should be enough, right?" I asked. "And here's another seventy-five dollars. That should cover anything else." I saw her look down and count it. I looked over at Geneva. She just shook her head, and I rolled my eyes.

It took only eight hours for us to go over the Canadian border. We flashed our passports at the border patrol, and they welcome us into their country. Our first stop was to Niagara Falls. We stopped quickly and took pictures in front of the gushing water. It was a beautiful sight, but we were more interested in getting to the party.

Toronto looked like any other big city. There was a melting pot of people of every race and nationality walking down the street, like in New York City. The only difference was it was really clean.

We were staying at a Sheraton Hotel near all the events. We entered our spacious room with two double beds, unpacked, showered, and changed our clothes. They both checked in by cell phone with their husbands. That was one part of being married I wouldn't miss. I could do without the constant "Hurry home," "What's for dinner?" and "Where are you?" No more cell phone checking in for me. I happily turned my phone off. I was a free woman and loving it.

It was time to see the city and we were all dressed and ready to go.

The city streets were full of Caribbean people adorned in their islands' colors. Jamaicans waved yellow, black, and green flags, and people from Trinidad and Tobago waved their country's red and black flag. I saw so many colors and flags, that it was almost dizzying. We were lucky our hotel was just a few blocks from all the excitement: we could drink as much as we liked and were close enough to be able to stumble back to our hotel. And the events we couldn't walk to, we would just catch cabs, because none of us were interested in receiving an international DUI.

We made it to one of the clubs called Coast Line and was ready to start our partying. After we showed the bouncer our

IDs, he opened the door to a club playing fast calypso music. It was humid and warm, and there wall-to-wall sweaty bodies shaking to the fast beat. We walked over to the bar and tried to order drinks, but there was a crowd of people ahead of us in the libation line. It didn't matter. I walked to the other side and managed to get the bartender's attention. I asked her for six apple martinis.

"Vette, why are you ordering so many drinks?" Stacey asked.

"So we won't have to get back in line."

"Girl, you always thinking. How much we owe you?"

"Nothing. This round is on me," I said as I passed them their light green drinks.

Stacey raised both her glasses and said, "Shout-out to my girl Yvette and her divorce."

"Yes, shout out to Vette's divorce. It is not the end, but a new beginning for you. You will get another husband, but you can't get another you," Geneva said and cheered.

"Exactly, shout-out to the men that don't know what they got until they are replaced. Let's drink,"

We all finished our first glasses of apple martini and were well into our second when Stacey pulled out her camera, and began taking pictures of us. We were being silly posing like models and making faces. She extended her arm to try to get all three of us in the frame. After my two drinks I was beginning to feel the effects of the alcohol. My body felt like it had to keep up with the tempo and began moving to the rhythm. I felt so liberated. I was in another country and didn't care about anyone, and I could do whatever I wanted, like dance by myself seductively in the middle of the floor.

It didn't take long before a man with excessive cleavage and a gold rope chain around his neck started dancing with me. I didn't care what country I was in; gold rope chains and man cleavage weren't in style. I danced with the gold-ropechain-wearing man, but after three songs I told him, "Thanks," and walked away. However, Fourteen Karat Gold wasn't done with me. For the rest of the night he kept following me around the club. When I looked up, there he was. I didn't want to be rude, but he needed to go somewhere. I dodged him in the bathroom and told Stacey to tell him she was my man, and he finally left me alone.

Once Fourteen Karat Gold left me alone, we were free to dance with these Toronto natives. They were all tall and cute, with long dreads. They were in their early twenties, smelled and looked good and were "dutty wining" us in every direction in the club. Geneva was keeping a safe distance away from her dance partner, while Stacey's guy had her pressed up against the wall. My guy had two-tone black- and brownish-gold-tipped dreads that were held back with a rubber band, and muscles popping out of his shirt. He kept biting his lip and flashing his abs at me. I grabbed them a few times, but I had seen tighter abs on Hector.

"What's your name, love?" he asked.

"My name is Toya," I lied as I smiled up at him.

"Beautiful name for beautiful girl."

I thanked him and didn't stop him as he spun me around and slow-ground on my ass. I kept backing away from him, but he still kept bringing me toward him. I was dropping and getting low all over my dance partner. I felt like a dance hall queen. My right hand was behind my head as I worked my hips on my dance partner, hypnotizing him with my movements. So much so that he was ready to make love in the club and I had to let him know it wasn't happening.

By the end of the night my dance partner, Henry, and I had really gotten to know each other. He gave me his number, and we hugged up like we were a couple in love when Stacey took a picture of us.

"Have a good night, ladies. Be safe. Toya, call me please tonight. We will meet up tomorrow."

"I will. I promise."

"You mean it?"

"Yes," I said as he finally released his grip on me. I caught up with my girls.

"He was cute, Vette, and all over you, too," said Stacey.

"I don't care. I'm not coming back here. I gave him the wrong number."

"Vette? You had two boyfriends tonight. Get it girl," Geneva noted.

"And I didn't want either one of them."

"Well, I like the guy I was dancing with, Xavier. I'm going to call him. He can get it before the weekend out."

The next morning it didn't matter that we hadn't had any rest. We were already at the main event, the Caribana parade. The parade was island themed, loud, festive, and fun. There were people everywhere still representing their island pride, singing and dancing with the paraders on the floats and along the route. The music and atmosphere were electrifying. Even the police officers, who were supposed to be controlling the unruly people, were joining in the party. A lot of the women were wearing creative, colorful, decorated bikinis and feather headpieces, with peacock back pieces like the ones Vegas showgirls wore. And it didn't matter how big or small you were. Women with and without fat rolls were having a good time dancing. It was one big party in the street that lasted for hours.

After the parade we went back to the room to recharge and get ready for another night of partying.

"Where are we going tonight? Won't you text your friend to find out what where to go tonight? They live here so they should know," Geneva said.

"I just texted him and, see, he said the Coast Line again, but we should get there before ten so we won't have to pay admission. He's already there."

"Okay, I'm not hanging out with grown men trying to get to the club to get in for free," I said. "Tonight is our last night. I don't want to go to the same place again."

"Well, I'm tired. I think I'm going to stay in anyway, let Xavier come through, and bring his friend Henry with him," Stacey laughed.

"Well we are going out, you can hang out with them if you like," I responded.

"I am. Let me get in the shower and get ready for my fun."

Stacey's guy, Xavier, and the guy I was dancing with the night before Henry arrived. I told them Stacey would be out the shower soon. I didn't know what type of shit she was into and really wasn't trying to find out. I guessed she was about to get her West Indies ménage à trois on, but I wouldn't be staying to watch.

Geneva and I left and on the other side of the door I started shaking my head thinking about the craziness that was about to take place in our hotel room.

"She is crazy. I hope it is all worth it."

"Don't be mad because she is about to get it in with two young boys. You have your own at home."

"I'm not mad at all. I swear I'm not. It's just me; personally, I can't do random dick," I said as Geneva and I exited the hotel.

"Me neither," Geneva replied. "Well, Stacey needs some excitement. She said her husband is so tired in the bedroom and he can't stay hard. I don't know how she could live like that. I have to tell Eric to get off of me."

"Yeah, me and Phil hated each other, but our sex life was fine, even during the cheating. That's on her. You never know who the real freaks are." I laughed and continued on. "Well, I hope she gets enough for both of us. All I know is I'm having fun. Thank you for convincing me to come."

"I knew you would. And it wouldn't have been the same without you."

We walked on the strip where there were a lot of clubs and people out, but the crowd looked much younger than the night before. Without our third wheel the party wasn't as fun, but we made up for Stacey's absence with extra drinks.

Instead of going into another club we found a bar, talked, and took shots until last call.

Hours later, Geneva and I returned to our hotel room totally drunk. The room was dark and Stacey was still booped up with Xavier. Henry must have had all his fun and left. "Shh. They're asleep," Geneva giggled as she turned the lights.

"Let's wake them up." I pulled the covers off of him and saw his naked body. I nudged Stacey awake. "Girl, tell him to get up and dance for us. If this is a divorce party, I am supposed to have a dancer. Tell him to dance for me."

Stacey lifted her head up and told us not to bother him. But between our drunken laughter and our movements all around the room, Xavier woke up, sleepy, trying to figure out why we were laughing and standing over him.

"Can you dance for us? I have some ones. I mean, well, I can't make it rain, but I can make it drizzle," I said drunkenly. I began pitching coins in his direction, waiting for him to dance.

Stacey slapped his ass. I think at first he was with it. Then, when he saw he was the joke, not the entertainment, he began to scramble for his boxers and jeans. Stacey couldn't hold her laughter in, and we all were laughing as he tried to leave the room. I was throwing pennies at him, and Geneva was in the corner, cry-laughing, and the last thing I remembered saying before I passed out was, "I need a water. Hand me a water."

That was several hours ago and I vaguely recall acting like I was twenty, but still didn't know how I ended up in the bathroom tub. I was feeling so very sick. I didn't know if it was the third, fourth, fifth, or sixth drink I had. My incoherence didn't stop Stacey from playing like she was the paparazzi, flashing the camera in my face.

"I can barely open my eyes. Stop taking pictures. It's not funny. Oh, my God, I have a headache," I grumbled. I got up out of the tub and fell onto the bed. Geneva came up and handed me a bottle of water. "Geneva, why are you walking around like you didn't have as many drinks as I did?"

"The key to not being hungover the next day is to drink water, eat something, and pop a aspirin before you pass out," Geneva informed me. "We learned that how many years ago? Plus, I'm driving back and have to keep my eyes on the road. Plus, my husband and kids are calling me nonstop. It is time to say bye to Toronto."

We packed and hit the road, and after I had food in my stomach, and aspirin in my system, I was feeling a little better. I couldn't wait to get home and just sleep my hangover off.

CHAPTER 7

Dana

Reshma and Zyeed must have invited everyone they had ever met in their lives to their wedding. There were hundreds of people seated in rows and rows of white-draped chairs with big bows behind them. Reshma came down the aisle escorted by her father. Her arms and hands were covered in henna tattoos. Her traditional Indian gown had vibrant hues of red and orange and was lined with beautiful beaded stones. The dress's rose-beaded embroidery accented her bridal nose chain. Zyeed waited for Reshma to reach him at the end of the aisle. He looked handsome dressed in a long gold suit jacket with a mandarin collar and a hanging scarf.

The wedding ceremony was amazing, but the reception was extravagant, like a Bollywood movie. I could easily say the wedding cost a couple hundred thousand dollars. The lavish reception was held at the Summerton Hill Country Club. There were elaborate, sparkling blue, yellow, white, and purple centerpieces and flower towers illuminated by white candles on each table, in addition to lovely silverware, plates, and napkins. During, the reception they did many Indian dances around her, and there was just so much love and family. I cried as her dad made a speech. He had a very thick accent, but it made me think about how proud my dad was going to be when he could finally give me away.

As traditional as the beginning of the wedding was, most of the music for the reception was hip-hop and dance music. Everyone was dancing and having a great time except for me. I didn't know anyone at my table and I was kind of lonely until Leah came over to my table and grabbed my hand and said, "Come on. Get up and dance."

"I don't want to dance."

"Yes, you do," Leah said insistently and pulled me up, anyway, and we began to dance.

I should have known it was a setup.

"I have this great guy I want you to meet," she said as she nudged me toward this okay-looking black guy. She gave me his stats as we danced over in his direction. "He is a doctor in the neonatal department at CHOP with Zyeed. A great guy and very single."

The closer we got up on him, the less attractive he became. He was shorter than me, pudgy in the gut, and had two prominent cowlicks in the front of his hair, but Leah did say he was a neonatal doctor. Plus, it was too late to avoid him, because she was already introducing us.

"Dana, this is Lavar. Lavar, Dana."

"Hi. Nice to meet you, Dana."

"Nice to meet you, as well," I responded.

Leah then awkwardly pushed us together and told us to dance. I got the impression I was not his type, because he never made eye contact with me and didn't seem that interested.

"So here, Dana. Take my card and call me. I'm not much of a dancer, but enjoy," he said instead of taking me to the dance floor.

"I will." I placed his card in my purse and took my seat back at my table.

No sooner had I sat than I gazed across the room, and

who did I see on the dance floor, Michael Jacksoning with a group of blondes and one brunette? I looked over at him and thought, *So you don't know how to dance, huh?* He must have felt me staring, because he glanced over in my direction and scrunched his shoulders up and kept dancing.

"So what do you think?" Leah asked when she came over to my table again.

"I don't think I'm his type."

"Really? Why do you say that?"

I pointed to him dancing on the dance floor with the ring of girls.

"Oh."

After the reception, I wasn't ready to go home yet, so I stopped over at Tiffany's cozy two-bedroom apartment. I entered her creatively decorated, comfy home and we walked straight to her kitchen area.

"You want a glass of wine or pasta salad?"

"No, I'm not hungry, but I will take a glass of wine."

Tiffany reached inside her pine wood cabinets and grabbed two glasses and began to pour us glasses of Moscato. "You look nice. Where are you coming from?"

"The wedding of my friend, Reshma, from work."

"Someone else at your job got married?"

"Yup. In the last year three people married. Four, if you count the gay guy Leonard's commitment ceremony."

"Everyone is getting married, and every man I meet has some type of issues. Nice," Tiffany grumbled.

"What happened with Mr. Art Guy?"

"Well, what happened was his apartment. I know this place isn't huge, but I stepped inside his and honestly, my kitchen is bigger than his entire place. I literally can extend my arms out and I am able to touch his walls. So I'm looking around, and then I see he had his goals on the wall. That was nice, I suppose. But you need more than goals on a wall. You need to put those goals into action. That might help, right?

While I was looking around his place, I wanted to say to him, 'You have a college degree, no car, and no children. Where is your money?' "

"Maybe he is paying back his student loans, and you know artists don't make that much in the beginning," I said with a shrug.

"Then he needs a second job, maybe even a third. And now I'm looking back at all that romantic stuff, like the free jazz festival and the open mic poetry night. He wasn't being romantic. He was just taking me on broke dates. And I just couldn't tolerate his being broke anymore. And plus, I was tired of him calling me queen. So I just told him not to call me anymore."

"You're mad at him for calling you queen? You are hilarious," I told her.

"No, I'm not being funny. I'm just being real. I just want to meet someone who is not crazy with issues, is not strapped for cash, or does not have a litter of kids."

"Well, you're not alone. Speaking of issues, I had to accompany Crystal to court because her awful baby dad said he is not the father."

"What? I swear, all these men are sad. It seems like either they were raised by a no-good-ass manipulative mom, and now they don't trust women, or they didn't have a father figure to show them how to be a good man. I don't know what we are going to do. I really want a husband by thirty, and now I only have, like, a year and a half left."

"It will happen," I assured her.

"I hope so, because I don't understand why I'm still single. I read an article that asked, 'Would you date yourself?' And I thought, *Of course I would date me.* I'm educated, in shape, pretty, and have good credit. I'm not asking for that much. Just that my potential partner comes to the table with just as much or more to offer. Is that too much to ask for?"

"No, that's not too much," I said.

"It must be. And it's not like I want someone to come and

take care of me. I just want my complement. All he has to do is come into my life and add to what I already have. But has that happened yet?"

"Yeah, that would be good," I agreed.

"It would be very good," Tiffany said. "Do you know how many young white teachers at my school come back after summer break every year as Mrs. So-and-So, and I still have the same old last name?"

"Yeah, that's pretty much how it goes. None of my coworkers are going through half of what we go through. They meet a guy, and within six to twelve months they say, 'Okay, let's do this. I love you, you love me let's get married.' No twist, shouts, or 'You better marry me or else.' Then they have a baby, and everyone is celebrating."

"Well, this other black teacher at my school—I think she is, like, thirty-seven—she said if she doesn't find a boyfriend, not a *husband,* by next year, she is getting artificially inseminated."

"Wow. Is that what it has come to? She can't even find someone to have a baby with? Please do not tell me anymore; that is so sad." I said between sips of wine.

"Isn't it? I hope it gets better than this, and soon, because I'm ready to get married. I'm ready for you to be my maid of honor and for us to go wedding-dress shopping," Tiffany said.

"Okay. First, we need to find you a boyfriend."

"Yeah, that's true. Well, I'm going to find me a guy one way or another. I think I'm about to date online. You know that website DateFairy.com? I'm going to sign up and meet someone. I don't care if they are Asian, Mexican or white as long as they are nice, because I'm tired of being single."

"So you are going to do the lonely girl online dating thing."

"Yes I am. And it is not lonely; it is smart. Everyone is meeting online now and there isn't anything wrong with it."

"I'd still rather meet someone in person. Plus, I don't think

I could date any other races. I'm not sure they would understand and get me."

"How do you know that? You never even explored it."

"No it is not for me. People online are crazy and it is just weird."

"I don't think so and I don't care what you say; I'm finding me a boyfriend. Watch."

"I hope you don't meet a maniac off that crazy website." I laughed.

"If I do, at least I'll have a man."

Chapter 8

Yvette

After a great mini vacation with my girls, it was time to get back to the job. I was already exhausted by the thought of all the work I'd left. Payroll had to be done by the end of the day, a stack of invoices needed to be paid, and there were over a dozen voice mail messages. The majority were from Edwin Mitchell. He had been out on disability for six months and was trying to get his doctor to sign off on another three months. If he was able to, that was fine; if not, I couldn't assist him with anything else. He would just have to work for a check like the rest of us.

It was going to be a crazy day. I could feel it. I'd been in my office only a half hour, but it was already time for a Dunkin' Donuts run. My caffeine fix was very necessary to accomplish anything. I picked up my bag and walked toward the showroom, and I bumped into Gene, who needed my assistance.

"Hi, Miss McKnight."

"Hey. What's going on, Gene?"

"My wife had the baby over the weekend. A little girl, eight pounds, eleven ounces."

"Wow! That's a big baby."

"Yeah, she is, but what I wanted to tell you is that I called the insurance company to add her, and they said she is not automatically covered or something."

"No, she should be. The hospital should have called the insurance company directly, not you. But just write down all her information, and I will contact them for you. I'll handle it when I get back."

"Thanks, Miss McKnight."

"No problem. Tell your wife I said, 'Congratulations.' " Just as I completed my conversation with Gene, I noticed my boss, Frank, walking toward me.

"I need to see you," he said very sternly.

"Okay, no problem. Let me grab my notepad, Frank. Also, did you get the message I left you last week about the trucks needing to be serviced?"

"I did. I'll see you in my office."

My coffee run was going to have to wait. I ran back to my office, dropped my purse, grabbed my notepad, and walked to Frank's big back office.

Frank immediately closed the door and went to his desk. He sat down, took off his glasses, and began rubbing the top of his forehead. He then began looking at me very seriously.

"Miss McKnight, I was trying to reach you a few times after our last conversation."

"You were? I didn't get it; my phone must have been out of range. It's been acting up lately."

"Understandable, but the main reason I wanted to speak with you is because . . ." He paused and took a deep breath. Then he said, "I received some really disturbing information."

"Disturbing information?" I repeated back to him.

I was lost when he said, "Ms. McKnight, you know my father started this company with nothing. He was an immigrant, and he believed in hard work and honesty."

"Of course."

"Well, quite honestly, I cannot let you or anyone else destroy this company. My father is very fond of you, and I think he was in tears when I told him about the information I'd received."

What the hell was he talking about? *What information?* I had to find out what the hell he was talking about, and I needed him to get to the point.

And then he continued, his eyes going back and forth. "Miss McKnight, last week I received several voice messages from an anonymous male saying there were criminals and drug addicts working for my company. Then the message also mentioned possible fraud, overtime abuse, and discrepancies in the payroll. Are you aware of any of this?"

"No, definitely not," I said as I shook my head no.

"Do you know if someone is on drugs or is a thief? If they steal from us or harm one of our loyal customers, we could lose everything." I was not following what Frank was saying at all. "As I said before, we tried to reach you to try to get clarity on this matter. We weren't able to reach you, so I reviewed the payroll records, and unfortunately, I found discrepancies."

"I'm sure whatever the discrepancies were, they were mistakes. I work long hours alone. It is quite possible I made a few mistakes here and there."

"There were numerous errors, as well as several employees who do not have a drug test or background checks on file. There is no possible way that these are honest mistakes, Ms. McKnight. Unfortunately, we are going to have to let you go."

"Let me go?"

"And at this time we are not going to take legal action against you. My father doesn't want to see you in jail. He really likes you."

I was unsure of what to do or say. Anything I could think to say would probably imply guilt. I knew exactly what he was talking about now; I was guilty of hooking a few guys up on different occasions when they ran out of vacation time. I hadn't been stealing, per se, or taking cash, embezzling hundreds of thousands of dollars, but I was guilty of looking the other way. A few of the guys had paid me to look past their dirty urine test results. And one of the drivers, Demetrius, had a record, but it was for vandalism—just for writing on a wall. I'd overlooked it. So what? He was eighteen when it happened and needed a job and had kids to feed.

"I think you are making a mistake, Frank, but okay." I got up out of my seat and began walking toward the door.

"This is effective immediately. If you can retrieve your stuff out of the office and make this as simple as possible, I would appreciate it."

I didn't say anything else. I was in total shock. Nine years of hard work for Zinoloi Rugs, Carpets, and Exotic Furniture, and now I was carrying my boxes to the car. Hector walked over to take a box from me.

"What's going on? Where are you going?" he asked.

"I was just fired."

"What?"

"Yeah, Frank just called me into his office, said he received a message or something that I was committing payroll fraud and hiring criminals. I don't know what's going on. This is crazy. Did you hear anything?"

"No, not at all, but your husband called me this weekend. Or at least I think it was your ex-husband."

I stopped my heart fell to my feet.

"What!"

"Yeah, I kept calling you, but your voice mail kept coming on. I left you messages. He called me, asking me all these questions. First he called and was, like, 'Who this?' so I said, 'This is Hector. Who is this?' He said, 'You know Yvette?' I asked why, and, anyway, we started getting into it. So then he said, 'Was you with my wife?' and I said, 'Yeah,' because I know it doesn't matter anymore. Y'all are divorced and all."

"Oh, my God." I felt my stomach turning and my entire head began to instantly throb. "Hector, I always told you, if anyone ever called your phone and asked about me to hang up. I can't believe you gave up information so easily. Why did you tell him anything?"

Hector saw that I was panicking and began trying to calm me down. "What's wrong? He's not your husband anymore."

I couldn't say anything else. I told Hector I would call him later. All I could think was, damn, all this time Phil knew I cheated, but he never knew who YB was, and now he did. So now I knew who the anonymous male was that had called my job. Phil knew that I didn't drug test everyone and that I had overlooked a record or two. We would always discuss how the "system" made it hard for anyone who had ever made a mistake to redeem themselves. We both agreed that it wasn't right and that some people deserved a second chance. He also knew that I would give myself overtime when I worked really hard and I didn't take lunch.

I wanted to get a few blocks away from my job before I called Phil and began screaming and cussing his ass out. I drove down the street, then pulled over and called him. He didn't answer. I called back several times. No answer. I was so disgusted and angry that he would call my job and tell on me that my hands were shaking. Since I couldn't reach him, I dialed Geneva. She answered. I didn't let her get a hello out before I cried, "Geneva, I don't know what the hell just happened. I can't believe this shit. I really can't believe it."

"You okay? What's wrong? Why are you crying?"

"Oh, my God, Phil left an anonymous tip on my job's answering machine, saying that I wasn't doing background checks or drug testing."

"What?"

"Yes, then he also said I was hooking people and myself up with overtime."

"You are lying."

"I wish I was. This doesn't make any sense. Girl, they fired me. I can't believe he took the time to call my job. We are divorced now. Why can't he just leave me alone?"

"I'm so sorry to hear this. I can't be hearing you right. You're telling me this bitch-ass man called your job and had you fired?"

"Yes, he did," I sighed. "Isn't this so fucked up? He somehow got Hector's number and called him, and Hector told him everything, and now he is mad."

"Oh, my God, this is crazy. I get off of work in an hour. I'll tell Eric to pick up the kids. What do you want to do to him?"

"I'm so ready to go and kill him, but I can't, because we are going to the settlement this week. But after I get my check in my hand, oh, it's on."

"Yeah, get your money, and then we are going to get his ass."

"Let me call the Realtor right now. I'll call you back."

I dialed the Realtor. "Hi, Ms. Womack. This is Mrs. McKnight.

"Oh, hi, Mrs. McKnight what can I do for you?"

"I was calling to see what day this week we are going to the settlement."

"Oh, Mrs. McKnight. Uh, yeah, you know we went to the settlement last week. I know you said you were going to come with your ex-husband, but he said you weren't feeling well, and everything was in his name, so your presence wasn't really necessary. I'm assuming you guys will handle the rest. You don't need me for anything, do you?"

"Yes, of course we will handle it." I got this sinking feeling in my stomach. I knew what it was already, but I was trying not to admit it, because if I did, I wouldn't know what I was going to do. I pulled over to the side of the street, prayed, and called Phil again. Whatever he said he was going to do would determine whether he was a living or a dead man walking. I held my composure as best I could. There wasn't a trace of rudeness in my voice.

"Yeah, Vette? Why do you keep calling my phone?"

"Oh, Phil, I wanted to see when we could meet up."

"We are meeting for what?" Just by the way he was speaking to me, I wanted to GPS his location and kick him in his face. He was sitting on the phone, pretending he hadn't called my job or already gone to the settlement without me.

"We are meeting so I can get my check. You went to the settlement last week, and I'm sure the check has cleared by now. So where and when do you want to meet?"

He didn't answer my question. Instead he said rudely, "Hold on for a minute." Then he came back to the phone and said, "Yeah, Yvette, my check did clear and I do have my money from the sale of my house. You don't have a check or any money."

"What? Phil, we both paid for the house. That house was just as much mine as it was yours."

He began laughing and yelled, "I don't owe you anything. I only verbally agreed to give you half, so technically I don't have to give you shit."

I didn't know how to respond, Phil had just confirmed that he didn't plan to give me my money. Before I could stop myself, I said, "Don't talk that technical shit with me. I put a down payment on that house and invested in all those repairs for the kitchen too."

"Do you have the receipts? You are not getting anything from me. Go get it from that dude, your YB. You know the one you were fucking at your job. My name is on the house. I don't owe you anything. And I don't know what to tell you. Maybe next time you get married, don't cheat and try to fuck over your husband."

"*I* fucked *you* over! You had an affair on me. And you know what? It doesn't even matter anymore, because we are not together. We are divorced."

"You're motherfucking right I divorced your cheating ass."

"Phil, *you* divorced *me*? Did you forget about the ignorant young chick that came to my house and told me she was pregnant by you?" I screamed.

His only response to that was to hang up. I kept calling

him back, but he kept sending me to his voice mail. That was when it all set in and I realized Phillip was trying to ruin my life. I was crying and crying, and then I realized I had to withdraw all the money out of our joint account. I called our bank, and there was only fifteen hundred left in there. I immediately drove to the bank and withdrew every dollar. There was no way Phil could get away with what he was doing to me. I was trying to stay calm and think rationally, but I just couldn't.

I called Phil back. As soon as he answered, I screamed, "Listen, Phil, it is bad enough you got me fired from my job. Now you are trying to take my money. You think I'm going to let this happen? You're going to give me my goddamn money, or you're going to have a problem."

"Yvette, I don't have any money that belongs to you, and I have nothing else to say. Stop calling my phone."

He hung up on me and I stood motionless outside the bank, looking at the phone, lost. Phillip McKnight had gone crazy, and someone had to talk to him before I murdered him. I called my dad. I didn't want to upset him, but he had to do something. As the phone rang and rang I began to break down. Once my dad finally answered I was hyperventilating.

"Dad . . . Dad . . . Dad."

"What's wrong, Vette?"

"Dad, Phil said he's not giving me my money from the sale of the house. And . . . and . . . .I don't know what I'm going to do."

"What do you mean, he's not giving you the money from the house? I thought you guys were going to split everything down the middle."

"That's what . . . what . . . what we were . . . supposed to do." I tried to catch my breath by taking a deep breath and began speaking again. "Daddy, he said since the house was in his name that I wasn't entitled to anything. I put up money toward that house's down payment and helped him do the kitchen."

"Did you discuss this with the Realtor? What about your divorce attorney?"

"We didn't use an attorney for the divorce. We did everything ourselves. I called the Realtor to see when the settlement was, and she was the one who told me it had already happened."

"I thought you had an attorney. You always have to get everything in writing, and then you always have to have an attorney review it to cover all your bases. There has to be something we can do. How much was he supposed to give you?"

"Twenty-five thousand."

"That's a lot of money."

"And, Daddy, he got me fired from my job, and he said he is not giving me any of it. I was using that money for me and the kids to move into a bigger place, fix a few things on my credit, and get another car."

"Twenty-five thousand? Oh no, he can't just take your money from you. Let me call him, and I'll call you right back."

I felt a little comforted. If anyone could talk some sense into Phil, it was my dad. He and my father had formed a strong father-son-like bond, and Phil really respected him. I said another prayer and walked into the convenience store across from the bank. I bought a bottle of water to soothe my aching throat. I got back in the car and tried to sit still, but my leg shook while I waited to hear from my father. My father called back.

"Dad, what did he say?"

"Uh, Vette, listen. You are going to have to hire a lawyer. He is talking crazy."

"Why? What did he say to you?"

"He said you're getting what you deserve and that you

were having affair and he caught you cheating with a young guy on your job and that you were stealing money and that's why you were fired."

"Dad, that's not true."

"I know it isn't. But really there is no talking to him. He kept me on the phone, repeating the same thing. Whatever happened between you two, he's still really upset over it. Give him some time to get over it. In the meantime go and speak to someone."

I couldn't believe any of this was happening to me. Phil was a man scorned and had declared war on my life, and I didn't know how I was going to fight back.

Chapter 9

Crystal

The test came back, and the truth was now undeniable. *You are the father!* I thought in my Maury voice as I stared down at our test results. The mailman couldn't have brought better news. I was now holding proof that Kenneth was my daughter's father, and now he could start taking care of her. I dialed his cell. He didn't pick up, so I called the house phone, and who picked up but that damn Syreeta. I started to hang up, but I thought, *Fuck her.* I needed to speak to her brother.

"May I speak to Kenneth?"

"Who is this?" Syreeta knew damn well who it was, but I still humored her.

"It's Crystal."

"Crystal, he's not here, and just to let you know, we got the same paperwork you did. So you don't have to call here checking up on nobody. When he ready, he'll do what he has to do. Until then, I'll tell you like I know. Stop begging a motherfucker to take care of your child. Do what you got to do for yourself and your baby."

There was no reason to respond to Syreeta. She was deranged, and I couldn't deal with her. I just called Kenneth's cell phone number again, and this time I blocked my number. It rang and rang, and then he finally answered.

"Kenneth?"

"Yeah. Yo, why you keep calling my phone and blocking your number, Crystal?"

"I didn't know it was blocked."

"What's up?"

"Kenneth, Syreeta said you got your test results."

"Yeah, I did. Listen, I want to take care of my daughter. All I needed was to know without a doubt she was mine. I already got her something and want to come by and get her."

"When?"

"Today. A little later. See, I'm gonna do the right thing now that I'm sure."

I started to say something, to tell him that he'd known she was his, but what was the point? As long as he came and got her . . .

"Kenneth, just call me before you come so I can have her ready."

"Matter of fact, I'm going to be there in, like, an hour."

I was shocked when I saw Kenneth's four-door silver Crown Victoria with dark tinted windows double-parked outside my house. I told Jewel to tell him that I would be out with Kori shortly. Instead of waiting outside, Kenneth came in my house. I heard his six-foot-two footsteps coming up my stairs and walking down my hall.

"Is my daughter ready?" he asked, entering my bedroom.

"Yes. I'll bring her out to you. And please do not just walk in my house or up my steps anymore."

"Yeah, all right," he said as he flagged me and went to use my bathroom.

He had a lot of nerve. I thought, *First, she isn't your daughter, but now she is, and you walking in my house like we are cool.* What made him think he could just roam around my house after three months of "I'm not sure if the baby is mine"? I didn't want to argue with him, but I would have to let him know he was no longer welcome in my house. I was furious while I was packing Kori up. I was beginning to have second thoughts about handing my child over to the enemy. Before I could change my mind, he grabbed her car seat and diaper bag. I watched as he placed her car seat in his car and strapped her in and drove off.

Since Kori was gone for the day, I wanted to take my other two children somewhere, but first I wanted to wash and fold clothes and have them clean the living room, which was covered with toys and game pieces.

"Get off the game, Nasir, and pick up all this play money and toys."

"I didn't have it, Mom. Jewel was playing with it." Nasir said continuing to play with his toys.

"No, it wasn't me. It was Nasir. You were the one," Jewel insisted.

"Both of you, get this living room together if you want to go somewhere today."

"Well, I don't want to go anywhere. I just want to play my game," Nasir said.

"Nasir, you still have to clean up." I walked over to the television and turned it off.

I supervised the cleaning from the kitchen, and then I texted Rell to say good morning. Since we met, I'd talked to him every day. We'd been to the movies and out to dinner once. He was a real sweetheart; he even came up to my job to see me on my lunch break. The one scary thing was that he kind of reminded me of Kenneth a little. They didn't look anything alike, but we were having a lot of fun, like Kenneth and I used to have. Instead of texting me back, he called me.

"Hey, just got your text. Good morning to you, Miss Turner. Where are your little ones? What is going on with you?"

"They're right here. I don't know what we are going to do yet."

"Oh, 'cause I was going to say, if you want to go, my brother and his wife have extra tickets to the Monster Truck Show."

"Okay. Sounds good. What time?"

"It starts at five o'clock. There's not enough room in the car for all of us, so I can probably meet you down there."

We met Terell in the parking lot of the Wells Fargo Center. There were families walking in, and it was very crowded. He spotted us and told me to come up to the door. He briefly introduced me to his brother, Shareef; Shareef's wife, Angel; and their son, Little Shareef. They spoke, and we waited in line to enter the arena. While in line I introduced Rell to the children as Mr. Rell, and he corrected me and instructed the kids to just call him Rell.

Once we were in, Rell bought Jewel and Nasir cotton candy and earplugs because the show was loud. We walked to our seats and viewed up close a gigantic green truck with huge wheels, revving its engine nonstop. The truck just kept racing up and down big mounds of dirt, smashing and crushing little cars and flinging mud everywhere. I didn't get it, but Jewel and Nasir loved it. Rell's nephew, Little Reef, was so excited, he was jumping up and down and cheering the drivers on. Rell and I didn't get a chance to talk that much during the show, but it meant a lot to me that he would think of my kids and take them out.

After the show Rell walked us to our car. I wanted to give him a kiss good-bye but didn't want to freak the kids out, so I texted him, Thank you.

He sent me a texted back. No prob. Can I see you tonite?

I texted him back that I had the kids still, but I would call him when they were asleep.

Kenneth brought Kori home, and I gave her a bath and her bottle, and she was ready for bed. Jewel and Nasir munched on pizza and were knocked out around ten, but I was so scared that I checked three times to make sure they were asleep before I opened the door for Rell. And even then I instructed him to be extra quiet. I did not want them waking up and Nasir coming downstairs, asking what the man from the Monster Truck Show was doing at our house.

"That was really nice to take me and my kids to that show."

"Sure. Your kids seem cool."

"They are."

"My brother and his wife really liked you."

"But I didn't even really get to talk to them."

"It doesn't matter. People can read people's energy, and they know good people when they see them."

"I am a good person, though."

"I know you are. That's why I'm here. You know what I was thinking about on my way over here?"

"What?" I asked, knowing that he was going to say something silly.

"I finally got the girl I wanted since middle school—Crystal Turner."

"You say the sweetest things, Rell."

"I know I do, but Crystal Turner, what are you doing to me?"

"I'm not doing anything to you."

"Yes, you are. I feel like I can't stay away you."

"Yes, you can." I laughed and tried not to think too much about how I was falling for Rell too!

Before I knew it, we were all over each other and he was inside of me knocking my insides out. It was like he kept going in deeper and deeper, and it was getting better and wetter, and I wanted to scream, but I didn't want my kids to hear me. I was telling him to be calm down and to go a little slower, but he was attacking inside of me like a beast and he wouldn't stop. Then it happened—a big, loud crash. The box spring was on the floor and my bed was hanging sideways off the frame. All we could do was laugh hard while still trying not to awake the kids.

"See what you did, Rell?" I said playfully punching him. He attempted to fix the bed but it wasn't working.

"I'm going to fix it in the morning. I'm sorry, I couldn't stop you got that extra good loving," he said placing the mattress back on top of the box spring.

After the bed fiasco I made sure everyone was still asleep and I made me and Rell a late night snack. We were already so comfortable together. We showered and watched a movie and talked all night, about him being in the Army and all the places he had traveled. It was so easy being with him, it was like meeting my best friend. I was going to enjoy Terell for now. The easy part was getting a man; the hard part was keeping him. It always started like this, fun and happy, but then something always happened.

CHAPTER 10

Dana

At Millennium Concepts Agency sometimes I felt like we were always in meetings, discussing the meetings we were about to meet about. I just came out of one meeting with long-winded Dennis Albridge. He was so annoying and only got away with his antics because he was with the company before the downtown office and seven-figure accounts. He was vital to the agency, and possessed a plethora of connections and loyal clients, but he really needed to bring his thoughts and ideas up to date because he was always made meetings boring as hell.

After I got out of my first meeting with Dennis I was ready to get my second meeting for Equalnoi Bars over. I walked into the next conference room and saw Reshma had a disgusted look on her face while trying to chew the bar at the table.

"So it's that good?" I asked.

"You should taste it."

"The wrapper is very different, unique looking," I said as I picked the cereal bar up off of the table and stared at the wrapper. I tore a big chunk of the bar off and ate it. It was horrible. There were too many nuts, and it tasted like dirt.

I looked around for a trash can to spit in. Reshma chuckled and poured me a glass of water, and I gulped it down. That was disgusting. I was glad I hadn't eaten it before I'd come up with the marketing plan. But it really didn't matter how much I didn't care for a product and that I wouldn't buy it. There was someone out there that would; I always remembered that lesson from my first marketing class. Besides, our company needed this deal. Even if it was a disgusting cereal bar, it would be displayed and sold in every health-food store in the tri-state area, and it was our job to make sure of it.

Three meetings in one day and I could not wait to leave the office, because I had a special evening planned with Todd. I realized I did overreact the last time I saw him and shouldn't have left in the middle of the night. I called him a few days later and apologized, and to make it up to him, I had planned a romantic night just for us. I got us tickets to our favorite singer, Wade Devon. He was this international, Grammy Award–winning R & B singer. I loved his music. We both loved the way he sang and played the piano . Todd had texted me three times today, telling me he couldn't wait to see the show.

"So what's the plan for the weekend, ladies?" I asked Reshma and Leah.

"Stephen and I are going away to a bed-and-breakfast place in Lancaster. We are going to relax and enjoy the country air," Leah said.

"Don't forget to take a buggy ride with the Amish people," I said jokingly.

"The Amish are not the only people that live in Lancaster," Leah replied.

"Well, I'm going to see Wade Devon under the stars this weekend at the Mann," I announced.

"Ooh, that sounds nice. Have fun," Reshma cooed.

"I will. And what do the newlyweds have planned?"

Reshma shook her head. "Not that much. Zyeed is on call all weekend, and I'll be entertaining his mom and sister."

"Well, have a good weekend, ladies. See you on Monday," I said.

I left the office and started getting ready for my night out. I picked up my favorite black dress from the cleaners, then drove home. I was going to take a quick shower, place a few curls in my hair, and get ready to meet Todd. While I was dressing, Todd called.

"Hey. What are you doing?"

"Getting ready to see Mr. Devon. You almost ready?"

"No, uh, I'm not ready." I didn't like the unsteadiness of Todd's voice.

Please, not again, I thought. "You're not about to stand me up again, are you?"

"Dana, please understand. I want to go, I do, but something came up at work. Remember I told you about how I had a conference next weekend?"

"Yeah."

"My boss's assistant messed up all the arrangements. She made a scheduling error, and we are supposed to be in Boston this weekend, not next. So I'm packing and about to leave now, and I won't be back until Tuesday. I will give you the money for the tickets, but I want you to still go and enjoy yourself."

I was speechless. I couldn't get mad. I should have known better. He always did this to me.

"I can't believe this. Why am I not surprised?"

"Dana, this is really not my fault. I'll forward you the e-mail so you can see it for yourself."

I didn't want to see any e-mail, and I didn't want to talk to him anymore, so I ended the call. Todd always disappointed me. What was new? I was so annoyed that perfectly good tickets were about to go to waste. Maybe my parents would want to go.

"Mommy, do you know who Wade Devon is?"

"Yeah, I think I heard of him."

"Do you think you and Daddy would want to go and see him in, like, an hour?"

"No, I don't like him like that. Why aren't you going?"

"Because I have to work to do," I lied. "Forget it, Mom. I know who I can give them to."

I dialed Tiffany.

"Tiffany, what are you doing tonight?"

"Nothing. About to watch all the shows I TiVoed. I may call the guy I met online. Why? What's up?"

"Do you want to go see Wade Devon? Todd can't go."

"What happened with Todd? Never mind. I'll go. But you have to come and pick me up since you taking me on a date."

"Yeah whatever girl, just be ready."

In front of Tiffany's door I texted Todd to let him know I decided to go to the show, and I hoped everything went well with his conference, and that I'd see him when he got back.

The Mann Center for the Performing Arts was an outdoor venue in the middle of Fairmount Park. The weather and the night sky were perfect for good music and love. Once we were there, I was happy I didn't waste the tickets.

We were seated in the orchestra section, in the third row, in the middle. Since we were fifteen minutes late we had to say, "Excuse me" to all these concertgoers before we could get to our seats. Tiffany was unfazed. She was just, like, "Excuse me. Thank you. Pardon me. Excuse me," down the aisle. As soon as we took our seat, I couldn't help but notice all the loving couples around us. There were old couples, young couples, Asian couples, black couples. They were holding hands, grinning at one another, and I was on a girlfriend date.

"I wonder if anyone thinks we are lesbians," I said.

Tiffany glanced around and said, "They probably do."

Then she grabbed my hand and began stroking it lovingly and laughing. I snatched my arm away from her and made the best of the situation.

Wade Devon came on stage and once I heard his sultry voice, it made me forget where I was and who I had come with. I was so excited to see him sing and play his piano. I couldn't think of anything else. He played each note so well and serenaded just me all night. I swear he winked at me a few times. I was in another place, relaxed, singing along to every song and enjoying the show until a text came in from Todd that read: I hope you have fun. Enjoy the show :)

I didn't know what was wrong with the text, but it ruined my mood. His text brought me back to the fact that he wasn't with me. It was finally beginning to sink in that I had been a fool for the last year and it wasn't going to get any better. Everyone's attention was on the stage, and not even Tiffany noticed the tears that were streaming down my cheeks. As fast as they ran, I wiped them off and concealed my pain. I was tired of being hurt by Todd and I couldn't take anymore.

By the time I dropped Tiffany off after the concert and reached home, I had come to the conclusion that it was time to have a heart-to-heart with Todd. Our relationship was going to change or end, one or the other, no more in the middle. It was late, but I was angry and could not wait until morning to let him know. I texted message after message about how I felt about our current situation. I didn't know how many texts I sent, but soon after my phone was going off and Todd was on the other end.

"What's wrong with you, Dana? Why are you sending crazy text messages this time of night?"

"What's wrong with me? Hmm. Let me see. I went to a romantic show with my girlfriend, when I was supposed to be with you, my man. Oh, that's right. You're not my man. You are what? My friend with benefits, my bed buddy? I'm not exactly sure what we are. Could you clarify exactly what we are, again so I can know? I need to hear it once and for all from you so I can know how to move on with my life."

"Dana, I don't know why you are so upset or what to tell you."

"Well, I need you to tell me something. Tell me things are never going to change. Tell me you are a selfish liar and that you are going to keep standing me up, and something, somewhere, somebody is always going to come before me. Tell me."

"Dana, you know how I feel about you, but I have to get my career going while I can. I'm sorry I can't be who you want me to be right now. And I really don't understand why you can't understand. Things are perfect the way they are. I really don't see what the big deal is. You were able to go to the show, and I'm giving you the money back."

"And that's it? You will never get it. Nothing is a big deal to you. Oops, sorry. Can't make it. Maybe next time. But now I see there will always be an excuse and a next time. Something will always come up."

"That's not true. It's just that things happen."

"You are right things do happen, but people make time for what is important to them. I have a busy career, but I still do my job and I do it well and I still find time to see you. Because you're a priority to me. I am not a priority of yours. Todd, I can't afford to waste any more time with you."

"Then don't waste any more time. I can't take hearing you say the same thing over and over again, and you're not going to make me feel guilty about things that I cannot control."

"Then don't hear it anymore." I took a deep breath and said, "If this is the way it is going to be, then I'll pass."

"So what are you saying, Dana?"

"I'm saying I'm not going to sit here and wait for you until I'm in my thirties. I'd wait on you and then you'd realize I'm not what you want and my life is gone. Because that's what you crazy men do. Suck the life out of women, make us wait, waste our good years, and then marry the next chick in three months. I don't think so. It is not going to happen to me like that. You can go to hell, Todd."

"I can go to hell? Okay, Dana, you are really in rare form tonight. You're not making any sense, so I'll call you tomorrow, when you are in a better mood."

I thought about it for a moment. I had to think if I really meant what I was about to say. "Don't bother. It's over. I've had enough. Don't call me anymore." I was surprised I said it, but it was exactly how I felt. It was something I should have told him a year ago, when he first downgraded our relationship, instead of waiting around.

"Are you sure about this?" Todd asked.

"I am," I said nice and clearly.

"Okay. Once again I'm sorry, but if that's the way you want it, then fine, Dana. Enjoy your weekend."

I stood with the phone in my hand, with a few more tears and a little bit of joy. I was happy that I had finally put my foot down, but sad I had lost the man I loved.

The next morning I didn't feel so joyful about telling Todd to go to hell and all the other things I'd said to him. I informed Tiffany that Todd and I were no more, and she let out a loud "Yea! Whoo-hoo!"

"You don't have to be that happy."

"Yes, I do. I hate Todd. You should have cut him out of the picture a long time ago."

"I know, but I thought he would eventually get it together."

"He wasn't ever going to be right for you. When a man wants something, they go after it. They won't make you wait, because they will be too scared someone else is going to get you. I'm glad you finally broke up with him. Forget him and listen to my good news. . . . I really like the guy I met online. He is so nice. We've been talking on the phone every day, and we are going to meet up."

Even though I agreed that I had wasted too much energy and time on Todd, I didn't think it was such a great idea for Tiffany to meet a stranger off the Internet.

"Are you really going to meet up with a stranger?"

"I sure am. What do I have to lose?"

"Maybe your life. What do you know about him?"

"His name is Solomon, and he lives in North Jersey, in Piscataway. He's an only child, and him and his mother are best friends."

"So you are going to another city to meet a momma's boy. Don't you know online people can be whoever they want to be? You're probably going to meet a killer posing as a man seeking romance or a bunch of teenagers playing a prank."

"No, he is really who he says he is. I have his work number and e-mail, and I even went to his company Web site, and he is in their directory with the same number I have. He is not a crazy man. Do you want me to read you his profile?"

"No, because whatever it reads, it is probably a bunch of lies, I'm sure. Tiffany, do you think he would write, 'I enjoy killing people and dismembering them. None of my dates are ever seen or heard from again, and I'm a psychopath'?"

"He is not a psychopath."

"I sure hope not, for your sake. If he kills you, I'm going to miss you."

"I'm telling you he is not. I did my research. I'm a good judge of character. I'm getting on the train now. I'll call you when I get there."

"Okay. Be safe."

That afternoon Tiffany texted me that she had arrived, but then I didn't hear anything else from her. The next day I was really worried. I kept calling her phone, but she didn't answer. Why did I let her go off to meet a stranger by herself? Why didn't I stop her or try to warn her more? I thought as I became more nervous. I was about to call her one more time. If she didn't answer this time, I was dialing 911.

The phone rang five times, and then I heard fumbling and she said, "Hey, girl. Sorry I didn't call you. My phone died. I was talking to Solomon the whole train ride, and I didn't bring my charger with me. We had to run and get a new one this morning."

"You couldn't call me from his phone? I was worried sick. Well, at least you're okay. So how is he?"

"I can't really talk, but oh yes, he is great. He is so gorgeous in person. We had the best first date."

"Well, it is not really a date when you spend the night." I laughed.

"No, we were up talking all night I lost track of time. Sorry for scaring you."

"Well, I'm happy you're safe, because I was about to call your mom."

"Why was you about to call my mother and scare her? What would you have told her anyway?"

"I don't know. Her daughter is missing. You sound so happy, and I'm here missing Todd already."

"Forget Todd. We are going online and getting you a man, too."

"That's not going to happen. I'm not doing any online dating."

CHAPTER 11

Crystal

Nervous didn't describe how I felt about going to Rell's nephew's birthday party. Not only did I have to make sure I looked nice, but I also wanted to make sure my kids looked right. I knew his family was going to be, like, "Who is this girl walking in here with all these kids?"

I usually did my own hair myself, but yesterday I got a wash and blow-dry from the hair salon around the corner. I wanted to be comfortable and casual, so I was wearing a long floral maxi dress. Nasir wore his blue polo shirt and shorts. I braided Jewel's hair to the side and added barrettes at the end, and she had on her sky-blue capris and blue and white Juicy Couture shirt.

The party was being held in a park. At first I couldn't find the party and was ready to call Rell, until Jewel said, "Mommy, I think that's the party right there."

And it was. How could I have missed the big sign that read HAPPY BIRTHDAY, KING SHAREEF? There were all types of activities for the party's seventy-five children, who were scattered around the park. It was like a mini carnival, with a moon bounce, an inflatable slide, and an actual pony.

I parked and lifted Kori out of the car, and Nasir, Jewel, and I began walking toward the intimidating crowd. I looked around for Rell but didn't see him. Then he appeared out of nowhere and walked up to me and grabbed Kori's car seat and gave me a peck on the cheek.

"Hey. What's up, princess and lil man? Y'all want to get in the moon bounce?"

"This is a lot. How old is he turning?" I asked, still looking around.

"Five. He is the only grandchild, and everyone spoils him. I told them he is going to be rotten," Rell replied.

Rell's brother was at the grill, but he spoke to us, and his wife, Angel, came over and offered the kids a hot dog. They both said no and were twisting in place, looking down at the ground, like they were shy. Rell pulled out a seat for me and then kneeled down to the kids and asked if they wanted their faces painted.

"I do," Jewel said, her head springing up.

Rell said, "Okay, let's walk over to that lady with that apron on."

"Mommy, I'll be back," Jewel called.

I had a seat, but Nasir still didn't want to leave my side. He just observed the other kids running around. I asked Nasir why he was acting shy, and he just said he didn't know. Rell came back over to me with this lady who had to be his mom.

"Crystal, this is Ms. Cheryl, my mom. Mom, this is my friend Crystal."

I said hello.

"How are you? Oh, look at that gorgeous baby. How old is she?" Ms. Cheryl asked.

"Thank you. She's three months," I replied.

"I remember when mine were that little. Can I hold her?"

I took Kori out of her car seat and handed her to Ms. Cheryl. She held Kori and started talking to me like she didn't just meet me.

"Nasir, are you going to go play or miss the whole party?"

He shook his head and grabbed my hand.

"How you going to be my big boy if you afraid to go play with the other kids?" I asked.

"Aw, that's what I used to call Rell, my big boy. Rell always was my helper and peaceful and just would come and lay on me and come and ask me if I was okay or if I needed anything. Shareef, on the other hand, was my ER baby—always was breaking something, like a leg, finger, ankle. I stayed in the emergency room with him.

"So Rell always been a sweetheart, huh?"

"Yup."

"Mom, maybe I could get a tiger painted on my face," Nasir said as he let go of me and joined the other kids getting their faces painted.

"Grandma, I want a hot dog. I'm hungry," Rell's chunky nephew Shareef said, walking up to us.

"All this and no one fed this boy? Shareef, go tell your mother to fix you a plate. She's right there," Ms. Cheryl told him.

Right after Little Shareef scurried off, a man came over, wiping perspiration off his forehead with a white paper towel. He looked like he might have had a beer or two. He was older, skinny with real baggy clothes on his thin body.

"Come here, nephew," he said to Rell, who was just walking up.

"What's up, Unc?"

"How come I'm the last to know you had a baby? Now it make sense why you came back home."

"No, Unc. This is my lady's baby."

"Your lady?" he said, puzzled.

"You heard what he said," Ms. Cheryl interjected. "Go somewhere, Billy. Go help Shareef finish cooking the rest of the food."

"I didn't know. What?" said Billy.

Rell shook his head. "Don't mind him. You okay, boo?"

"Yeah, I'm fine," I answered.

The rest of the day kids played nonstop. They were so exhausted when the party ended. They did face paintings, hit piñatas, bounced all around. I didn't think they ever ran free for six hours straight before. Rell's family was real nice, especially his mom. She worked at Kids & More on the boulevard and told me I could come and get a discount for the kids' clothes whenever I wanted. They were really good people. I dared not introduce Rell to my Denise and James. Oh, hell no. My dad had already made it very clear that he didn't want to meet any more of my boyfriends or friends, only husbands and fiancés.

The next day I was drained from the party, and so were the kids. I tried my best to get in the ACR building on time, but Jewel was sluggish and Nasir couldn't find his shoes. Then when I got on the expressway there was an accident that everyone had to drive past slowly. The minute I got to my work floor, I ran over to my desk and tried to log on to my phone as fast as I could. It was 8:33. I was only three minutes late. . . . Hopefully, it wouldn't be noticed. I caught my breath and readied myself to answer my one hundred plus calls for the day.

"Thank you for calling ACR Cable Vision. This is Crystal. How may I help you today?"

"Yeah, Crystal, how you doing? Uh, I need to know why my bill keeps going up every month. The bill is suppose to be ninety-nine dollars, 'cause that's what it was advertised as when I signed up. So why the hell is it one sixty-seven now? Explain that to me."

"Yes, ma'am. One moment." I knew the caller on the other end didn't know I wasn't fully awake. It wasn't her fault, but I did have to place her on hold, because she was yelling at me like I was the one who had ordered all the pay-per-view movies on her account. "I'm sorry, ma'am. May I place you on hold while I research your account?"

"What?"

"Ma'am," I said, "may I please place you on hold while I research your account?' "

"Yeah, go ahead, but I'm tired of this bullshit every month."

I snatched off my headset and put my head down. I looked over at the pictures of my kids on my desk. They were the only reason I stayed at this job. Right when I was thinking *Why me?* Rell texted, I think I love you, Crystal Turner. You're doing something to me.

I responded, I think I luv u too, Terell Glover.

Seeing Rell's cute text made me smile and I was now able to deal with the crazy lady on the line. I was in such a good mood that I removed all the charges for the movies she said no one ordered, and she hung up happy.

Right before lunch I was still feeling good. I was happy I'd met Rell, and thrilled I had someone special in my life again. But my joy was short lived, because my supervisor Delphine placed a write-up on my desk and told me if I had any questions to see her before I went to lunch. She needed to take her points-counting ass somewhere and sit down. She was on Weight Watchers and had lost hundred pounds and needed to lose a hundred more. I don't know why, but me and her just didn't click. I guess because I don't kiss her ass. I come to work, do my job and that's it. I wanted to ball up the write up but I didn't.

I strolled to her end of the row, to an extra-large cubicle. I was protesting this write-up. "Delphine, I don't deserve this write-up."

"Okay, let me look into your file."

She pulled something up and said, "Let's see, Crystal Turner. You were late today, and actually, it's your fifth lateness this month. So, you should be on probation, but I'm only going to recommend peer coaching. Do you have any other questions?"

I rolled my eyes at her and then said I didn't have any

other questions. I began walking away from her desk, and she said, "And Crystal, if you are late in the next ninety days, then you may be suspended. You have to sign here."

I didn't want to sign anything, but I didn't want to lose my job, either. I signed it and got out of that stupid building. I walked across the street to the lunch truck and ordered a soft pretzel, hot sausage and Snapple ice tea. I was going to enjoy my lunch peacefully in the park and ignore Delphine's stupid ass when I got back inside. Rell rang my phone right as I began to eat

"How's your day going, boo? You're at lunch, right?" he asked.

"It's going. Yeah, I'm at lunch."

"What happened? You sound upset?"

"Nothing. I just got written up and I feel like slapping my supervisor. I got a write up and I was only three minutes late this morning. I can see if I was, like, ten, twenty minutes late, but three minutes? That shouldn't be enough to go on my record. I think they should have some kind of five- or ten-minute grace period."

"If they had a five minute grace period everyone would know they had an extra five minutes, and no one would come on time. They can't do that, they are running a business."

"I know, but it's just some bullshit. I hate that stupid bitch anyway."

"You just better be glad you are not in the military. Up and at 'em every morning, five o'clock. Working out before you get a chance to eat. You wouldn't last a day in the military with your attitude and mouth."

"I probably couldn't."

"Yes, you could. You can do anything. You just have to start being on time."

"Yeah, I guess you're right."

"It will be all right, but I'm going to start calling you in the morning so that you can get up. Okay?"

"All right."

"Now, go back into work with a smile on that pretty face, and I'll see you later. Maybe we can go to dinner."

"Okay, I have to see if my mom will watch my kids for me."

"If she doesn't, then we can just stay in. As long as I'm with you, I'm good." Hearing Rell say he just wanted to spend time with me made me feel so special. For the second time in one day Rell had lifted my spirits, and he didn't even know it.

My mom said no to babysitting so I couldn't go out with Rell. I was upset, but he wasn't; he just suggested we take the kids out to Chuck E. Cheese's and let them play, and we could go out another night.

At Chuck E. Cheese's he loaded Jewel and Nasir up with tokens and played on the games with them. I watched him interacting with them and he seemed almost unreal. He was twenty-nine, had no kids, which meant no baby mama, no ex-wives, and his ex-girlfriend lived in another state, meaning she couldn't pop back up anytime she wanted. I did do something of a background check on him. I asked Portia, and she said he was a good guy and no dirt was on his name anywhere. I was so lucky, I thought as I looked over at my kids and new man.

Saturday morning and I wanted to make the most of my day. I planned on doing the laundry and making the kids and Rell breakfast. As I eased out of the bed, Rell grabbed my arm and asked me why I was leaving him. "I'm about to make some breakfast."

"Wait. I need you to keep holding me."

"You know, I think I should call Shareef and tell him how much you like to be held," I joked.

"I don't care tell him. I just need five more minutes with you." He then wrapped my arms around his body. I closed my eyes only to hear Nasir yell outside my bedroom door.

"Mommy, I'm hungry."

"All right, Nasir. Okay. I'll be right down to make your cereal."

"I don't want cereal. I want pancakes."

I came downstairs, popped sausage and pancakes into the microwave, and prepared a bottle for Kori. I even changed her Pampers without waking her and then got back in the bed with my boo bear.

But just five minutes later, Jewel screamed, "Mommy, Aunt Dana's here."

Dana. Damn, I thought. I didn't want her to meet Rell yet. She was too nosy. She would ask me too many questions.

"Okay. Let her know I'll be down in a moment." Once I was dressed, I came down the steps.

"Hey," Dana said. "I wanted to take the kids to the movies. And I haven't heard from you guys, and I just wanted to check on you."

"You should have called me before you came. I could have had them ready."

"It's okay."

"Where is Kori?"

"Still asleep," I said.

"Wake her up. I want to see my niece."

"No, I'm going to let her rest. Uhm, but I'll get the kids ready for you. Jewel and Nasir come put your clothes on."

It was my house and I could do whatever I wanted to, but still I didn't need Dana asking me any questions. She didn't know I had company and wouldn't have known if Rell hadn't gotten out of the bed and walked to the bathroom.

"Who's upstairs?" Dana asked eyeing my stairs,

"Rell."

"Who the hell is Rell?" Dana questioned me like she was my mother.

"A friend of mine."

"You got a man here already and you just had to take a paternity test? Who is this guy? Where does he live? Where does he work?"

"His name is Rell. He went to Wagner with us, he is a good man, and he is looking for a job right now."

"Looking for a job? Really?" she said as she followed me into the kitchen with a scrunched-up face.

"You are unbelievable; weren't you just in court with Kenneth. I guess you never learn your lesson. Do you, Crystal?"

"Dana, listen. I know what I'm doing; please mind your business."

"Well, how about you please use protection this time and get on some birth control, before you're pregnant again."

"Dana, you can leave my house and stop talking trash."

"Trash? No, that's what's up in your bed, Crystal. Anybody can come over and get in the bed with you. When are you going to learn and stop making the same mistakes over and over again? You have to be one of the dumbest people I ever met. I really can't stay here and watch you ruin your life again. Can you tell my niece and nephew I'm outside waiting for them?"

Dana walked out of the house, and I thought about not letting the kids go with her, but they were already getting ready. How did I just get cussed out in my own house?

After they left with Dana's evil behind, I flopped back in the bed, took a deep breath and tried to get back into relaxation mode.

"Who was that, Crystal?"

"My stupid sister Dana."

"Why were y'all arguing?"

"No reason. She is just always talking a whole bunch of mess."

CHAPTER 12

Dana

I loved visiting my parents' home, even though I was older and so many things had changed in my life. When I was back in the house, it always seemed like time stood still. My mom was still sitting at the kitchen table, watching the little television on the counter, and the magnets from all the vacations we took were still on the refrigerator.

"Mom, how you been?"

"Good, even better since your daddy gave me this," my mother said as she held out her arm.

"Mommy, that's a nice bracelet. Daddy is always picking you something up." I took a glimpse of my mother's newest piece of jewelry. I grabbed an apple out of the countertop fruit basket.

"Are you hungry?" my mom asked.

"No."

"You sure, Dana? Because I have plenty from last night, and you know your daddy don't eat leftovers."

"I bet if you don't cook anything else, he would eat it. But, no, I don't want any. Does Daddy ever cook?"

"No."

"He needs to sometime."

"He doesn't have to, I cook for him. You'll see when you finally get a husband."

"No, I won't; my husband is going to cook for me."

I loved my parents, I loved their relationship, but I didn't want a relationship exactly like theirs. I think my mom relied too heavily on my dad in all aspects of her life. Growing up, I would ask if could I do something, and she would always say, "Ask your father," like she didn't have an opinion of her own. I don't know. . . . I guess it had worked for them for thirty-five years. But I didn't think I would ever submit to a man like that. I'd be damned if my children came to me and I said, "Ask your father." I just thought in this day and age a relationship had to be more equal.

"So, you know Crystal has a new boyfriend already," I said.

"Huh? How do you know?" My mom was surprised.

"The other day I went over there to take Jewel and Nasir out for a few hours. I call myself, giving her a break, and I heard something upstairs, and I asked her who was it and she said it was a friend."

"Oh, I'm going to have to have a conversation with her."

"Yeah, you should. Because that's, like, the last thing she should be thinking about. Being with another man. You know she gets pregnant easily." I took another bite of my apple.

"That damn Crystal, always doing something dumb. Then this fool Phillip hasn't gave Yvette her money yet. He better hope I don't catch up with him."

"Mom, what are you going to do?"

"Something. I don't like how he doing my child."

"Yvette's strong; she will find another job, and she can just take him to court for her money."

"I know, but it just isn't right. I called her a few times, but she doesn't answer my calls," my mom said, like she was worried.

"I've been trying to reach her, too. I'll call her later."

My dad came strolling in the house. I walked over to him and gave him a hug.

"How have you been, sweetheart?" he said.

"Fine. I just came to say hey to Mommy. Then I'm going home."

"Stay for dinner," he replied.

"No, I have to go, but Mommy has something she needs to tell you about Crystal. You are not going to believe it."

"Please tell me she is not pregnant again."

"Mommy will tell you. I love y'all. See you later."

On the ride home I tried to get in touch with Tiffany, but she was still busy with Solomon, her online sweetie. Surprisingly, he was not a weirdo, but Tiffany's perfect match. Every weekend she was on the train, going to see him, or he was coming to see her. I had to admit I was wrong about her meeting an online killer. Life was so funny. I had finally cut off Todd, and she had met the man of her dreams. I missed Todd so much, and it had been hard to ignore all his "Hey, yous" and smiley faces texts, but he couldn't give me all, so I'd take none. I wish he would have been able to get it together. But since he never will, I'm back at square one, looking for love again.

Once I was home I opened my laptop and signed up for DateFairy.com. If Tiffany could meet someone online, I could, too. The site made you answer twenty-five personality questions. Simple things like likes and dislikes. But what made this dating Web site unique was you had to judge everything in terms of personality and compatibility, and not from photographs. The site encouraged its daters not to share any pictures until after they had communicated first.

After answering all the questions, I had several matches. I was so excited to read about my matches. One was a divorced father of five. *Next. Not trying to be a stepmom.* My second match said he was in the gym six days a week. *Never.* I kept scrolling down, and my third match was perfect. He was a six-foot-five chef who lived in Delaware, had no children, did not smoke, and his hobbies were weight lifting and movie watching. I read the rest of his bio, and I liked what he had to say. So I messaged him.

My date from Date Fairy was named Rob, and we were coming face-to-face for the first time at a waterfront restaurant in downtown Wilmington, Delaware, about twenty minutes outside of Philadelphia. I did feel like such a hypocrite. I had given Tiff so much grief about meeting someone online, and now here I was, doing the same thing. But when you met online, you did get to learn a lot about them through e-mails and texts.

I already knew I liked Rob just from our messaging, or at least I did until I saw him walking toward me. I didn't judge people by the way that they looked; however, Rob hadn't exactly been truthful when he described himself. In his defense, he was six five and had light brown skin, but because he was tall, I hadn't bothered to ask him how much he weighed. Big mistake, because he was a giant. He look like he belonged on one of those "Help me. I need to lose weight before I die" shows.

The first thing I wanted to do was run. The second was act like my name wasn't Dana. I shouldn't have told him what I was wearing. Then he wouldn't have been able to come right over to my table and say, "You must be Dana."

"Hey, Rob. Yeah, Dana," I said as I digested this big giant that was in front of me.

How could he be a chef? He probably ate all the food before it got to the table, I thought. My first clue should have been that he was a weight-lifting chef. That was an oxymoron in itself. I couldn't run, so I was going to have to stay and endure the date. I shook my head as he got comfortable and opened the menu. Then I heard the most repulsive sounds imaginable each time his lungs inhaled air. He was breathing so heavy, like there were pizzas and cheesecakes clogging his windpipe. I thought he was going to have an asthma attack or pass out from lack of oxygen.

"Are you okay?" I asked.

"Yeah, I'm fine, just a little out of breath. I could tell by your voice you were going to be cute. So what do you think about me?" he said.

"You're good."

"So tell me some more about you, Dana."

"No, uh, you go first." I didn't care that much to tell him anything about me.

"Well, I've been a cook at Olive Garden for the last four years, and I like movies and I lift weights."

But you don't do cardio, I thought.

"So what are you getting?" he asked.

"I'm not sure," I said as I covered my face with the menu.

I pulled my phone out and texted Tiff. My date off of Date Fairy is a giant heavy breathing disaster!!!!

She texted me back. OMG. Ha-ha. LOL. Next date will be better.

I told her I knew it would and put away my phone, even though I didn't care if was being rude or not. When our waitress came over, I ordered a salad and he ordered cashew chicken.

Our food came right out, and I was ecstatic, because I wanted this date to hurry up and be over. However, this fat boy was taking his time eating his chicken. I didn't know why he was fronting—slicing and dicing his chicken up. *Keep it real, and shove the breast in your mouth so I can go,* I thought. I wanted to go home and watch television, anything but be here on this date with him. *Yuck.* And then the waitress asked if we would like to look at the dessert menu, and he said yes.

"Do you want dessert?" he asked.

"Oh, no, sorry. I can't. I have to get up early tomorrow."

"I understand. I won't get any, either."

I gave him a half smile.

He paid our bill and began walking me to my car.

"So did you have a good time? You want to do this again?" he asked.

"Oh, yeah, great time."

He tried to give me a hug, but I pulled away and said, "See you next time."

But there will be no next time, heavy breather.

Chapter 13

Yvette

I was trying not to lose hope that I was going to get my money back from Phil. Over the last few weeks I'd called, begged, threatened, and prayed that he would return my money. When none of that worked, I called his father to see if he could talk to him. I explained to his dad all the reasons why his son was wrong, and he agreed with every single one, but all he had to say was that Phil was grown and he couldn't make him do right. Which was true, but sad at the same time. Everyone had been calling, but I didn't feel like talking to anyone, because they all kept asking me the same questions about Phil. "How is it possible?" "Why didn't you have an attorney look over your paperwork?" "Can't you do something?" If there was something I could do, I would have done it already.

The only thing I was certain of was that none of this would have happened if I hadn't gone to Toronto. I should have stayed home, paid my bills, and been at work when Phil was making his anonymous phone calls. If I had been there, he would have never got through and Frank wouldn't have had the chance to snoop through all my files.

So far I'd had consultations with two different attorneys, and they both had said the same thing—that our home was community property before we were divorced, and I would have to show proof that we planned to split the proceeds from the sale of the house, since it was sold after the dissolution of our marriage. It was going to be costly and hard to get my share, but it could be done. However, I would need at least five thousand dollars for a retainer. So basically, to get my money, I was going to need money, but I had none.

In the meantime, while I was waiting for Phillip's dumb ass to come to his senses, I had bills to pay. I'd already paid my August rent, but I didn't know how I was going to pay September, and I had so many other bills and the children to take care of.

And speaking of my children, I couldn't wait until they went back to school. It was hot, and they were driving me crazy with their constant bickering and fighting and bugging me like babies in this little apartment.

I applied to at least ten positions a day. Most companies wanted you not only to submit a résumé, but also to fill out an application on their Web site. I couldn't understand why, if I had my résumé and it had my name and address and everywhere I ever worked on it, I had to fill out an application, too. At the moment I was applying for an administrative position at Drexel University, and I began inserting my information into the application, because I wanted to be hired. During the process Mercedes came in, interrupting my concentration.

"What do you need, Mimi?" I asked.

"Mom, I'm bored."

"How are you bored? You have your toys, books, television. You'll have to find something to do, because I'm on the computer and I'm not in charge of your entertainment, Mercedes. Go out and play."

"All my good toys are at that storage place, and I don't

like the kids around here. I want to go back to our old neighborhood. When are we going to move to our new house?"

"Soon. Go play."

A few moments later she stuck her head in my bedroom again and said, "Mom, uh, I wanted to know what we were having for dinner."

"I don't know. Let me finish this, and then I'll tell you." I turned my attention back to my application.

She left my bedroom, and a few seconds later she knocked on my door again. Without looking up I said, "What do you need now, Mercedes?"

"No. It's me, Mom. Can I go out and play ball with Semaj?" Brandon asked as I lifted my head up.

"You can go, but come back in an hour so you can eat."

The verdict was still out on his new friends and this neighborhood. Our Germantown neighborhood seemed pretty good, but it really was either-or. If you went three block south, there were nice large colonial houses, but a couple of blocks west and boys were hanging on the corner in front of several liquor stores and Chinese stores. Semaj was Brandon's age, but way more thuggish. I'd met his mom. She looked like a baby herself, and I knew she had, like, four younger kids, so her attention was definitely not on him. I got the feeling he did whatever he wanted.

Sixty-two minutes and several space and tabs later, I finally completed the application and hit UPLOAD. I felt like I'd accomplished something, until an error message appeared and then the screen froze. I'd sat here for an hour, filling out that application, and it didn't even get saved. *Forget it,* I thought.

It was time to make dinner. I walked into the kitchen and then went into the living room, and Mercedes began to tell me everyone who had called me.

"Mom Mom and Pop Pop both said to call them. Aunt Crystal said to call her when you get up, and Miss Geneva said it is real important and that she needs to talk to you."

"Thank you. Just continue to say what I told you to say whenever anyone calls. I'm asleep or in the shower."

"Okay. Can I sit on the steps?"

"Go ahead. Take your dolls or a book out with you."

Mercedes gathered a few of her dolls and went to sit on the steps. I watched her from the front window and began to make dinner. I looked down at the ringing phone. It was Geneva again. I finally decided to pick it up myself.

"Hey, Geneva. Sorry I haven't called you. I've just been out of it, trying to figure all of this out."

"I know. Are you okay?"

"Yeah, I'm good. A little frustrated, but good. It's really crazy that he has every dollar I have in his possession and won't give it to me."

"I know, but can't you cash one of your CDs or go into your savings?"

"I wish. That's all gone. I used everything I had saved on our down payment for the house and on remodeling the kitchen."

"You don't have anything left?"

"Nothing, and I know I could probably get money from my dad, but I don't feel like asking anyone for anything."

"I know. Well, it is not a lot of money, but I can loan you a few hundred. I would give you more, but Eric is the only one working right now."

"No, I'll be fine. You have your own family. Don't worry about me. I'll be all right."

"I know you will, but I've been trying to think of ways to help you. How about if you try talking to Phil?"

"Geneva, I tried. He doesn't want to hear anything I have to say, and I'm not trying to get any angrier."

"Well, I think he is doing all of this because he is upset. And probably is still in love with you. You know men can dish it, but can't take it. Maybe if you apologize, he'll forgive you. You were his wife just a couple of months ago. And do you think he really wants to see you and the kids without? I doubt it."

"You might be right."

"Just really try to reason with him. Break down and cry if you have to. Change your approach and you might get new results."

"All right, that's what I'll do. I'm going to try to talk to him. It can't hurt. I'll do it tomorrow."

If insulting and threatening hadn't work with Phil, I would try another method, called tears. Geneva had a point. He did once love me. So maybe if I went to him crying and upset, he would get weak and help me. I knew I had to confront him one-on-one and catch him off guard. I decided to meet him at his job, right before he got on the bus he drove. His 52 bus pulled out of Wynnefield Station promptly at 7:09 Monday through Friday. I arrived at 6:37 a.m. and waited for him to drive up.

I was looking for his Chevy pickup truck, but to my surprise, he pulled up in a shiny new white Ford Explorer. He backed into a parking space a few cars in front of mine. *So this was how he was spending my money*. He was wearing his bluish-gray uniform and a navy sweater vest over top of it. He took his duffel bag out of the trunk, hit the alarm, and then threw on his sunglasses and headed for his terminal. I got out of the car and began jogging up to him. I think I startled him, but I began crying and leaning into him before he could react.

"What the hell are you doing here, Vette? You can't be showing up at my job."

"I know. I just wanted to talk to you."

"I'm at work. We can't talk right now."

"But, Phil, please. I need to talk to you, and your bus doesn't leave for another fifteen minutes."

"Okay. What do you want?"

I grabbed his arm and hugged it, burying my face in his shoulder. "Look, Phil, I'm sorry if I hurt you, but what you are doing right now is affecting not just me. You're hurting Mimi and Brandon. How am I supposed to take care of them with no money and no job? I know you are mad at me, but this is not the way to get back at me. Please, stop all of this. Please." I lifted my head and let him see all the real emotion displayed on my face. I thought I saw something that looked like a hint of remorse.

Then he stepped away from me and said, "You are really going to have to figure it out, because there is nothing I can do for you."

"What about the couple of thousand I put toward the down payment and the money I put up for the kitchen? You can't keep that money, too."

"Vette, I don't want to talk about this anymore. You have to leave, and I don't need you causing a scene."

"Please help me, Phil. I don't know what I'm going to do. I don't have any money; I don't have anything."

He just shook his head, as if he didn't have any control over anything.

"So you really are going to let me sink. You'd rather see me fall than help me." I cried more and sobbed louder, still hoping to get a different reaction out of him.

Instead he yelled, "I don't care either way, and you need to get out of here." His yelling infuriated me. I couldn't pretend any longer.

"I wouldn't be here if you weren't a thief."

"Don't call me a thief."

"That's what you are if you take something that is not yours. What does that make you? A real man does not steal from a woman, only one with female tendencies. You fucking bitch." I was furious, and I wanted my money.

"Listen, I don't have anything for you. You can get out of here with all of your nonsense. And don't come back up here, because next time I'm going to call the cops on you."

Phil left me standing there and boarded his bus and took off. I walked back to my car, feeling even more frustrated than when I arrived. I didn't know how I was going to take care of anything. Just thinking about my situation I became angrier and angrier, and I felt like I had to do something to him and now. I got in my car and caught up to his bus. He was going to give me mine and now. I had tried the nice way. Now he was going to pay up or get fucked up. I followed his bus a few stops. Passengers were boarding the bus and getting off.

I wasn't sure what I was going to do. I was thinking about pulling in front of his bus and blocking it from traveling, but he could possibly go around me. I decided to pull over. I threw my car into park, hit the locks on the doors, and sprinted over to the bus. An elderly couple was exiting the back of the bus, and when they got off, I hopped on. A few people were looking at me as if to say, "Why is this lady sneaking on the bus?" I didn't care anymore if anyone was looking or listening. Phil was looking at me through his rearview mirror. He shook his head and told me to get off the bus.

"I'll get off this bus when you give me my money, you crook. You are going to give me my money, now Phil or else."

"Vette, get the hell off my bus before I call the police."

"Call the cops! I dare you. So I can tell them to lock your ass up.

"I'm warning you, Yvette."

"Fuck your warning, Phillip. How about I tell all your passengers how you stole my damn money, you bitch. Huh? Or tell them how you smoke weed every day. Call the police so I can tell them to give your ass a drug test. I know you still roll up every weekend. Excuse me, everybody on the number fifty-two bus. I'm sorry y'all have to start y'all's morning like this, but I need to let everyone know that your driver, Phillip McKnight, is a drug addict and a thief, and he likes to date girls that are barely legal—so that makes him a borderline pervert, too. He owes me twenty-five thousand dollars and he needs to pay or I'm going to whoop his ass right now."

One lady was on my side she said that wasn't right. But most of the passengers weren't interested or amused; they just wanted to get to work on time. I became a little apprehensive when I saw a girl pull out her cell phone and start recording, but unfortunately, it didn't stop me from causing a scene. I began walking toward Phil.

"That's it. I'm calling the police." He pulled the bus over and pulled out his cell phone.

"Call them, you punk ass. You want me off this bus, then give me what you owe me." People were still looking, and I was getting closer to him.

He must have seen the anger in my eyes, because once I was a few feet away, he said, "Don't do anything you will regret," and got ready to block a punch, which he knew I would throw at any moment.

"I'm not going to regret anything. I don't give a fuck. I'm going to show you I'm not playing with you. I want my money. I should have known better then to have married you. Your mother and father ain't shit. So why did I expect any better of you." I lifted my hand and let my palm make contact with the bridge of his nose. The smack was so loud, the entire bus jumped. He ducked in the corner of his driver's seat, making sure not to hit me back or allow me another good shot.

I got in a few kicks and punches before I heard sirens. I didn't want to get arrested, so I pressed the button to open the door and ran back to my car. I saw an ambulance, not a police car, going the other way, but I was still scared and got the hell out of there.

I knew Phil's punk ass was going to call everyone and tell them I had lost my mind and needed to be put away, and I was right, because my father called me, screaming, "What the hell is wrong with you, Vette? I just got a call from Phil, and he said you came to his job and slapped and kicked him."

"I didn't, Dad. He is lying."

"You can't be acting like this. Why would you go to that man's job and start all that trouble?"

"He deserved it. He owes me."

"Well, I hope it is all worth it, because when I was on the phone with him, he was talking to the police. You better pray they don't come and lock you up."

"Daddy, I don't care. He took my money."

"Yvette, forget about that money. Is twenty-five thousand worth you going to jail? Leave that man alone. If you go to jail, you won't have anything. I know you are mad, but you can't go and get your own revenge. You have to put this in God's hands. Let him go and do whatever he is going to do, and be sure that God is keeping score."

My dad was steady preaching about God and all these other churchy things, which I was not trying to hear. I was so angry, and I had to calm myself down before I bought a gun and killed him. Phil was going to give me mine or handle the penalties that came with playing with my livelihood. I was determined to get even, and I was going to do so by calling his job. If I wasn't going to get my money, then he was going to lose his.

I called the main number for SEPTA and asked for the human resources director's office. I was transferred to his assistant. A cheery voice answered, and I started to give up all the information, true or not, I had on Phil.

"Yes, I would like to report a driver, Phillip McKnight. Uh, he's a driver on the number fifty-two bus. I'm just a concerned person and don't want to see any innocent passengers get hurt. So I just wanted to report that he is an alcoholic and is on crack cocaine and smokes a lot of marijuana. I would drug test him immediately."

"Okay. You said his name was what?"

"Phillip McKnight. He drives the number fifty-two bus."

"Okay. Thank you for your concern. We will look into this."

"Yes, you're welcome, because I know he is a ton of lawsuits waiting to happen."

After the call I felt a little better. *Bitch, you are fired, too,* I thought. Now all I needed was to figure out a way to get my money back.

CHAPTER 14

Dana

Reshma walked into my office, upset, and was flustered when she spoke. Her speech was very fast, and it was hard to understand what exactly she was saying.

"I can't take her anymore. She doesn't do her job. I don't understand."

"What's wrong, Reshma?"

"That intern, Courtney. She broke the copier and then she left early, and we need copies and pamphlets made for tomorrow's meeting with Connelly Brothers. And I really don't want to ruin someone's internship. I know she needs to get credit, but I'm about to report her. I can't take it."

"Calm down. I'll take care of it. Don't worry. On my way home, I'll stop at that big copy center on Fortieth Street."

"Are you sure?" she asked, relieved.

"Yeah, I'm sure. Relax, finish everything else up, and I'll get here early and help you set up."

"Thank you so much. Still, Dana, we must do something about her."

After work I rushed over to the busy copy center. There were about five people ahead of me, and I needed the five hundred brochures expedited. Even though I had assured Reshma that it could be done, I was nervous. I stood in line patiently as the copier techs waited on other patrons. A well-groomed, light brown–skinned man with shades, wearing a black T-shirt and jeans, asked if I had been waiting long.

"No, I just got here."

He looked down at his watch and said, "All I want to do is pick up my postcards. I'm not placing a new order."

"They seem like they are moving pretty fast."

"They need to move faster. I need to get to the airport. I have a client waiting for me. I have my own security company, and if they get off the plane and I'm not there, I'm going to have a problem."

"What kind of security company?"

"My company does security for most of the nightclubs and big events in the city. Every time a celebrity comes to town they call me. Here. Take my card."

I read his card. UNTOUCHABLE SECURITY AND EVENTS—CEO & OWNER, GENE RICHARDS. I thanked him.

"Do you have a card?"

I handed him mine. He went up and said something to one of the copier guys, got his order, and smiled at me on his way out. Just out of curiosity I wanted to see what the CEO was driving. *Not bad,* I thought as he drove off in his black Range Rover.

I didn't think much of meeting Gene until he called me a few days later.

"Hello, Dana. This is Gene. When I can take you somewhere nice?"

"I don't know, tell me what you had in mind?"

"I wanted to take you to dinner. Maybe to Buddakan or maybe get seafood at McCormick & Schmick's?"

"How did you know they were two of my favorite restaurants? I think we can make that happen."

"Okay, then meet me at Buddakan tomorrow around six."

* * *

A little after six the next day I got a call from Gene saying he was sitting at this table by himself and for me to hurry up. Although Gene wasn't my normal suit and tie type, I was still going to give him a chance. I appreciated that he was showing immediate interest. However, when I got to the restaurant, I didn't like what he was wearing. Who went out of the house wearing a white T-shirt and basketball shorts and flip-flops? Why would he ask me to this nice restaurant and dress like he was about to go sit next to a pool? Damn, I was disappointed again. Gene was on a call when I sat down. I ordered a saketini and tasted one of the shrimp and scallop spring rolls sitting on the table. I overhead him discussing a meeting he had to attend after our date. He ended his call and then thanked me for coming and said I looked nice.

"Thanks. So, where do you have to go after this?"

"I have a meeting with this big financier that wants to invest in my company. As soon as we are done, I'm going to meet up with him."

"You're not going to go home and change your clothes?" I asked looking his attire over again.

"No, why should I. What's wrong with what I'm wearing?"

"I just wouldn't go to a meeting dressed like that."

"Dressed like what?" he said, looking at his white outfit.

"Never mind. Forget it."

"I'm dressed fine. I can go anywhere in this city and get respect. It doesn't matter what I'm wearing; people know who I am."

"Oh, okay," is all I could muster out. This date was starting off badly. I shouldn't have said anything. I couldn't tell if he was offended or not. I didn't say anything else about his pool outfit, but the date still went from bad to horrible. "I'm sure they will be very impressed with your business skills."

"Yeah, I know they will. I know how to talk business and what not. But let me ask you a question. When was the last time someone made your toes curl?"

"I haven't had my toes curl. It's been a while." *What kind of stupid disgusting question was that,* I thought.

"I don't believe you, because you answered that too fast. That's how I know you are lying. I know somebody is making you feel good beating that thing up"

"No, I'm single."

"For real. All of that is going to waste. That's a damn shame. You too fine not to have a man."

I tried to change the subject. "So, Gene, have you ever thought about maybe taking some classes and getting a degree in business? So you could learn how to expand your business, without investors." Again I thought I was saying something positive but I got a negative reaction from Gene.

"No. Why would I do that? My business is already making money."

"Well, it wouldn't hurt."

"Yeah, I don't need college. I made six figures last year without a degree."

"That's impressive."

"Yeah, I bet it is. I probably make more than you."

"You might." There was definitely some tension in the air. How did me suggesting he takes some classes turn into an insult? I stopped talking, ordered my meal, and for the rest of the date I didn't ask him any more questions. He didn't even notice he was having a conversation by himself. I laughed at a few things that weren't funny and agreed with him on things he was obviously wrong about. I could have left, but my grilled lamb chops and saketini were too good to leave.

The check arrived, and I thought I had done a pretty good job of faking a date.

Gene stood up, pulled out a big wad of hundreds and twenties, and said, "Well, Dana, it was nice meeting you. I can't say it was the worst date, but I can't say it was the best." He threw down eighty dollars on the table. I looked down at the check. It was a $155.00 tab.

"Gene, this bill is a hundred fifty-five dollars, and you only left eighty."

He looked down and said, "Oh, I did. I'm sorry. I didn't leave the tip. Oh, and you can pay your own half."

"What? I don't have any cash on me."

"Reach in your bag, and use one of those cards. Man, y'all stuck up bougie bitches all the same. Don't worry about how I'm dressed. Worry about why you ain't got no man." Gene walked out the restaurant and I sat in disbelief. I didn't understand what had just happened.

The waiter came over to the table and asked if everything was all right.

"Yes, it is," I said, reaching in my bag and pulling out my wallet. I located my Visa card and paid the bill. I folded up the money and put it in my wallet. *What an asshole,* I thought.

The waiter came back with the receipt. I signed my name and gave him a generous cash tip.

"Thank you so very much, and do come again."

"I will. Thank you." I stood up, and tears began to stream down my face. This was what I got for dating someone like him, a guy without enough class to dress right. I had to call someone and tell them about my date from hell.

I dialed Tiffany as soon as I reached my car. I explained to her what had happened and she couldn't believe it. She kept trying to make excuses for his bad behavior. "Maybe he didn't have enough money on him and didn't know how to tell you."

"No, he pulled out a big knot of money. Damn fake CEO. I'm getting so tired of this bullshit and all these crazy men," I whimpered.

"I know you are not crying over that crazy guy."

"No, I'm not crying over him."

"I can tell by your voice that you're crying."

"I am crying, but not over him. I'm crying because if he and people like him are all that is left out here, I'm going to be single forever. You know he had the nerve to call me a stuck-up, bougie bitch and told me to go in my bag and grab my credit card and pay for my own dinner. I've never been talked to that way, and it is not fair. I should have just stayed with Todd; at least he was respectful. I knew what issues he came with and what he was capable of.

"No, you shouldn't have. It sounds like a really bad date. You're not stuck-up or bougie. You have just been running into a few crazies lately, but there are good men out there."

"I don't believe that. I am really starting to think all men are insane and there aren't any good ones left."

Chapter 15

Yvette

I was served an order to stay away from Phil, his family, and his place of employment. Like I was some kind of stalker, killer, or even wanted him. I didn't want anything to do with him. I just wanted my money. I felt so dumb and embarrassed. Simply put, even if I didn't agree with the order, if I violated it, I would be jailed and fined. Every time I thought about my situation, I got upset. My every thought was about my plans for that twenty-five thousand. It wasn't a lot of money, but it would make my life a lot easier. Without my money, I had to think about how I was going to pay Mercedes's tuition, and I still needed to pay my September rent, my cable, cell phone, electric, Internet, and gas and get groceries. I had eight things to do, but enough money for only three. I had applied for unemployment. Hopefully, I'd be approved, because I didn't know what I was going to do.

When we moved into this apartment, it was temporary. I knew it was small and couldn't fit all our belongings, but now I found myself constantly running to the storage to get something we needed. I was going crazy thinking that we actually might have to live in this small apartment long term and I might not be able to get out. I sat and cried for a moment. I placed my hands in my lap. I had no idea what I was going to do.

Mercedes ran in my bedroom, screaming, "Mom, Brandon saw me watching television, and he came and changed the channel." She didn't get the reaction she wanted. She took a look at me and asked me if I was crying.

"No. I'm not crying, but stop yelling."

"It looks like you were crying. Brandon, Mommy was crying."

Brandon ran into my bedroom. "Mom, what's wrong?"

"Nothings wrong, I'm not crying. I have allergies."

"Oh, well, tell this dummy not to change the channel," Mercedes stated.

"Mimi, stop calling him out of his name. Both of you cut it out before I don't take you school shopping and I take a nap instead."

The mall was busy with back-to-school traffic. I didn't know about all the parents, but I was so happy. With the kids out of the house, I could get peace and would be able to think. Thankfully, Doug had sent some extra money this week, which would help cover some of the back-to-school bill. Mercedes was easy to shop for. I bought her two uniform shirts and three pairs of pants to start off with. Now, Brandon was different. He was entering high school and was going to be a little more challenging to clothe because of his husky size and big feet.

At Foot Locker Brandon tried on a bunch of sneakers. He thought he wore a ten, but the salesman measured his foot and it turned out he had gone up another size since the beginning of the summer.

"Mom, I want these." I turned the shoe over and almost fainted at the $145.00 price tag. My budget was only $150.00 for them both.

"How about these, Brandon?" I said, suggesting black

Nikes that looked like they would last for a long time and conceal the dirt once they were older and were much cheaper.

"No, Mom. I really like these. Can I get these in an eleven?" he asked the salesman.

I didn't want to pay $145.00 for one pair of sneakers, but I didn't want Brandon to be the corny kid, either. I remembered how that felt, to want a certain look and hear my dad say, "I'm not buying that," so I gave in. I would have to make the money up from another bill.

I felt like I'd accomplished something. They had uniforms and sneakers, and I had enough money to pay the most important bill, which was shelter. And after I paid that, I wouldn't have any money. Everything else would have to wait.

A few lights away from the mall, my Chevy Malibu started making noise and smoking, and before I could pull it all the way over, it just gave out; steam was rising from the hood. Mercedes asked if we had run out of gas, and Brandon got out of the car and asked me to pop the hood, like he was a mechanic.

"Boy, get in here. You don't know what you are looking for."

"Yes, I do. I can push you out of the street."

"I can help him," Mercedes said as she took her seat belt off and got out of the car.

"Both of you, get back in the car." It was embarrassing enough to have a car smoking on the side of the road. I didn't need two kids pushing it. I got out and pulled out my cell phone and tried to think of someone who could help us. A tow truck driver pulled up next to us and asked if we needed a tow.

"I'm not sure. How much is a tow?"

"I can take you wherever you want to go for a flat fee of seventy-five, but before I tow you, do you know what's wrong?"

"No, it just gave out on me."

"Do you have a mechanic?"

"No."

"There is a shop not too far from there, and I can tow you there."

At the auto repair place, we had a seat and waited for the mechanic to come back with the results of my car's diagnostic.

"It's your head gasket, and with parts and labor, it's going to run you like four-fifty. Let me show you." He walked me into the dark, oily garage and pointed to connected metal parts inside my open hood. "See right there? That's your cylinder block, and that's connected to the head gasket. You have water in your gas, and once the water's in there, there's a fifty-fifty chance your engine is going to go. Now, I would suggest you get a new engine, but then you are looking at about a thousand dollars, or just get the gasket fixed for four hundred dollars. If you decide to get it fixed, I can have it ready by this evening."

I needed my car, but I needed to pay my rent. But if a job called, I wouldn't be able to get there if I didn't have a car. I chose to get the car fixed and was going to have to get more money from somewhere.

The car was fixed, but I needed rent money ASAP. I broke down and called Hector. I knew he would help me, but I was really angry with him and didn't want to talk to him. I was sure that if he hadn't opened his mouth, I wouldn't be going through any of this. But he had said to call him if I needed anything, and I did.

"Where you been, Yvette? Everything all right with you?"

"No, not really. I have a lot going on right now."

"You know I'm here. What's up?"

"My ex didn't give me my half of the money. He stole like twenty something thousand from me"

"Can't you do something?" He was asking the same annoying question everyone had asked. I didn't feel like going through the motions again.

"No, Hector I can't. If I could, I would. I'm calling you because I really need money."

"Like how much do you need?"

I didn't know what to say. I needed, enough to pay my rent, storage, and buy food, but I knew he didn't have that kind of money.

"Uh, whatever you can give me."

"Come on, give me a number. Like, what you need? A couple hundred, five hundred? What?"

"Five hundred is good."

"Okay. I have to stop at the bank after work. I'll give you a call when I get off."

The next day I met Hector at a BP gas station near my old job. He was grinning hard when he gave me a hug and handed me a skinny white bank envelope.

"Here, it's only three hundred. I forgot I had loaned my brother some money."

"That's cool. It will help," I said, but I'd been counting on the entire five hundred.

"I know you stressing, but when am I going to see you and my lady again? I need to feel you, Vette. I miss you and need that." He didn't know sex was the last thing on my mind. I could care less. "Let's get a room."

"No, Hector. No offense, but I'm tired, stressed, and drained and don't feel sexy."

"You need some of this; it will release all that stress."

"I'm sure it will, but I'm good right now. Listen, thanks for the money. I will call you."

I walked towards my car and left Hector at the gas station putting his fingers up to his ear like a phone, mouthing *make sure you call me*.

CHAPTER 16

Dana

Tiffany was dragging me to a professional happy hour called Second Fridays. She claimed there were going to be distinguished gentlemen in attendance and said that I should get dolled up. I told her I was coming straight from work and wasn't getting any better dressed. Whoever was going to be at this happy hour could take it or leave it. And I was glad I followed my instincts, because I would have been mad if I had got pretty for a bunch of women.

It was the typical sixteen-to-one ratio. I saw it every time we would go out. There would always be a roomful of attractive professional black women huddled in groups, buying and sipping their own drinks, waiting, hoping, wishing for a half-decent man to approach them. Meanwhile, the few men in attendance would stand around, pretending to be gods, figuring out which women they wanted to pursue, since they had a large selection to choose from. And I guess we got chosen this time. Lucky us. Tiffany met a seemingly nice man. She told him she had a boyfriend, but that made him more interested. He asked us if we wanted to have a cocktail with him and his friend.

I said no, but Tiffany said yes. So we met them at the Walnut Room, a lounge a few blocks from the Second Friday event. Tiffany's new friend was keeping her attention, and I had to be her wing woman and babysit her new friend's friend. His friend was not attractive at all. He was dressed well but I couldn't see past his creature like features. I was already in a bad mood and didn't care to exchange pleasantries with anyone. I ordered my own drink and had a seat.

"So, what's in your glass?" asked the friend's friend.

"Wine," I answered very dryly.

"Well, excuse me. Did I say something wrong?" He looked around, as if someone was going to answer him. "What's your name?"

"It's Dana."

"Okay, Dana, you ain't have to say it with such an attitude. I'm Leon."

"No, I don't have an attitude. I guess I'm just a little tired. I came straight from work."

"Oh, okay. What kind of business?"

"I'm in marketing."

"Oh, that's cool. I thought y'all were nurses or something. Where did you go to school?" he asked.

"Maryland Eastern Shore."

"I went to Lincoln. So you married? Divorced?"

"Neither."

"How many kids do you have?"

"None."

"No kids? That's good," he said, surprised. "How you manage that?"

"Easy. It's called birth control." Where was Tiffany? I was becoming increasingly irritated.

"Really, yeah Dana I think I like you. No kids, good shape. 'Cause I'm really getting tired of seeing these ugly chicks with big guts and bad shapes."

"Is that right?" He must hadn't look in the mirror in a long time.

"Yes, it is, but I like you. You're relaxed and calm. I like that. I'm glad you are not a vulture like a lot of women out here. Most of the time these women be all over a good black man."

"A good black man," I repeated almost choking.

"Yeah, you know, desperate scavengers. Like all those chicks, at that second Friday. I mean of course it is way more of y'all than it is of us, but damn, give a brother some room to breathe." He continued, "Most of the time I always have to say slow down, let me get to know you. I usually take them on one date and then they want to know if I can be their boyfriend. Then on the second date, they want to know my plans for marriage. I've seen so many women mess up really good relationships by talking about marriage," he said, shaking his head and laughing to himself. "Or they want you to pay their bills, and I'm thinking, How were you paying your bills before you met me?"

If anyone was trying to marry you, you should have probably said yes, I thought.

"Plus, I have a few years before I settle down, anyway," he continued.

"How old are you?"

"I'm thirty-eight. I probably get serious about forty or so. When I do it, I want to do it right. I'm trying to find a good girl that don't mind spoiling and taking care of her man."

I couldn't be hearing him right. He was thirty-eight and wanted someone to take care of him, and he had a few years before he would be ready to settle down. I was laughing so hard inside that it seeped out as a cough I couldn't control. He had absolutely no reason to be conceited. I toyed with the idea of knocking down his ego, but I didn't even have the energy. I just got up from the table and said, "Nice meeting you."

"Nice meeting me? What's wrong? What happened?" he asked.

I let him sit at the table and figure it out himself. Tiffany was still carrying on her conversation, but I tapped her and told her I was ready to leave. She said good-bye to her new friend and came running after me.

"What's wrong?"

"Tiffany, I'm so tired of all these losers. I'm totally convinced there aren't any good men out here. It is not us. It is them. Like, really, that man was none of that, and someone has him thinking he is a gift. He said he was happy I wasn't a vulture."

"Hold up. A *vulture*?" She laughed.

"Yes, all the women are all over him, trying to get with him." I was walking so fast, and she was trying to keep up. "I'm not going to let these men continue to beat up my self-esteem. There is absolutely nothing wrong with me. I'm a professional with a home, a nice car, no children. I should be happily married or beating off men. I'm really getting tired of these horrible black men and their fucked-up egos. They want you to baby and coddle them. They don't want a commitment and if you ask them about a relationship they'll say 'Oh, hell no, you trying to tie me down. I'm still in my prime.' They think they are hot until their ass is, like, forty-five and nobody else wants them! That dude is crazy; he said he was looking for a good girl to spoil him. He must be on drugs, ugly fuck."

"That's not true. All men are not the same. You just haven't come across the right one. Me and Solomon are still new, but he is a good guy."

"Well, you need to keep a hold of him. All I know is you don't see white women or Asian women going through all of this. And you know why? Because they are not dating crazy-ass, spoon-fed black men. I'm not patting anyone on the back and declaring him a good man because he is not the status quo. Because he has a good job and provides for his family. That's what the hell you are *supposed* to do. I'm tired, Tiffany. I'm so tired of our men. I am not dating another ego tripping, backward thinking black man. Fuck them all. Fuck black men and all their bullshit. Fuck the black women that chase after them, acting like they are an extinct species. And fuck the horrible ones that think they are prize and ain't. I'm not doing it anymore. Fuck black men, all of them. I'm going to date others from here on out."

"Well, if you feel that strongly, maybe you should try the other side," Tiffany said, because she knew she couldn't argue with me.

"It is not a maybe—I am."

Chapter 17

Crystal

Kori's cries awoke us. I got out of bed to grab her bottle. By the time I returned to the room, Rell was already next to the crib, patting her back. I picked her up and put her in my arms. He watched as I fed and burped her. I wondered how it made him feel to be awakened every night by a child that wasn't his. Rell had really been a blessing in my life, especially since all the trash Kenneth and Syreeta were talking about me. I think I was starting to believe that no one was going to ever want me or accept me and my kids. I didn't think it was possible to be this happy and feel this loved. I thought it was going to take me years to bounce back from Kenneth. Love must have come into my life, because I wasn't looking. It really just came and wrapped its loving arms around me in the form of Rell and hadn't let go.

It had been a few weeks and we were still getting to know each other, but I could already say he treated me better than anyone I had ever met. It was like he gave me the same amount of love I gave him. He always told me how smart and beautiful I was, and didn't judge me at all. He knew the story behind all my kids' fathers, and he didn't care. He thought they were all fools for passing me by. I loved the little things and big things about him. Like the other day he was at the sneaker store, and he asked me what size the kids wore and brought them all sneakers. And he paid my mortgage this month, and he didn't even live here. I told him not to, because the job hadn't called him yet and it was not even like he had money coming in. He was spending what he had left from the military on us.

He was a good dude with a good heart, and that was worth a lot. I kept telling myself, *Something is going to happen.* I had never had a relationship go this well. I hoped I didn't mess it up, like I somehow always did.

My boo bear was watching his ESPN, and I was ironing and planning what everyone was going to wear for the week. While it was on my mind, I called my mom to check on her.

"Mom, what are you doing?"

"No, the question is what are you doing? I want to discuss this man you have around the kids."

"Huh?" I looked at Rell and walked out of the bed room. "Mom, what are you talking about?"

"I hear you have a man staying over there with you, and Kori's not even six months yet, and he doesn't even have a job, and your father and I are upset."

"Mom, that's not true."

"Well, I sure hope it's not, because I know you more responsible than that, because the last thing you need is to get pregnant again."

"Mommy, I'm going to call you back."

I already knew who told my mom about Rell. I called Dana and when she answered I tried not to raise my voice so Rell wouldn't hear me in the bedroom.

"Hey, Dana. For starters, I think you should start worrying about your own life, and not mine."

"What are you talking about?"

"You know what? I don't appreciate you telling Mommy

and Daddy about anything that happens in my household. What I want them to know, I will tell them myself."

"I didn't say anything about you having a boyfriend. Mommy asked me."

"Dana, I know you said something. You've been a snitch your whole life. I don't need you to judge me."

"I'm not judging you. I just don't understand how a man without a job can help you. I just want the best for you and those kids, and I want you to stop making the same mistakes over and over again."

"You know what? Please Dana, whatever choices I make in my life—and who I decide to make them with—are none of your concern. Okay? So I would appreciate it if next time you just mind your own business and worry about your own affairs."

"Don't say anything when you got a big belly and are sitting alone in the labor room again. Don't call me, because I don't have time to keep going to court with you."

"I won't ever call you, bitch," I shouted and hung up on Dana.

Rell walked into the hallway. "What's wrong?"

"My sister and mother are talking a lot of crap."

"Like what?"

"Like I shouldn't have anyone around the kids, and you don't have a job and you going to use me, get me pregnant, and leave me."

"Do you think that?"

"No."

"Well, I'm not going anywhere."

"I know you're not, Rell."

It was hours later, and I still was thinking about the conversation I had with my mom. Everyone was asleep; the house was quiet except for the sound of the television. I got out of the bed and walked to the bathroom. Rell turned over and asked what I was doing up.

"Just turning off the television and going to the bathroom."

"We need to talk, Crystal. I don't want you to get in any fights with your family over me."

"Rell, it's no big deal. They trip about every guy I date."

"But I'm not like everyone else, I'm different. I don't want your people thinking you with some loser that's going to hurt you and play games."

"I know you're not," I said.

"Look at me. I'm not leaving you."

"Okay." I didn't know where the conversation was going, but I listened as Rell spoke.

"Crystal, I know there is something special about you and I never fell in love this fast. But I do know I don't want to be without you. I want to make you feel comfortable and reassured. I was thinking the only thing that could make that happen is if we get married."

"Married?"

"Yeah, married. We can go to West Chester. It only takes a few days for the license to get approved. I want you to be my wife."

Was he asking me to marry him?

"But, Rell, we've only known each other for a short time."

"It doesn't take months and years to realize you love someone. I want you to be my wife. I want you to know I'm serious about you and this," he said as he pointed around the room. "I don't want you to have to argue with your family about me. I'm real, and I'm dedicated to us."

"Yes, I will marry you." I wanted to ask him how he could fall in love with me in such a short time and how was he sure and why he chose me and what made me special. But I didn't. I just wanted to be happy, and maybe this was my chance.

I went to work the next day full of anticipation. I couldn't concentrate on my peer-coaching session. I tried to go over the 110-page ACR Cable Vision employee handbook like I cared, but I didn't. And I didn't like my coach, Tricia. She was talking to me like I wasn't smart and my job wasn't easy. I had been doing it for years. I nodded my head and listen intently, but the only thing I wanted to contemplate was that I was going to be Mrs. Terell Glover today.

I took a half of a day off from work, and at noon Rell was outside waiting for me. I was so nervous. We drove to the West Chester courthouse to fill out paperwork. We handed over a sixty-dollar money order to the courthouse clerk. She then stamped our paperwork, made a few copies, and told us that we could come pick up our marriage license in three days.

"We don't get it today?" I asked.

"No, there is a three-day waiting period, and here is a list of judges and ministers who can marry you," the clerk explained.

We thanked her, and we walked out of the courthouse.

"So in three days you will be all mine."

"I'm all yours now, Rell."

"You know what I mean—officially. I love you, Mrs. Glover."

"Mrs. Glover. I really liked the sound of that."

CHAPTER 18

Dana

Now that I was open to new things and on a black man hiatus, Leah invited me to the Poconos with her boyfriend, Stephen, and his friend Adam. According to Leah, Adam was my perfect match. He was thirty years old, an accountant, and very good-looking. Leah thought it would be a great idea for us all to go to the Poconos together and to get know one another. The only issue I had with going was the start time. I had to be at Leah's at the crack of dawn.

"I don't usually get up this early on the weekend. So this better be worth it," I told Leah.

"It will be. Adam is so nice. I promise you will like him. We're going to do a little rafting, biking, and hiking. And Stephen reminded me you guys already met before."

"When?"

"Last year, at Stephen's birthday party. You probably don't remember him. He was there with his girlfriend, but he is single now."

I wanted to get an advance look at my perfect match. I peeked out the window to see a nicely tanned, tall guy with brown, curly hair and eyes that were a blend of green and brown. He kind of reminded me of the actor Bradley Cooper from one of my favorite movies, *The Hangover.*

We all crammed into Leah's silver Toyota Prius. Her car was good on gas but not on space. Stephen and Adam sat in the front, while Leah and I enjoyed girl talk in the back. Judging from Adam's hello, a love connection was highly unlikely. I didn't know. . . . His "Hey" was very basic. It was polite, but not like "Hello. How are you?" I wasn't upset. At least I was going to have a little sun and relaxation.

We reached the scenic mountain destination. In the distance between the greenery of the wilderness in every direction sat a peaceful stream of water. I was still sleepy and needed to stretch my legs once we were out of the car.

"I think I might forgo the hike and just relax by the river," I notified Leah.

"You can't. We have to sign in and find our tour guide," Leah announced.

"Leah, why exactly do we need a guide? Don't we get to do a little of this and a little of that at our own leisure?" I asked.

"Yeah, something like that. I'll be right back," Leah responded.

A few minutes later Leah came back with a perky tour guide. She was short, but full of energy. "Are you ready for today?" the guide asked.

Ready for what? I thought.

She didn't wait for an answer and said, "Great. I want you guys to make sure you stay hydrated, and let's get ready for the Big Day Out."

We boarded a yellow school bus, and it dropped us off at a bike shop. There were bikes of all shapes and sizes. We all had to choose a bike, get the correct seat, and then start up the trail. I tried to get my footing right on my bike, but I kept losing my balance, wobbling back and forth.

After an hour of biking on the nature trail, I asked one of the guides how much longer we had left. It honestly seemed like we'd been biking for miles.

"Oh, we've already done about twelve miles or so."

"Well, how many miles do we have left?"

"Nine more miles. Then we will stop for a break, but you have to pick up your pace a little," the guide informed me.

My legs immediately began to cramp when I heard the mileage we had left. Who told Leah I wanted to ride on a bike for twenty-one miles or that I was a trail-mix kind of girl? She knew that I grew up in the city and that nature wasn't one of my friends. Adam was in the back of the pack with me, he seemed to be struggling else well.

"Are you okay?" he asked.

I said, "Are you? You don't look that great yourself."

"Honestly, I wasn't expecting all of this, but we will make it," he said.

Our reward for our twenty-one miles of bike riding was a brown bag lunch that included one bottle of water, a dry turkey sandwich, a small orange, and a bag of chips. I was quiet as I looked over at the water. It was tranquil. It was too shallow to swim in, but it was an incredible view.

"Are you having fun?" Leah asked me.

I nodded yes without making eye contact. No need to tell Leah how this "Big Day Out" was going to be the end of our friendship. She would find out soon enough.

After lunch we were off on the second phase of our journey. Which was hiking. We entered the path there was a sign that read BEWARE. ENTER AT YOUR OWN RISK. HIKERS HAVE DIED.

Oh, really. That's where I draw the line. "Leah, I'm not hiking on a trail that people have died on," I protested. The guide came over to me and said it really was not that bad. And I believed her, like a fool. Before today I thought hiking meant there might be a few hills and a few inclines, not rock climbing. For about two hours I swatted insects, gained about eight pounds of muscle mass in my calves from climbing steep, never ending terrain. I cried silently as perspiration poured into my eyes. Leah, Adam and Stephen were ahead of me and I was just taking my time and I didn't care how long it took me to get to the top, which seemed like forever.

At the top of the hill, I have to admit the view was amazing, but now that I was up, I had to get back down. Again, I silently cussed Leah out for calling herself my friend and making me endure pain and almost die of exhaustion.

We biked for twenty-one miles, climbed a mountainside, and it was not over. It was time for rafting. Yes, rafting. I entered the small water boat with my orange life vest on and tried my best to keep up with everyone. We went downriver, and my heart was in my throat because I had to dodge rocks and heavy splashes for several miles. I didn't know how deep the water was, but I hoped the boat didn't flip over. We paddled all the way to where the journey first began, and I felt lucky to be alive; I survived the Big Day Out. They gave me a T-shirt and a mug as proof. It was over. I had done it. I couldn't wait to get to our hotel and pass out on clean, nice sheets, take a shower, order room service, go to sleep, and never speak to Leah again in my life. I secretly thought, *Is this why Leah comes back to the office chipper? Because she's happy she didn't die?*

"Where is the hotel? I can't wait until I get back and get a warm shower," I said.

"The campground is a right up the road. We will set up the tent," Leah said cheerily.

"The tent?" I started laughing. I was nice all day, but Leah had to be out of her mind if she thought I was going to pitch a tent and sleep in the wild after the hard day I had just had. I laughed so hard, tears started running down my cheeks.

This was where I drew the line. This was where nature lovers and city people differed. This was *not* fun. Overexerting yourself, getting bitten by bugs, being hot, sweaty, and out of breath all seemed like work and were not relaxing.

"Leah, are you really out of your mind?" I yelled. "Do you really think I'm going to sleep out here? My body is aching, and I am not sleeping on the ground. I'm getting a hotel room."

Leah shrugged. "Okay, well, we can drop you off on the way to the campground."

To my surprise, Adam chimed in and said, "Hey, guys, if you don't mind, I'm going to do the hotel thing, too."

Great. I'm not the only one who hasn't lost their mind, I thought.

We drove up to a hotel, and Adam and I trudged inside. We told the clerk we both needed a room.

"We have one room left with two double beds," the clerk informed us.

"Thank you, but we need two rooms," I said, then began walking back to the car.

"Hold up," Adam said, coming after me. "We can get a room together. I'll take the sofa; I just want to rest," he said as he held the door open for me. I went back and told the clerk we were taking the room.

Once I was back to civilization, I took an hour-long shower. I would have been longer, but I knew Adam had to get in.

I was going to order room service and see what cable stations were available. First, I checked my phone and texted Tiffany to tell her everything that had transpired that day. I was still on the phone when Adam tapped on the door and said he was going to the store and asked me did I want anything. I yelled out no, but then once I tried to move my right leg, I felt this horrible pain. I let out a loud shriek. I felt tears streaming down my face. Adam came in the room and asked me if I was okay. I told him my body was in such pain, like I had been beaten by a prizefighter and had been hit on both kneecaps with a brick. He left, then came back into the room and tossed me a bottle of Tylenol at me.

"No, I'm fine, I will be okay. I'm too young to take Tylenol. If I take those I will feel old."

"Taking Tylenol doesn't mean you're old. It means you don't want to be a pain."

I laughed and accepted the pain pill.

He came in with water to help me swallow it. "Do you want me to try to rub it?"

"No, I'll be fine," I said after swallowing the pill.

"You have to rub it. My mother is a runner. Trust me, I don't get turned on by knees."

We both shared a laugh, and I told him I would pass on his massage. He instructed me to let him know if I needed him.

Leah and Stephen arrived bright and early to pick us up from our hotel. Both of them had a shocked expression on their face when Adam and I came out of the same room. I was still in a little bit of pain.

Once Leah and I were both in the backseat and on our way home, I leaned over to Leah and whispered, "I slept with Adam. I don't know what happened. Just one thing led to another."

"You did? Wow, that was fast." Leah wasn't being judgmental, but I could tell she was wondering how everything had progressed so quickly. It was like she wanted to say something, like "Why would you sleep with him on the first night?"

"That was funny. You thought I would really go there. No," I said, letting her know I'd been pulling her leg.

"Well, you never know. Oh, well, are you still upset with me?"

"Very, and I will be until I can walk pain free again."

Chapter 19

Yvette

I saw on the morning news that there was a big job fair being held at the Embassy Suites Hotel. The reporter said there was going to be two hundred companies and some of them would be hiring on the spot. I knew one of them needed to hire me. It was crime that I had to beg the sisters of Holy Redeemer to allow Mercedes to start school without paying her tuition. I had confided in Sister Olivia, and she said the sisters would say a prayer for me. I hoped their prayers worked, because I was almost out of money. Hopefully, I'd get a job today and have a check in maybe two to three weeks. The only thing in my way of getting to the fair was finding something to wear. I must have gained weight, because all my work slacks, suit jackets, and even my shoes were snug. I had no idea you could gain weight in your feet. I took my clothes on and off trying to find something to wear. This extra weight must have come from all this pressure. I had to lose the weight, but one step at a time. *First step, find something that fits and get to the job fair,* I thought.

There were plenty of companies at the job fair, but triple the amount of well-dressed job seekers. I was surprised there were some really polished, nice-looking people. All these people could not be unemployed. They probably were looking at me, thinking the same thing. *Why doesn't she have a job?* Then there were really smart, young kids that looked like they had just graduated college. All I had was experience. Now I was wishing I had gone back to school and had at least got an associate's degree. It really didn't matter. I had to get something.

I handed my résumé out a few times, I applied for an assistant manager at a pharmacy and even at a telemarketing company. I felt so discouraged. Every time they would give me the same big smile and say, "Thank you. Here's my card, and we will be in contact." Then they would throw my résumé on top of a big pile of résumés.

The job fair was like a day of work. I came in, took my shoes off and flopped on the love seat. Hopefully somebody would call me for an interview. Brandon was on the video game and Mercedes was sitting at the kitchen table doing her homework.

"Did you do your homework, Brandon?"

"Yes."

"Okay, because this school year we are going to start off right. You in the ninth grade now. Start yours, Mercedes. Let me check your homework."

"Yeah, you in the ninth grade," Mercedes repeated. "No one should have to tell you to do your homework."

"Just do your homework, Mercedes, and leave your brother alone."

After their homework was done and dinner was eaten, it was time to head for my rendezvous with Hector. I took a shower and changed into some tight jeans and cute baby t-shits and heels.

"Where are you going, Mom?" Brandon asked.

"I'll be back."

I had agreed to meet up with Hector. I did need a distraction from my crazy life. We met at a Days Inn. The hotel room was basic with a capital *B*—one square bed with white sheets and a tan coverlet, a back-in-the-day television, and a dingy mirror hanging over the dresser, but we weren't spending the night or staying long. I just needed him to relax my mind, make me forget about my worries and troubles, then see me home to get a good night's rest.

"What's up with you, Mami? You get another job yet?"

"No, still waiting. Did they replace me yet?"

"Yeah, three times. They got some old lady in there now, and she ain't going to last, either. Can't nobody do your job. We all was, like, 'They might as well bring Yvette back in.' "

"That's not going to happen."

"So did you miss me?"

"Yeah I did. Now come over here and show me I didn't waste my time driving over here." I took my clothes off and began to lie lazily on the bed. I wasn't going to do anything. My arms were folded, resting behind my head. Hector did what he was told and came over to me and began kissing on my stomach and then I watched as his head disappeared under the covers and just the shape of his head was visible. His tongue felt amazing. I was trying my best to be into it, but something was off. He flicked out his tongue, worked his lips, his fingers, but nothing happened. I wasn't excited. He came up for breath after trying hard for thirty minutes to get me aroused. I just looked at him; as much as I wanted to, I couldn't get into it. I was still thinking about all my issues and my problems. Hector sensed I wasn't myself, and was taking it personally. He kept asking me if I was okay and what was wrong. I told him I was fine. He got off his knees, walked over to his pants, took out a condom in a gold package, and peeled it apart. He strapped it on and came over to the bed and crawled on top of me. He dug deep inside of me. I closed my eyes and tried to connect with him until he was finished and I could go home.

Chapter 20

Crystal

Seventy-three hours had come and gone, and I was about to get married. I was so happy, excited, scared, even though I knew I was doing the right thing. I had never imagined myself eloping. I'd always thought when I finally got married, my dad would walk me down the aisle in my off-white dress and I would be surrounded by my family. But life didn't always turn out the way we wanted it to.

Our courtroom wedding judge read us our vows. Rell and I repeated our vows to one another, promising to cherish each other till death did us part. Rell slipped on the simple silver band that we got from Wal-Mart on the way to the courthouse. It wasn't a fancy ring or a big diamond, but it meant so much to me. By placing that ring on my finger, he shut up all the naysayers. No one could talk about me anymore. Not Syreeta, my sisters, or my dad. Once the judge pronounced us husband and wife, our lips delicately connected and the moment got the best of me.

"Don't cry. Boo, I'm gonna make you so proud to be my wife."

"I know you are, Rell. I already am," I said as I held back my tears.

Rell asked the judge to take a picture of us. He snapped the picture, congratulated us, and left the courthouse.

I glanced at our wedding picture. We were smiling. "Babe, we look cute."

"We do."

"I'm sending this picture to everyone." I gave the picture the caption "Just Married" and texted it to him, and we shared it with all our friends and family. Instantly, congratulations started coming in, and Rell's phone rang.

"Yeah, we did it, Reef. I got a ball and chain now, too."

I smiled and punched his arm as he put Shareef's call on the speakerphone.

"Welcome to the family, sis," said Shareef. "You are a Glover now. And that last name comes with a lot of responsibility. And remember, Rell, you got to do everything she says now. Happy wife equals happy life."

"I know, man, I already told her. I'm going to make her proud to be my wife."

"Did your parents call back yet?" Rell asked.

"No. I don't know if my mother got the message. She is really not that good at texting."

"Now you see I love you, Crystal. Do you feel more secure now? I'm not going anywhere."

"I do," I answered just as my phone began to ring. "Hey, Daddy. Did you get the picture?"

My dad didn't say what a father was supposed to say to a new bride.

"Just married to who? What the hell? Are you crazy? You got married, and I never even seen this Negro before. Who the hell is he? And Dana said he doesn't have a job, so why would you marry him? Are you on drugs, Crystal? You gotta be, 'cause ain't no other explanation why you just keep making all these problems for yourself."

I didn't want to answer my dad in front of Rell, and I wasn't about to be lectured. I was grown and able to make my own decisions, whether he agreed with them or not.

"Daddy, you don't understand what's going on. You don't know," I said.

"I know enough. I know a man don't marry a woman he known for, like, a month unless something wrong with him. I know he better stay the hell away from me."

I kept the phone cradled close to my ear so Rell couldn't hear what my dad was saying about him. When my dad was tired of reprimanding me, he handed the phone over to my mom.

"I guess you know what you are doing. But don't you think we would have wanted to be there?"

I heard my dad still fussing in the background, saying "I wouldn't have wanted to be there and witness that mess. It ain't going to last."

"Mommy, I'm grown, he is grown, and we don't have to check in with anyone. I'm sorry you weren't there, but this is something we decided we wanted to do on our own."

"Well, it doesn't make sense. I'm giving the phone back to your father."

"Crystal, come get your children. We sure wouldn't have watch them if I knew it was because you were going to get married."

"No problem. I'm on my way. I can't do anything right in your eyes, anyway, so does it really make a difference?"

I drove up to my parents' house, and I saw my dad's car in the driveway. I didn't want to talk to him or hear his yelling. He was not going to ruin my happiness.

"Do you want me to come in?" Rell asked.

"I don't think that's such a good idea right now," I said as I exited the car.

I was trying to escape my father's wrath, not walk into it. I wanted to get the kids and get out the door, but I couldn't make it out of the house quickly enough. He pulled me into the kitchen. My mother was sitting at the table like she was praying, like I was the worst child and had committed an atrocious crime.

"Crystal, we raised you so much better," she said. "It's like you don't have any values. You let a stranger you don't even know marry you, and look at that worthless piece of metal he put on your hand. Don't you know you deserve better?" my mother said scolding me.

"Forget the cheap ring. He didn't have the decency to ask me, your father, if he could have your hand."

"Daddy, I live by myself with three kids. It is not like I'm a little girl on a farm. This is not back in the day. I pay my own bills. I didn't need your permission."

"You didn't need my permission? Fine. But how can you marry a man that you just met? I understand if you want to be dumb, but why not think about your children?"

"He is really good with the children."

"Most child molesters and pedophiles are good with kids, Crystal!" my mother screamed. "Do you know anything about him? Where is he from? Who is his family?"

"Yes, I do know all of that."

"How is he going to support you, Crystal?" my father said. "Where are y'all going to live? A real man don't move in with a woman. A man is supposed to move you out, not move in."

"Daddy, you always come down on me. You always have something to say about what I do. You never say anything to Dana, and you especially don't say anything to the princess child, Yvette."

"I wish you'd stop saying that. I love all you girls the same. If it was Dana or Yvette, I'd tell them the same thing."

"That's a lie. The only one you always come down on is me."

"That's not true, Crystal," my mother asserted.

"Mom it's true. I'm done. I'm getting my children and leaving." I called up the steps. "Jewel, get Kori's bag and tell Nasir to come on."

"Mommy, you married to Rell?" Nasir asked when he came downstairs.

"Yes."

"Mom, now that you married Rell, is he going to take my room, or do I have to share one?" Nasir asked as I tied his shoe up.

I looked over at my dad. He was still staring down at me. "No. He is going to get his own bed in my room. Don't worry. It's going to be a little different, but a good different."

"See? This is what I'm talking about. You didn't even sit these kids down and talk to them. They are already confused. I just don't understand you, girl," my dad yelled loudly as he stomped up the steps.

The questions hadn't stopped by the time we reached the car. Jewel asked if I was having another baby.

"No, Jewel. Why would you say something like that?" I asked.

"That's what Pop Pop and Mom Mom said . . . that you were probably going to have another baby real soon."

"That's not true."

It was amazing. My dad was always saying, "You need a husband. I don't want to meet any more boyfriends, just fiancés and husbands." And now that I had a husband, no one was happy for me.

Chapter 21

Crystal

To celebrate our new life together, we invited our families to breakfast. It was sort of our reception, but we weren't expecting any gifts. We just wanted everyone to meet. It was Rell's idea, but I knew once my parents met Rell and his family and saw him interacting with the children, they would have a change of heart. I was sure of it. I even forgave Dana and invited her. I was just ready for my family to meet my new family.

I wanted everything to be perfect, and I'd been up since six preparing everything. I feverishly chopped onions, green peppers, two five-pound bags of potatoes, and I cooked two cartons of eggs. I boiled some of the eggs, scrambled some, and made omelets. I also made turkey bacon, hot beef sausage, pancakes, grits, and waffles. It was a feast, and there was enough for everyone.

I came to the door and saw Big Shareef, Little Shareef, Angel, and Ms. Cheryl. Ms. Cheryl gave me a big hug and handed me a gift bag.

"Thank you, Ms. Cheryl. Come in. You can have a seat. There's orange juice and apple juice on the table." I could see them eyeing the food in the dining room and hovering around it. "We'll start eating in a few. I'm going to give everyone else a few more minutes to arrive. Babe, get some more spoons, while I call everyone to see where they are."

I stepped into the kitchen and dialed my parents. Angel came in the kitchen, asking me if I needed any help with anything.

"No, thank you," I said as I looked in the refrigerator and pulled ketchup and hot sauce out. "Mommy, where y'all at?" I said into the phone.

"Sweetheart, we are not coming."

"You're not?"

"No. I tried to convince your father, but he is still very upset."

"Well, Mom, can you come by yourself?"

"I can't do that. Your father will have a fit. I think Yvette is still coming. I don't know about Dana."

"That means no one is coming. I'll talk to you later."

I hung up and called Yvette; she said she couldn't make it and Dana didn't answer her phone. Oh well why was I shocked—no one ever supported me anyway. I felt like crying, but I had to put on a happy face for my husband and family. I held my tears back and walked back into the dining room and announced to everyone that they could help themselves and placed more plates on the table.

"You don't want to wait on your family?" Rell asked.

"No, they are . . . Uh, my mother said they are stuck in a little traffic. She said for us not to wait on them."

"Oh, okay. Well, everyone, grab hands," Ms. Cheryl said. "Rell, come bless this food."

Rell walked over, grabbed my hand, and then his mother and everyone closed hands, and Jewel and Nasir closed the circle on the other end.

"Thank you, God, for bringing us together and blessing us with this amazing food. Thank you for my mother, my brother, and family. But mostly importantly, thank you for bringing my wife and our children into my life. Please bless our lives and our marriage. Amen."

Everyone said, "Amen," after we let go of each others' hands, and charged the food on the table. As everyone made their plates, I made an effort to remain composed. I didn't want to cry. No one noticed when I left the room. I needed my family to be here. I tried my mom again, hoping that she would change her mind.

"Mom, can you please come? Can you do this for me? Can you support me this one time? I look foolish in front of his family. His brother and mother are here supporting him, and I don't have one person from my family here for me."

"Crystal, congratulations. I love you, but I'm not coming."

Chapter 22

Dana

After a little over a month of knowing a man, she married him and got mad because no one wanted to support her. Crystal was an idiot. I loved my sister, but she was the same moron that just had to establish her baby's paternity. I called Yvette to inform her of her sister's latest idiotic decision. My mom said I needed to apologize, but I didn't apologize to stupid people. The only people I felt sorry for were our poor nieces and nephew. They had to pay for their dumb momma's mistakes.

"So, I know your little sister is a newlywed."

"Yeah, I got her text message, but I didn't know what it was about," Yvette replied.

"She eloped, and Mommy and Daddy are mad. They haven't even met him yet. I asked Mommy if Crystal got dropped on her head as a baby, because I really can't understand her thought process. She makes these irrational decisions."

"Yeah, well, it is her life. That's on her. I have so many things happening, I really can't concentrate on anyone else.

I'm still trying to find another job and figure out a way to get my money back."

"Really? Well, if I come across anything, I will let you know. Have you been on any interviews?" I questioned her.

"Not yet."

"Well, if you need anything, I'm here," I said.

"Thanks, that is good to know. I'll talk to you later."

After I hung up with Yvette, Leah came in my office, smiling like a deranged person and I knew she was up to something.

"What's your sneaky smile about?"

"Well, apparently, you should be smiling, too, because of the love connection you made with Adam," Leah revealed. "He wants to know how he can contact you again."

"That's nice. Give him my number and e-mail."

"Okay. I'm so excited and glad you guys are going to be a couple. Now we can all go on a double date."

"Leah, we haven't even talked yet."

"But you will, and then you'll go out, have a great time, fall in love, get married, and have the next president."

"Okay, that is enough. Out of my office."

Adam and I were going on our first unofficial date. Due to our hectic schedules, we would have our first official date sometime next week. I met Adam in Rittenhouse Square, a little park downtown. People were sitting on park benches, reading books, walking dogs, and throwing Frisbees, taking in the last warm days of the year. Adam was dressed in a collared blue shirt, navy slacks and black shoes. He took his sunglasses off and gave me a soft hug.

"Well, don't you look like nice," I joked admiring his good taste in clothing.

"Yeah, have to wear a suit to the job."

"No, you look really nice."

"I do? Well, you look very beautiful yourself. You are a little taller than I recall. Maybe it's those nine inch heels you're wearing."

"They are five inches."

We traveled down the street to a small café. It was an easy breezy type of place with a Starbucksesque quality. People were typing on laptops, listening to iPods, and reading books.

"I know this is different, but I wanted us to be able to meet up quickly before next week."

"No, I think this is fine; I like this place. I'm glad you were able to squeeze me in."

"No, you're squeezing me in, remember? So how is your knee doing?" he asked.

"It feels fine now. But I've had recurring nightmares of coming down that mountainside. Only Stephen and Leah would think any of that was a good time."

"Yeah, Stephen and Leah are an interesting couple."

I didn't know what I wanted to order. I looked at the menu, then back at my lunch date. *Cute,* I thought. He ordered the brick-oven pizza, and I had a salad. We took a seat by the window and the waitress brought over our food.

"So tell me something I should know about you," I said.

"What do you want to know?" His eyebrow rose, and he smiled.

"Have you ever dated someone like me?"

"Are you asking me if I ever dated someone stunning? No, not as beautiful as you."

"Cute, but you know what I mean."

"No, I've dated just about every race except African American," he said. "Have you dated a white guy before?"

"Does summer camp count?" I joked.

"No, it doesn't."

"Then, no, so we will be each other's experiment."

"I wouldn't say experiment, because then it is like a trial period."

"I think you are correct about that one."

"I am right. Most of the time I am, anyway. No, I'm kidding—is there anything else you would like to know?"

I shook my head.

"Because I'm really not that interesting. I'm an accountant, and my uncle Henry is an accountant. I've been working with him every summer since I was sixteen. I have two sisters, was raised by the greatest woman in the world. I'm the middle child. I have an older sister—she is an actress—and a baby sister about to go to art school."

"I have two sisters, also, and I'm the baby of the family. Middle children are usually the weird ones."

"Yeah, they are, but I'm not. I was the only boy, so my mother gave me attention. Let's see, I'm gradually taking over my uncle's business, because it is time for him to retire and see the world. He has a bunch of his older clients that have been with him for the last twenty, thirty years or so. What else? I've been single a few months, because my last girlfriend was a bit off."

"Now, Leah did mention that. How exactly was she off?" I asked.

"Let's just say she used to have auditory hallucinations."

"What is that?"

"She used to hear voices. I hate even talking about it."

"You started. Now you have to complete the story," I insisted.

"Okay, I met a normal girl. We were going out for a few months. Pretty good relationship, and then one day she just wasn't there anymore. I was out with her, and she went into the restroom. I was waiting for her, and she was taking a long time to come out. I approached the restroom, and I heard her crying and screaming. I knocked on the door a few times, but she didn't answer. So I had security open the door. I went inside, and there she was, having the biggest argument with herself. I thought maybe someone gave her something. So I'm freaking out. I called her parents. They met us at the hospital, and they broke the news to me that she was bipolar and schizophrenic."

"That sounds like a lot to deal with."

He nodded. "It was. At first I didn't want to stop dating her because of it. So when she would have her episodes and she forgot to take her medicines, I would just go along with it."

"That seems crazy. How did you go along with it?"

"She would say, 'Did you hear that?' I would just say, 'Yeah, yeah, I heard it.' But eventually it just got too heavy, and I couldn't do it anymore."

"I bet."

"But enough about that. Let's plan our official date before we both go back to work."

"I'll let you take the lead with the planning. Just tell me where to meet you, and I'll be there. By the way, I prefer steak over seafood."

"Okay, sounds good to me, I'll think of something."

Our lunchtime date was different and cute. I learned a lot about him in a short period of time. A love connection? I was not sure about that, but he was fun and interesting. I'd be glad when I never had to go on anymore first dates and I was in my relationship, happy and satisfied. Then I could call off my man hunt.

CHAPTER 23

Yvette

"What are you doing here?" I asked, shocked, as I opened the door for Crystal and a man. I was not expecting any company. I invited them in and pushed down my hair to make myself look more presentable.

"I came to get Mimi, remember?"

"Oh yeah, I forgot." Mercedes ran up to Crystal and gave her a big hug.

"Auntie Crystal, I already took my shower. All I have to do is put my clothes on."

"Hurry up, Mimi. Sorry she is not ready I really forgot when you talked to me last night—I was half asleep."

"It's okay, and, Vette, this is my husband, Terell."

Her husband greeted me, and he and Crystal had a seat.

"Oh, and guess what? He used to like you back in school," Crystal revealed.

"Really? Me?" I asked, playfully brushing my hair back down some more, not feeling very likeable. "Is that true?"

Terell nodded. "Yes. I told Crystal, everybody in the neighborhood used to like you." My first impression of Terell was that he didn't seem like half the loser Dana had described.

"You sure you want Mercedes to go? She is a piece of work," I said.

Crystal smiled. "Yeah. You know I want my Mimi over. Jewel and Mimi, they will just drive Nasir crazy. I'll probably take them to Chuck E. Cheese's or something, and we are going to pick up Rell's nephew, Shareef, too." She paused for a moment. "Vette, tell me why Dana running her mouth like she normally do. Did she say anything to you about me getting married?"

I shook my head. "Uh, no, not really. You know Dana thinks she knows everything. If I were you, I wouldn't pay her any attention."

"I know, but she keeps hyping stuff up to Mommy and Daddy. We haven't even been able to sit down and talk to them sensibly since we've been married."

"Don't worry. They will come around. Daddy doesn't like it when you run off and get married. Remember I did it."

"You know what? I forgot all about that. How could I have forgotten when I caught the wrath of God?" Crystal said. " 'Daddy can I go to the store?' 'No! You might run off and get married.' Daddy started picking me up from school, and I wasn't allowed to go anywhere. All because of her, babe. I use to cry, because anything I wanted to do she had already did and got in trouble for."

"I wasn't that bad."

"Yes, you were. Remember the time Mommy and Daddy told you not to go out, and you snuck out and went to that teen club dance, and they came to the club? Daddy got onstage, looking for you. You were so embarrassed and was hiding in the bathroom. I was, like, thirteen, and I was just happy to see the inside of the club."

I laughed. "Oh my God, yes. I do remember that. Oh well, what can I say? Those were the days."

We had a few more laughs about growing up, and then Crystal changed the subject. "So you know my baby was in the army. Served in Afghanistan twice and Iraq. Wasn't Doug there, too? Babe, her ex-husband was in the army, too!"

"Where was your husband stationed?" Rell asked me.

"In Pine Bluff, and then from there we moved all around."

"Oh, I know people there," said Rell.

"Oh, and, Vette, he got the kids cleaning up like they in the military. Right, babe?"

He grinned, and I just told her that was good. I don't know why, but I got the impression that Crystal was trying to sell him to me, which was unnecessary, because she had already bought him. It didn't matter if I like him or not.

Brandon came strolling in the living room, letting me know he was going out. He gave Crystal a hug and shook Terell's hand, then walked back toward the door.

"Where are you going?" I asked.

"To the court," Brandon replied.

"Not in that dingy white tee, you are not. Throw on something better," I told him.

"Man, but I'm only running ball," he muttered.

"Stop with the 'mans,' and you look crazy and dirty. Put on something better to walk down the street, or don't go," I ordered.

"I don't see what the big deal is," he said, looking down at his own clothing.

"You heard what I said, Brandon."

"Let him live, Vette. He's fourteen now. You sound like Mommy and Daddy. You don't get dressed up to play basketball, do you, baby?"

Terell shook his head no.

I frowned. "I don't care how old he is. He does and wears what I say."

Mercedes was now ready to go. She had her purple overnight bag and another bag full of her belongings. Terell took the bags and said he would be waiting in the car.

"Okay, Vette, so what do you think about my husband?" Crystal asked the moment he left.

"Does it really matter, Crystal? You are already married to him," I said.

"I know, but I still wanted to know what you think."

"He seems really nice."

"And he is, and he is so good to me and the kids." She paused and then dug around in her bag. "Oh, and before I forget, here," she said as she handed me two hundred dollars.

"What's this for?"

"Daddy told me to give you this. He said to answer your phone, and Mommy wants you to call her."

I didn't want to let on how happy I was about the two hundred dollars, but I was. I walked them to the car and called my dad and left him a thank-you message. I was happy he didn't pick up, because I still didn't want to speak with him. Before long I began to enjoy Mercedes being gone. I was just relaxing on the love seat with the remote. Brandon came in the house and stood right in front of my *Law & Order* episode.

"Move out of the way Brandon."

"Oh my bad. Uhm, Mom, can I go to the movies? Semaj's mom is dropping us off and picking up."

"Call his mom so I can talk to her."

He dialed Semaj's mom. I spoke with her to confirm she was dropping them off at the movies and would pick them up. I gave him twenty dollars for the movie and told him to have a good time. Later on that night Brandon called me, asking if he could spend the night at Semaj's after the movie so he wouldn't have to come home late. I thought he was being responsible by calling, and I didn't really want him to be walking around at night. So I said that if it was okay with Semaj's mom, he could stay.

That was last night. This morning I received a phone call from Semaj's mom, thanking me for letting Semaj stay at my house overnight. I told her I thought they were at her house, and we began to call around for both the boys. I couldn't believe Brandon was dumb enough to try to get one over me. When I caught him, it was going to be a wrap. He was crazy. I thought, *Like, really, you are going to try to stay out all night at fourteen? At least wait until you're sixteen or seventeen. And even then you won't get away with it.*

That afternoon I was furious when Brandon came through the door like everything was fine.

"I give you money to go to the movies and you stay out all night? Where have you been all day?"

"Out at the court."

"You smell funny," I said as I walked up on him and sniffed his clothes.

"I wasn't doing that. That was Damon and Semaj."

"They were smoking weed!" I exclaimed.

"Yeah."

"Then you can't be with them."

"Why not?"

"Because they will have you smoking it, too."

"I'm not going to smoke it. I know how to say no."

"So where did you spend the night?"

"We were at Semaj's, but then we walked to Damon's house. You can call his mom."

"I'm not going to call anyone. You asked to go one place and then took your behind somewhere else. This is why I can't trust you and you can't do anything." I yelled at him, getting all in his face and finally smacking him upside the head. He flinched a little. I couldn't tell if it was a reflex or if his arm was purposely coming in contact with mine. Just the thought of him thinking about trying to hit me back enraged me.

"Act like you want to hit me back. You know everything that I'm going through, and you still want to act like a fool. I give you what I don't have so you can go out and have a good time, and what do you go and do? You go out all night, to who knows where, and you come back smelling like a bag of weed. Don't you know if you get caught at the wrong place at the wrong time that it is over for you? You will be another black boy in jail. Or another black boy dead. Stop putting yourself in situations."

"Are you done?"

"Am I done? Who are you talking to, Brandon?"

He didn't say anything. He just stood there. I reached for my phone and called his father. I knew with all the stress I was under, I would smack him again, and he wouldn't be able to get up off the ground.

"Doug, you might have to come and get your son, because if he acts like he is not going to listen to me, I'm going to send him to one of those juvenile facilities for baby criminals."

"You can't send him away, Vette."

"Yes I can. I'm not going to have a kid that lies and doesn't listen in my house. I'm doing my very best and he is running around following after people. I keep telling him it is so easy to get caught up. I'm tired."

"Vette, don't talk like that. As soon as I get some more money, I'm going to send for both of them. Give him the phone. I'll talk to him and we will work it out."

"I sure hope so, Doug, because I can't take him right now. Come get this phone and talk to your father."

Brandon talked to his dad saying "No sir" and "Yes sir" for a few minutes, then handed the phone back and said that he was sorry, and then went to his room and slammed the door shut. I didn't go after him, because if I did I would be in handcuffs.

Chapter 24

Dana

I was meeting Adam for another date. We had been on our official date, which went well. And since then we'd been on two other cute half dates. Tonight he was taking me to one of his favorite places. He said it was a special place his mother would take him and his sisters. I was excited, not knowing what to expect. I felt so special that he thought so highly of me already. That was why I was confused when we were standing in front of an drive-up ice cream place near a corner bus stop in a residential neighborhood. There were moms walking past with strollers and a baseball team getting a treat—I suppose for winning a game.

"So you say your mom used to bring you here, but you can't sit down or go inside. So where did the memory occur?" I questioned him, still confused.

"Are you kidding me? They have the best mint chocolate chip ice cream."

"Really?" I folded my arms in front of my body and said, "Adam, I'm trying to figure out if this is a cheap date or a cute date."

"Do you think I would be cheap with you, Dana? I'm not like that."

"Well, you are an accountant. There is a rumor that you guys may be a little on the cheap side."

He laughed. "Absolutely not. That's just a stereotype. I really like this place. My mom and sisters love this place, and I really thought you would like it. They have the best ice cream in the city."

"Okay, I'm going to take your word for it."

I still was unimpressed, but after eating the ice cream and talking with Adam, I considered it to be a cute date and not a cheap one. He filled me in on life growing up in Bucks County, right outside of Philly. His parents divorced when he was young. When his dad left, he married another woman and didn't help out his mother very much. He referred to his mom as a supermom because she took him everywhere and exposed him to everything, even though they had very little. It wasn't until she remarried that she was able to go back to school and get a better job. We just walked and talked and didn't realize how far we'd walked until it began to drizzle. Adam showed me he was a real gentleman when he gave me his jacket to cover my hair. He noticed how upset I was becoming about it getting wet. Once we reached my car, we ended the date with him giving me a romantic wet kiss in the rain and asking me on another date, to a Phillies game.

I met Adam outside newly built, gigantic green Citizens Bank Park. It was so big, it looked like its own planet. It was loud, and people were calling out to the players. Our seats were fairly nice. I wasn't very familiar with baseball outside of gym class at school. Adam couldn't believe I had lived in Philly my entire life and had never been to a game. I told him I grew up on football and basketball.

All the die-hard fans were dressed in blood red baseball jerseys with their favorite player's name and number in white on the back. The game was easy to follow, but there wasn't as much action as in other sports I've watch. This player Jimmy Roland hit a home run while the bases were loaded, which meant four people scored at the same time. A guy in front of us caught the ball. Adam was so excited, he began jumping up and down, while other people in the crowd were swinging T-shirts and screaming, "Go, Phils!" I jumped up also, and in the middle of all the excitement Adam playfully grabbed my face and gave me a really nice kiss. The Phillies won, and Adam wanted to meet up and celebrate the win with Leah and Stephen. We decided to meet them at a well-known sports bar called Chickie's and Pete's and enjoyed the rest of the evening.

Chapter 25

Crystal

I was still becoming accustomed to having Rell around full-time. I loved being married. A lot of things had changed in my life and I just felt so much happier. It seemed like since Rell had been here everything had been much easier. Nasir and Jewel had been making their beds and putting away their toys, without me asking. Rell helped me out so much, he even helped them with their homework and took them trick-or-treating. Even Kori was in line; now she went to bed at 9:00 p.m. and didn't wake up until the next morning.

It also felt wonderful getting to work fifteen minutes early instead of late. I got to get breakfast, talk with my coworkers a little, and just relax before logging in my phone. I kind of became cool with my cubicle mate Gloria. She was nice, and I kind of spoke to Delphine now, too!

So life was so good. The only thing that hadn't improved was my relationship with my parents. I still hadn't been able to make amends with them. I did, however, attempt to. I spoke to my dad briefly. He asked me if I was ready to apologize and if Terell had a job yet. I told my dad the truth: he was waiting for a company to call him back. So for being truthful, my dad insulted me some more and told me I wasn't his daughter anymore.

I entered our home. "Hubby, I'm home," I called out to Rell. I checked the mail and noticed that the entire house was clean, and it smelled of powdery fresh dryer sheets. I heard noise coming from the basement.

"Rell, you down there?" I asked as I came down the basement steps.

Rell was washing and folding clothes. He had allotted half of the basement space to the kid's toys and had filled the other half with all his army and workout stuff. I reached the bottom of the steps, and Rell welcomed me home with a tight, warm hug, followed by a few kisses. When we parted, I noticed the huge television in the corner of the basement.

"Babe, what made you get it?"

"I don't know. I was in Walmart and saw the TV. I had one just like it in North Carolina, so I bought it."

"This is nice. The kids are going to love this thing. How big is it?"

"Sixty inches. That's why I said, 'Wait until Nasir sees it'; he can play his games. I want to go get a rug and a few chairs from my mom's to put down here so it can be a real man cave And babe, I need your car. Shareef came and picked up his car."

"Is he going to give you the car back?" I took the keys off the ring.

"No, he is keeping it. I had it forever. I'm just going to have to grab something else."

I followed him back up the stairs in to the kitchen

"Oh, and I made dinner. Some dirty rice."

"You did," I said as I sampled the rice with pepper and ground beef dish. "This is good."

"It's nothing special. It comes in a box you just add

ground beef. My brother makes it the nights Angel works late."

"Thanks, babe. This looks good. I'm so lucky I have a great husband that cooks, cleans and is so good to me."

"No, I have a great wife. That's why I'm going to do everything I can to make her happy."

CHAPTER 26

Dana

So far, I liked how "swirling" my chocolate mix with Adam's vanilla cream made the perfect blend. I liked his company, and we really enjoyed ourselves when we were together.

It was a little different dating someone of another race. We got the occasional glares of disapproval from black and white people, but we both ignored them. Honestly, I forgot that he was another color until someone else reminded me or my arm rested next to his and I saw the contrast.

What I like most about going out with Adam is that we were really dating. Like real dates and, to be honest, I wasn't used to it. Adam even called me in advance to ask me out. Most men thought a date was coming over and watching a movie. He was so down to earth, sweet, sincere, honest, and I was beginning to feel very comfortable with him. And what I like most about him is he never stood me up and was always on time. We would make plans to meet at five, and he would be there at four-fifty. I've been the one who has been running late on every date. He also calls me regularly; not, like, to check in on me or with me, just to say hello throughout the day. He's cooked me dinner, massaged my entire body without trying anything, surprised me with flowers at my job and even wrote me a poem. Okay the poem was a little corny, but he is a great guy, and I love the attention he shows me. I don't think I could date any man that doesn't treat me well again. Having someone like Adam in my life makes me want to say I'm done with black men altogether. That's a joke—it is, but it's not. I honestly do feel like it's a big difference. The difference is I'm being pursued; I don't have to come on strong, or remind him that I am a good catch. Dating him, I feel like I get the freedom to be a lady. I don't feel like I have to put up with his shit, because there isn't anyone else like him. The truth be told, there are plenty of guys like Adam, and that is refreshing to know. No more chasing the prized black men.

Tonight we were meeting at Marie's Kitchen, an authentic Italian restaurant.

"Is it okay if I come on your side of the booth?" Adam asked, as he smiled brightly at me with his seductive green eyes.

"Of course." I greeted him on my side of the booth, and our lips met quickly.

"I like this side better already. I get to sit next to an amazingly beautiful woman."

"I know you do." I snuggled up on him in our comfortable booth and we read off of one menu trying to decide what we wanted to order.

Now that Adam was on my side of the booth, he kept leaning into me, giving me quick kisses at the dinner table.

"Have you decided on what you would like to order yet?" the frustrated waiter asked for the second time.

"Whatever she wants," Adam said, giving me another kiss on my cheek. I playfully pushed him off of me and looked down at the menu.

The waiter gave us an uncaring smile, as if to say, "Stop playing, and hurry up and order."

"Dana, what are you ordering?" Adam asked.

"I don't know. Let's just get an appetizer for now."

Adam looked over at the waiter, and we placed our drink and appetizer order.

Our food arrived, and we both nibbled off of my plate of calamari and seasoned stuffed meatballs.

"I still can't decide what I want. What are you going to get?"

"I'm not going to get anything else. I'll be leaving soon." He looked down at his watch.

"You're not ordering? Are you going back to work already?" I asked, becoming a little sad that our fun was ending so soon.

"Yes, but I had to take a few hours away from work to spend time with you."

"Well, I appreciate you taking time for me."

"You are very welcome, but I am going to get out of here. So I'll see you maybe this weekend?" Adam asked as he put his coat on. He left money on the table for the bill, gave me one last kiss on the lips, and told me to call him when I arrived home.

I asked the waiter for a to-go container, and while I waited, a woman approached my table. She was honey brown, well dressed, cute and slightly younger than me. She was smiling really hard and I didn't know why.

"Hi, I know you don't know me and I know this is a little awkward but see my friends over there?" She pointed to a pretty group of brown women.

I looked over, and they waved. "Well we just wanted to know how is it?"

"How is what?" I asked completely dumbfounded.

"You know, dating a white guy. Your boyfriend is gorgeous, and we all have been considering it, but we are a little scared," she said as she sat down at the table with me. "Well, they are scared. I'm not. I'm tired of our men."

"Um, it's a little different; after a while you don't see color, you just see a great guy."

"That what I was telling my friends, people are people, but they are scared of what people might say and don't want to feel like sellouts."

"At first I was a little scared about what people might think, but I got over it. And black men date whoever they want and it's time for us to stop limiting ourselves when it comes to dating too."

"Exactly, because when black men date white women, it's an upgrade, and when black women date white men, they try to say we are with the slave master. I don't think any of that is true. Thanks so much for giving me hope."

"You're welcome. Good luck."

CHAPTER 27

Crystal

After giving ACR Cable Vision eight hours of my day, it was too cold to be standing outside my job. I shouldn't have to and wouldn't be if Rell was here. He was driving my car, so he could have at least tried to be on time. I called Rell eight times, with no answer. When my phone finally rang, I answered it with an attitude.

"Yeah, Rell. How far away are you?"

"Crystal, it's me, Portia, girl."

"Hello. Oh, my bad. Hey, Portia. I'm sitting here, waiting for Rell to pick me up. What's up with you?"

"Nothing. Just checking in on you. You and Rell still hanging in there, huh?"

"Yeah, we are. We're married. What's going on, Portia?" *What kind of question is that to ask somebody?* I thought.

"Oh, nothing. I just wanted to give you a heads-up about some information that came my way on Rell. Because if I knew he was like that, I wouldn't have introduced y'all or let you talk to him. I'm sorry I even have to come to you with all this."

"All what? Portia, what is it?"

"Well, supposedly, Rell used to hustle down Brickyard in Germantown back in the day, and everybody that was down there still in jail except for Rell. So people are saying he is a snitch and he might get dealt with now that he back."

"Hustling? Rell? Are you sure, Portia? Me and Rell talk about everything. He never mentioned selling drugs."

"Oh, well, maybe it is the wrong one, but they said that Rell went into the navy or something, and wasn't he gone for a lot of years?"

"Rell was in the army."

"Well, I guess that's a coincidence, then. Anyway, I want you to be careful, because you know how people might still be away but can get somebody else to handle people for them, and I don't want you and the children in the house and get caught in anything."

"That's not going to happen, but thanks for the heads-up." I was in a semi-trance, and I hoped that what Portia had just told me was incorrect. *If it is true, oh my God, here come the I-told-you-sos,* I thought. I looked up the street, and I saw Rell driving fast toward me. He pulled over, and I got in the car.

"Sorry I'm late, boo. I just got some bad news. One of the guys I was stationed with killed hisself. Nathan was my man for real, boo. And I was on the phone with his mom. I'm really messed up right now. I can't believe it. I lost track of time. I don't know why he didn't talk to anyone?" he said all in one breath.

I looked over at him to see if there was any hint of a liar or a drug-dealing hustler that someone was looking for. "Why did he kill himself?"

"Because his house is getting foreclosed on and he couldn't find a job, his wife is pregnant. I guess the last straw was when they repossessed his car last night."

"I'm sorry to hear that. That's really crazy; he had a lot going on."

"Yeah, but not enough to take hisself out. I can't believe he left his wife here to hold it down alone. That's some sucker shit, but a lot dudes come home and get dumb. That PTSD is real."

"What's that? Postwar stress stuff?"

"Yeah. Now I got to wait for this other bull that was stationed with us to get everyone's ideas together on how we are going to help her."

Rell was steady talking, but I wasn't really listening. As much as I loved him, if someone was looking for him, we couldn't be together and we were getting a divorce.

I couldn't wait for Rell to come home so I could have a serious conversation with him about everything Portia had told me. He'd dropped me off earlier and then went back out. It was eleven thirty, and he still hadn't come in yet and I was growing impatient and called him.

"'Sup, wifey?"

"Where are you?"

"Out with Reef, having a drink. You all right?"

"Yeah. Rell. I just have a question to ask you when you get home."

"Okay. I'll be there soon. I love you, Crystal."

"Okay."

"No, for real, Crystal. I really love you."

"Rell, I'll see you when you get home."

Rell came in kind of tipsy.

"Are you drunk, Rell?" Why did I bother asking him if he had been drinking when I already knew he had been?

"I had a beer or two, but I'm not drunk. I'm so glad to be home." He started taking off his clothes and kissing all over me. "Boo, when we was out, they were all saying how they didn't want to go home, and I told all of them, 'I can't wait to get home to my wife. I love my wife.' "

"That's what you said? Uh, Rell, we need to talk."

I didn't believe what Portia had said. I didn't know how to bring it up without offending him, but I also couldn't risk being shot at. He was drunk, so he would be truthful. I turned to him, and started hitting him with questions. I needed answers.

"Rell, uh, Portia called me today."

"Okay. Yeah, what about her?" he asked, scratching his head.

"She said that you use to hustle and snitched on all these guys. And that they all are in jail and you are the only one out, and now people are looking to kill you."

"What. That's not even true. I never snitched on anyone, and no one is looking for me. I hate when people talk about things they don't know anything about." Rell's friendly demeanor was gone in an instant. I could tell he was upset and irritated. "My cousin Monk was getting money back in the day. He would pick me up from high school, buy me stuff, and let me drive his car. So everyone automatically assumed I was hustling, too, but I wasn't. So when they all got locked up, I was arrested with them.

"The state tried to hit me with conspiracy charges. However, they had no witnesses or evidence, and my charges were dropped. And when my charges were dropped, my mom took me down to the army office and made me enlist. She said it was either that or get kicked out and she would never speak to me again. So I joined the army. Nobody made me run, no one is looking for me, and I never sold drugs. My cousin Monk is about to come home in, like, two years. So tell Portia not to call you with any more nonsense."

"So where is she getting this story from?"

"I don't know. This is the first I've ever heard of it, but I'm not surprised. I guess it does look suspicious since I am the only one home."

"So why didn't you tell me?"

"I don't know. There's a lot of stuff you don't know about me yet, and there's a lot of stuff I don't know about you, but the one thing I need you to do is never doubt me. You are not married to a liar or a bad dude. Don't ever doubt me, Crystal, for real. It makes me real mad that you would believe something Portia said and would think I would put you or the kids in danger."

"I didn't believe her, Rell. I was just asking. I'm sorry." I felt like a complete idiot for even bringing this mess to Rell. I should have knew better than to listen to Portia.

Chapter 28

Crystal

My dad apologized to Rell and me, and it felt like I hit the lottery. My father actually came to my house with my mom and stepped up to Rell like a man. Rell had to say only one thing to shut up my father. Rell said, "Sir, I plan on taking good care of your daughter. I will not disrespect her. If those were my intentions, then I wouldn't have married her." That was enough right there, but then he said something that had my mom in tears. He said, "Sir, I, like you, only want what's best for Crystal and the children, and I'm a man. I'm going to take care of them."

My mom said, "Crystal, honey, I don't know where you found him, but he is a winner." I knew she was right. It felt so good to have my mom back in my life. I missed our conversations, her wisdom, and her babysitting.

Rell's mom, Ms. Cheryl, said she would watch the kids, but I didn't want to put that on her. She was my new mother-in-law, and I didn't want to start using her up already. No, but Ms. Cheryl was my girl. She sent clothes over for the kids all the time, like they were her grandbabies, but there was nothing like having my own mommy back in my life. I loved my dad, but we didn't always see eye to eye. But my mother always had my back. Well, at least 90 percent of the time.

We were still waiting for the call. You know the call for that job that still hasn't panned out yet. Yeah, that one. Anyway, Rell said the job should be calling him any day. He was convinced; I wasn't. But once he started working, we were going to need a car. Instead of sharing my car, we were going to put our money together and get a cheap little car for the time being.

As we prepared to go to the car lot, guess who decided to give my phone a call? Dumbass Kenneth. He hadn't called for Kori in almost two months. His timing was horrible.

"Yes," I answered with no type of enthusiasm.

"Yeah, I'm about to come past there and get my daughter."

"Huh? You haven't even called to check on her or given me any money for her and you think you can just come and get her."

"I know. I've been busy, but I'll be there in, like, forty- five minutes."

Before I could say, "Oh, no, you won't," the phone went dead. I started getting Kori ready and pulling out her clothes. Rell came up the stairs, asking me if I was ready.

"No, uh, I have to get Kori ready."

"For what? Who was that on the phone?"

"It was Kori's father. He's about to come and get her."

"Okay, well, he needs to call you in advance when he wants her. He doesn't know if you had something planned or not."

"You're right, Rell, but he is still her father, and they do need to bond."

A half hour later I heard Kenneth's horn beep, and I tried to get down the steps as fast as I could, which wasn't fast enough, because Kenneth came strolling in the door. I heard him say, "What's up?" to Jewel and Nasir. And he would have continued up the steps if he hadn't seen Rell on the top step, holding Kori. I was right behind him, clenching my teeth. Kenneth looked like he'd seen a ghost. He took a few steps back down. Rell didn't give Kenneth an opportunity to speak. He came down the steps with Kori in his arms. I yelled for Jewel and Nasir to come upstairs and use the restroom before we left. I wasn't sure what was about to be said.

"Hey. How you doing, fam? I'm Rell. I'm Crystal's husband."

"Yeah, hey. How you doing? W-what's up?" Kenneth stammered.

"I know in the past y'all been having some disagreements and whatnot," Rell stated. "So now I just wanted you to know any problems or issues, you can go through me. I'll handle it. You know, because I don't want her upset, and it will help us out a lot if you can pick a day and time when you going to get Kori so we can plan our day."

Kenneth looked at him and then over at me and bitched up something crazy. "Oh, definitely. I feel you. Like, me and Crystal don't really have no beef no more. It is more her and my sister. I appreciate what you saying."

"Let me get her bag," Rell said as he handed Kori over to him.

Kenneth held his daughter in disbelief. I was about to excuse myself, because I was really trying not to laugh in Kenneth's face.

"What time are you bringing her back?" Rell asked.

"About seven."

"Okay, that's good, because she is on a schedule. We'll see you then."

Kenneth couldn't even wait three minutes before he started lighting up my phone with explicit text messages. He typed in, *Fuck u bitch. Who the fuck is that nigga? Who the fuck do you think you are? You a dumb-ass smut. You got married, you whore.* And then the text that made laugh the hardest was, *Ain't no otha man gonna be round my daughta.*

Was I reading right? This was all too much for me not to laugh at. Didn't he say just a few months ago that she wasn't his? Now that I got a husband in the house, it was a problem.

His texts and calls kept zapping in and I just kept ignoring them. Rell was driving, so he wasn't paying attention to the barrage of lewd texts. Then miss cosigner extraordinaire Syreeta began calling. I didn't answer, so she left me a message. "Your ho ass then went and married someone? Your stank ass ain't even wait a whole six months before you start sitting on someone else dick! You're wrong as hell, Crystal! That's some fucked-up shit you on, for real. But I'm going to let you know you ain't going to play my brother. I'm not having it. We are going to go back down to court and taking that baby from you."

I didn't have a response for their madness. I erased the messages. I was totally amused that Kenneth and Syreeta were upset that I was married and they thought they had a chance at taking my daughter from me. The first thing I thought of was when she was yelling at me in court that no one would ever want me. She now knew that she was wrong about that. All I could think was that Kenneth and his sister were so crazy, and I wished I had never met him or known them. It scared me that I would, in some shape or form, be in contact with him for another eighteen years.

Rell interrupted my thoughts. "Crystal, babe, tell that dude to stop calling you."

"It's not him. It's his sister."

"Yo, you might have to sit down with both of them, because they're not going to keep calling you all crazy over nothing. Something has to be done."

"You're right," I agreed and shut my phone off.

The car lot had a big sign on the gate that read BUY HERE. PAY HERE. Neon green stickers covered the front windshields of rows of shiny waiting-to-be-driven-home cars. The salesman came out. He was a young Middle Eastern man. He asked us what kind of car we were looking for today.

"We just need a small, reliable car that's good on gas."

"Okay. I got the perfect car for you." He walked us over to a small Ford Focus.

"Not that small," I said as a navy Chevy Tahoe caught my eye. "Oh, babe, look at this. I can't believe something this nice is only nine thousand dollars."

"Yeah, this is nice. It's, like, five years old. It looks new, though," Rell said. We both looked inside the truck and began admiring its features. There was a navigational system, a sunroof, CD player, and heated seats.

We took the truck around the block. It was much more car than we were looking for, but the car payment wasn't going to be that much. The tan leather interior was spotless and everything else was clean. It was like brand-new. I looked down at the miles.

"It has a hundred and forty thousand miles. That's a lot right Rell?"

"Yeah, but the miles don't matter as long as the last owner took good care of it. It runs nice."

"It does. Do you like it?"

Rell asked the man if we could have a few minutes to decide whether or not we were going to buy the car. He said sure and we walked away from the salesman.

"What do you think? I think it is good. We should get it," I said.

"He wants nine for it. We can talk him down, put two down, and then just pay off the rest. We would just make the car payments in the meantime."

"Mom, I like this car. Rell, are we getting this one?" Jewel inquired.

"I don't know yet. It is up to Mommy. She makes the decision. It's nice, babe. You will look real good driving it," Rell said.

"Mom can we get it please?" Nasir begged.

"Rell, can you drive me to school in it?" Jewel asked. They both were jumping up and down screaming, "Please, Mommy."

"So what do you think, Mommy?" Rell asked.

"Okay. Let's get it."

CHAPTER 29

Dana

"Look at the two of you. You guys look so cute, like you have been dating forever," Reshma gushed.

"We do look cute, don't we?" I looked down at the picture in my cell phone of "us." Yes I was now an "us" and no longer an "I."

Already Adam and I had a little collage of pictures from our dates. I think I had one picture of me and Todd, and he wasn't even looking at the camera. "I'm so happy you are seriously dating. All of this time I thought you were not going to find anyone."

"And she has me to thank," Leah said as she pretended to turn up her collar.

"Yes, you did a great job, matchmaker," I admitted.

"Reshma, are you coming out with us tonight?"

"I can't. Every time I think about going anywhere, I get nausea."

"Too bad, but we can't wait until you have that baby. We're going to spoil it like it is our own."

"Yes, I'm ready," said Reshma.

"Well, good-bye. And I'll see you later, Leah," I said as I left the office.

Adam and I were meeting up with Leah and Stephen. We were going to the newest club, Mixer. The club was in Northern Liberties, a very trendy area with new clubs, boutiques, and cafés. There were write-ups all over about it. Mixer was supposed to be the it place. They even required a reservation for entry, to keep the list and the clientele somewhat exclusive.

The crowd was a diverse mix of professionals in their late twenties to early thirties. I was impressed with the club's old European, Gothic decor. It had enchanting chandeliers, high ceilings, and cathedral-type windows. The hostess chaperoned us to our table and told us our mixologist would be with us shortly. We sat in high-back chairs upholstered with maroon velour. The music was a mixture of dance music played loudly over hip-hop fused beats.

"This place is great, every lush's dream. We get our own mixologist," I said.

"And they have every drink you can name on the menu," Leah said, reviewing the extensive drink menu.

"Why does everyone have to have a fancy title? She is not a mixologist. She is a bartender," Stephen asserted.

"I like that they call them mixologists," Leah added over the loud music.

Stephen shrugged. "Why did we even come here? You know I hate these kind of self-important places. Look around at all these people. They think they are important, and they are not."

"I like it. It's nice, and I think it is cool that we can ring a bell instead of waving to the bartender all night. Lighten up, Stephen. We're here. Enjoy it," Adam replied.

"I'll try to," Stephen said.

Our mixologist kept our lemon drop martinis and shots of Cuervo topped off all evening. Friends, drinks, great conversation . . . and I was with a guy I really liked. We played a few shot games and were really grooving and enjoying ourselves. We took turns leaving our table and going to the dance floor. Unbeknownst to Adam, tonight was our night. After several months of dating, check, good guy, check, I was ready. Adam had waited long enough. Tonight I was going to give him everything.

A few shots and my hands became extra friendly all over Adam's lap. I slid my hand under the table. I was making him firm, stroking him back and forth. I was toying and playing with him, while he tried to keep a straight face while Leah was steady discussing who knows what.

Stephen made it known that the shots were getting to him and he needed to hit the restroom. Adam stood up and said he had to go to. Before he left the table, my tongue reached out and shook hands with his.

"Don't be too long," I whispered.

He bit his lip at me and stared at me and said, "I won't."

"Cut all the PDA out," Stephen muttered.

"Stephen, don't be mad," I told him. "Why are you in such a grumpy mood tonight?"

Stephen just shrugged again, and the guys walked off toward the restroom.

Leah sighed. "Stephen has really been so irritating lately. But did I tell you I love you two together?"

"Yes, many, many, many times," I said, mimicking her.

Stephen and Adam reappeared fifteen minutes later, with a girl clinging to Adam's side. The woman was wearing a hugging, strapless rust-colored dress. I didn't want to be alarmed, but I was interested in learning who the mysterious woman was. Stephen must have read my disturbed look.

He came over, tapped me, and said, "Dana, that's his crazy ex. It's really nothing. I'm trying to rescue him."

Stephen walked back over to where they were standing, then took the woman's crab claws off of him. Adam then freely returned to the table, looking very flustered. The ex had decided she wasn't through, and stumbled right behind him over to our table. Her presence didn't please Adam or Stephen. Up close I saw her mascara had run, and false eyelashes were hanging halfway off her lids. She also needed to retouch her red lipstick.

"Heather, I thought we told you we would see you another time," Stephen said.

Her speech was slurred and almost inaudible. "I know. I'm about to leave, Stephen. I just wanted to see which one of these ladies is dating my Adam."

No one said anything. I was scared to move. She looked like the kind that might carry a little pistol in her clutch.

Adam becoming increasingly annoyed and said, "Do you want me to call you a cab, Heather?"

"No, I can drive myself home. Well, since you won't introduce me to these beautiful ladies, I will introduce myself." Turning her attention to Leah and me, she said, "Hi. I'm Heather. I used to date Adam, but he broke up with me because, he says, I'm crazy." She put her finger up to her temple and made a circular motion. "But I'm not crazy, and I still love this guy." She was swaying from side to side, slurring her words. "Whichever one of you is dating him is so lucky. He is the best."

"Okay, that's enough. Time to go. Do you need me to call you a ride, Heather?" Stephen pulled out his phone.

I was waiting for Adam to say something, to help her out. He just looked past her and downed the last of his drink and acted as if she wasn't there.

"What's wrong? Did I say something? I just want to see what my replacement looks like," Heather said. She walked over to Leah and said, "So how is he in the bed? Still good, right?"

"I wouldn't know that. I'm not his girlfriend," Leah said, blowing my cover, thinking it was funny.

Heather turned from Leah to me and said, "Wow! Adam, you did good! She's so gorgeous. She looks just like Beyoncé.

No. You know who she looks like? That model Tyra Banks. Yeah, you look just like her."

"Beyoncé and Tyra Banks. That's so funny." Leah laughed.

I couldn't help but laugh, too, since Beyoncé and Tyra Banks were probably the only two good-looking black women she could reference.

"Heather, it was really nice seeing you, but we're going to see you later," Stephen said sternly.

"Okay. Bye. Have a good evening." Heather walked away from our table.

"That was interesting, Adam," Leah joked.

"It was very heavy," I added. "Now I'm ready for another drink. Call that mixologist over and let's have another round on me."

At the end of the evening Adam's hands were all over me, and I hoped we would be able to make it home. I thought about taking him in the bathroom and letting him bend me over the sink, but I would just have to wait until we made it to my apartment. Coming out of the club, we saw Heather sprawled across the hood of a car. People were walking past like it was an everyday occurrence to see a drunk lady asleep outside. My first reaction was to tell Adam to help her, but I didn't think he was going to take her home, which is what happened.

Once I was home alone, I regretted being so kind to his drunk, crazy ex-girlfriend and felt so stupid. I thought I was helping a crazy girl out, but now I'm thinking it might have been her insane little plan all along to get him to go home with her. I didn't know what about Adam being responsible and not letting his ex get robbed or raped made me angry. Of course, he did the right thing by making sure she was safe, but what about me? I was upset and alone, instead of having crazy, wild, unapologetically loud sex all night long. I was sad, sleepy and alone.

I sleepily answered the phone to hear Adam's voice on the other end.

"Dana, are you up? I'm sorry I left you. It's just that I didn't want to see anything happen to her. I shouldn't have allowed her to ruin our evening. I know I was supposed to be coming over there tonight."

"It's okay. You can still come here if you like."

"Okay. I'm on my way to you. Please don't be mad at me."

I sprang out of bed and made myself sexy again. I couldn't wait for Adam to arrive. We were going to turn the heat back on exactly where we left off in the club. Ten minutes later Adam called back to say he still could not locate his keys. *Okay what gives and what dark force didn't want me to have sex and was keeping us apart,* I thought.

"Adam, where did you put them?"

"I don't know. I came right in and I swung them somewhere." I wanted to scream. I was ready, he was ready now, and a set of keys were in our way. *Keys, appear so Adam can come over here now,* I thought.

"This doesn't make any sense. I need you Adam."

"I want you so bad too, Dana. I'm ready to catch a cab, but I wouldn't be able to lock the door. Damn it shit fuck. Where are those damn keys?" I could hear him moving things around in his apartment.

"Adam, how about I'll just come there."

"No, it's too late. I don't want you walking to your car this time of night."

"Then I'll catch a cab over there. I won't come out of the apartment until the driver says he is outside."

Twenty minutes after picking me up, the cabdriver turned onto Adam's block. He was waiting outside his apartment. He opened my door and paid the driver. I felt everything begin to tingle; I could not wait for him to make passionate love to me.

"I'm really sorry," Adam said.

"Just make it up to me now."

Once inside we tore each other's clothes off. My nipples bunched in his mouth and he feverishly kissed all over them.

I pulled his pants down and licked on his stomach. He took a deep breath. My tongue grazed in a zigzag motion up and down and near his pelvis. I teased him by going near his lower region, but stopping just before I reached it. Then when I didn't want to make him wait anymore, I kissed the tip of him and nibbled at the top. He was ready for entry in my warm awaiting mouth. After a few long deep pulls of my cheeks, he snatched his self out of my mouth and snapped a condom over his peach-colored, plump, thick member. His body filled mine to capacity. With no warning he plowed through my juicy pussy's interiors. His motions were invigorating, pleasurable, and it almost felt like he wasn't even wearing a condom. It felt as if his body was made specifically for me. He focused on my needs. Him wanting to please me made me eager to give him more. He made love to me up against the wall, on the floor, in the shower. We were in sync. He pushed up and I pressed down. Each time we would retreat and then meet up again, fast and hard. There was no doubt that we had an incredibly organic sexual connection. The more satisfied he became the harder he became, until he couldn't take it anymore. He climaxed in a violent, loud groan. He kissed me and then we started all over again.

CHAPTER 30

Yvette

I leaped out of the kitchen and ran to the window because I heard the rattle of a diesel engine and the beeping of some type of service truck, which was backing up in front of my door. I peeked out the window and saw the electric company's utility van. I was scared. I hoped they weren't coming to turn off my service. I was behind on my bill and hadn't paid it in two months. I didn't even know how much I owed, since I'd been too scared to open any bills. Just seeing a crazy past due bill that I had no way of paying gave me a headache. I didn't know how long it took for them to cut you off, but I imagined I didn't have very long. My landlord, Mr. Jimmy, had been understanding, but he wanted his rent. He'd come by here a couple of times, and I just didn't come to the door. As soon as I started working again, I was going to pay him everything I owe.

The electric company worker got out of his truck, and he looked down at his silver clipboard. *Please don't come here,* I thought. He looked up at my address and then began walking across the street. *Whew.* I couldn't live like this forever; it didn't feel good to be so nervous and worried that at any moment your utilities will be shut off. I closed the blind and walked back to the kitchen and opened my laptop. I had to find a job and soon, before it was my house they stopped at. Something had to give, because my checking and saving accounts had almost nothing in them, and my unemployment had been denied.

Everyone was still calling me, telling me not to sulk, but what else was there to do? I was embarrassed. I was scared, and I didn't want to ask anyone for anything. How would it look if I said, "Daddy, I need some money," or if I asked my sister with three kids of her own for something? I was not going to do that. I was just going to get a job and recover from all of this. At least I hoped I would bounce back. Because right now I was in anguish, wondering, *Why me?* I questioned what the hell I did to deserve all of this. And I couldn't think of anything.

All I could think of was that it was all Phil's fault. Dumbass Phillip was the reason I was unemployed, broke, and had to transfer Mercedes out of her school. I wanted Mercedes to stay at Holy Redeemer, but there was no way I could pay her tuition. Yes, maybe I should have planned better, and then I wouldn't have had this avalanche fall on me, but it was still his fault.

I had daily thoughts of killing that son of a bitch, Phillip McKnight. If there was any way I could murder him and get away with it, I would do it. However, every time I thought about planning his death, I realized how much I didn't want to wear an orange jumpsuit and cornrows to the back for the rest of my life. But God knows he was going to pay for this shit he was putting me and my kids through.

I closed my laptop and went to take a shower. I brought the phone in the bathroom with me just in case an employer called. The phone began ringing. I got out of the shower, and I saw an unusual number on the phone's screen. I prayed it was a job. In my most professional, pleasant voice I answered.

A woman's voice at the other end said, "Hello. May I have Yvette?" It was a little informal for an employer, but I was still hopeful.

"Yes, this is she."

"How you doin'? This is Mr. Jimmy's daughter."

"Hi," I said, confused. What did Mr. Jimmy's daughter want with me?

"I'm calling you because my dad said you were having issues with paying your rent."

"Yes, I spoke to your father about that."

"Okay. You can speak to me, because we are going to need some kind of payment immediately."

"I know. Uh, I'm not like that. I really don't have any money. I'm not working right now, but I told your dad that as soon as I start, I would give him my first check."

"That's sounds good and all, but everyone has a story, and I just have to let you know that if you don't get caught up, we will start the eviction process."

"Eviction process? No, that won't be necessary. I should have all of my rent soon."

"I sure hope so. We don't like to kick people out, but you can't live anywhere for free," she said and then hung up.

Damn. I had to get some money. There was no way me and the kids could be on the street. *What if me and the children have to move? Where would we go? I can't move back in with my parents or go into a shelter. I need something to happen. I have no money. I feel like a complete bum. What if my life remains like this forever?*

I stepped back in the shower, and the phone rang again. I got out of the shower again. I didn't recognize the number; hopefully, this was really a job. Once again I picked up the phone with wet, slippery hands and answered enthusiastically.

A professional male voice said, "Hello. May I speak to the

parent of Brandon Turner?" I was disappointed it was not an employer again, but Brandon's school.

"This is she. What's wrong?" I asked, knowing schools didn't just randomly contact parents without there being some kind of issue.

"Hi, is this Brandon's mom?"

"Yes, it is."

"I'm Mr. Walker. I'm the vice principal at the Leadership Charter School, and I'm calling to inform you that Brandon was just suspended for a fight and cutting class."

"He was fighting? Is he all right?"

"Yes, he is, but unfortunately, he will be suspended for the role he played in the fight. If you can get here by ten o'clock, today could count as the first day of his suspension." I took the phone away from my ear and looked at the time on it. I had exactly thirty minutes to get to Brandon's school.

"Is he with you in the office?"

"Yes, he is."

"May I speak with him, please?"

"Yes, one moment." I heard the phone being exchanged.

"Mom, I didn't do anything," Brandon whined.

"If you didn't do anything, then why are you suspended, and why were you fighting?"

"Mom, they kept saying stuff to me. And he said he wanted to fight me. He put his hands up, so I threw up mine."

"You threw your hands up? What is wrong with you, boy? You know what? It doesn't even matter. Tell your principal I'm on my way. Boy, when I get there . . ." That was all I could get out. I hurried to get dressed and headed for his school.

I was beyond upset as I entered the Leadership Charter School building. A woman sitting behind a desk stationed in front of the auditorium instructed me to sign her log, then handed me a yellow visitor's pass and pointed me in the direction of the office. I stormed into the office and saw Brandon sitting there like a dunce. His head was hung down.

He let out a weak "Hi, Mom."

"Boy, come on. Let's go."

"You have to sign me out over there."

Just as I walked over to the counter, a nicely built and well-dressed man came out from behind the office desk.

"Hi, I'm Mr. Walker, the vice principal. I just spoke to you on the telephone."

"Yes. Hello."

He looked over at the big, round clock hanging on the wall and said, "I'm glad you were able to get here before ten. So today does mark the first day of his suspension, and you can reinstate Brandon on Wednesday. We're giving him a two-day, instead of three. The third day was unnecessary, and I already had a talk with him about what is expected of him. Right, Brandon?"

"Yes," Brandon said with his head down.

On the ride home Brandon knew he was in trouble, but he wasn't sure how much. He was nervous, though, because every time I moved, he flinched. I just really didn't have the strength to deliver any blows to him. We walked in our apartment, and I just exhaled loudly.

"All I can say to you, Brandon, is that I have enough problems. I don't need any more."

"But, Mom, can I tell you what happened?"

"I don't care what happened. You are suspended, and that's all I need to know."

"But, Mom!"

"There is no 'But, Mom.' Just do the right thing. Get your work done, and stay out of trouble. It is the beginning of the school year. You know Phil took my money. You know things have been tough. So don't add to my pressure."

"This is not right. You not even listening to me."

I continued to ignore him. Then I decided to let him have his say. "Okay, tell me what happened."

"Well, I did cut class, and that was wrong. But only because Semaj said we had a substitute and we weren't doing anything. So me and Semaj went and was just hanging out in the lunchroom. Then this guy in the eleventh grade just came over to us for no reason and told us to move. We said no, and we all started fighting."

"Okay, first, would this all have happened if you were in class?"

"No."

"Okay, second, was Semaj suspended?"

"No."

"Exactly. He is at school, in class, and where are you? You're here. You should be in school, learning, preparing to be a man, so you can one day have a job and a career to take care of yourself. What do you even want to do with your life?"

"I don't know. I want to run stuff or something."

"Oh, run stuff," I repeated after him and sighed. This was too much. "Brandon, you want to be a company owner, not just run stuff. In order to own a company, you can't be following behind someone. Point-blank, if you were in class, you wouldn't have had a fight. That's it. I'm not saying anything else. I know one thing. I'm not coming up to that school any more this year. Do you understand?"

"Yes."

"I'm not saying, 'Be a punk,' but people are going to say things every day. You cannot throw your hands up each time. If that was the case, you would never stop fighting. If they don't physically touch you, walk away. It is called self-discipline, and you need to get some, because all the tough people that can't control themselves end up in the jail."

Brandon seemed a little regretful of his actions, but I wasn't sure if I had got through to him. I was going to have Doug and my dad talk to him some more, too.

* * *

We needed groceries, and I had only sixty dollars left in my savings account until Thursday, when Doug deposited money into my account for child support. I transferred the money out of my savings and into my checking account. How was I going to feed three people, for four days, three square meals I didn't know, but I had to make it work.

I made my way to ShopRite, grabbed a circular, and began to see what on my list I could afford. I opened the circular and strategically shopped, buying everything that was on sale. I was happy that I was able to fill my cart with sale items. I thought I should be right at sixty dollars. I walked to a line where there wasn't a wait. I began placing my eggs, milk, apple juice, and chicken wings on the belt. While the cashier swiped each item, I kept up with the calculations on her register's screen. I got up to $58.97, and I told her she could stop. I had to put one of the bottles of salad dressing and the dinner rolls back, but that was okay. At least I hadn't gone over my budget. I swiped my debit card to pay for my groceries, and instead of APPROVED appearing on the screen, it read DECLINED. I knew that was a mistake, so I asked the cashier to try it again. I knew the money was there, because I had just transferred the money, but I had to get out of the line and call the bank. The bank's 800 line had a series of prompts and numbers I had to press before I could speak with a live person. Once one was on the line, I read off my account number and verified all my information.

"How may I help you today, ma'am?"

"My card was just declined, and I know I have money in the account."

"Yes, I show you had a deposit entered today, but it won't be available until tomorrow," the woman said.

"I don't understand. It was a cash deposit."

"Yes, it was cash. However, it was deposited after three,

which makes it fall under a new business day, and the funds will not be ready until tomorrow."

"Okay, I don't understand. You're saying I can't put cash in and take the same cash back out on the same day?"

"Yes, that is correct. This is our policy."

I was beyond fuming mad. I wished I knew where the call center was, because I would go and choke the lady for telling me I had to wait for cash to clear.

"Well, I've never heard of such a thing, and I'm in the market, trying to buy my groceries, and I need the funds to be available now, and when I checked online, the money was there, so someone has to do something."

"Well, as a courtesy, I can make the funds available, but please go to our Web site and read our new policy, put in place this year."

I said, "Yeah," but I thought, *Whatever. Just make this shit go through so I can walk out of this damn market with groceries.* The customer representative made my funds available, and I felt validated. I walked back over to the register and paid for my groceries.

After grocery shopping I picked Mercedes up from school. I sat in front of her school, trying to determine where she was in the crowd of running children who were all happy that it was dismissal time. She found me first, got in the car, and put her seat belt across her chest.

"Hey, Mom."

"Hey, Mimi. Did you have a good day?"

"Yes, I had a good day. I just want something to eat. Can we stop and get something to eat?"

"Why are you hungry, little girl?"

"The kids stole my lunch. I forgot to give it to the teacher. Mom, these kids at this school are bad. They don't listen to the teacher, and if you don't give your lunch to the teacher, they take it out of your book bag."

"What? Did you tell someone?"

"Yeah, the teacher and the lady in the lunchroom gave me a ticket to get a lunch, but they had something nasty. I didn't want it."

"I'm sorry that happened to you, but I just went to the market. There are snacks in the bags. We will make you one when we get in the house."

"Okay, and, Mom, can I go to the hairdresser and get my hair done?"

"I'll make you a snack, and I'll straighten your hair out after dinner."

As promised, I washed and blew out Mercedes's hair. Neither of us had been to the hair salon or nail salon in months.

"Look in the mirror, Mimi. See if you like it."

"Oh, I look like I went to the real hairdresser. Oh, Mommy, can you paint my fingers, too?"

I could tell Mercedes missed being pampered, and so did I. What I wouldn't do to have someone wash and style my hair. And a manicure, pedicure—that would be amazing. I would love to place my feet in hot soapy water and get my cuticles cut and the dead skin sloughed off my tired feet. I couldn't wait to start working again, because I did miss the simple little things.

"Sure. Go get the polish off my dresser."

She ran to my bedroom to get the polish and returned with an aqua color.

"This is pretty, Mimi," I said as I complimented Mercedes on her choice and dipped the brush and covered her nails with the sparkly green color. I had got to her third nail when a light knock at the door interrupted my stroke. I walked to the door, where I found a young, nicely dressed couple.

"Yes?"

"Hello. Does Sammie live here?" the young guy asked.

"No, sorry. No Sammie lives here."

I began to close the door and the young guy asked, "Are you sure? He has curly, short braids. And they said he lives here and he hangs out with a brown-skinned, husky boy."

"You mean Semaj?"

They looked at each other.

"Yes, that's his name," the guy said.

"He doesn't live here, but that's my son's friend. What happened? Is there something wrong?"

"Well, miss, he broke into my car and stole my husband's work computer," the young woman said. "He really needs the computer back. All his work files are in there."

"What?"

She went on to say that other neighborhood kids had placed Semaj at the scene. They'd seen him running away from the car with the computer bag. I called out for Brandon. He didn't come fast enough, so I called him again.

"Brandon, get out here!"

He came to the door. The couple looked him over, shaking their heads, letting me know he wasn't the one. I told them right where they could find Semaj and his mother and angrily closed my door.

"That's it. No more Semaj, Brandon. He is stealing computers out of people's cars. Plus, he is having you cut class."

"You can't tell me who my friends can be," he yelled back.

Mercedes stood up and said,. "Mommy can tell you whatever she wants, Brandon, and you better listen."

"Mercedes, be quiet. I don't need any backup. Brandon, until you are eighteen years old, you can listen to me, or I can send your ass to Florida with your father. You will not turn into a criminal under my watch."

"Man, I'm not going anywhere. Those people lying, and I didn't even do anything. You're yelling at me for nothing."

"Go to your room, Brandon, because if you don't, you will be so sorry. I don't want to see your face." I was so angry that my son was so dumb and just didn't get it. His life could change with one bad decision. That was it. He had to go. I called Doug and told him to come and get his son.

"I'm not dealing with him anymore Doug. All of a sudden

he thinks he is so tough and hanging with the wrong kids, getting in trouble. I'd rather you come and get him."

"Vette, listen, if I could, I would send for him now, but I can't."

"Doug, he said I couldn't tell him who to be with. Anytime he can tell me, his mother, what I can't tell him . . . that means he's grown, and since he is starting to think he is grown, he can go. Come get him or send him a bus ticket."

"If you tell him who not to be with, he is going to want to be with those kids more. He's being rebellious. Don't give up on him. If you want to send him, send him, but I think you should wait until the end of the school year. I will take them for Christmas break."

"I really don't know if I can wait until then."

CHAPTER 31

Dana

Adam's brown love seat was so comfortable, and I was enjoying the peace of not doing anything. I was flipping between the pages of his *Maxim* and *Men's Health* magazines, and he was on his laptop. We'd just come in from working out at the gym. We had both run seven miles. Well, he did seven miles. I walked maybe half of a mile, but I still felt very energized. We had had a light breakfast, had showered, and were going to watch the football game between naps and lovemaking. I was still learning Adam's body and he mine, but I enjoyed every moment of us being together. That's why I looked down at the screen of ringing phone and shook my head as my phone chimed loudly, "It's them again, isn't it?"

"Yes, it's them."

Them was Stephen and Leah. I loved Leah, I was glad she had introduced us, and she was still my girl at work, but I'd come to the realization that she was extremely clingy. She wanted to be a part of everything. I really thought *they* or *she* thought they owned us. The couple dates were cute at first. Over the last month we had done everything from bar crawls to bowling, but enough was enough. Now we were tired and couldn't take any more.

"Don't answer."

"Okay, I won't." I knew Leah couldn't see me, but I still felt guilty for not answering. A few moments later Adam's phone started buzzing on his dresser.

"Leah, leave us alone." Adam laughed. Then my phone rang again.

"Oh, it's not Leah. It's Tiffany." I answered. "Hey, Tiff."

"Where are you?" Tiffany asked

"At Adam's. Are you okay?"

"Not really. I've been crying since Wednesday. I didn't want to tell anyone, but Solomon stopped calling me. He called me every day, all day, and now nothing. I haven't received one text message from him in four days. Dana, I don't know what I did wrong. It makes absolutely no sense. Like, why wouldn't he call me? I knew it was impossible for both of us to be happy at the same time."

"I don't know. Did you call him?"

"Yes, I left him a message, and I've been waiting for him to call me back, and he hasn't, and something must be wrong. I'm telling you, somebody better be dead," she groaned.

"No one is dead. He just got tied up. Tiffany, don't always wait for a man to take the lead. I think you should call him. That's the only way you're going to find out what exactly is going on."

"I'm not calling him. I tell you one thing. I really believed that this one was going to work. Now I'm single again."

"And it still might. You'll never know unless you call him. It's only been four days."

"I'm so scared. I'm really scared. I think when I call him, he is going to tell me what I already know . . . that it is over."

"It's not over. Call him. You're being silly and crazy."

"Okay, I'll call him, but ask Adam if he has any friends, since I'm single again."

"No, I'm not asking him that. Call Solomon, and then call me back."

"What's wrong?" Adam asked as he came up to me from behind, kissing me on my neck.

"Tiffany's boyfriend hasn't called her in a few days."

"Yikes. What did she do?"

"She didn't do anything."

"Then he probably has a valid excuse or explanation for her."

"I sure hope he does." I saw Tiffany's number across my cell phone. That was fast.

"So what happened?"

"Well, his grandma died and the funeral is on Friday."

"I told you. You should go up there and support him."

"I am. He said he really needs me. Oh, tell Adam I said, 'Never mind.' "

"I will." I hung up the phone and was so thankful that Solomon was not a jerk and that someone really had died. I wasn't happy his grandma had passed, but, wow, it was possible for us both to be happy at the same time.

Chapter 32

Yvette

Not even a week passed before Brandon's vice principal was calling again. Brandon was now fighting Semaj. I think he wanted to see how much it would take to drive me crazy. If that was his intent, it was working. I couldn't say anything but that I was on my way. *This makes no sense,* I thought. What if I was a normal person with a job? Then I would not be able to run back and forth to his school every day.

We had just had a long talk about self-discipline, doing the right thing. His father had talked to him, my mother had talked to him, and so had his grandfather. And he went right back to school and forgot everything we discussed. What was the damn problem? I had tried talking to him like they said you were supposed to, but today I was going to use excessive force and kick his ass. I had too many things going on to have to run up to his school every day.

I threw on my clothes, washed my face and brushed my teeth, and left the house. I tried to calm my nerves and turned on the radio, and at the next light I heard something pop and then the car started smoking. I coasted to the side of the road. I put my head in my lap and took a deep breath. *Why? What now?* I thought. I closed my eyes. This couldn't be happening. I got out of the car and popped the hood open. I had no idea what I was looking at or looking for. Cars were riding by slowly, looking at the steam and smoke coming from my car, but no one stopped. I couldn't stay there forever. I called my dad and started crying.

"Daddy, where are you? My car broke down."

"Do you have AAA?"

"No, I don't. It's smoking bad, and it won't start up. I'm a few blocks away from Brandon's school. Off of Chelten Avenue."

"I'll be right there."

My dad came right away. He had already called a tow truck company, and they were on their way. While we waited for them, my dad put my hazard lights on and we went to his car to get out of the cold.

"You need some tires on that car, Vette."

"I don't have any money for tires, Dad. I don't have money for anything."

"Well, you can't ride around with those. They are going to bust at any moment. Your front tires are fine, but those rear tires, you need to change them."

"Dad, I don't have money to pay my rent. Phil took my money. The car broke down. It's just so much. Brandon keeps getting suspended."

"Don't worry about all of this. I'll take care of the car. We will go get Brandon. I can loan you money. I have it. You're my child. You're going to get it together. I'm going to take Brandon with me. Let's just take the car down to my mechanic first."

"Thank you, Dad."

After all this time I was still Daddy's big girl, and he was still rescuing me. But all I wanted was to be able to rescue myself.

My dad went inside to get Brandon at school, while I

waited in the car. Brandon came out and knew he was in trouble. His face was balled up, and he was looking down.

I met him on the sidewalk. "So what's your excuse, huh Brandon? Your mom was on crack and wasn't there for you? You didn't have a dad in your life? I mean, really, were you abused? Because you're going to need some excuse when you are a loser and someone asks you why you haven't did anything with your life."

"I'm not a loser," Brandon yelled back at me.

"Well, you're sure are acting like one."

"Man, you don't know."

I punched him dead in his chest. "I'm tired of you, boy. You need to get it together. First, you want to be with Semaj. Now he is your enemy."

He bowed over, and my dad grabbed me off of him.

"Leave him alone, Yvette."

"No, Dad. Stay out of this."

"You're taking all your anger out on him," My dad said as he tried to wrestle me off Brandon.

"I'm not, Dad. He just has to has to stop acting like he doesn't have any sense."

"Leave the boy alone. He will learn."

My dad was right. Brandon was going to learn right now—learn to stop having the school call my phone and interrupt my day.

Chapter 33

Dana

"How do I look, babe?" Adam asked. His beard was coming in a little scruffy.

"You look good. Your beard is sexy." I fixed Adam's tie in the mirror as we got ready to attend his uncle's retirement party. I was wearing a pretty ivory cocktail dress. I knew I looked great, but I wasn't prepared to meet his two sisters and his mother all at once. I didn't know why I was so nervous, because I met people all the time and could sell anything, so I knew I could sell myself.

We arrived at the upscale banquet hall in Bensalem, Pennsylvania. There were people standing around the reception area, drinking out of champagne flutes and wineglasses. Adam's mother came over to us and kissed her son on the cheek. She had a short blond cut, was petite like me, and had very light blue eyes. She was in her fifties but looked a few years younger. She was followed by his sisters and his aunts.

"Everyone, I want you all to meet my girlfriend, Dana," Adam said as he kissed me on my cheek proudly.

"I haven't heard much about you. Where do you live and work, Dana?" his mother asked.

I looked over at Adam, puzzled, and before I could respond, he said, "Mom, she works downtown, at a marketing agency, and lives in the city, and I have told you about her."

"Oh, a city girl. Nice," his mother said, and I noticed her eyes cut over to his aunts.

"Like, really in the city?" his sister Amanda asked.

"Yes, Philadelphia," I said.

"Whoa. I would be so scared to live there," Amanda stated. "I watch the news every day. It seems so scary to live there. It's like every night someone gets shot or robbed. And the last time I was down there, we rode the train to the game and a homeless guy asked me for a dollar and I gave it to him, and then he came right back and asked for a cigarette. So then I finally told him I didn't smoke anymore, but then he came back and asked me for ten dollars; it was very scary."

"Oh, that's interesting. That's real interesting," I said, sort of lost for words. I scratched my head because I didn't know why she was telling me this horrible story.

"Being as you're a city girl, you probably see that all the time," said Adam's mother.

"Actually, I don't in my neighborhood, but you know, over in Adam's neighborhood it's a little rougher. I have a doorman." I looked straight in the witch's face. I got her "city girl."

Adam interjected, "Yeah, we city people like it there, Mom. Let's go and find Uncle Stuart and congratulate him on his retirement."

All evening his mother kept referring to me as a city girl, like the entire city was one trash can that I had jumped out of to run to this party. This lady was not behaving like the supermom of the year I had heard so much about. She was a rude bitch, and I wasn't sure if I was a city girl because I lived in the city or if I was a city girl because I was black. I wanted to confront her, but then I didn't want to act like a city girl, too. So instead I just smiled, and I managed to maintain my composure and got through dinner with his mother and his sister Amanda asking me ridiculous questions.

The next morning in the conference room I was still in deep thought about the evening before. Leah was presenting our ideas on a Smart Board to the executives at Quench 0 Calorie Drink. I was supposed to keep up with her, but all I could think of is that I finally had found a great guy that I liked, but our relationship might not work out because his mother was a racist. After the meeting was over and the executives had left, Leah, Reshma, and I stood around talking. I was still moving in slow motion, trying to get my thoughts together.

"What's wrong Dana? Who did it?" Reshma asked with her little belly starting to poke out; she looked so cute in her Pea in a Pod maternity jumper. I couldn't help but touching her belly.

"It's nothing, well. Adam's mother kept referring to me as a city girl. She was really a bitch," I complained. "All night she said things like, 'Give the city girl another drink,' and 'The city girl is going to the restroom.' It was so embarrassing, and what made it even worse was Adam didn't say or do anything about it."

"Do you think she is prejudiced?" Reshma asked.

"You know, I'm not sure if she is, but something is wrong with her and she was so shamelessly rude."

"I wouldn't worry about it. You're dating him. Forget his mother. Stephen's parents don't care for me. They'd much rather he date a Jewish girl," said Leah.

Reshma frowned. "I didn't know that. I love Zyeed's parents. I couldn't imagine not liking my in-laws."

"I think they are concerned about when we are married. I'm Christian, he's Jewish, and it's hard raising children with two different religions," Leah explained. "The whole kosher thing makes everything complicated."

"Wow. Well, I'm going to say something to him," I told them.

I took their advice and dialed Adam once I was back in my office. I had to let him know his mom's behavior bothered me and it was unacceptable.

"Babe, last night your mom said a lot of things I didn't take well. Does she have something against me? Is she maybe a little prejudiced?"

"Dana, absolutely not. No, she is not prejudiced. I'm her only son. She has hated everyone and anyone I have ever dated."

"Oh. Are you sure? Because she kept referring to me as a city girl."

"My mother was born in the city, in South Philadelphia. My grandfather is Italian. My mom has a lot of—"

I stopped him mid-sentence. "Don't say it, Adam."

"Don't say what?"

"Don't say, 'My mother has a lot of black friends.' It's the first thing every racist person says when they are trying to defend themselves about being called a racist."

"Okay, I won't say it, but she does have a lot of black friends. She pushes buttons on purpose. I'll call her now."

"No, you don't have to." Before I could stop him, his mother's deeply annoying voice answered on the three-way call.

"Hey, Mom," Adam said. "I meant to ask you last night . . . What did you think about my girlfriend?"

"I thought she was okay. Nothing jaw-dropping." I waited for her to say something really reckless. "But you know my opinion is different from everyone else's. She was okay to me, but your sisters seem to like to her. What do I know?"

"Mom, how come you don't like any of my girlfriends?" Adam asked.

"Because I don't. But I will say she is a vast improvement over the other one. At least she is not on medication."

"All right, Mom. I will call you a little later."

"Bye, son." His mother hung up.

"See? She loves you."

"That's love? Watch when you meet my parents. You'll see how easygoing and nice my family is. You'll see love."

"When will I get to meet your family?"

"I don't know. Soon. My dad is really funny sometimes. He really only likes to meet husbands and fiancés. At least that's what he tells us."

"I'm going to be your husband one day, right?"

"Maybe you will be one day, maybe not, but right now I'm completing my workday. I will talk to you later. I'll be over around seven."

After hanging up with Adam, I called my mom. I hadn't talked to her in a while. Between work, being in a relationship, and just everyday life, there wasn't enough time to keep up with everyone. She answered on the fourth ring.

"Mommy, what are you doing? Why did it take you so long to answer the phone?"

"I was upstairs fixing up that back room. Everything is okay the same I suppose. I'm just really concerned about Yvette and the kids."

"What's been going on with Vette?"

"Everything. Every time I call her, she still doesn't answer. I leave her messages and we've sent her money and she doesn't respond. Your father said her car broke down on her, Brandon is misbehaving in school, she still hasn't found a job or got her money from that nothing-ass man, and he also said she put on some weight. It's like the world is coming down on her, and I don't know how to help her."

"Really?"

"Yeah. Dana, just call her or go past there please for me."

For once I was worried too. I was going to have to make sure I called her.

"I will."

"Oh and Dana, Thanksgiving is at Crystal's," my mother informed me. "And, when you get a chance, I want you to help me pick out new luggage. We are leaving this cold weather and going to the Florida Keys."

"Thanksgiving at Crystal's? Can she even cook? Is she still married?"

"Yes, she can cook and her husband Terell is a real good guy since we've gotten to know him. I told her I didn't feel like making all the food, and she volunteered. She is doing good now. They bought a new truck and everything. You need to apologize to her. You have to give credit where credit is due."

"I don't care. I'm dating someone now, too, and I'm bringing him. I still say it won't last—I give them to the end of the year."

"That's not nice, Dana."

"It's not nice, but true. Mommy, I'll talk to you later, and I'll take you to get luggage this weekend."

CHAPTER 34

Yvette

I felt so behind, like I was drowning and trying to reach the surface. I was getting there, taking a breath, and then some force of nature kept pulling me back down again. I was getting tired of the fight, but I didn't want to die. I needed someone to pull me out of this water and rescue me before I sank to the bottom. I'd been praying and praying and praying. And hopefully, the interview I was about to go on was the answer to all my prayers.

Finally, one of the companies from the job fair had called. The position was for a human resources director for an insurance company. If I got it, it would be perfect. It was right downtown. I could catch the train. And the salary was just about what I was making before.

I pulled apart hangers and tried to search through my closet for something that fit and was interview worthy. I'd tried on a few suits for my interview. My suit jackets were tight, and my pants felt like they were about to split open. I settled on a blouse and black slacks that were a little wrinkled at the bottom. Hopefully, they would iron themselves out by the time I got to the interview. Being on time was more important than a getting rid of a few wrinkles.

I left all the clothes I'd taken off the hangers on the bed and rushed downtown. My plan was to park in a parking lot, but the parking prices right around the office building were extremely high. I didn't have fifteen dollars for the first half hour, so I circled around and parked seven blocks away for free and walked to my interview.

I reached the office building ten minutes early. I checked in and went to the bathroom to check my appearance. I looked nice. I smiled at myself, took a deep breath, and hoped they hired me. I had to make a great impression, because I needed this job. I had my entire future paycheck spent already in my mind, and I hadn't even got the job yet.

An older white man name Samuel Creighton was my interviewer. He was wearing skinny, black-rimmed glasses to look over my résumé. I knew all the questions he was going to ask me, because so many times I had been on the other side of the desk, asking the questions. I had a seat and Mr. Creighton went right into going over my job history.

"So why did you leave your last job? You were there for a very long time."

"Yes. Unfortunately, they were downsizing, so I was a salaried employee and they couldn't afford to keep me, so they laid me off and brought in an outside company to handle their payroll."

"A lot of companies are doing that today. That's unfortunate," he said as he gave me an understanding glance and further studied my resume.

"Yes, it is," I agreed.

He asked me a few more questions. Then he said that he was very impressed and thought I would be the perfect candidate, because they needed someone to start immediately. Mr. Creighton explained he had a few more interviews this week, but he would know something by the end of next week and be in touch.

I think the interview went well. I drove home excited and hopeful. I felt good about the prospect of having a job again. The possibility of having employment again gave me the courage to open my bills. As soon as I was home I took the stack of bills and opened them one by one. When I moved here, I forwarded my mail here, and Phil's mail to his father's address, but somehow his got mixed in with mine. I could have been nice and put his new address on it; instead I tore his shit up. *Fuck him,* I thought. One thing was for certain, I couldn't keep letting the bills pile up and not do anything about them. I opened the electric bill and called them immediately; I was scheduled to be shut off in two days. Thank God I called them first; they allowed me to make a payment arrangement. Then I contacted the gas company and was able to make an extension. The last thing I needed to handle was my storage company, because their notice read that they have been trying to reach me.

"Stanley Storage. How may I help you?" a male voice asked.

"Yes, I was calling to see how much I owed on my storage unit." I gave the man on the other end of the call my name and he put me on hold. He came back on the line and said, "With late fees, the total amount on this account is three hundred and twenty-one dollars and two cents. You have until the twenty-sixth to pick it up."

I wrote the information down and thanked him. I was happy to be finally getting everything in order. In less than an hour I had the status of three bills under control and felt a lot calmer. Just as I got up to contact the bill collector, Geneva called.

"Hey, Geneva."

"Don't 'Hey, Geneva' me. I want you to stop avoiding me and come out and have a drink with me and Stacey. I want to get you out of that house."

"I can't even afford a drink right now, though I need one."

"Come on. I'm treating. Get out. Eric has the kids. We can laugh, talk. I promise you will feel so much better if you come out."

"Okay, I'll go."

I didn't have anything new to wear, because I hadn't bought myself anything in months. But I looked in the back of my closet and found a cute shirt I hadn't worn and threw on jeans and heels and met up with my girls.

Geneva looked so pretty, and so did Stacey. Their hair and nails were done. Their shoes were cute. We ordered our first round of mango margaritas with Patrón Silver, and I began to feel at ease.

I sipped a little of my drink. "This is good. Whew. I really needed this," I said, pointing to the drink.

"So what's going on? Girl, how are you managing?" Stacey inquired, stirring the pureed mango at the top of her drink.

"Managing by the grace of God. Besides the world coming for me, I'm doing okay. I think what keeps me going is the fact that I know that this can't last forever. And things are already looking up. I had a really good job interview today."

"Yes, they are. The sun got to shine sometimes, right?" Geneva said and laughed. "You are so strong, and all you have to do is just keep praying and God will send you that miracle."

"I know. It is just hard while you waiting on the miracle. I think not being able to pay for Mimi's tuition was the hardest thing. Then Brandon got suspended twice. I just keep thinking, 'Why me?' And then my car broke down again. It's just a lot . . . That's why I don't even feel like talking to anyone. I just want to be alone."

"Well, that's not healthy. That's what friends and family are here for."

"Yeah, but I just I can't ever remember being this broke,

it's really depressing. Not even when I was young and married to Doug, and we were poor. And speaking of Doug, he has been so good, sending me extra money for the kids. If I didn't know better, I would think Phil put roots or something on me. He is the devil."

"You believe in that stuff?" Stacey asked.

"No, I believe in God, but how and why does all this stuff keep happening to me? I don't know that devilish man."

"Phil's not the devil, but he's damn sure one of his agents and works for him. It will get better," said Geneva.

"It will. You know what you need in the meantime?" Stacey asked.

"What do I need?" I asked sarcastically looking over at her.

"To get some."

"Please. That's not going to work. It's something about not having money that kills my libido I don't know about you, but I don't feel sexy when my bills are not paid. Hector kept pressuring me, and I met him at a hotel and did not enjoy myself. After that he gave up, just stopped calling me, and I'm glad. I'm just really trying to get me back together again. And secondly, since I gained this weight, I've noticed fewer men have tried to talk to me."

"Whatever, but you did put on some weight. How much did you gain in total?" Stacey inquired.

"I don't know . . . like twenty pounds."

"Damn, what are you doing sitting home eating your troubles away? That's a lot," Stacey said. "I was going to say, 'Take those marbles out the side of your mouth.' Damn, so Phil just ruining your life all the way around. If I was you I would just sell some pussy, to get some money," she laughed.

"Huh, what the hell are you talking about, Stacey, who is a trick selling pussy? First, I'm never selling anything, and second it's so many chicks giving it out for free, I don't think it would work. You know, like when they go on vacation."

"Yeah, but you got to do something to get some money.

I'm not saying trick, just meet a guy with money and tell him you need your bills paid."

"Right, I'm not doing that, but you try it and let me know how you make out. Anyway," I said as I popped my eyes out at Geneva so she could check her girl. Stacey was getting on my nerves and I was getting ready to tell her off. I decided to change the topic. "So how are the children, Geneva?"

"Home with Eric. I'm surprised he hasn't called yet, asking me how to use the microwave. You know he is domestically challenged."

"Yeah, he is."

We talked a little more, then the waiter came over and asked if we wanted another round of drinks. I had already had one. I wasn't exactly buzzed, but a second drink would seal the deal. I took three big swallows of my drink and said, "I'll take another."

"She doesn't need another drink. One is enough. She don't have any money," Stacey said loudly.

My eyes went directly to hers. I couldn't believe that she had said I couldn't have another drink because I didn't have money.

"Wow, really, Stacey? Are you serious?" Geneva said.

"What I'm joking, give us all another round." Stacey said to the waiter. At this point I didn't care if Stacey was serious or not—I was totally offended. I wanted to reach over and slap her.

Geneva tried to intervene. "That was uncalled for, Stacey."

"No, don't say anything, Geneva. Stacey, you have a lot of damn nerve. When I had it, it was never a problem. Drinks were always on me. I hope you're never in my situation. But thanks for letting me know who my real friends are."

"I swear I was only joking," Stacey replied. "We joke all the time. You're being so damn sensitive."

"Yeah, well, watch what you say. I've never been a broke bitch." I left the table. *I've paid my way my whole life. I'm not going to let some no-name, corny bitch disrespect me. I always have paid my way and always will,* I thought as I walked out of the restaurant.

Geneva came up behind me. "She didn't mean it, Vette. I know she didn't. Don't leave."

I stopped momentarily and said, "It is better that I leave before I beat the shit out of her. I came out to get away from everything and she is sitting here making jokes. This shit ain't funny." I said as tears began to flush out of my eyes. Geneva consoled me and started patting my back and more tears poured out.

"I'm getting tired, Geneva. This is hard. Like, I can't pay my bills. I'm fighting not to break down. Trying to stay strong for my kids. Every day I wake up thinking, this is the day my life is going to be normal again. Thinking positive and nothing is changing. I don't know when it is going to end. When will I be me again?"

"I know it's been hard, but you have to pray. You have to just keep staying strong."

"I've been praying. I don't know if God has a waiting list or what, because he hasn't answered me yet. I really can't take any more and that's why I'm leaving. I have enough problems. I don't need a fake friend kicking me when I'm down."

"I know. No one knows how it feels. But don't give up on your faith. I promise you, when you least expect it, He is going to bless you."

Chapter 35

Crystal

The last time I had a conversation with Kenneth, he was cussing me out, telling me not to call him anymore and to let my husband be Kori's father. We tried to be civil with him when he brought Kori back that night, but ignorance was all he knew. He said, "Forget you, your husband, and our daughter." Actually, he said something a lot harsher but, anyway, I told Rell not to worry about him. I didn't want them getting into anything. And that was easier said than done, because Rell had taken it personally that Kenneth had disrespected him, his wife, and his stepdaughter. I knew Kenneth and Syreeta were crazy, but Rell was not having the disrespect at all. That was why I wasn't sure if I should allow Kori to go anywhere with her dad for Thanksgiving.

I was sprinkling layers of cheese and bread crumbs over the top of my macaroni and cheese when Kenneth and Syreeta called, asking to have Kori for a few hours. I asked him if he was going to be in or out of her life. Kenneth promised he was in it now for good, so I would allow him one last chance to be her father. He came over to get Kori, and it was too cold to have him stand outside, so I invited him in while

I got her dressed. I didn't think nothing of it, really, until Rell came home and saw Kenneth. With a shocked look on his face, he demanded that I come upstairs with him.

"Rell what's wrong? I'm getting Kori ready."

"What the hell is he doing here in my living room?"

"He was waiting for Kori; it was cold so I told him to come in. He is her father."

"I know who he is. You told me everything he's done and said to you. He's not allowed in here—let him wait outside. Let him turn his heat on."

"But it was only for a few minutes."

"I don't care. You heard what I said he's not allowed in this house anymore. What, you still like him or something? Why are you taking up for someone who don't give you any money for his daughter, and disrespects you anytime he gets ready."

"No, I don't. I just thought . . . He asked for Kori for Thanksgiving. I was giving him one last chance to do right by her."

"I don't care. He can't just decide when he wants to be a father. Matter of fact, I don't want to see this dude anywhere near her, you, or this house. She is not going with him. Go tell him to leave, or I will." Rell was angry and I didn't want him to say anything to Kenneth and then they would start arguing.

I went back downstairs and scratched my head. "So, Kenneth, uh, she can't go with you. I've decided I want her to stay here with me and my family for the holiday."

"What? This is my daughter too. Ain't nobody going to tell me I can't take mine. Now, Crystal, finish getting her clothes. Let me take her, and I'll bring her back, like, at eight."

Rell came down the steps.

I was scared for a moment, like it was about to be a problem, but Kenneth just got up and left. Within a few moments

Syreeta began calling my phone. I didn't want to answer, but she kept calling back.

"Answer your phone, Crystal; stop acting scared of him."

"It's not him; it's his sister again."

"I'm really getting tired of them," Rell said as he grabbed my cell phone.

"Rell, stop—I'll answer it." I answered and all I heard was yelling and screaming.

"Uhm, Crystal, didn't Kenneth just talk to you a few hours ago and you said he can come get that baby."

"I did but some things came up and I changed my mind."

"Well, you can't just tell people one thing and do another. You let my brother come all the way the hell over there. What the fuck kind of shit is that? I don't mean no harm, but your little husband needs to mind his business when it comes to my niece and what's going on between you and my brother. We just want to come and get Kori for a few hours. We ain't got no family. It's me and him and my kids, and he wanna come and grab his daughter. I don't see what the problem is."

"Syreeta, he can't. He just can't do things when he wants to. My husband doesn't have anything to do with this. She can't go, and that's it."

"Crystal, my brother is on his way back over there, and you are going to send the baby out, or else."

"Or else what?"

"Bitch, you don't even want to find out."

Rell snatched the phone from me. "Listen, this shit is over today. You and your brother don't run shit and you not going to keep disrespecting my wife. If you want to see Kori so bad, tell your brother to go see a judge and get a visitation order. Until then stop calling my wife and tell your brother to stay away from my family." After he ended the call with Syreeta, he fussed at me some more for still tolerating them.

* * *

Thanksgiving was being held at my house, and I was happy. I had to pretend like Kenneth and Syreeta didn't almost ruin everything. I would deal with them later. I pulled all the food out of the oven as our guests started to arrive. I hadn't seen Dana in a while. I wasn't mad at her anymore. She brought pies, and when she came in, I just gave her a hug. All was forgiven.

"I'm sorry," she said.

"I know. I'm sorry, too," I said as I hugged my sister. I knew she meant well but didn't know exactly how to express herself.

"This is my boyfriend, Adam. Adam, this is one of my big sisters, Crystal," Dana said.

"Hello. Nice to meet you. That's my husband, Terell," I replied. Her boyfriend, Adam . . . Wow, so much had changed. I was married, and Dana was dating a white man.

I told them to have a seat and waited for everyone else to join us.

Dana picked up Kori and remarked, "I missed y'all. Look how big she got!"

My parents arrived next, and Daddy said hello to Adam. I think Daddy was a little surprised, but he played it off. He instantly bonded over the game with him.

I never thought the day would come that my husband and my father and Dana and her white boyfriend, Adam, would all sit happily in front of my sixty-inch television, watching the game in my house.

My father was so accepting of Rell now, and for the first time I thought he approved of my life.

Just as I had that thought, my mom said, "I'm so proud of you, Crystal. I was just telling your daddy how you got your husband, a new car, and how your life is really coming together. And I love that big television downstairs."

"Thank you, Mom. Is Vette coming?"

"Yeah. Where are Vette and the kids? Let me call her. She was supposed to bring that other salad."

CHAPTER 36

Yvette

I didn't want to go to Thanksgiving. Thanksgiving was for giving thanks. I knew I had a lot to be happy about—my life, my health, my children—but I didn't feel like celebrating anything. Payment arrangements, extensions, speaking to a supervisor . . . I didn't want to do any of the above anymore. I needed money. I needed a job. These past few months had been pure hell, and, well, I didn't want to be around anyone. That man I interviewed with, Mr. Creighton, had guaranteed me a second interview, and all I got was a form letter saying that they went with another candidate.

My mom had been calling me all morning, making sure I made my red potato salad for Thanksgiving dinner. I'd made the salad, but I still wasn't going to dinner. I didn't really want to disappoint everyone, but I didn't want to make everyone miserable, either. I'd rather keep my drama to myself. She started calling my phone nonstop. I finally answered.

"Mom, I'm not coming to Thanksgiving, but you can pick up the potato salad," I told her when she called again.

"Why not?"

"I don't feel too good. I think I'm coming down with something."

"Yvette, you can keep staying in the house, isolating yourself from the rest of the world, acting like a hermit, but it doesn't help. I think you might be depressed."

"I'm not depressed , Mom, really. I don't want anyone else to catch what I have."

"Well, at least let me pick up the kids, because Crystal made all of this food, and they can bring you a plate home. Okay?"

"Sure, Mom. I'm sure they want to come." When I got off the phone, I called out to Brandon and Mercedes and told them to get dressed.

Fifteen minutes later my mom called back. "Yvette, I'm outside."

Damn, I didn't want to see her. I was hoping she'd beep the horn and keep it moving. I sat up and squinted my eyes so I could look sick. Then I went to the door and let my mom in.

"Mom, your hair looks nice." Her curls were tight, like she had just taken her rollers out, and the gold hoops matched the brown pantsuit she had on.

"I went and had it done yesterday." She studied my face. I knew she was trying to determine if I was really sick or not.

"You must be sick, because you look a mess." She patted my wild hair down for me.

I began to cough and sniffle, and she backed away from me and I said, "Yeah, I am. I don't know what I came down with."

"Well, if you change your mind, just call and someone will come back and get you."

"Okay." I coughed once more.

They all left, and I was free to do nothing. I made sure the door was locked and turned off all the lights. I went into my bedroom, flicked the television on, and put the covers over my head and closed my eyes. I rested for two hours and then had a change of heart and decided to go to Crystal's and surprise everyone.

Daddy had two men to watch the game with him, and Terell seemed to be fitting in just fine with my father. I was happy I'd come, but I did feel out of place. At least I showed up. Now I could leave. I felt like my sisters' lives were on track and mine was still a wreck. My mom was kind enough to make made me a plate, but I only picked off of it. I wasn't hungry; I was miserable.

"So are you going shopping with us in the morning?" Dana asked.

I shook my head. "No."

My mom said, "Why not? We go Black Friday shopping every year. I have to get some things. Your dad is taking me to the Florida Keys for our anniversary."

"Oh, that's nice," I said. "I forgot you guys' anniversary was in a few days. Yeah, but I'm not for all that pushing and rushing around the store. This year."

"I saw on the news that the stores are opening up at midnight tonight. So it might not be as crowded," Crystal said.

"Go with us, Yvette," my mom insisted.

"Well, I don't feel like getting up early, I don't feel well, and I have things I have to do. Actually, I'm about to leave now." I didn't get why they kept asking me to go when they knew I didn't have any money.

My niece Jewel tapped me on my leg. "Aunt Yvette, can I come over and spend the night?"

"No, sorry. Not tonight."

"Then, Mom, can I spend the night over here and go shopping with them in the morning?" Mercedes asked.

"No, Mercedes."

"Mom, why not? There is no school tomorrow. And we always go shopping."

"I'm getting tired. I'm about to get out of here," I said.

"Well, if you want them to stay, they can, Yvette," Crystal said.

"Okay. Just drop them off tomorrow." I put on my coat, told everyone good night.

"If you want to go shopping, I have money for you to go," my mom whispered to me as she caught up with me at the door.

"I can't go shopping. I have bills, Mom."

"Well, still take this. Take care of your bills. And I was talking to your father. . . . Listen, we have space at the house. I'm tired of seeing you struggle. You have family. Why don't you just come back home? Brandon can take your old bedroom, and you and Mercedes can go in the back room."

"Mom, I don't want to move back home. I'll be okay, but thanks for the offer. When I get everything together, I promise I will pay you back all the money you and Daddy have been loaning me."

"We know you will."

CHAPTER 37

Yvette

My parents were on their way to Key West, Florida, I'd just dropped them off at the airport. And now I was off to take care of all my business with the money my mother loaned me. I was en route to the storage facility to pay my storage bill in person, and from there I planned to go to the market, and then it would be time for the kids to get home from school.

I walked into the U-Haul storage center. It was a big multilevel warehouse. There were people loading boxes, and the phones kept ringing. The woman at the counter asked how she could help me.

"I'm here to pay my storage bill."

"Last name and unit number?"

"It should be under McKnight or Turner-McKnight; it's unit 178."

"Okay, let me see. I'll be right back." She came back and said, "Miss, you sure that's your unit number? Because that unit is showing as empty."

"Why would it be empty? That's the number on my paperwork."

"Let me see it. Let me check this other system." Her fingers tapped fast on the keyboard. She picked up the phone and made a call, told someone to check my unit. They radioed back that it was empty. "Hold on," she told me. "Maybe they moved it."

Why would they move my belongings? I thought.

"Okay. I know what's going on," the woman announced. "Every month we have an auction, and unfortunately, your stuff was auctioned yesterday."

"Whose stuff was sold yesterday? What do you mean? I called down here, and y'all told me that I had until the twenty-sixth."

"No, it was the twenty-fifth, ma'am. Maybe you didn't hear him correctly."

"What do you mean? Get a goddamn manager! Are you kidding? This has to be a mistake."

"Miss, you must have misunderstood them."

"I can hear very well. I wrote it down. I need my belongings. Everything I ever owned was in the storage unit. My life . . . What I need you to do is find my stuff."

A manager came from the back, and he started explaining what had happened. He began to get loud with me and talk down to me, like I didn't matter.

"Ma'am, I'm going to need you to calm down," he barked.

"Calm down? You calm the fuck down! I'll calm down when you find my goddamn belongings!"

"If payment is not made in one month, we send out a notice. After sixty days we sell the contents for payment. Read your contract," he grumbled.

"I didn't have to read a contract. I only owed you two months. I had thousands of dollars worth of clothes, furniture and everything else"

He shook his head. "I'm sorry. There is nothing we can do." I stood still and began to cry the young girl behind the counter must have felt sorry for me because she offered me tissue to wipe my face.

* * *

They'd sold my stuff. They'd sold all my children's stuff. They'd sold all my pictures. Everything I had worked for was gone. My whole, entire life was gone. I couldn't understand why or what I was doing wrong. I didn't deserve this bad cloud that was following me. I wasn't going to cry. I couldn't cry. I was out of tears and numb. I drove home, exited my car, collected my mail, and tears started to flow. I opened my bills. There was a lot of junk mail, a cell phone company wanting me to switch to their company, and a postcard from my travel agent. It mentioned a survey about my recent trip to Rio de Jinero, Brazil. They must have made a mistake. I'd never been to Brazil, especially not recently.

I flipped the card over and saw the words *Phillip McKnight and guest. Phillip McKnight and guest. Wow!* I was sitting here worrying about how I was going to pay everything. And he was having the time of his life in fucking Brazil—with a guest. I had just had my every possession sold, and *he* was in Brazil. Okay. That was it. I didn't care if I went to jail. I had had enough. I'd been struggling all these months and this bitch had been living the glamorous life. He was about to pay with his life for ruining mine Just to confirm I wasn't mistaken, I dialed the number on the postcard.

"Hello. This is Mrs. Phillip McKnight. I wanted to answer questions about my trip. When did we take the trip again? We travel so much." I recited a code on the postcard to the agent.

"I show that you used our agency for a five-night stay in Brazil in October. How were the accommodations? If you could score them on a scale of one through five, with five being the highest."

"It was excellent, a five," I answered.

"Thank you, and would you recommend this property again?"

"I sure would." I hung up before she could ask me another question. I had somewhere to go. I was going to do something to that son of a bitch. Slashing his tires was not enough. Busting his windows . . . I might get cut myself. Set his motherfucking house on fire—that just might work.

I entered Auto Zone, a woman on a mission. I was looking for one of those red containers with the black spout and handle to put gas into. A young man wearing a red shirt welcomed me into his store.

"Welcome to Auto Zone. How can I help you today?"

"Thank you. I need a gas container."

"Oh, you ran out of gas? Are you nearby? Do you need any help?"

"I'm good. I have help. Thank you. I got this," I said, smiling.

He directed me to where I could find them. I had a choice between a small one and a big one. I thought about it for a moment. I needed a big container. I purchased one.

With my gas container in hand, I drove to the gas station and filled it up. I was now going to light Phil's ass up. At least when I violated my stay-away order, it would be well worth it. I had it all planned. I'd pull up in front of his door, wait for him to get out of the truck he probably bought with my money. Then I'd walk up behind him, open the gas can, tap him on his shoulder, wait for him to turn around, and then throw the gas in his face. While he was bent over, screaming for mercy, I'd strike a match and let him burn.

Only it didn't work out that way. Phil came home like he was supposed to, but the sneaking-up-on-him part didn't happen. He must have felt my presence, because he turned around, saw me, and ran in the house. I chased him and banged on the door and screamed, "You want to play with my damn life! I can't feed my kids because of your stupid ass. I'm going to make you pay, bitch. Come back out here, bitch. You went the fuck to Brazil with my money. Really, bitch? You are going to pay you son of a stank dirty bar-stool-sitting bitch. And where the fuck your dirty dick ass dad at? Tell him to come out here so I can light his ass up, too." I demanded for Phil to come out a face me, but he refused.

He wouldn't come back out but kept screaming from the second-floor window, "Yvette! I'm going to call the police."

"Fuck the police when they get here! I'm going to tell them what you did to me, and they probably are going to say, 'Okay. Go ahead. Burn his ass, miss. He deserves it.' Bring your ass out here so I can light your ass up!" I kicked the door a few times, because he wouldn't come out. I was ready to go in. I walked back to the car to get a match. In a few moments I wouldn't have to worry about Phillip McKnight anymore. I had the gas can, but I couldn't find any matches. *Fuck!* I thought. I forgot to bring matches. I saw a man walking down the street.

"Excuse me. Do you have a lighter?" I called.

"Naw, sorry. I don't smoke."

"Okay." *Shit,* I thought. I would just have to go to the gas station to get a matchbook.

On my way to the gas station a few blocks away from his house my phone was ringing back to back. Why was he calling me now? Why did he want to talk now? He hadn't had anything to say all these months. I answered so I could tell him that he was going to get it once I got a lighter or a match. It was Dana, not him, this time.

"Yvette, what are you doing? Daddy just called me and said that you are at Phil's house, screaming you're going to set him on fire with a gas container. The police are on their way. If they catch you there with gasoline, you are going to jail forever. I don't know what's going on, Vette. But listen, whatever you are about to do, it is not worth it."

"It *is* worth it. I don't care about going to jail. Everything I ever owned is gone. My life is gone. This son of a nasty bitch has fucked with me for all these months, and now it is time for him to pay. He is buying trucks, going on vacations, and I'm sitting here figuring out how my kids are going to eat. That money belongs to me. So now it is time for me to get even," I cried.

"You're not getting even. I'm on my way to you. Please, where do you want to meet, Yvette? I'll meet you anywhere you want, just get out of there. He probably told them what kind of car you driving and if they pull you over you are going to jail."

"Dana, thank you but I don't care. I have to get him. I have to get his ass. He has to pay, Dana, he has to pay. I got to make him pay."

"You can't fight crazy, Vette. He is crazy, and you know that. You're fighting him, but you are getting beat up. The only thing you can do is walk away; he is going to get his. What goes around always comes back. Didn't Daddy use to always say that to us. You remember that, Vette?"

"Yeah I remember, but, Dana, my life is fucked up. He took everything from me. I have nothing."

"Let him have it. You can get everything back."

"No, I can't. I have to go."

"If you do anything to him, he wins."

"I don't care."

"Yvette, come on, you're talking crazy. You are not getting your money back. Get the hell over it. He is not going to give you your money, so you have to make another way. You've been stuck sitting around the last couple of months, saying how he wronged you. You need to take that same energy and hate for him and put it into you and fixing your life. You're my big sister. I looked up to you. I always wanted to be like you. You were the one to show us, and now you are allowing him to pull you down. He won already, and he will have the last laugh when you are crying behind bars for the rest of your life. He will be taking more trips, and your kids will be out here without a mother."

I wouldn't respond, but Dana kept talking. "Yvette, I never thought I would see you lay down and die and let him take everything from you. He already got your house, your money, your memories, and now you about to give him your life. You set his house on fire, you're going to jail. Think about Mercedes. Think about Brandon. Who is going to take care of them? Huh? Get rid of that gasoline, and go home."

I was hearing her, but I wasn't. I had to do something to him and now. I didn't need my baby sister telling me what to do.

"Dana, I have all these bills. I'm about to get kicked out of my apartment. He ruined my life. My life is over anyway! How do I come back from all of this?"

"No, it is not. It's never over. I'll write you a check; I have money. I'll pay your rent and bills. You can pay me back later when you get on your feet. I will help you, but please don't throw your life away."

"I'm tired, Dana. No one understands how tired I am."

"I know you're tired, but I promise I'll pay everything. Just get out of there now, before the cops show up."

Just her telling me she was going to help me take care of bills was enough to bring me to my senses. Nothing was going to get shut off. *Thank you, Lord.* I had to get strong again and turn things around. Instead of getting the matches, I took the gas container and left it near a gas pump, got back in the car, and began praying. *God please help me. Please Lord have mercy on me. I need help, please forgive me for anything and everything I ever did. Please put my life back together.* I didn't know what else to do or say, because I needed help. I really wanted to hurt Phil, but instead I went home.

CHAPTER 38

Crystal

"This truck takes eighty dollars to fill up, Rell?" I said as I grimaced at the number nine pump.

"Yeah, like eighty to eighty-five. Just fill it up and add it to whatever I already owe you. How much do I owe you now?"

"Rell, I don't know. I'm not keeping track."

That was a lie. I wanted to be a good wife, but I was starting to resent having to pay for everything for us. I got out of the car and paid for the gas, and Rell pumped the eighty dollars into the tank. We were coming back from an evening that was supposed to be some old-fashioned alone time. My mom was watching the kids, and I thought this was what we needed, because lately Rell had been aggravating me. We'd needed a second car, but now it didn't seem like that was the smartest thing for us to have done. Now I was thinking, Why did I take on an extra car note and insurance when my car was fine? Rell needed a car, not me.

When we first met, I saw all this energy and drive with Rell, but now that I was married to him, I thought I had probably made a mistake. I didn't want to tell anyone, and even during Thanksgiving I was pretending to be so happy.

Paying for everything was getting real old fast. If he was working, it would make my life a lot easier. And please let's not talk about Shareef's stupid-ass job. They are not calling Rell. He's been waiting for how many damn months? He could have found nine other jobs instead of counting on that stupid position to come through. I kept saying to Rell, "Look for another job, we have bills." But his answer to me was to be a little more patient. Patience is bullshit. Patience will have my lights off. The way these bills were stacking up, I might have to ask for some extra hours. I got back in the car, and Rell was just staring straight ahead, appearing to be troubled.

"Listen, Crystal, babe, if this job don't call me by next week, I was thinking about reenlisting." Was he reading my mind? Did he hear all the shit I was talking about him in my head?

"What? Rell, what am I going to do if you are not here?"

"I don't know, but we won't be struggling. I would go back over there and make a lot of money. I blew the other money, but this time I'll send it all to you. I know dudes that paid off their kids' college tuition and almost their house by keeping going back. It is not that bad. It will be only for a year."

"Rell, if you reenlisted, I would not be happy at all. I don't think I can do it."

"I don't know, Crystal. I just might have to. If this job doesn't call me back, that's what I'm going to do."

"Why don't you start looking somewhere else and say, 'Forget that job'? Put some other applications in other places. There are other places to work."

"Yeah, but they don't pay any money."

I wished I had someone to talk to. This was when I wished I had some good girlfriends. I couldn't mention this to my mom or my sisters. There was no way I would be home writing letters, waiting, watching the news, hanging yellow ribbons, walking around praying that he was okay. While he was in another country, fighting a war, I would be here fighting alone. What if he got caught in friendly fire or one of the terrorists threw a bomb out of a moving car at him? Oh, I praised all the people that fought for us, and their family members, but I didn't want to be one of them.

That evening in bed I turned my back to Rell. I was not in the mood to have any physical contact with him. I didn't want to speak or even know him right then.

"Don't do that to me, Crystal. I want you. Boo love, what's wrong?"

"Rell, you can't even think about leaving me and going back in the service. What if something happens to you? And I need you here."

"But we need money, and nothing is going to happen to me. Earlier today I didn't feel like a man when you had to put gas in the car. That's my responsibility. I'm a man, and I have to do whatever I have to do."

"Then get two jobs here. Wouldn't that be easier, Rell, than going to another country at war?" Rell made me so angry and was becoming an idiot. I couldn't take anymore. I took my blanket and went to sleep in the kids' room.

Chapter 39

Yvette

I was very upset about my things being auctioned off, but they were gone. What made me feel better was that my mom had copies of a lot of the pictures I'd lost and I realized that everything that was in storage could be replaced. I could buy myself and Brandon and Mercedes more clothes, bikes, televisions, and furniture. It was just stuff. I had to think of it like that; otherwise I would go mad. Dana writing me a check to cover my bills gave me a sense of peace.

Brandon had been fine. Mercedes was still adjusting to her school. She had made a few friends and was beginning to like it. I'd been applying to jobs every day and praying someone called me. I was happy Doug had said he was still taking the kids for Christmas. I hoped I was working then so that we could have a good holiday and I could have something for them when they came back from Florida. I made a bunch of follow-up calls to make sure the people that had my resume knew I was still looking, and it worked, because when I came home there was a message for me.

"Hi. This is Tina from Service Air. You sent in your résumé. I know you were looking for more of a clerical position, but I know we spoke and you said that if I had any openings to give you a call. So I do have an opening. It is only a seasonal position, but you would start immediately. Please give me a call if you're interested. Thank you, and have a great day."

I called her back, and she said the position was a driver's helper, and if I was interested, I could start on Monday. It was only from December to March, but I didn't care. I would have a check.

On my first day as a driver's helper, I was introduced to the driver I was assisting. His name was Kirk. He was short and stocky and wasn't that friendly. I didn't really like the uniform. It was straight up and down brown work pants, and not flattering at all. However, I tried to make myself look cute by doing my hair and makeup.

A typical day at Service Air began at 7:30 a.m. We came in, and first, we did our stretch and flex to make sure our bodies and muscles were ready for the day. And then we scanned and loaded. Most of the men that had women helpers loaded and the women scanned, but not Kirk. He believed in equal rights. He had me breaking my back loading, while his lazy self scanned.

Once we were in the truck, we had about forty packages that had to be delivered on time between 9:00 a.m. and 10:30 a.m. In order to be timely, I would jump off the truck, knock twice, and if the customer didn't answer right away, they got a yellow slip. Some of the people on our route complained, but they needed to answer their doors quicker if their packages were that important to them.

Chapter 40

Crystal

Rell got the J-O-B! He was finally an employee of Seisman's Bread. I was shocked but so happy. I thought they weren't ever going to call him at that damn job and that he was waiting in vain. But I'm glad I was so wrong. It was his first day and he was so excited when he left out for work. He called me on his break and I quizzed him about his day.

"How is it so far?"

"Babe, it's good. From what they showed me it's not hard at all. And Reef said I can get overtime when I'm done training. And you know that is time and a half. He said I could jump on as many shifts as I want to. So you know I'm going to tear that OT up. And don't worry, baby, my first check, I'm going to give it all to you. I don't know how much it is going to be, but pay the bills and keep whatever is left. I want you to get you and the kids something. Jewel was telling me she wants this Barbie doll. It's quiet—where are they at anyway? Is Shareef still there?"

"They are all downstairs playing. I'm going to call Angel in a little bit to come and get him. He's fine, I'm just happy for you."

"Babe, I'm so happy this came through for us. I love you. I have to get back to work."

"Okay, babe. I love you too. Congratulations."

I went downstairs, and I caught Little Shareef pulling on my daughter's hair.

"Shareef, you can't pull her hair!"

"She hit me."

"Even if she hit you, you can't pull her hair. You have to come and tell me, because you are way bigger than her and can hurt her, okay?"

I had three children, and most of the time when I'm not working, I was home, but that didn't mean I wanted to watch Little Shareef. Like what the hell? Where did they get off just leaving him with me every weekend. I told Rell it was okay, but really I don't want his bad ass over here anymore.

"Okay, Shareef and Nasir, clean this room. And get all y'all's stuff, Shareef. I'm taking you home." I called Angel to let her know I was about to bring Little Shareef home.

"We not there yet. As soon as we get back around there, I'll call you," she said.

"Okay." I wasn't going to get a break, but at least my baby had a job. I walked in the kitchen and started dinner. I pulled out some chicken wings. I was going to fry them and make some yellow Goya rice and cabbage.

"Mom, somebody at the door!" Nasir screamed out. I hoped it was Angel coming early. I peeped out the blinds and saw Kenneth. I wasn't sure what he wanted. He didn't appear to be angry, but I still wasn't sure if I should call the cops or run. I backed away from the blinds and I heard him yell "I just wanted to talk to you." What could he possibly want to talk about now. I opened the door slightly to find out.

"Hey, what do you need?"

"I just want to talk to you for a moment. Can I talk to you right quick?"

I came out the door, and Kenneth began speaking. "Look, I can tell you're happy now, and I just want to be there for my daughter, nothing else. I didn't want to do all that stuff to you. Syreeta just was all in my ear, telling me this and that, but I shouldn't have put you through it, and I don't want to go through this anymore.

"Well, that's in the past and I'm sure we can work out something so you can get her sometime. Just call my phone—the number is the same."

"Okay, I probably call you the weekend. But do you think I can see her for a few minutes now?"

"Yeah, let me get her dressed and I'll bring her out to you."

I carried Kori to his car. Before I could tap on the window, he was already out attacking me and Kori with a tight hug. He squeezed us so hard Kori started crying.

"Kenneth what are you doing? Get off of me."

"I'm sorry about everything that happened between us, and I wish things might have turned out differently, Crystal. I shouldn't have done what I did and I fucked up. You're my women—this is my daughter and those are my kids." I kept trying to get away from him, but he wouldn't let me go.

"You know I was going to marry you, right? I just never got the chance."

"Oh, you were? Before or after the paternity test? Get off of me, Kenneth." Just as he released me, Shareef and Angel pulled up. I spoke to them both, and Angel got out to collect her child.

"Shareef ready?" she asked, looking over at Kenneth.

"Yup," I said.

"Now, you know we will take yours next weekend. We can have, like, a babysitting club," Angel replied.

"Okay. Sounds like a plan. Let me get Shareef."

I fetched Little Shareef, they climbed in the car, hit the horn twice, and pulled off. I was still standing with Kenneth. I asked him to leave and that he could have Kori the weekend.

Dinner was ready, and the kids were asleep. I couldn't wait for Rell to come in and tell me more about his first day at work. While I waited for him, I put some makeup on and added a few curls to my hair. I wanted him to always come home to a put-together wife.

My mom used to always put her perfume and her makeup on and be waiting by the door for my dad. We would all run up to him and hug him when he came in. I wanted to do the same for my husband. I heard Rell come through the door. I rushed downstairs to greet him.

"Baby, dinner is ready. You want to get in the shower while I warm up your food?"

"I'm actually going to take a long bath. My back hurts a little."

Rell spent an hour in the tub. I open the bathroom door and sat on the side of the tub. I took the hot washcloth and wiped it along his back and neck, letting the warm water drip.

"Your body hurt, babe? So how was your first day?"

"I don't really feel like talking right now. Excuse me," he said as he reached for a towel.

"What's wrong?" I said when I met him in the bedroom, bewildered about why was he acting like he was mad about something.

"Crystal, I could have sworn I just told you not to have that dude up in this house. Why was he here again?" he asked, very jealous.

"What are you talking about, Kenneth? He wasn't in this house. He showed up at the door and asked for Kori. And I brought her out to him."

"So why was y'all hugging, and why did you jump when you saw Shareef's car?"

I didn't see what the big deal was, but now I guessed it did look suspicious. "That's not what happened. He was just trying to see Kori, and he said sorry to me."

"I don't understand why he has to keep coming here. Doesn't he have his own place?"

"Yes . . . Well, he lives with his sister. but I don't see what the big deal is."

"The big deal is we have to set limits for this dude and all your baby fathers. You think each time one of your baby fathers decides to come around, they can just pop up? Jewel's dad be home in a few years. Or what about when Nasir's dad starts playing his part? They all can just walk in and out of this house freely?"

"No, they can't, and I can't believe you are going there. I just don't really trust Kenneth with her for long periods of time."

"Well, maybe you should have thought about that, before you had a baby with him. Forget it. I just don't want to see him around here anymore. You figure out how you are going to handle it. Just don't bring it my way."

Chapter 41

Yvette

You never knew what to expect when delivering packages; every day it was something new and crazy. There were so many holiday shipments. That kept us busy and made the day go by fast. I'd seen some interesting things happen on this job. Who knew that people sent drugs through the mail? Last week this man shipped two pounds of weed and got busted when he signed his name. The police were waiting for him. I didn't even know I was part of a sting operation and they were watching me make my delivery. Then there were so many crooked people in the world: neighbors signing for packages and then telling their neighbor it never came. And between the fraud and the drug bust, we had the bad kids throwing rocks at us. But the job was not all bad, because since I'd been jumping on and off this work truck, going up steps, and lifting boxes, I'd gone down a size.

Even though it was not the best job, I thought just leaving the house every day was so refreshing. I'd been so busy, I hadn't even thought about Phil. When I got enough money, I was going to hire an attorney. I didn't forget about my money, but I wasn't letting it run my life anymore.

Kirk and I had a delivery of nine big boxes to Lena's Soul Food on Germantown Avenue, and there weren't any available parking spaces. Kirk double-parked, blocking the narrow, heavily trafficked street. I raised the door, stacked the packages on a dolly, and pushed then into the dimly lit restaurant. Inside were about a dozen prelunch customers scattered throughout the establishment. I walked over to the hostess's desk.

"I have packages for Mr. William Nelson."

The thin hostess told me she would be right back to get the owner to sign for the delivery. An older, well-dressed man came out from the back.

"I need your signature here, sir."

"Oh, these are my new light fixtures I've been waiting for, now?" he said as he instructed the hostess to count the boxes. Then he attempted to lift one of the boxes up and then placed it back down. "Wow, these are heavy. I can't believe they got women lifting these big boxes now? Do you know how many boxes I am supposed to have?"

"You have nine boxes and, yes, they do have us ladies lifting boxes and stuff now and, by the way, did you know we can vote now, too?"

He laughed and said, "I should have eleven boxes, miss."

I looked down and realized two boxes were missing, and he was right. "I see that; I'll be back. Let me go to the truck and check."

I went back out to the truck and told Kirk we were missing boxes. He got off his ass and located them all the way in the rear. I walked back in with the two packages, and the hostess said the owner would be right back out. I looked down at my watch—it was time to go and he needed to hurry up.

"So have you ever ate here before?" the hostess asked as she wiped off menus. I told her no. I wasn't with the small talk; I was just trying to get to the next delivery. "You should come here for lunch one day. We have really good food."

"Yeah, maybe one day I'll try it. Uhm, do you know how much longer it will be?"

"I'll go check for you."

Ten more minutes passed, and I was still waiting for a signature. The owner came back out, carrying two hot plates of food, and told me he would be right with me. He delivered the food to a table and then said, "Where do you need me to sign, pretty lady?"

"Right here would be good."

"I'm so sorry for having you wait. But come check us out sometime. On Wednesdays we have a live band and fifty-cent buffalo shrimps and wings. Take a menu."

"Okay, I will."

I finally made it back to the truck.

"What took you so long? You know we got all these other deliveries, and your phone keeps ringing," Kirk grouched.

"The owner had me waiting for his signature."

Kirk cranked the diesel engine back up, and my phone began ringing again. I grabbed it out of my bag, only to hear Brandon yell, "Mom, these boys keep bothering me. I'm trying to do the right thing, but I'm about to really go off on one them. It's Semaj and these other two boys."

"Ignore them, Brandon. Don't get in trouble again. Just go to the office and talk to the principal."

"Mom, I'm really trying. I don't want to get suspended again, but if they swing on me, then I'm going to defend myself . . ."

Brandon, just go to the office. I'm calling up there now."

"Okay, Mom I'm going there." I felt a sense of peace that he was on his way to the office and had avoided a fight, or so I thought.

The next thing I knew, Brandon said they were coming up to him, and I heard kids in the background saying there was about to be a fight. I called his name, and the phone call ended.

I called his school and they said they would call me back after they had everything under control.There was no way I could get off this truck and run to his school. This was a new job, and we were miles away from the distribution center, where my car was parked. I tried to call my dad, but he didn't answer, so then I dialed Dana and asked her to go get Brandon at school. Her phone rang and rang and tears dripped down my cheek. I was so angry and felt so stuck and then Dana answered.

"Hello, Dana, I can't leave work. Brandon was in a fight. Can you please go up to his school? These boys keep bothering him?"

"Don't worry. I'll go up there. No one is going to touch my nephew. I'll call you when I get there."

Chapter 42

Dana

Yvette called me, crying hysterically, asking me if I could go to Brandon's school, because he was in a fight and these boys wouldn't leave him alone.

I arrived at the busy school. The office phones were ringing, and the sound of students filled the hallway. I spotted Brandon.

"Nephew, are you okay? What's going on? Who were you fighting?"

"I'm okay. These bulls just be talking crazy, and I had to let them know that I will fight all of them."

Just as he was explaining to me what had happened, I heard a student who was sitting at the opposite end of the office say, "Look at him. Got his mommy to save him. He don't know I beat people's moms' ass, too!" I turned around to see who he was talking to.

"Excuse me. Who are you talking to, little boy?" I said.

As clear as day he looked over at me and said, "You bitch."

I looked around the office to see if some authority figure was watching or had heard what he'd just said, and before I could respond, Brandon was on the boy, punching him in his head.

"Don't be calling my auntie out of her name. Bull, I warned you." I struggled to pull Brandon off of my verbal attacker. Security came up, and suddenly all the adults in the school office were paying attention.

"What kind of school is this?" I yelled as I held on to my out-of-control nephew, who was still swinging.

"Ma'am, calm down. We have everything under control," a man said as they gathered the other boys and pulled them out of the office.

"Well, it sure doesn't seem like it. That boy just verbally attacked me and threatened my nephew! So don't tell me to calm down. This is a disgrace."

"Ma'am I'm sorry you feel that way. I'm Mr. Walker, the vice principal. Please step in my office." I followed him, and I remained standing.

"What kind of insane asylum are you running, Mr. Walker?"

"We didn't allow Brandon to be attacked. I believe the altercation is stemming from some ongoing disagreement. Brandon, what is going on with you and Semaj?"

"Man, he keeps saying things to me every day, and I've tried to ignore him, but he wanted to fight me, and he thought because he had Jahlil and Damon with him, I was going to back down."

"Brandon, you're going to have to find another way. All this fighting could get you suspended, if not expelled," Mr. Walker replied.

"They attacked my nephew! You're not going to suspend him for defending himself."

"I didn't say I was going to suspend him. I said he could be suspended. Because Brandon was not the aggressor, he won't be. However, in the future, Brandon, you will have to try to stay out of these types of situations."

Brandon nodded. "I know. I tried, Mr. Walker. That's why

I called my mom, and I was on my way to the office when they came at me."

"But you have to control your anger," Mr. Walker advised. "Some people make me mad every day, but I can't go around knocking and punching people out. If I did, I wouldn't be able to be here, because I'd be in jail. So what you have to do is learn to control your anger and attitude. Because this is high school, and it's time to be responsible and start thinking about your future. What do you want to do when you graduate?"

Brandon looked at him with a straight face and said, "I was thinking about going pro playing either basketball or football."

"Basketball or football, Brandon?" I looked over at my nephew. I didn't want to break his poor little heart, but the last time I saw him on the court, he wasn't that good. Especially not good enough to play professionally.

I guessed I wasn't the only disgusted person in the room. Mr. Walker closed his office door and said, "Brandon, that sounds good, but you always have to have a backup plan. Just in case something goes wrong. What else would like to do?"

"I don't like to do anything besides hang with my friends and play ball."

"Brandon, you're interested in other things, right?" I asked.

"No, all I want to be is either be a basketball or a football player, or maybe a rapper."

A rapper? Really, Brandon? I thought as I became alarmed. I couldn't believe that my nephew had the same dumb fantasy as a million other little black boys.

"Again, that sounds good, but what are some other possible career choices, other than in the entertainment field?" Mr. Walker asked.

Brandon shrugged. "I just really want to make a lot of money, and I know football and basketball players make money."

"But attorneys make money, and so do doctors," Mr. Walker pointed out. "They make a lot of money, and their careers are longer, because they can't get cut because of an injury or because they are not fast enough. My brother Micah is a neurosurgeon. Do you know what kind of doctor that is?"

"No."

"Well, he is a doctor that operates on his patients' brains, and he makes more money than most football players.

"Really?"

"Yeah, really. How about you start hanging out with me on Saturdays, so I can introduce you to my brother and people like him so you can get some other ideas of what you might want to do? How does that sound?"

Brandon nodded. "I guess all right. How long do you have to go school to be a doctor?"

"Well, you have four years of college then four years of medical school. Then you have your residency. Maybe ten years give or take a few, but then you have a career for a lifetime."

"Okay, I want to meet your brother, but I have to ask my mom."

"Okay, we will arrange it."

"His mother won't mind. He can attend. Thank you for inviting him, Mr. Walker."

I was really impressed with Mr. Walker. He was able to get Brandon thinking in a matter of minutes. Brandon wasn't going to be suspended and I could return to work.

"No, thank you. It takes a village, right? I'm glad you were able to come up and support your nephew," he said, smiling as he looked over at me and then back over at Brandon. "You'd be surprised how many times you call a student's house and no one shows up."

"No, we won't do that in my family. Any problems, just call me and I'll be right up."

"I'm not even going to have to call your aunt, am I, Brandon?" Mr. Walker asked.

"No," Brandon assured him.

"No, what, Brandon?"

"No, sir."

"Well, it was very nice meeting you," Mr. Walker said.

"Likewise. Again, any issues, call me. His mother is working, and I might be able to respond quicker," I said and gave him my card.

"Will do. Brandon, walk your aunt to the door, and come back to the office so I can write you a note to go back to class."

CHAPTER 43

Dana

"Good morning. May I have Dana Turner, please?"

"This is she."

"Yes, this is Mr. Walker, from your nephew's school."

"Is he in trouble again?" I sighed.

"No, not this time. As a matter of fact, I haven't had any issues with Brandon since we met. He's been stopping in my office, and we've been talking about things. I was calling to see if you were interested in participating in a career day panel of women in business for our young ladies. I saw that you are a marketing executive on your business card and, well, our girls need to see examples of successful women."

"Of course. What do I need to do or bring?"

"Not much. I just want our students to get an idea of what your everyday workday is like for you, and you could possibly just answer a few questions."

I wrote the time and date down and thanked him for inviting me. I guess I could give the students a few hours of my day.

I remembered career day when I was in school. It was just an opportunity to get dressed up, not to have to go to class, and be bored to death by peoples' parents talking about their job. I hoped my job was interesting enough to keep the students' attention.

The Career Day was set up in the large library of the school. On my panel there was an attorney, a police officer, and a veterinarian. We all spoke about what we did and then the students were able to ask us questions. At first no one asked any questions, then a young lady stood up and said, "I want to know: are y'all rich and what kind of cars do you drive?"

The other women on the panel didn't answer, so I took the microphone and responded. "What's your name?" I asked.

"Charae."

"Okay, Charae, to answer your first questions, I do make a very good living and I drive a nice car, but I'm not rich." I heard someone yell out if you're not rich then you're poor, and the other students started laughing. I laughed a little because it was funny.

"My job is to make you want to buy something I'm selling." I looked at the audience of attentive students and asked Charae to come up to the front of the library. She walked up to me, and I picked up a thick book I saw to the side of me. "Now, what I want you to do is sell me this book."

She bent over and laughed nervously and said, "Hold on, okay? Hold up. What do you want me to do?"

"I want you to tell me why I should buy this book, why I have to have it, and make me want to buy it."

She spoke into the microphone. "You should buy this book because it is nice and it is thick and it's green."

"Now, that was good, Charae. How many people would buy Charae's book?" A few students raised their hands. "Now, let me show you how I would sell this book. I would say, 'Charae, you need this book. It has four hundred and thirty-six pages. Have you ever had a book with this many pages? Do you know how much you will learn with this text compared to other books? This book is green and goes exactly with your beautiful eyes. Charae, this book is made for you.' Now, would you buy my book?"

"Yes."

"Why?"

"Because you made me think I needed it."

"Exactly. Good job. Everyone, give Charae a round of applause." Charae walked back to her seat, and other students' hands shot up. I tried to answer as many questions as I could before the next guest took over.

After my panel I walked to my table, where two young ladies were waiting to speak to me. Both were pretty and innocent looking. One was short, had light brown skin, and had her hair up in a long ponytail. Her browner, taller friend wore her hair in two French braids with a headband over them. I smiled, ready to answer all their marketing career questions.

"So how are you ladies doing?"

"We're fine," the taller girl said. "We just wanted to come over and tell you we liked your speech and wanted to tell you that your hair is cute."

The shorter girl asked, "What kind of hair is it?" It was not a question I was expecting, but at least I had people interested in me. The veterinarian was typing into her phone, waiting for someone to talk to her.

"Well, thank you again. It's a Remi Loose Deep Wave."

"So, like, is it fun at your job, selling stuff, and do you get dressed up every day?" the taller girl asked.

"I do, and it's fun most of the time."

"It seems like it is, and I like your shoes, too. My cousin got the same kind. They are Jessica Simpsons, right?" said the shorter girl.

"Yes, they are."

"I told you," she whispered to her friend.

I answered every question they had about my career and

style until they ran out of them. By that time Mr. Walker had approached the table, clapping his hands lightly.

"Bravo, Miss Turner. You were great. I'll buy whatever you are selling."

"Thanks. It is my job."

"I just had a young lady come up to me, saying, 'Mr. Walker, I think I want to be a marketing executive.' "

"That's great."

"I'm sure this morning, before you came, she didn't know what a marketing executive was. And now she does. People do not realize the importance of seeing a visual in front of them," he said.

"That's good. You're making me feel like I did something special today."

"You did, you really did, and I'd like to thank you. If you are not busy, I would like to invite to you one of my Temple alumni events, Real Men Sizzle, next Saturday."

"Oh, I've heard of that event. I'll try to make it. I'll bring my boyfriend," I said.

"Great. I'll expect you, then. And I will e-mail you with all the details."

"Thank you. I'll look for it. And right now I'm going to sneak out and go back to work," I said. Mr. Walker thanked me again for coming, and I began making my way out of the school.

Adam had plans to go see his sister Melissa in a play already, so I dragged Tiffany to the Real Men Sizzle event. The event was held at the African American Museum. There were photos and artwork of different eras of black history on the walls.

We walked in and I immediately spotted Mr. Walker. He looked so handsome and refined. His creamy whipped-mousse brown skin was flawless.

I waved to him. He began walking in our direction. He

was wearing a taupe suede jacket, with a peach shirt underneath.

"That's Brandon's principal."

"Wow, he is cute," Tiffany said.

"Thank you for coming, Ms. Turner. Make sure you get some of this good food."

"We will, and you're welcome. I'm a person of my word, and I have to support you, because my sister said she can see a change in Brandon already. Mr. Walker, this is my friend Tiffany. She is also an educator."

"Where?" he asked.

"Smedley Elementary in South Philly," Tiffany told him.

"I used to be in that district. I taught at Bryant. I enjoyed it, but I wanted to make a difference on a broader level. Eventually, I want to start my own school or nonprofit," he revealed.

"So you really want to save the world?" Tiffany laughed.

"You could say that, one kid at a time. I don't subscribe to the whole 'I made it, I'm good, and forget everyone else' mentality."

Tiffany nodded. "I say that, too, but then I look at my paycheck and say, 'Is it all worth it?' "

"Of course it is worth it. You make a difference every day. My parents were educators. They didn't make a lot of money, but they stressed that education was everything." He paused for a moment. "It is not about us. You really can't have the mind-set 'I have mine.' No, because what will happen is the same kid that you didn't help will hit you in your head in ten years and rob you. I don't know—maybe it is me, but I can't eat in front of a hungry man."

Tiffany nodded again. "I agree."

"One of my brothers is a surgeon, my sister is completing her law degree, and my baby brother is a freshman at Morehouse."

"Your parents must be proud to have four successful children. How did they get all of you to do well?" Tiffany asked.

"No sports or outside activities until our school work was done. And it paid off. They raised us to make a difference. My attitude is this: I can easily get my corporate six-figure job." He looked over at me and gave me the eye. "No offense, Ms. Turner."

"Mr. Walker, none taken. I don't exactly make six figures yet." I laughed.

Then he continued on. I wanted to scream, *Can I be part of the conversation?* They were going back and forth about theories and solutions to the problems with education, and I couldn't add anything to the conversation.

"I'll be back," he finally said, placing his hand on the small of my back. Moments later he returned with a gorgeous caramel-skinned man.

"Ladies, this is my very good friend, Jacob Price. He is one of the city's best attorneys. If you ever get into a situation, you should give him a call."

"We try to stay out of trouble," Tiffany joked.

"That's true, but sometimes trouble can find you." Mr. Walker's handsome friend reached in his suit pocket and handed us both his business card.

After some small talk Jacob began, filling us in on his last horrible relationship and how he was looking for a girlfriend. But it was hard for him to date with his long hours. I couldn't imagine why he was single; he was perfect.

Tiffany whispered to me, "Oh my God I'm in love."

I said, "Me too."

I wasn't sure who he was interested in, but then he made his move on Tiffany. He looked in her direction and asked, "So, do you think we can go out see a movie or whatever you like?"

"Sure, okay. When?"

"Whenever; give me a call any night, but Thursdays I teach a law class at CCP, so any other night."

"Okay, sounds good." Tiffany smiled, and Jacob walked

away. As soon as he was a couple of feet away, Tiffany ripped up his card.

"Why did you do that?"

"Because, I don't need any temptation. I don't want to cheat. Where was he when I was single and alone?"

"So you are not single anymore?"

"No, I am not. Solomon and I had the conversation, right after his grandmother's funeral. How about you and Adam?"

"Well, we never had the talk, but I'm there all the time, and he introduced me to his mom and his sisters as his girlfriend, so I guess I'm his girlfriend."

"Well, isn't this amazing? The two single girls both have men, and now we are at an event with a room full of all these good-looking, successful black men in suits."

"Tiffany, I was sitting here thinking the same thing," I said as I looked around the room.

"And they're not married, either. I've been doing hand scans, and no rings. I've never seen so many men I would date in one room. We were looking in all the wrong places. Shit. Don't we have some girlfriends to call to tell them to get down here right now? And Brandon's principal, he is great. Whew, that man looks good."

"Yeah, he is a good-looking man," I said, inhaling all of him from across the room.

Throughout the evening Mr. Walker came to check up on Tiffany and me, making sure we were comfortable.

"Thank you for inviting me out, Mr. Walker," I told him when Tiffany and I were getting ready to leave.

"I'm glad you were able to make it. Uh, Ms. Turner, I know I'm being a little forward, but is it possible for me to see you again, outside of Brandon and school?"

"No, I'm sorry. I'm involved. But thank you."

Chapter 44

Yvette

The kids had left for two weeks. They were with their father in Florida for Christmas break, and I was about to cash my first paycheck. It wasn't a lot of money, but I was so happy. I was so blessed to be working again. It was going to take me a few months to pay everyone back, but at least now I could see the light at the end of the tunnel.

I wanted to get out and treat Geneva for being such a supportive friend. Everyone needed someone like her to have their back. I invited her to try the soul food place that I had delivered to on Germantown Avenue. We met at the bar inside the restaurant and were immediately seated at a table by the window.

"You look good," she said as she gave me a quick hug.

"I feel good. I feel like the weight is starting to lift, literally and figuratively."

"That's great. I started to invite Stacey, but I didn't know how you would feel."

"I'm glad you didn't."

"You don't understand how sorry Stacey is."

"I don't care. If she didn't mean it, fine, but she shouldn't have let it slip," I said. "Plus, she is more your friend than mine. If you are not around, I don't call her. I remained friends with her all these years because of you."

"Well, I'm so happy everything is good now. I was getting scared that you might really kill Phil and go to jail, and then I would have to put my house up to bond you out."

We both laughed, then I said, "Then I won't tell you that I almost burned his dad's house down. I had the gasoline, but not the match. He doesn't know how close he came to being in the burn unit."

"What the hell, Yvette? I'm not sure I even want to know."

"Yes, you do not want to know. I'm now only having positive thoughts," I said as I bowed my head playfully, like I was praying.

"So what's good here?"

"The owner said they are known for their buffalo shrimps and wings. I don't know where the waitress is."

The gentleman that owned the restaurant was going from table to table, checking on his patrons. He came over to our table and said, "Ladies, how you doing this evening?"

"Better if we had some drinks in front of us," I snapped. "And I should get better service because I'm your delivery lady, Mr. William Nelson."

"Call me William. I hate Mr. Nelson, and I recognize that pretty face. Let me take your drink order, since no one has been over here yet. My apologies—we are a little short-staffed tonight."

A few minutes later he came back out with our drinks, and the waitress rushed over to take our dinner order.

After spending so many months in the apartment and not being able to treat myself to dinner, it felt so good to be served and to catch up with my friend. The food was delicious, and we couldn't finish everything and had the remainder of our dinner boxed and bagged. I asked the waitress for our bill. She told us the owner had taken care of it.

I was touched. "Aw, that was nice. Let me go over there and say thank you."

I approached William and said, "Just wanted to say thank you, and the food was really great. I'm going to tell everyone about your establishment."

"Thank you. I would appreciate that. Here. Take a few cards. I was wondering if I could possibly take my delivery lady out."

He wasn't my type, but I gave him my number. I walked back to Geneva and told her he'd asked for my number.

"That would be good—a nice, distinguished gentleman. He's not that bad looking, either. I would give him about forty-something. You know he has money. He owns the place."

"We'll see. I don't really feel like being bothered by a man right now."

I knew William was over forty, but someone should have updated him on dating protocol. But anyone should know that after your first half a dozen calls went unanswered, you should leave a message and wait for your call to be return. He wasn't getting the hint, so I answered.

"Hey. How you doing, Yvette? This is William."

"I'm good."

"I've been trying to reach you."

"I know, but I have children and a life; so I'm sorry, but I'm not always near my phone."

"Right. Yeah, I know you're a busy woman, and I see you a feisty one, too. I just wanted to say hello and tell you it was real good to meet you. I wanted to say something to you when you came in last week, but I wanted to keep it professional. So when I saw you again, I couldn't let you pass me by."

"Is that so?"

"Yeah, so when will you be available for me to show you a good time?"

"I don't know—give me a call, maybe Friday or Saturday."

CHAPTER 45

Crystal

Rell's middle name now was work. He worked so much, like he was making up for lost time. I was happy he had a job, and it was making everything a lot easier on me. But I missed having my boo bear with me, and not at work, but you can't have everything. I was decorating my white Christmas tree with bright, colorful lights and ornaments, trying to get things done for the holidays. I would get so much more done if Rell wasn't fixing everything that Little Shareef broke and was able to help me.

I went into the kitchen to check on him, to see how he was making out with the stopped-up drain. Shareef had put something down there. I saw Rell plunging the sink with long, hard strides, yet the water still would not move. And the only thing I could think was, *If Little Shareef breaks another got damn thing in my house, I don't know what I'm going to do! Angel and Big Reef still think I'm their babysitter. Hello, I have three children of my own.* She always said, "Girl, I got you. We are going to babysit for you," but this had not happened yet.

After numerous attempts at plunging the sink, Rell realized the clog wasn't budging, and it was time for him to get ready for work. He left the sink full of undrained water. I followed him upstairs and said, "I don't know why Little Shareef has to come over all the time and break everything."

"Mercedes is over here just as much as Shareef, and he doesn't break things on purpose."

"But my niece doesn't punch holes in the wall or stop the sink up. I'm not used to this type of stuff in my—"

"In your what? Go ahead and say it. In your what? Where is all this 'my stuff' coming from lately, Crystal? That's my nephew and he is a kid and they break things. It happens."

"All right. I'm not saying anything else, but what time are they coming to get him?"

Rell scrunched his shoulders, tied his black work sneakers, buttoned his evergreen-colored work shirt, which had GLOVER stitched on the pocket, and said, "I don't know. I'm going to work. Call Angel and tell her to come get him."

I followed him to the front door. "And what about the sink, Rell?"

"I'll get on it when I come home."

As I watched him walk out the door to the truck, I realized there were some things I really had to get used to. One of them was waiting on a man to do something. I'd been on my own since Jewel's father went to jail, and I was just so used to getting things done. I was not waiting for him to come home to have this sink fixed. I did not have time to look at a sink full of dirty water. I was going to call a plumber.

By the time I heard Rell come in the house, I was exhausted from dealing with the plumber, kids, decorating, and washing clothes. I heard him call out from downstairs, "Eh, Crystal, how you fix this sink?" I came down the steps to see him standing in the kitchen with this metal coiled pole thing in his hand.

"I called a plumber."

"Why would you do that? Didn't I tell you I was going to

fix it? You had me drive across town to pick this thing up, when you could have at least called me and said that you got it done."

"Well, Rell I didn't know what you were going to do. I didn't have time to wait. I had to cook and wash clothes."

"But I told you I was going to do it. Next time say something so I won't be running around."

Christmas morning, our house looked like a toy store. There were big, colorful, blue, green and red metallic wrapped boxes with bows on the top.

Last night, on Christmas Eve, while we were wrapping the last of the gifts, Rell surprised me with an early gift. He took my hand and removed my wedding ring and replaced it with a big diamond cluster ring. I was in tears when he said, "Every year, boo, I'm going to upgrade you."

I felt good, because I had a real wedding ring, and then bad, because I had bought him only a robe and more slippers for Christmas, but he told me he'd wanted something comfortable to wear when he came in the house after work.

As for Nasir, I think he stopped breathing when he discovered Rell had got him a PlayStation 3 and an Xbox, a bike, and cars. And Jewel, she had dolls' clothes, a little computer, and a little pink cell phone There were bikes, games, and Barbies. He bought Kori clothes and a bunch of baby toys. I didn't know how he'd managed it. I knew he made money at that job: the overtime made our Christmas look like we were rich. I wasn't really expecting all of this. With my gifts and the kids' gifts, there wasn't enough space hardly to walk.

"So I have one more gift for y'all," Rell said. "Nasir, put on shoes. Jewel, you going to love it."

"Oh my God, Rell. What is it?" Jewel asked. They were jumping all around the living room.

And then I went from happy to what the hell? Rell had a nasty dog with a bow run into my house.

"A puppy?" Jeweled shrieked.

Rell nodded. "Yes, a dog."

Nasir got on the floor with him and was playing with him and hugging him.

I didn't want to end the love session with man's best friend. But I had to tell Rell, "Babe, no dogs in my house. I hate dogs."

"But I'll clean up after him. Look, the kids love him."

"No, Rell, they are dirty and they stink. I hate animals. I don't want no filthy animals in my house."

"Fine, I'll take him back."

Chapter 46

Yvette

William was far from the kind of guy that I would date and that was exactly why I thought I should go out with him. I couldn't get it right any other time, so maybe I needed to date differently. At least it was worth a shot and I wasn't doing anything else.

He was outside my door promptly at 6:30 p.m. He opened my door and closed it like the gentleman he was. Up close William was a medium shade of brown, with a little darkness underneath both eyes from long hours and hard work. His aura seemed older, not like my dad, but a lot different than what I was used to. I wasn't sure if I liked it yet.

"Did you have somewhere special you wanted to go? Because I was thinking maybe we'd ride down to Atlantic City, get a bite to eat. Get on the table for a little bit."

"Okay, that sounds good," I said.

He was driving a black Mercedes-Benz S-class with white interior. The inside smelled like strawberries, and the car rode smoothly. The whole forty-five-minute drive he played old-school R & B. He was in his own groove, bobbing along to music I kind of remembered from back in the day.

"So do you go to AC often?" I asked him, breaking the silence.

"When I can. Believe it or not, this drive is relaxing for me. Takes me away from all the craziness of the restaurant."

"Why don't you have more help?"

"Do you know how hard it is to keep good people? I'm constantly hiring and firing people. I'm forty-seven. I've been working since I was thirteen. When I was growing up I knew I had to work if I wanted something. But this younger generation don't know or understand hard work. They come in and play around. They want to get paid for showing up."

"I know what you mean. I used to run an HR department, but then I got divorced from my second husband and had to find a new job."

"You've been married two times, and I've never met anyone I loved enough to marry once."

"Yes, second means two," I answered, becoming slightly irritated.

"Whoa. Should I be concerned?"

I wasn't about to let this old man make me feel any kind of way for being divorced. Since he wanted to be a smart, I decided to play the insult game with him.

"No. I think I should be more concerned about a man that's forty-seven that has never married. But to be honest, you don't look forty-seven. I've never dated an older man."

"I'm going to take that as a compliment. I'm like a good-running car. You wouldn't know what year I was unless somebody tells you. I get thirty-five, sometimes forty."

"I definitely wouldn't give you thirty-five with those strands of gray hair."

"This I had since I was twenty-seven." He laughed and I laughed and the game was over.

We arrived at the busy casino. He turned his car over to the valet, and we walked into Harrah's casino. He went to a table and laid down stacks of one-hundred-dollar bills and the dealer dispensed him stacks of chips. Before he started playing, he handed me ten twenties and chips to play with. There was no way I was going to gamble all the money away. He would never know if I lost or kept the money.

I cashed in the chips and walked around the casino floor a bit, and then located William at the craps tables. His sleeves were rolled up, and he was shaking dice in his hand. It appeared like he was doing well: his chips were in a few rows stretching in front of him. He must have rolled the right number, because the second the dice hit the green table, the entire table erupted with a big, loud "Yeah!" The man next to him gave him a high five.

"What just happened?" I asked William.

"I rolled my point, and we all had a few hundred on it."

"So you are winning?"

"I'm making out pretty good," he said as he turned his attention back to the dealer, who was giving him back the dice once more. My father used to always say, "Never bother a man while he's gambling." William was gambling and winning, and I didn't want to break his flow, so I left the table.

I made my way over to a blackjack table. The dealer handed me twenty-one a few hands in a row, and then the dealer turned on me and I lost back-to-back hands. I was done with blackjack and was off to the slot machines. I went and had a seat with all the senior citizens on the slots. I slid in a twenty and then pulled the handle aimlessly. I would probably give William another hour before I let him know I was ready to go. I looked around to see what the other people on my senior citizens' row were doing. I kept pressing the buttons and pulling the lever. So far I had won forty dollars. Not bad, but after an hour of hitting the minimum bet of a quarter, I was back down to zero. I slid another twenty dollars in, and began pressing the buttons and pulling the lever again. Shortly, after the machine started making noise and three sevens appeared on the screen in front of me. All these people started surrounding the machine and me.

The older woman that was sitting next to me said, "You just won seventy-five hundred dollars."

"Seventy-five hundred?" I repeated to her. "Are you sure? I only put one dollar on the line."

"That's okay. You still won the jackpot."

People were coming over to me, congratulating me. Then an attendant came and asked me for my license. I was shocked and about to cry. My luck had finally changed.

Chapter 47

Yvette

The New Year would be here in a few hours, and I could not wait. My children called me earlier to wish me a Happy New Year and tell me that they were going to the fireworks with their father. I was comfy on the sofa reflecting on how crazy the past year had been. Geneva had invited me over to bring in the New Year with her family, but I wasn't leaving the house. All I wanted was my glass of wine, a little television, and relaxation. That would be the perfect New Year. The phone buzzed on the floor and I answered to hear William say, "Good evening, beautiful. Do you have plans?"

"Hey, William. No. I will probably be asleep when the clock strikes twelve."

"Oh no. I don't want you to be alone on New Year's Eve. My buddy and his wife are having a New Year's get-together. Why don't you join me?"

I thought about it and said, "Why not?"

I met William at the get-together, which was a really an old head cabaret. Which meant everyone had to bring their own food and liquor for the guests at their table. It was held at a hall that hadn't been renovated since the eighties. I think the average age of the attendees was fifty-two. I couldn't believe that William had brought me out of my house to witness this "Step in the Name of Love," "Cupid Shuffle," old-head line-dancing fest. It was horrible. All the men were dressed in their Sunday best Easter suits with the hats to match. The ladies were snapping their fingers while line dancing in kitten heels. No one would be able to tell them they or their wigs weren't sharp. I felt like I was with my sugar daddy, the way William was prancing me around the party, introducing me as his lady to everyone he knew. A lot of the men gave him approving looks; a lot of the women weren't as kind with their stares.

We had a seat at his friend's table, and he asked me if I wanted anything to eat and drink. I said yes and asked him to get me a double shot of Hennessy and some macaroni and cheese. I was going to need something to keep me interested in this party. One of the ladies from Cupid Shuffle line came over and asked William about the restaurant and his granddaughter. As soon as she left, I inquired about him being a grandfather.

"Yeah, I have custody of my granddaughter."

"Why do you have custody of her?"

"My son and her mother are in jail. What can I say? I sent him away to college. He wasn't doing what he was supposed to. I told him to come on home. He stayed down there and got himself in a bunch of trouble."

"Wow."

"Yeah, he didn't even tell me he had a baby. Of course, I went to get her when I found out Child Services were about to place her. I figured I'd keep her for a few months until their trial was over, but now it's been seven years," he said, shaking his head

"How long is your son going to be away?"

"Another three years, but I'm so used to her now. I don't

know if I will let them take her when they are released. She is nine and in the fourth grade."

"My daughter is the same age. Maybe they can meet up."

"That would be good. She needs other girls her age to be around. She is so quiet and never goes out to play."

"So who has your granddaughter now?"

"I have a lady that picks her up for me. She used to work for me and needed a job."

"So she's like a nanny."

"Yeah, Connie's way more expensive, but I need her. I'm constantly checking in on my businesses, and the restaurant keeps me very busy. She didn't have a car, so I had to buy her one, and I give her gas money to get Jalena around to all her activities." I drank my second shot of Henny and began to enjoy William's company more. By the end of the night he got me on the dance floor, stepping and twirling the night away. We even had our picture taken by the picture man after he bought me a rose from the flower guy. I had a good time bringing in my new year with William.

Chapter 48

Yvette

Whew! That seventy-five hundred was so needed, but it also went as fast as it came. I think I had like four hundred dollars left. I paid everyone back, bought the kids gifts, treated myself to a few things, and that was it.

I was just getting off work and was on my way to Lena's to see William. We'd been spending a lot of time together the last month or so. He may have been forty-seven, but he didn't show his age, and he was really sweet and attentive. The other day we met at a day spa. I didn't know how he knew my body needed that attention. He was there getting his monthly deep-tissue massage and invited me for the works. After our massage he stopped in Neiman Marcus to pick up his suit, and we ended up shopping for me also. I didn't want anything. I mean, I did, but I didn't want him to spend a bunch of money on me, but he told me he liked to spoil whoever he was with. He had one of the salesladies come over to me and help me shop. I stopped fighting it and let him spend two thousand dollars on me and another fifteen hundred on himself.

When I stepped into Lena's, everyone catered to me like I

was a queen, because I was William's friend. While I waited for the hostess to get William, the new bartender placed a napkin in front of me and began flirting. He was clean-shaven and smelled good. He had a bald head and almond-colored skin. He would be my type of guy if he wasn't working for William.

"What are you having, beautiful?"

"I don't know. What do you recommend?" I asked.

"I think you might like my famous tropical rum. It's sweet, it goes down smooth, and it makes you want more."

"Sounds good to me. I'll take it."

Right as I said, "I'll take it," William came out and kissed me on my cheek. He asked me how my day was going while giving my neck a quick massage. The bartender placed my drink in front of me, and William said, "By the way, Andre, I see you have met my lady."

"Yes, Mr. Nelson, we just met."

"Okay. Watch how you observe her when she comes in here." I was embarrassed, and the bartender laughed nervously.

"No, Mister Nelson, I was just making her a drink."

I tapped William on his hand and told him to stop. "So how is business tonight?"

"Business is always good on Thursday nights. It starts picking up. Are you cooking tonight?"

"No, probably not."

"Order something for yourself and kids. Here's the menu."

Looking down at the menu, I said, "I don't know if I'm going to be able to be with you."

"Why not?"

"Because you'll have me fat with all this food."

He laughed and said, "No need to worry. I like a thicker woman. Plus, it is too late. I'm already into you. And all my friends said we made a beautiful couple. They couldn't believe I had a girlfriend who's thirty-three."

"So that's what I am. A young, sweet thang to you," I joked.

"No, you are much more. Order something and call me when you get in. I have to hurry up and get back in there. You know we are short staffed again." He left, then turned back to me and reached in his pocket, pulled money out, and handed me four one-hundred-dollar bills.

"What's this for?"

"For you. Treat yourself to something."

"Okay, but I don't want you to think every time I see you, you have to give me money."

"You didn't ask. I gave it to you. Now take it," he said as he gave me a deep, strong squeeze of a hug and returned to the back. Before he left, he joked with the bartender that he was still watching him. The sexy bartender didn't even look over at me anymore.

I went home, and the apartment was clean. Mimi was doing her homework, and there was a bowl of chicken noodle soup, garlic bread, and hot tea waiting for me. Although I had dinner for them already, I didn't want to disappoint them and not eat the lovely meal they had prepared for me.

"Mom, I know you had a hard day at work. We cleaned the house and made dinner for you. Dad told us to start helping you out more," Brandon said.

"I really appreciate this. Thank you." I gave them both hugs.

"Oh, Mom, I forgot to ask you. Is it okay if I go with Mr. Walker to the art museum? He is on his way over," Brandon said.

"That will be fine," I said. His vice principal, Mr. Walker, had been mentoring him and you could definitely notice the change in him. Brandon had a dad, but it was good to have someone close who could get through to him. Doug asked me what was up with Mr. Walker and why was he paying so much attention to Brandon. I told him I didn't get the pervert vibe from him at all and that he was just a good principal going the extra mile.

Mr. Walker knocked on the door. I greeted him and asked him to come in.

"I thank you so much, Mr. Walker. Does he need money for anything?"

"No, we are only going to be gone for an hour or so, and I'll bring him right back."

"I really appreciate the way you're helping my son. He doesn't get to see his dad often, because he is in Florida. So it is really nice for him to be around a strong male figure. Since you've been mentoring him I've noticed a change. The other day he said he was thinking about going to college, then law school to become an attorney. That's amazing, because before he just wanted to run stuff, and now he wants to be a lawyer."

Mr. Walker laughed and said he was glad he could help.

Chapter 49

Dana

"Aunt Dana, me and Mr. Walker are at the art museum. Can you meet up with us?"

"Uh, how long are you going to be there? I'm still at work, trying to complete a few things, Brandon."

"Mr. Walker said we should be here for about an hour."

I agreed to meet them. After my long day at work I really didn't feel like going anywhere, but I wanted to support Brandon.

I met them on the steps of the art museum, the ones that were made famous by the movie *Rocky.* Immediately, I noticed my nephew was dressed like a miniature, casual version of Mr. Walker. He was wearing a navy blue peacoat, pants, and hard-bottom shoes.

We walked around the museum, admiring the artwork. Some of it looked like something I or one of my nieces or nephew could have drawn, but beauty was in the eye of the beholder.

We stopped in front of a collection by a painter named Bartolomeo Vivarini. He was a painter from the Renaissance era. While we were admiring the large paintings on the wall,

Brandon went to the restroom, leaving me alone to talk with Mr. Walker.

"Ms. Turner, do you know anything about this painter?"

"No."

"Do you see the texture? His painting reflects anger. His mother abandoned him, and he was an orphan on the streets of Paris. That's where all his inspiration came from."

"Really?" I asked, seeing new depth in the picture and seeing it with a different set of eyes.

"No, I just made all of that up. I don't know anything about him."

"You're really funny, Mr. Walker. So are you making my nephew a clone of you?"

"No. I had some old things, and I gave them to him."

"That was really nice of you. He really needed a male role model in his life. He pays my father no attention. I can see the change in his demeanor and behavior already."

"Your sister mentioned the same thing earlier."

"Well, I'm glad I met up with you guys. I haven't been here in years, and this was really nice," I confessed.

"When I drop Brandon off, would you like to get coffee at Brownie Joe's and discuss you possibly mentoring some of the young ladies at the school? They are still talking about you. You made a really big impression on them."

"They are? Okay. I'll meet you at the Brownie Joe's on Nineteenth Street."

We met at the Brownie Joe's coffeehouse. It was a small café with delicious desserts and great coffee. Mr. Walker was still trying to convince me to become a mentor, but I told him I didn't have the time.

"So, Mr. Walker, do you pay this much attention to all your students? How do you do it?"

"Yeah, I do, especially the students I see with a lot of potential and who have pretty aunts."

"So are you trying to use my nephew to get to me, Mr. Walker?"

"Maybe, and Brandon is gone, so you can just call me Marcus."

"Like the porn star Mr. Marcus?" I said jokingly.

"Exactly, like him. Are you familiar with his work?"

I blushed and said no, and we both laughed as my phone began to ring. I answered without looking, still giggling, and said, "Hello."

"Hey, babe. Where are you? I called you a few times," Adam's voice said from the other end.

"Adam, I had to meet up with my nephew and his mentor. I'll call you when I get home."

"It's pretty late for a school meeting."

"Yeah, its running a little over; we're almost done. I'll call you when I get home." I hung up the phone and Marcus began inquiring about my relationship.

"I'm assuming that was your man."

"Yup, it was."

"How long have you been together?"

"About four months."

"Only four months. So you are still getting to know him. Adam—that's a different name. I don't know any black Adams."

"I know a few, but my Adam is not black."

"That's interesting, because you don't take me as the kind of sister that would date other. No offense, but don't you want a strong man that looks like you standing next to you? I have nothing against interracial relationships, but I just only date black women. I'm not attracted to any other kinds of women. My boys date the rainbow, that's them. I don't."

"Well, for us it just happened, and I think you have to be open minded. And my last boyfriend was a black man and he was a jerk. I bought me and my ex tickets to see Wade Devon. I love Wade Devon. He knew that and, anyway, an hour before the show he called me while I was getting dressed to tell me couldn't make it."

"So you did you get to see Wade Devon?"

"Yeah, I did, but it wasn't the same seeing him with my

girlfriend. He offered me money for the tickets, but I was just, like, it's over. At that point I'd had enough of him. So when you get a good guy, his race doesn't matter."

"Well, I'm glad you found someone who treats you well."

"I am too! How about you, Mr. Walker? Where is your girlfriend? I know you had ladies beating down your door since you were a kid."

"No, not exactly. I was a weird kid. Some might say a geek. I didn't really start coming into my own until college. You know what else I used to think when I was growing up?"

"What?"

"That the news people knew God, because they knew the forecast. I said, 'Hey, they must call up God and say, "What's the weather tomorrow and the next day?"' And I think I believed in Santa Claus and the tooth fairy until I was in the eighth grade."

"That's funny."

"Don't laugh at me, Ms. Turner, Brandon's aunt. So I think I missed the whole game most men learn. You know pickup lines, how to act with and attract pretty women." He smiled as he looked across the table at me. "To be honest, I'm ready to get married. I can't wait to start a family."

"It will happen."

"I know it will. I witnessed a good marriage. My parents'. My father loves my mom. They've been married almost forty years, and I just want the same."

"Wow, my parents have been married thirty-five years, and my dad really loves my mother, too. I think relationships today are just a lot different. Men do not know how to be men. If my dad sees a woman on the side of the road, he stops and helps her out, doesn't ride by her. Or I've seen men let a door swing right in a lady's face, instead of holding it open. I've had that happen."

"But you know what, Mrs. Turner? It all boils down to examples and what you see. If people don't know, they can't do better."

"And you're very right about that, Mr. Walker—I mean, Marcus."

There was something so alluring about Mr. Marcus Walker. He was tall, dark, handsome, worked in the community, and wanted to start a family. He was the man I had wanted and had dreamed of before I met Adam.

CHAPTER 50

Crystal

"Get in the car. I have to show you something," Rell instructed me.

I wanted to sleep in on my Saturday, but he insisted, so we all loaded in the car. I didn't have any idea where he was taking us, but twenty-five minutes later the car stopped in front of a single brick home with a driveway in Springfield, Pennsylvania.

"Who lives here, Rell?" I asked.

"Just come with me." He grabbed my hand, and we all followed him to the front door of the home. I thought he would ring the bell or knock. Instead he took a key out of his pocket and opened the door.

"Boo, on my way to work for the past month or so, I saw them working on this house. I kept saying, 'That's a nice house. One day I'm going to get a house like that.' So then I saw this sign go up for rent. I called the number and got a tour inside. I started looking around and was like, 'I really like this place.' I didn't sign anything, but I told the owner I had to show it to my wife. But what do you think, boo?"

"It's okay, but why would you make a decision like this

without me?" I said, arms folded, looking around the freshly painted white rooms.

"I didn't sign anything yet. I just think this is what we need . . . a place of our own. It has four bedrooms. Come look at this big yard, and the basement is already finished."

"I don't know about this. What I want even more than a house is you. It seems like all you ever do is work now, anyway, and with a house like this, you will work even more."

"Come here. I'm doing all this work so you . . . so we can have what we want. You deserve to have everything."

"I know, but I'd really rather just have you. This neighborhood looks really expensive. How much is the rent?"

"It's only fifteen hundred. I was talking with the landlord about my deposit."

"You gave the man a deposit, Rell? You just said you didn't. That's too much money!"

"Yeah, I did. I gave him the first month's rent."

"You're kidding me, right?" I said as I looked around. "What would make you do that?"

"Crystal, you know, eventually, we are going to need more space, and the kids can play back here. I can get them another dog."

"What about my house? And I don't want a dog around my baby. Dogs stink and you have to constantly clean up after them. You will be working all the time, so who is going to clean up after the dog? And what about my house?"

"I'll clean up after the dog and you can rent your house and this can be ours. And we can make the rules in our house, and it can be our new beginning. The owner wants to sell in a few years so we can eventually buy this."

"No, Rell, this house is nice, but I'm not interested, and I hope you get your money back," I said as I marched out of the house and back to the car. Who would go and do that? He was so damn stupid sometimes.

On the way back home, Rell was acting like a spoiled baby, and I did not care. He would get over it. I didn't want to move right now. I liked it where I lived now, and people didn't make rash decisions like that without speaking to their significant other.

Later that evening, I was in the bed waiting, for Rell to get in. I wanted to explain to him why I felt the way I did. He took a shower, put on his boxers and t-shirt and flipped on the television without acknowledging me. I knew he was still upset about the house, but I didn't really care.

"What's wrong with you, Rell?"

"Nothing," he said as he pointed the remote at the television and changed stations.

"There has to be. I'm sorry I didn't like the house, Rell. But we are a team, partners, and you need to tell me when you make a decision that is going to affect all of us."

"Like you always do, right? Please, Crystal. It's not the house. It's us. I feel like you are not the same person I met. It's, like, I can't understand you. I feel like we are hitting a block. Something has changed. Do I even make you happy any more?"

"There is nothing wrong with me, and I don't know what your problem is. Rell, come on please. I'm tired. I'm not going to argue about something so stupid."

"Crystal, do you want this marriage? Do you want me to leave?"

"What kind of question is that to ask me? I don't like a house you picked out on your own, so that means we should break up? I don't want you to leave, but if you want to, then fine."

"No, I don't want to leave."

"So why would you ask me something so damn ridiculous?"

"Because you have crazy mood swings, and I'm doing everything for you, working hard, making moves. I really am, Crystal, and yet all you do is complain about everything."

"What did you do for me that was so special? I've been on my own since twenty, and I can take care of myself. I don't need you or anybody else. Okay, Terell?"

"What did I do for you? Let me see. I married your ass for one. So your family could stop talking about you. Then I've been working, giving you money for the bills, paying for the car, making sure you had a ring, the kids had a nice Christmas, and I even tried to go out and get us a new house, and you just shut it down. Didn't even bother to look around the house. That's crazy."

"So I'm crazy now?"

"Look, I didn't call you crazy, but you always have to find the negative in everything. If I didn't know better, I would say I think you've been trying to force me out of here. It's like it scares you when there's no drama, like you don't know how to be happy."

"Yeah, whatever. I like drama. You sound stupid."

"It's not your fault, though. All you know is drama. Since I met you, it's been one thing after another. The bitches at your job, drama with your dad, your mom, your sisters, your baby father. Crystal, you argue with everyone. Do you want us to fail? Because it's like you trying your damnedest."

"Whatever. I knew all you were going to do was try to use me and leave me."

"I'm going to *use* you?" He chuckled. "I'm going to use you for what? Before I met you, I was a single man with no responsibility, and I'm trying to use you or get over on you? I need you to think about that. Ask yourself if that even makes sense."

I lay there in silence.

"Crystal, use you for what? Has it ever crossed your mind that none of those kids down the hall are mine, but each day I'm growing closer to them and loving them like they are my own, because I love their mom? Huh? Do you think about that when you talk that crazy shit? Are you happy with me,

Crystal? Because if I'm not making you happy and you don't need me and you can do everything on your own, anyway, I'll leave. I love you, but I don't want to be miserable."

"That's your choice, Rell. I really don't care if you stay or leave. You didn't do me any favors by marrying me. I was doing perfectly fine without you. You can do whatever you want."

"So you don't care if I leave." He sat up. I don't know if he was testing me or not, but it was not working.

"Not really." I said holding my ground.

"Ok, then. I'll leave since you don't give a fuck." He jumped out of the bed and started pulling his belongings out of the closet and drawers.

"I didn't say that, but since you are packing, fuck you and fuck this ring," I yelled, taking the ring off my finger and throwing it across the room.

"I see," Rell looked over at the ring on the floor, and just twisted his lips and marched over to the closet and filled his duffle bag with more clothes. I still didn't care.

"And just to let you know. I don't need you or any man. I've been holding everything down by myself for years. So pack your shit like you doing and go back to your mother's house."

"Okay, no problem. I will."

"Bye."

"Ok, if that's the way you wanted."

"I do."

"Yup, well if you have any questions and need to figure out why your life is the way it is, just look in the mirror," he said as he picked up his bag and walked out the house slamming the door so hard I could feel the vibration on the second floor. I looked out the window at him pulling off. He was gone, and I was not fazed.

CHAPTER 51

Yvette

William had slipped and fell at the restaurant and needed to stay off his ankle. He asked me if I could take his granddaughter to get her hair done since he couldn't get out. A little girl with big, bright, wide eyes answered the big double doors at William's home.

"Hello. You must be Jalena. I'm Miss Yvette."

She smiled at me and then screamed, "Daddy Pop, your lady friend here."

"So I'm your lady friend?" I said when William walked into the foyer.

"No. I told her to listen out for the door, because I was expecting you."

"Oh, so are you okay? Your ankle looks pretty bad."

"I'm feeling as good as anyone would feel after twisting my ankle on ice."

Eyeing his cane, I asked, "So do you have to use that thing?"

"No. I'd rather limp than walk with a cane. I don't need you calling me an old man."

"I didn't say anything. If you need it, you better use it. This is a big beautiful house." I was admiring all of the high ceilings and big windows that were allowing sunlight in.

"Thanks. Five bedrooms, but we only sleep in one. Jalena refuses to sleep alone so I pulled her bed in my room. Here's the money for your hair, and thanks for coming to get her. When you are ready for me to pick her up, I will. I have to come to Philly today anyway."

He walked us to the car. Jalena had these big, brown eyes and was so sweet and well mannered.

"Be good. Listen to Miss Yvette," he told Jalena.

"Yes, Daddy Pop," she said in a sweet baby voice. She got in the car, slid her seat belt across her legs, and began talking with Mercedes. They both were smiling and already talking about television shows they liked and their favorite subject in school.

The Dominican shop had salsa music playing to drown out the loud blow-dryers. It smelled of hair being pressed, hair sprays, and perfume conditioners. Luckily, it wasn't that crowded. We came in, and a lady speaking with a Hispanic accent said, "Have a seat, Mami. We will be right with you."

Mercedes and Jalena were still talking quietly among themselves. Jalena was first in the chair to be serviced. She must have been tender headed, because the entire time she got her head done she looked like she was about to cry.

"Ms. Yvette, it hurt!" Jalena moaned. "They burning my scalp." I tried to tell the woman styling Jalena's hair not to be so rough, but she didn't understand English very well, so another stylist came over and translated for her.

After having their hair conditioned and pulled, they both looked like little princesses, and they knew it. I got just a wash and a set, and from the hair salon, we went to the nail salon. It was time to get our manicures and pedicures.

After a day of beauty, the girls were making so much noise in that room back at home, like little animals. I walked in the room and they were jumping on the bed and giggling loudly.

"What are y'all doing?"

"Nothing, Mom, we are just seeing who can jump the highest."

"Stop jumping before one of you get hurt." My lecturing at them was interrupted by William ringing my phone.

"I'm on my way to come get her," William told me when I called him.

"She is fine. They are having a lot of fun. Here. Talk to her." I turned and yelled, "Jalena, your grandfather is on the phone."

She came running and took the phone. "Hey, Daddy Pop. Can I stay a little longer? I'm having fun."

She handed the phone back to me after a second, and then I asked him, "How is your ankle feeling?"

"It's feeling about the same. Well, I'll be getting out here shortly and I'll call you when I'm on my way."

William came to pick up Jalena and I didn't know how Brandon would react to meeting him. He had known only two men in my life. His dad and Phillip. After William got to my place, he walked up to Brandon and introduced himself.

Brandon stood up, said, "What's up?" respectfully, and shook his hand.

"Nice firm grip, that's what I like. How old are you again?"

"Fourteen."

"Okay. Maybe next summer you can come work for me," William told him.

"I want to work. My mentor, Mr. Walker, said that I should start looking for a summer job now. I'm going to tell him I already found one. Thank you. So what do I have to do?"

"Don't worry. You have the job. I really mean it, Brandon. Your mom won't let me forget."

Chapter 52
Dana

I was waiting at our place. The place that after months of dating, we had agreed we liked the service, the ambiance, and the selections. It was 6:15 p.m., and Adam hadn't arrived yet. Adam was never late, so I dialed him.

He answered, "Babe, I'll give you a call back in five minutes."

"But, Adam, hold up. I'm waiting at table twenty-seven for you. We were supposed to meet here at six."

"I was? Are you sure?"

"Yes, you asked me to put it on my calendar."

"I did, sweetheart? Oh, wow, I did. I'm so sorry. Listen, I can't make it. Dana, this is the beginning of our busy time of the year, and I'm swamped with work. With my uncle retiring, he sent all his people to me. I can't get out of here. I hope you understand."

"Of course I understand."

"Okay, I will call you later and maybe we can meet later in the week." I don't know why, but when I hung up with Adam I wanted to cry. Maybe I was having flashbacks of being played by Todd, or I was becoming accustomed to having a great boyfriend that never stood me up. I don't know what it was. However, I did know that Adam could not start make cancellations a habit. Because if he did, the next thing he would do is start start standing me up all the time and then start saying our relationship was getting too heavy and he needed space and it wasn't me. It was him. I was not going to allow that to happen. If he wanted to work, fine, but that didn't mean I was going to stay in the house, waiting on him. I made that mistake in my last relationship. Mr. Walker had invited me to go out with him. I'd declined, but now I was going to call him and tell him I could.

I met Mr. Walker at a trendy restaurant lounge in the Liberty Towers skyscraper, R2L. I rode the elevator to the thirty-seventh floor. Mr. Walker was waiting at a table overlooking the city. He stood up and gave me a quick hug. His cologne smelled so delicious, and his hug was so warm.

"What a beautiful view," he said.

"It really is pretty nice. It reminds me of place I ate at in LA. Yeah, it's almost identical . . . ," I said as my voice began to trail off as I looked out at the panoramic view of the city.

"Not that view. You."

I blushed and said, "Mr. Walker, you're starting early this evening."

"I am. Why wait? If I see something I want, I go after it."

"As you should, but not when you want is not available."

"My parent taught me nothing was out of reach. Were they wrong?"

"No, but . . ." I was saved by my ringing phone. Adam's timing was always perfect.

I didn't answer the first time, and then he called back.

"Dana, I feel real bad about standing you up, so let's meet up. Are you still downtown?"

"Uh, I am. I met Mr. Walker, Brandon's principal." He waved as if Adam could see him.

"Where are you?"

"We are at R2L."

"What are you doing there? That place is nice."

"Him and his girlfriend were in the area, and they were having drinks, and she is a mentor, so you know, babe, they are still trying to get me to join their mentor organization."

"Okay, well, just meet me at my office." I told him I would see him in a bit.

"You're a great liar, Ms. Turner. So our date is off. I feel kind of sad."

"You shouldn't. . . ." Before I could say anything else, he grabbed my face and began passionately kissing me. He pulled back. If I hadn't liked it so much and hadn't been mesmerized, I would have slapped him and told him I was involved and he could never do that again.

"Did you feel that?" he asked.

"Feel what?"

"That?" he asked, then reached over and kissed me again. I pulled away. "Mr. Walker, I have a boyfriend. I'm in a relationship and everything is not in your reach. Again some things are just not available. Have a good evening."

I walked out like I was angry, but I wasn't. I was more intrigued. I wanted to know more about Marcus. Why, why, why was I being tempted by this man? It was not fair.

CHAPTER 53

Yvette

"What if he is on Viagra or the other one, Cialis?" Geneva said, giggling on the other end of the phone. I began to picture erectile dysfunction commercials in my mind.

William was my friend, and the man I'd been seeing regularly and whose granddaughter I'd been taking care of, but I had not been having sex with him. He hadn't made a move on me yet, and I hoped what Geneva was saying was incorrect.

"Don't say that. He is only forty-seven. I like him, but if he said, 'Hold up, honey. Let me take my pill first' that would spoil everything."

"Are you attracted to him?"

"I am. I really am. He is growing on me."

"If his man equipment doesn't work, could you be in a sexless relationship if everything else is on point?"

"No, if it doesn't work, then that is a deal breaker."

"But he has all the other components of a good man."

"I know, but I still don't think I can be with him. We'll see. It hasn't come to that yet. Let's not talk about that anymore.

Well, you know I'm unemployed again. Tina in HR over there said she was trying to get me in, but I haven't heard anything yet. I'm a little uneasy about not having steady income."

"Something else will come through and your hard times are over, especially now you got William in your life."

"Yeah, I know." I looked down at the screen on my phone. "You talked him up. I'll call you back. That's him calling me now."

"Hey, William," I said after hanging up with Geneva.

"Hey, love. What are you doing?"

"Nothing. I was talking to Geneva about not hearing anything back from my job. And I don't want to go too many weeks without working again."

"Don't worry, they will call."

"Yeah, hopefully. What are you about to do?"

"I'm about to go and ride and see my son in Maryland; how about you go with me. It's only about two hours away."

"Okay, I'll go."

"All right. Well, I'm getting dressed now, so I'll be there in a few and, Yvette, wear something simple, not anything too revealing."

The Maryland State prison walls reached far into the sky, keeping the inmates inside. I had never stepped inside a prison before, and I thought I wouldn't ever again. The minute you got inside, it felt like your spirit was crushed. William and I entered and had to show identification, put all of our keys, money, and cell phones into a locker, and wait for our visit to begin. There were so many rules concerning what we could or couldn't do. Like no phones, nothing in our pockets, no pictures. They should have just made a big sign that read NO ANYTHING. The guards treated us badly, like we had committed a crime. We sat in the waiting room, and a hating female guard came out and said I had too much cleavage showing and needed to go in the restroom and pin my shirt up. I was going to protest, but I really didn't want to mess up William's visits with his son.

"All of this would make someone not want to come," I said as we waited for his son to come out.

"I know that's what they want you to do, get aggravated and not come back anymore."

We waited almost an hour for William's son, Tyron, to come out.

"What's up, Pop?" he said as approached, smiling. He gave his father a hug, spoke to me, and then took a seat. He was way smaller in person and didn't look much older than Brandon.

"This is my lady, Yvette."

"Hi, Yvette. My dad said Jalena been coming over your house a lot. Many thanks. She needs a woman to be around, instead of this old guy."

"You're welcome. She is such a sweet little girl."

"So how are you doing, Dad?"

"Same ole same ole. You?"

"I'm good. They have me in this program teaching classes, since I had college credits. It's good. It makes the day go by fast. I'm doing whatever I have to do to make this time pass fast."

"I know, son. You don't have that much time left. You can come home and let me retire."

"I will, Dad. When I come home, I'm doing the right thing."

We left the prison, and as we drove back, I thought about how I had to keep my own son out of there. How William was a real good father and grandfather for taking on his granddaughter. How laws were made for bad people, but usually they missed the big-time drug dealers and the little guys got caught and did all the time, like Tyron. He shouldn't have been selling, but he was good kid and shouldn't be in prison, either.

William interrupted my thoughts. I could tell William had a lot on his mind as we were leaving.

"You okay?"

"Yvette, I was thinking. Don't worry about that job calling you back. How about you come help me out?"

"Doing what?"

"Everything. Managing and putting a woman's touch on the place. You know I need the help."

"I don't know. I never worked in a restaurant atmosphere before."

"Well, just try it out. See if you like it. I do pay real money. You get a salary and a paycheck every week."

"I know, but how do you think your other employees would feel about the boss's girlfriend ordering them around?"

"I don't care. You can go in there and fire everyone. Just make it work."

Chapter 54

Crystal

I was on a call, and all of a sudden it hit me that my Rell was gone. I loved him and he did everything for me, and I just wanted to be a bitch, have dumb arguments, and fight for Kenneth to see Kori, when he'd never wanted to be a good dad before. I broke down at work. I needed my husband back. I took a fifteen-minute break. I walked to the restroom and went into a stall and began to silently cry. What was I arguing about? Why was I angry? I didn't know. I couldn't even answer my own questions.

Rell left that night and hadn't called me since. Rell hadn't called me, and he'd changed his number. I couldn't even call him to say I was sorry. It was so unreal.

I knew I'd made a giant mistake, but I didn't know how to fix it. I wasn't sure if I was married anymore. I didn't know what it took to get a divorce. I didn't know what to tell the children. At first I'd said that Rell had gone back in the army for a few weeks to get the rest of his belongings, but that had only further upset Nasir. I didn't know how long I could keep the charade going. Yesterday my dad called for Rell, and I couldn't be honest with him. I told my dad someone had stolen his phone at the job and he had been pulling doubles and I would have him call him when he got his rest.

I came out of the stall. I got a paper towel. After work I was going to go to his mother's and try to talk to him. My mom agreed to pick up the kids, and I was going to see what I could do to make it right between me and Rell.

When I was finally off work, I was so nervous. I didn't know where Rell was, if he was at his mom's or at work. I was going to try his mother's first. I didn't know if Ms. Cheryl knew that we had broken up. But my plan was to try to siphon as much information out of her as possible. I knocked on her door. She didn't answer, and I didn't see Rell's car. I didn't want to call her. Maybe she was at work. But I tried her, anyway.

"Hey, Ms. Cheryl."

"Hey, Crystal. I haven't talked to you in a while. How's my Kori?"

"She's good."

"I'm so happy for you. Rell showed me y'all's new house when he came to get the rest of his stuff the other day. It's nice. When are y'all moving everything in?"

"I don't know yet."

"Well, I think it is just wonderful that you two have found each other and are living the life you are supposed to be. I really am happy to have you and Angel as my daughters."

"Thank you, Ms. Cheryl."

"Yes, and you know, soon as you get in and settled, you have to make us all a big breakfast again."

"No problem, but I have to go and get the kids, Ms. Cheryl. I just wanted to say hello."

"Okay, baby. Talk to you soon."

I had just learned a lot from my brief conversation with Ms. Cheryl. Not only did Rell have a new cell phone number, but he had moved to the house in Springfield without me. It was really over, and I was too late. He had already moved on.

I sat crying in my car in front of my parents' house. Today had been a hard one. However, I didn't need to share it with my nosy parents. I pulled it together and entered the Turner house.

"Dad, where are the kids and Mommy?"

"She went out to the market. I need to talk to you, anyway, Crystal."

"About what, Dad?"

"I talked to Terell today. He called me to give me his new number. He said you guys are separating. What's going on with you two?"

How ignorant! I thought. *Give my dad your number and not me, and tell him we are separating?* I was thinking of another excuse or lie I could tell my father, but I just couldn't hold it in anymore.

"I don't know, Daddy. I think I chased him away. He didn't do anything wrong. He wanted us to move, and I didn't. When he asked me if I wanted him to leave, I said, 'I don't care.' And now he has moved into the house without me and has changed his cell phone number. He started working too much. I don't know why, but I kept pushing him and pushing him some more, seeing how far I could go."

My dad began comforting me as I broke down. "Crystal, marriage takes work. No two are the same, but the moment they get rough, you cannot say, 'I quit,' and walk away. If every married person left at the first sign of trouble, the world would be single. Me and your mother had our times, but we knew those were temporary and the marriage was for the long haul. I wasn't sure about him at first, but Terell is a real good guy. You have to go and talk to him. Here's his number. Call him."

Chapter 55

Dana

Why did Marcus Walker keep bothering me? He could walk down any street, go to any club in any major city, and have his choice of women. They would rub his back, cook for him, wash his clothes, and love him unconditionally, but he kept calling me. I wanted to stay away, but I kept feeling this strange pull toward him. But I knew I was in love with Adam, but it was just insane, and I just thought about Marcus all the time

Marcus left a message and said he had a really big surprise for me and if I could just meet him out once more he would leave me alone. I sat on my white bed, debating whether or not I should go. He was just a temptation that I needed to stay away from.

Against my better judgment, I met him in East Falls, at a private fund-raiser. He looked so good, but I played it cool, like I wasn't impressed and had come just because he kept calling, not because I was really interested in exploring us more.

"Mr. Walker, what is this little event?"

"You'll see in a minute." He held his arm out for me to

hold on to. I placed my arm on his, and we walked to a room with three dozen round tables and chairs.

We had a seat and my heart dropped when the fundraiser's performer walked onto the stage. I couldn't believe it was Wade Devon. He sat at his white piano and began striking each key. Astonishingly, I was a few feet away from my favorite singer. Wade Devon was singing, and I could hear the tremble in his voice when he hit a high note, and I could almost reach out and touch him. I turned around and I grabbed Marcus's hand and told him thank you.

It was enough just to be so close to the singer I loved and played almost daily. I almost passed out when, in the middle of the third song, Wade Devon said, "Is there a Dana Turner celebrating her birthday tonight?" How did he know my name? It wasn't my birthday but he had just invited me on stage with him and I couldn't move my feet to stand. I looked over at Marcus, and my eyes began to well up. Marcus whispered, "Just go along with it," and walked me over to the small stage. Wade Devon sat me next to him and began singing two of my favorite songs to me, "Last Night You Left" and "It's Another Day." I didn't know how I didn't cry. I wanted to scream and tell him how much I loved him and how his songs made me feel, but I didn't. I kept my composure and sang along with him, and then the entire audience sang "Happy Birthday" to me.

After the show was over, I was still in awe. I thanked Marcus several times and joked with him about his lie. He said he had to say something special to make it happen. I didn't think it could get any better, and then he told me to hold up and let the crowd dissipate. A few moments later the drummer came off stage and walked over and shook hands with Marcus.

"Marcus Walker. What's good, brother?"

"Good show, man. Thanks for making that happen."

"Yes, good, really good show. It was amazing," I interjected.

"You ready to meet Mr. Wade?" Marcus asked me.

Marcus grabbed my hand, and we followed his friend back stage. I thought I would pass out. People were taking pictures, and when Wade Devon was done with them, he came over to us and said, "Happy birthday, beautiful. You make a beautiful couple. That's what I do, everybody. I promote love."

"Thanks, but she hasn't even agreed to be my girlfriend yet. You're putting pressure on me." Marcus laughed as he gave the singer a handshake, told him it was good seeing him.

Wade Devon gave me a hug. He smelled just like I had imagined. And then we took a group picture.

"So okay . . . so what am I supposed to say to all of that, Mr. Walker?" I asked after we left the room.

"Uh, 'you are the man,' maybe. Or 'thank you.' Maybe a kiss right here." He tapped the middle of his cheek. I bypassed his cheek and gave him a long passionate kiss on his lips. He was very surprised. I was too. But I felt like he deserved it; never had anyone done anything so special for me.

"How did you organize this?"

"My brother Micah went to school with Tim, Devon's drummer. I heard they were having a private show and fundraiser. I knew I had to bring you after that sad story you told me. I had to make sure you saw him again, this time the right way."

"Thanks. Wow, that was really amazing."

"So you know we can't disappoint—Mr. Wade said we made a beautiful couple."

"I'm in a relationship."

"Exactly, a relationship, not a marriage. You could break up with him in three months and say, 'Damn I never got to see the potential of what I could have had with Marcus.' "

"Or I could break up with a great boyfriend, take a chance on you, and you turn out to be the worst thing that ever happened to me."

"Or you could take a chance on me, and I could be the

love of your life, the best husband and father to our children, and you'd be so happy you took a risk. But you never know unless you try."

I wanted to tell him to leave me alone, thanks for the show. I knew it was wrong to be at Marcus's apartment and to not answer Adam's call. But I wanted to explore Marcus more. His body, his soft hands and tongue. I wasn't supposed to rest in his arms and allow him to pleasure me in every way except for actual access into me. I didn't want to, but I couldn't help it.

Chapter 56

Yvette

We were in Atlantic City. William was downstairs, gambling, and I was preparing myself for what was about to occur. Intimacy was something that normally just happened, but I knew I was going to have sex with William. However, I was very concerned about him being able to keep up with me. I never considered myself to be a freak or even a nympho, but I did know there wasn't any way I would be able to stay with him if his equipment didn't work.

I hoped he could satisfy me and didn't need pills. If he wasn't any good, we would have issues moving forward. That even sounded too stupid to say aloud, but a healthy sex life was very important. I opened the minibar. I needed a drink. I took a shot to prepare myself either way. I tried to relax. I flicked on the television with the remote. I took a nice hot shower, and when I exited, William was already waiting for me. He gently kissed me and began to pinch my nipples softly. Instantly they perked up. When he was done fondling them, he placed the pair in his mouth and began to relish and taste them. I felt like I could climax just from his kisses and his attention to my ladies. But he was just getting started.

He walked me over to the bed and peeled my legs apart and his lips were moist and delicate and he gave my pussy the best French kiss she has ever had. If his equipment didn't work, I would be happy with just his touch and his oral skills. But he took the remainder of his clothes off and placed me on his lap and made me ride his strong, hard manhood. With each stroke he assured me that it worked well and he didn't need any assistance. After he was done with me, I lay on the bed and I could see the lights of the skyline of Atlantic City and I was in awe.

I would like to say that I knocked William out, that he was tired and lay sprawled out on the floor, but none of that would be true. William actually put me to sleep, took a shower, and went back downstairs and completed his gambling. I was sore; that was what I got for underestimating him. Geneva was wrong, and I felt silly for feeding into everything she said.

Chapter 57

Dana

Marcus sent pink, red, and yellow roses to my place of business. Why? He just wanted to confuse me more. I already felt guilty for spending the night in his arms. This whole entire situation is getting crazy. The other day I was with Adam, and I was thinking about Marcus. Now I was taking in the floral arrangement in front of me, until I saw Leah reading my card. I tried to snatch the card from her, but she read it, closed my office door, and started inquiring about the sender of my flowers.

"Mr. Walker? What's going on? These are not from Adam. I hope you're not playing games with him, because he is very serious about you."

"No. I'm serious about Adam, too."

"Then why are strange men sending you flowers?"

"It's nothing, really. It's just my nephew's principal thanking me for coming to their career day."

"Wasn't that a while ago?"

"Yeah, but I guess he is just getting around to thanking me."

"Oh, good, because Adam he is very serious about you. So serious, he had Stephen and me help pick out your engagement ring. He is about to ask you to marry him. It's big, too. You're going to love it."

"He is? But we just met."

"That's what Stephen said. How do you think I feel? We got in a really big argument. Actually, we broke up over y'all."

"How? Why? What do you mean you broke up, Leah?"

"Well, he said I've been putting too much pressure on him to ask me to marry him, but I said, 'It's been two years. What are you waiting on?' And he said, 'We need time apart.' "

I couldn't believe she was telling me this.

"What? No. I'm so sorry, Leah." She began to cry on my shoulder.

"It's been two of the hardest weeks of my life, and I couldn't say anything to you, because I didn't want to ruin your surprise."

"You'll get back together."

"I don't know. I think we are over. I never should have pressured him."

After comforting Leah, I again had to process all the data she had given me. She had broken up with the love of her life, Adam knew I was the one after five months of dating, and Mr. Walker was sending flowers and wanted me, too. The only person that could help me sort this out and would understand how I felt was Tiffany. But she hadn't been answering her phone lately. I tried her, anyway, and miraculously, she answered.

"Tiffany, oh my God, I wish you would start answering your phone. I have so much to tell you." I tried to give her the condensed version of my crazy life. Tiffany took it all in and laughed and said she was just as confused as I was.

Well, you know I do like Marcus, but oh well you are about to getting married, girl. Yay! Okay, so when do you want to go dress shopping?"

"He hasn't proposed yet. I don't know, Tiffany. It's a surprise engagement. And I am beyond confused; don't you think it is too soon for marriage? And should I marry him if I'm having feelings about another man?"

"Forget about Marcus, you don't really know him. He is not ready to make a commitment to you. He probably just wants you because you are already taken."

"You're right, but he said he is ready to get married, Tiffany. He has said everything I've been waiting for a man to say to me for years."

"But saying it and doing it are two different things. Adam is doing, and Mr. Walker, well, we don't know yet and we will never find out 'cause I'm going to be a bridesmaid." Tiffany start singing and then placed me on the speaker phone so Solomon could congratulate me too.

"Tell him I said thanks and I'll call you later."

"Now that both my favorite ladies are here, let's celebrate," Adam poured from the bottle of champagne, that was on the table and said, "Mom isn't she beautiful? One day I'm going to marry her." His mother did not object and just smiled. We exchanged I love yous and enjoyed our dinner.

Adam didn't propose tonight, but something better happened. I realized I had a great guy that I wasn't going to give up. Just being in Adam's presence brought me joy. I was so happy for so many reasons. We went back to his place, and I made up for almost cheating on him. I kneeled down in front of him and kissed each spot on his thigh. Once I reached his smooth peach rod shape dick. I devoured it taking long deep, intense, pulls with my cheeks. As my head move side to side and up and down his lap, he slid my panties off and inserted two of his fingers and moist warm fluids gushed down my legs. And when I thought I couldn't take anymore, he flipped me over, held open my lips with his finger, and let his tongue give my insides a lashing. I was so excited, I released immediately again. He then picked me up and was carrying me to the shower when my phone started ringing a bunch of times like it was an emergency.

"Turn you phone off and meet me in the shower." Adam stepped in the shower, and I ran to my bag to answer my phone.

"Why haven't I heard from you today?" Marcus asked. I was so nervous I dropped the phone. I picked it up off the floor, then hung it up again and he called right back.

Mr. Walker, stop calling me, I thought when the phone rang. *Marcus, leave me alone.* I answered the phone.

"Listen, you have to stop calling me."

"Why is that?"

"Because I can't see you anymore. I'm in love with a great man that is going to propose to me and it is not right if I'm still seeing you when it happens."

"So you are going to give up on us just like that?"

"I'm not giving up on us. There is no us, Mr. Walker."

"Mr. Walker, huh? Dana, won't you come out and meet me. You've been on my mind. I can't stop thinking about you." He was being really persistent, and I didn't like it.

"Stop it. Please stop it. Okay? Stop all of this. The calls, the flowers, the shows. I'm taken."

"Dana, I want you to be mine. A few months is not a real relationship. We are destined to be together. You know that, right? You are the type of woman I have dreamed of, and you would make a great wife and be a great mother to our children. Dump your boyfriend, and develop what we have further."

"Are you serious? I can't do that. As I told you before, I am in a serious relationship. Besides there are plenty of single women in this city. Go find one."

"You're probably right, but I want you."

"You want me," I laughed. "Please don't contact me anymore."

"Okay if that's what you want, but you can break up with tomorrow and you'll be so upset that you never got to see the potential of what we can be."

"No, I won't have any regrets. Goodbye." I peeked in the bathroom to see if Adam had overheard any of my conversation. He hadn't. I turned off the phone, slipped out of my clothes, and joined Adam in the shower.

Chapter 59

Yvette

Everything familywise and with William had been wonderful. Mercedes and Jalena acted like they were separated at birth. They really acted like twins and couldn't take a day apart from one another. Brandon was still doing really well. Service Air didn't get back to me, so I accepted William's offer to manage the restaurant, and it was going okay. I'd made some mistakes, or had some learning experiences, as William liked to call them. I could not do any wrong in his eyes, anyway. I ordered too many cases of lettuce. They were a good price, but I forgot that lettuce didn't have a long shelf life. Then I didn't order enough wings and sauce for Decker College's alumni weekend.

Other than that, I would give myself a B-. I'd made a few changes so far. The staff liked me. I'd changed their uniforms and I'd added complimentary breadsticks to the menu. I'd been approaching everything with the thought, *What would I appreciate, and how do I like to be treated?* Today I had Dana come in to give us her ideas on what else we should change. She brought Adam with her. They were such a cute couple. I was happy my sister had found someone really loved her. They sampled things off the new menu, and then Dana began giving me some of her thoughts. Adam was silent, but his steady smacking was assuring me he was enjoying the food.

"Vette, these appetizer are good, but like, everyone doesn't want all this high-fat, caloric food. People are trying to be more and health conscious. I would include some vegetarian dishes and more salads on the menu. I think you should register with the site Daily Deals, and I will call someone I know over at NBC Ten to see if you can be featured on *Neighborhood Eats*."

I nodded. "That would be good. Now, tell me more about Daily Deals. And what do you think, Adam?"

"I think everything is great. I'll have to bring my mother and sister here."

My phone began ringing. I excused myself from the table and took the call. The number looked familiar, but I couldn't remember the voice when I heard it.

"How you doing, Yvette? This is Mr. Jimmy's daughter, Ebony." Why was she calling me? I was paid up on my rent, and I didn't have any repairs that needed to be taken care of.

"I'm fine. I'm at work." I needed her to say whatever she had to say quickly.

"Well, I have some news for you. My dad is ill. He's in the hospital, and I'm going to be taking over all the properties."

"Is he going to be okay?"

"Eventually, yes, but unfortunately, I don't want the responsibility of being a landlord, so I'm selling all my dad's buildings. The new owners are willing to renew leases with all the current tenants, and I wanted to call you and give you that option."

"Well, that's something I'm going to have to think about. Is it okay if I give you a call later?"

"Sure, but I'm going to need a definite answer by the end of the month." I told her I would think it over and call her. Now, I had something else to think about it.

Chapter 60

Crystal

I was a crazy person. How did I let my husband go? He was doing everything he was supposed to do, and all I could do was complain. Yes, we had problems, like everyone else, but I was the one who'd been acting crazy. I was the one who had been looking for any reason to give up and say, "Never mind."

I had to fix us, but I really didn't know how I was going to. I took a chance and called him. Maybe he would want to talk. Maybe he missed me like I missed him all of these weeks and wanted to talk; at least that was my wish. I called his phone and all I heard was long drawn out rings and then he answered whispering, "What's up?"

"Rell, where are you?"

"I'm at the movies, can I call you back?"

"Okay, but I wanted to talk to you about a few things."

"Yeah, all right, well, when I get out of here, and don't worry. I'll come and get the rest of my stuff by next week."

"That's not what I wanted to talk to you about. Can I meet up with you after you leave the movies?"

"Uh, I don't know how long I'm going to be."

"Could you just call me when you're done? I can meet you."

"Yeah, I guess. I'll call you."

Two hours had passed, and Rell hadn't call me back. Most movies are only an hour and half long. My mind started wondering. Who was he with and why hadn't he called me yet? I couldn't wait any longer to speak with him. Although he said he would call me, I dialed him again.

"Yeah Crystal, what's up?"

"Can you meet me, Rell? It's real important."

"All right, Crystal. I'm down Columbus Boulevard, where are you?"

"I'm not too far away. Can we meet at the Wawa in twenty minutes?"

"Fine."

I was so nervous, but happy that he agreed to meet. I arrived at the Wawa in fifteen minutes and three minutes later Rell pulled up beside me. I wanted to get out my car and hug, hold him, and tell him my life has been hell without him. I was waiting for him to get in my car, but he just stood outside the door and put his hands up signaling me to get out and saying what's up at once.

"Hey Rell," I said as I exited the car nervously.

"You wanted to talk, so talk, Crystal. I have somewhere to go after this." I didn't like the way he was speaking to me, but I had to put it all on the line.

"Can you get in my car?"

"No, I don't have time for all that. Say what you gotta say."

I didn't want to pour my heart to him in a busy convenience store parking lot while people were walking past us, but Rell wasn't giving me much of a choice. I was a beggar and I couldn't be choosey. If I wanted him, I had to tell him how I felt. I took a deep breath and began to utter every emotion I felt inside of me.

"Okay, Rell, first I want to tell you I'm sorry. I'm very sorry for everything I said to you."

"That's what you called me out here for, Crystal? You could have called me on the telephone to say that."

"No, Rell that's not it; just listen to me. Ever since forever I had people saying things about me, from my family to my friends. They would say Crystal dumb, Crystal always getting pregnant. Crystal got all them kids and none of the fathers with her. And I don't know why, but I started believing some of the things myself. Like, I didn't think I would ever meet anyone that would love me unconditionally. I didn't think love came without a catch and then you came into my life. You didn't care about how many kids or kids fathers I had, you just loved me and my children and I'm sorry Rell, 'cause I wasn't used to that. I kept telling myself you were too good to be real. I don't know. . . . Maybe I was talking myself out of believing that I deserved happiness. So when things weren't going right, my first thought was to give up, but now I know you can't do that with a marriage. A marriage is about sacrifice. It's about giving a little and taking a little. I didn't understand that then. I see how it is to be without you, and I don't like it. Can you please come home, Rell? Please, baby, I need you. I really need you, the kids need you. We miss you, and I never want to live without you." I felt tears gushing down my face and my heart opening up. "Baby, I need you—please come home. Rell, don't leave me. Please come home?"

He pulled me into him. "Stop crying, Crystal. I don't like to see you cry. I'm sorry, too. Boo, I probably shouldn't have left the way I did, but it just didn't feel good with us arguing all the time. You know I love you and you know I love the kids."

I felt all this stress leave my body. I leaned into him, and he wrapped his arms around my body tighter. He held me up against his chest, and his phone began ringing. I guessed it was whoever he was supposed to meet, he probably was about to leave and tell me he needed some time to think. I wanted an answer now, but at least we were on speaking terms again. I would just call him tomorrow. He picked up his phone and said, "Yeah, no I'm not going. I'll catch up with you another time. I have to go home with my wife."

Chapter 61

Dana

You can break up with your boyfriend tomorrow, and you'll be so upset that you never got to see what we can be. Marcus's voice was in my head, and I was debating whether or not if I should give into temptation. Even though I told Marcus to leave me alone, he wouldn't. He called and texted more and if I didn't like him I would think he was crazy. But I did like him, he did intrigue me, and I loved his persistence and attention and was finding it hard to say no.

He had a fancy hotel room reserved for us and wanted me to spend the night with him just once. There were so many thoughts spinning in my head—should I? Shouldn't I? I wanted to but I couldn't. I needed to make the right decision. Adam was only my boyfriend, not my husband. I didn't know if we were going to last forever. What if I really was passing up my soul mate? Then again, Marcus was my nephew's mentor, and he could just be saying anything to capture the final prize he wanted from me. He said he wanted to meet me on neutral territory, so we could see once and for all if we were meant to be. I wasn't going to go and I was going to call him and let him know.

"Are you ready, Dana?"

"I'm not sure I'm coming, that's why I'm calling you."

"Don't flake on me now, Dana. All I'm asking is for is one night. Just one. If you don't like it, I'll leave you alone and you are free to go and marry what's his name. But if we have the chemistry that I know we do, then you have to give us a fair shot. Deal?"

"No deal." I wasn't agreeing to anything with him. "No, one night of sex is not going to determine whether or not we are destined to be together."

"You are right. It is only the final piece to the puzzle. We already know we are mentally and spiritually compatible. The only thing that is left is the physical. I know you are just as curious as I am, and I know you want me, too. I'll see you at eight at the airport A Loft hotel."

"Okay, I'll see you then." Why did I agree to meet him? I was so confused. I was so in love with Adam, but when I spent more time with Marcus, something changed. I wanted him badly. I wanted to know how our bodies would feel intertwined as one.

I met Marcus at the hotel. He was happy I'd come and showed his appreciation by giving me a tender hug and asked me if I wanted anything to drink.

"No, I'm fine." I sat on the chaise chair in the corner of the room. I felt very awkward, like we were in a movie and the director screamed action and we were supposed to start the scene. Marcus didn't wait for any cues. He pushed me on to the bed, and suddenly his tongue attacked me. Like a snake, it sprang into my mouth and began whipping around wildly. "Oh my God," I kept repeating while his face made its way to my pelvis, licking, torturing, punishing it with numbing licks. We both undressed and we both were ready. I slid up against him. Our skin was smooth, wet. I felt his every vein and his plumpness. At any given moment it was bound to slide in. Everything felt like it was meant to be. Like I was right where

I belonged. I didn't know how I was going to tell Adam I loved him. I was breathing heavily.

"Where is the condom?" I panted in Marcus ear.

He jumped up, grabbed his pants, and searched his pockets. My eyes were on his clothes. I was ready for him. I couldn't wait. And he was fumbling around. I was all set and now he was taking forever.

"What's wrong? Why are you putting on your clothes?" I groaned.

"I have to go to my car."

"For what?"

"I left the condoms there."

"The vice principal, a responsible man, left the condoms?" I snickered and sighed and fell back on the bed, wrapping the sheets around my body.

"I'll be right back."

"I'll be waiting."

Ten minutes passed. He was taking so long. I reached for my phone and saw a message from Adam I just wanted to let you know I love you, and don't make any plans next week.

My heart sank. Oh my God, Adam was going to propose next week and here I was, about to throw it all away for Marcus Walker. I read the message again. I had to get out of here. I had a great man that didn't deserve this. I had waited for someone like him, and I wasn't going to lose him.

Everything happened for a reason, and Marcus not having his condoms was a sign for me to get out of there. I wasn't supposed to be with him. But then other thoughts raced through my head. I glanced at myself in the mirror. I had to make up my mind whether to stay or to leave. After a few moments I decided to leave. I dressed swiftly. I didn't want to be here when Marcus returned. Once on the other side of the hotel door, I questioned myself again. Did I make the right choice?

Before I reached my car, Marcus was calling me nonstop. Finally I answered.

"Where are you?"

"I left. I'm sorry. I'm confused, and none of this feels right, Marcus."

"You really are settling for safe."

I had to belt out, "And you are so dangerous, Mr. Walker?"

"No, I'm not dangerous, but I'm a risk. You are scared of the unknown."

"No, but you're asking me to give up someone who loves me and wants to spend the rest of his life with me for . . . I don't know what."

"If you marry him, I'm going to show up, run down the aisle, and yell 'Stop' at your wedding."

"What! You won't know when and where it is." I laughed at the thought.

"I'll ask Brandon. Come on, Dana. Come back to the room."

"No, seriously, I'm really ending us this time. Good-bye, Marcus."

I left the hotel and when straight to Adam's place. He opened the door and asked me what was I doing there. At first I couldn't look him in the eye. I had a seat at his kitchen table.

"What's up Dana?"

"We need to talk, I have a few things I need to share with you."

Something in me felt like I had to be honest with Adam and tell him the truth about what had happened. Actually, I didn't have to. I probably shouldn't, but I didn't want to start the next chapter with Adam based on deception and lies.

"What are you talking about?"

"You know Brandon's mentor, Mr. Walker?"

"Yeah. What about him?"

"Well, I've kind of been seeing him."

"Okay, this is crazy. What the hell are you talking about? Kind of been seeing him?" he said as he stood up covering his face with his palm. "Did you sleep with him?"

"No, not exactly."

"Then why tell me, Dana?"

"I don't know. I just feel like I should be honest with you. Because when you ask me to marry you, I don't want there to be any secrets."

"Dana, I didn't ask you to marry me. How do you even know? I need to have a seat."

"Leah told me that you bought me the ring already."

"Well, I was going to ask you to marry me. But right now, I'm not sure if that's a great idea. You didn't sleep with him, but do you love him?"

"No, I don't love him. I'm not sure why I even considered it."

"Dana, this is not making any sense."

I had a seat next to Adam. I didn't want to cry, I had to tell him the truth. I took a deep breath. "Adam, listen, you have to understand—before I met you, my dream was to meet and marry a strong, educated, successful man, and I always just assumed he would also be black." I stood up and walked away from him. I took another deep breath. "Adam you're strong, educated, successful, but you're not black. So when I met him, I was like why would God bless me with you, everything I ever wanted and then send him, too?"

"I still don't get it, Dana. I'm there for you. I treat you with respect. We have never had an argument, and you know I'm madly in love with you."

"I know, Adam, I know, but he represented what I thought I wanted and had to have—a good black man. But now I'm certain all I need is you, a good man."

"I don't know what you want me to say to all this. So after everything we've been through, it really comes down to black and white."

"No, you know what I realized tonight? That I love you, Adam and when I'm with you I don't see color anymore. I just see you. I love you for who you are, and I want to be with you because I can't see myself without you. I want to see you when I go to close my eyes every night and awake in the morning."

"Do you mean that?"

"I do."

Chapter 62

Yvette

Since I've been managing Lena's, the business has picked up. I made all the changes Dana had suggested. The menu has a broader selection and is not all soul food anymore. Plus we have a new Caribbean chef and he is very creative. He added seafood macaroni and cheese to our menu and it is delicious. It has lobster, shrimp, crabmeat, sweet cream and five different cheeses. I had a couple last night, purchased extra orders to take home and freeze. I added before-4:00 p.m. specials and after-10:00 p.m. specials. But what really is driving in our patrons is that Daily Deals Web site. Because of that site we have reservations booked all the way into next month.

And it's also the simple changes I've made, like I notice a lot of customers receiving tickets, so I got the church across the street to let us rent their parking lot on busy nights. I also brought in promoters and made Mondays comedy night and Tuesdays karaoke competitions. Wednesdays were still buffalo shrimp and chicken night. Everything had been falling into place. I just had to find another apartment. I'd been looking all over the city, and I hadn't found anything that I liked. I spoke to the new owner of my building, and she was willing to give me a new six months' lease, but I wasn't sure I wanted to sign anything. I was in the middle of another busy night at Lena's and every table was filled and we had about ten more parties still waiting to be seated. I had even pitched in to clear tables. After I placed napkins and silverware on the table William grabbed my waist and kissed me on my cheek. "You don't have to that, that's why we have a staff."

"I know, but I don't just want to stand around giving orders. I'm hands on."

"You do enough. We are having another great night, thanks to you, sweetheart."

"No, it's thanks to that website and the write-up in the paper."

"No, you are the change. By the way, I need to see you in the back office for a moment. I have something to discuss with you."

"Give me a second, babe." Instead of following William, I grabbed two menus and seated the next guest. I returned to see another table that needed to be cleared off. "Corrine, how long before that table is available? Can you get Joey out here?" Then I saw the bus boy, Joey, slowly walking towards the messy table. "Joey, come on, we have to turn these tables around faster. We have guests waiting to be seated. Pick up your pace okay?"

"I'm sorry. They had a spill in the back. I was helping them get it up," Joey explained.

"No problem, let's just get it done."

After I seated more guests, I went in the back to check on what William wanted. He was sitting in his chair and told me to close the door and have a seat.

Oh boy what did I do? I thought. I had a seat and asked William what was going on.

"Okay, first, let me say that you have really been a joy to have in my life. Yvette, I'm older, and I know what I want and what's missing. I say all that to say, why sign another lease at an apartment you hate? You have a man with a big house and a bunch of extra bedrooms. What I'm trying to say is, I want you in the kids to move in with me and Jalena."

"William, we are in the middle of an extremely busy night. Let's talk about this later."

"No, I need you listen now. At least consider it, Yvette. The children can go to better schools. We can be together, and it would make everything much easier."

"William, I care about you a lot, but I'm not sure if I'm ready to move in together. Let me go back out there, and we will discuss this later, okay?"

"Yvette, seriously think about what I'm saying. I don't want you struggling anymore. I don't want you in a crammed-up apartment. I want to take care of you and provide you with the best. I'm going home to pick up Jalena. Please think it over." He put his jacket on, grabbed his keys, gave me a peck on the cheek, and told me to call him once we had closed up.

Back out front I didn't know what to make of the conversation I had just had with William. I felt cold hands cover my eyes and heard a voice say, "Is the boss lady available?" I took off the hands covering my eyes and turned around to see Geneva standing there with Eric.

"Hey, girl. What are you doing here?"

"Date night. We are hungry. How long do we have to wait for a table?"

"You don't have to wait for a table. Follow me." I grabbed menus and seated them at the same table Geneva and I had sat at when we first had dinner here. "How you been, Eric? I haven't seen you in a long time."

He greeted me.

"This table looks familiar," said Geneva.

"It should." I laughed.

"Where is the man?" she asked, looking around.

"I gave him the night off," I joked. "He went home to pick up Jalena. The nights I'm here late, he gets to spend more time with her and to have just a night or two for himself."

"That's nice of you."

"Yeah anyway, let me get you guys some bread and something to drink." I walked over to the kitchen and I grabbed Geneva dinner rolls, and then I had the waitress send them over a bottle of wine. Between running around, serving, I managed to take a break and pull a chair up to Geneva and Eric's table.

"You're working. You can't sit down with us," Geneva said.

"What? Remember, I run this place. I can do whatever I want to."

Eric got up from the table.

"Where are you going, baby?" Geneva asked.

"Have your girl talk for a moment. I'm going to take this call," Eric said and excused himself. With Eric gone from the table, I took full advantage of the chance to catch up with my best friend.

"So have you found a place yet?" Geneva asked.

"I still haven't found a place. Everything is so expensive. I might as well wait until I can buy a house again. But you will never guess what William asked me tonight. He wants me to move in with him and Jalena. He gave me a speech about how he knows what he wants. He is getting older and wants to build a future, and he doesn't want me struggling anymore. I just don't want to feel like I need or am using someone. Then I think he needs help with Jalena."

"Didn't you say he had a nanny for her? And you aren't using him. Hell, you are using each other. Everyone needs something from someone. He needs you just as much as you need him."

"I suppose. But what I'm most afraid of is turning control of my life over again to someone. After everything I've been through with Phil, it makes it a little hard to trust anyone."

"He's not anything like Phil. Phil took and William gives."

"I know, but what if I move in with him and then we break

up and then me and the kids are homeless and I have to find another place?"

"Only you know what you are ready for. Do you love him? I think he is a good man. He has already proven himself. Look how your life has changed since you met him."

"I don't know about love, but I care for him deeply and, yes, my life has changed drastically. Girl, I was thinking about that yesterday—how hard of a time I was having. I'm so glad I'm out of it."

"I know. I'm happy to see you smile again, Vette, and I think it is win-win and win. You'll have security again, because he'll be an excellent provider. The kids will be in good schools, and he has someone to help him with his granddaughter."

"I know. That's all the things I thought of."

"Just pray on it."

"I will, because there isn't any way I'm moving in with him *and* working for him. It's one or the other."

Chapter 63

Crystal

Four months later . . .

"Happy Mother's Day, Mommy. We made you breakfast," Nasir said as he ran into my new spacious bedroom and jumped on the bed.

"Mom, I made you that," Jewel said, pointing at the cereal and toast then she set on the side of the nightstand.

"Mommy, you like your surprise breakfast?" Nasir asked.

"Yes, I love it. Thank you so much." I sat up and munched on a piece of toast and gave both of them hugs.

"Where are we going for Mother's Day today, Mommy?" Jewel asked.

"I want to go to the indoor water park. No. Dave and Buster's," Nasir declared. Rell walked in and leaned over and kissed my forehead and said, "Okay, let Mommy enjoy her breakfast, and go get ready." The children left the room racing towards the bathroom arguing about who was going to take a shower first.

"Jewel, let Nasir in the shower first." Rell called out. "And go pick out what you are going to wear."

"Okay," Jewel answered back.

"Is Kori still asleep?"

"Yeah, she is."

"Thanks for my breakfast."

"You're welcome. They tried to make you pancakes. I said, 'No Mommy likes cereal.' Oh I forgot to give you this. Happy Mother's Day." Rell pulled out a red square box.

"What's this? I said opening the box and saw a necklace with all five of our birth stones dangling down in a clump and at the bottom in cursive it read *family*.

"It's beautiful—thank you, Rell."

"You're welcome; didn't I tell you I was always going to upgrade you?" he playfully said as he wrapped the necklace around my neck. I got out of the bed to see how it looked. Staring in the mirror I began to clam up.

"And you know it's more room for our son that we'll have one day and oh and the kids' doggie."

"Our son, yes, one day; the doggie never," I smiled trying not to cry as Rell stood behind me in the mirror.

"Are you okay, Crystal? You like it."

"Yeah, I love it. It's just sometimes I get scared."

"Scared of what?"

"Scared of what life would be like without you."

He hugged me then, turned me around, gently grabbed my face, and said, "What did I tell you when I first married you?"

"To never doubt you and that you weren't going anywhere."

"And I'm not. I'm never leaving you. I love you, Crystal Glover, and I'm always going to be here for you. You understand?"

"Yes, I do."

Rell exited the room, and I fell back in the bed under the covers for a moment. I began reflecting on how happy I was with my life and how far I had come. I thanked God daily for my new life, my children, and my husband.

When I first met Rell, I was scared to give up control or surrender to a man. But in reality I wasn't surrendering to him. I was instead becoming his partner, and there is a difference. Rell stepped in and took the heavy bricks off of my back and now he is carrying them for me. I know it's not always going to be easy or perfect, but to know Rell is by my side makes me the happiest women in the world. Rell was my boo bear, my friend, my protector, and my husband. I wished I had noticed him in sixth grade and had avoided Jason, Maurice and Kenneth, but then, I thought, I wouldn't have my children and I had to go through all of that drama to appreciate the man I was married to now. All the mistakes, all the heartbreak were all worth it, and I would do it all over again if Rell was my prize.

CHAPTER 64

Yvette

I heard a truck backing up. I peeked out the window to see a moving truck. I opened the door and told the movers that they could take the stacked boxes on the porch and that more were coming.

"Brandon, Mercedes, the truck is here. Start bringing the rest of the boxes out here."

"Mommy, I'm so happy we are finally moving," Mercedes exclaimed.

"Yeah, I am too!" Brandon huffed, carrying the remainder of the big brown boxes to the door.

Seeing the movers load the boxes onto the truck gave me a sense of satisfaction. I knew I wasn't going to live here forever, but I didn't know when I would be able to move and get things together again. I was just so happy that they were. I felt like I was getting another chance at life and this time I'm going to live it right.

I had to choose between working with William or living with him. I couldn't do both, so I was going to continue to manage the restaurant.

I was moving to a town house I was renting in my old neighborhood. I had thought long and hard about moving in with William, and I realized I didn't know him well enough and our relationship was too new. And, more importantly, I didn't want to put myself back in a situation I would later regret. And before I move in or marry again, I want to work on me some more. I signed a one year lease. Everything has truly come full circle, and in a year maybe I will move in with William, but right now that's not for me.

One thing is for sure: God made you go through some things sometimes so you could realize how blessed you were. I'd learned so many lessons from this whole experience, like I would never take anything for granted. I would always put something up for a rainy day. And I thought I was going to be a one-woman man. I was not going to mess up this relationship with William. I've also learned you can't pray against your enemy, you must pray for them. God takes care of people when he is ready and not when you are. For months I had waited, hoping and wishing that Phillip got his. All I had to do was sit back and wait. When I stopped worrying about Phillip, my dad called me and told me to get the paper, because Phil was in it. I grabbed the paper and read the headline: TEXTING AND DRIVING SEPTA CRASH. My heart sank. Karma had finally slapped Phillip in his ass. He was texting while driving his route and ran into three parked cars and a convenience store. He injured five people and was in the hospital with a broken pelvis and leg. The accident was under investigation, and he was out on leave. That meant he was getting fired. Which further proved to me that what goes around always comes back around. The one thing that amazed me about all of this was that, if Phil hadn't stolen my money and got me fired, I would never have worked at Service Air, walked into Lena's, and met William. I just didn't understand it. I hated to say it, but maybe it was a blessing in disguise.

As the movers loaded the last of the boxes onto the truck, I took a mental picture of the apartment that I'd called home for almost the last year and then happily closed the door and that chapter of my life.

Chapter 65

Dana

"Okay, are you sure, Dana? Once I drop them, there is no turning back."

"I'm sure, Adam. You are the person I want to see when I close my eyes and when I opened them, and in the November I will officially be your wife." Staring deep into my eyes he asked was I sure once more.

"Positive. That's why I accepted this," I joked as I gazed at my engagement ring, with its three-carat, gleaming oval stone.

"You did. Well, it is settled, we're getting married," he said as he released the mailbox handle and the door swung closed. He opened the mailbox door once more to make sure all the cream-colored save-the-date envelopes had fallen to the bottom of the mailbox. We kissed and then held hands and walked to the car. Adam opened my door; once I was in, I reached over and opened his. When he started driving, I leaned over and kissed my man again.

Adam is so special and loving and I don't want to be without him. After I told him the truth about Marcus, a lot of men might have left me. And I was scared that he was going to. But I knew I had to tell him the truth; I didn't want it to come up later. I figured we would just continue to date and go from there. So I was totally shocked when Adam blindfolded me in the car, drove, dropped to one knee, and proposed in front of the same inn where we first spent the night, and I accepted with no hesitation. We spent the night there and the next morning he had my parents, my sisters, and his mother and sister meet us for brunch. Adam is not perfect; he has his quirks and he is still a man, but he is about me and us and that's why I love him.

They say every encounter is for a reason or a season. I don't know who they are, but I do think they are right. Mr. Marcus Walker came into my life for a season. I enjoyed, cared for, and adored Marcus, but I didn't love him. I couldn't deny that I had thoughts about him. I did wonder what he was doing and how he was making out, but I was sure he was going to make somebody really happy one day. Who knew what would have happened if I had met him first? But I did know that you never left a sure thing for a what-if. But I believe the reason he came into my life was to prove to me that there are plenty of great and wonderful black men that were doing the right thing. If I hadn't met him, I would have probably kept buying into the myth that there weren't any left. But now I knew better. And good men and jerks come in all shapes, sizes, and colors. Tiffany lucked out with a great man in Solomon, and they are on their way to setting a date. And Leah got a dumped by a jerk like Stephen. He still hasn't given her any explanation as to why, no closure at all. She was heartbroken and felt like she wasted so much time, but she was getting over it and dating again. While you are dating you never know what kind of hand you're going to be dealt, but I know I would tell any single lady, have fun, date, explore your options, live your life and stay away from time wasters—aka the Stephens and Todds of the world. I know for sure there is a man out there who will give you his all, not stand you up, introduce you to his family, make you his wife—and if he won't, another man will.

A READING GROUP GUIDE

ANOTHER MAN WILL

DAAIMAH S. POOLE

ABOUT THIS GUIDE

The suggested questions that follow are included to enhance your group's reading of this book.

DISCUSSION QUESTIONS

1. What lessons, if any, did you learn from *Another Man Will?*

2. Do you think there are good black men left in the world, or are they all taken?

3. If Dana had chosen Marcus, do you think it would have worked?

4. Why do you think Dana chose Adam over Marcus? Who, in your opinion, was the better man?

5. What are you thoughts on Terell and Crystal's relationship? Did Crystal take a big risk, and was it worth it?

6. Do you think Yvette will become bored with William? Will she eventually move in with him or marry him?